By
Tom Barber

*****

The Sam Archer thriller series
by
Tom Barber

NINE LIVES
26 year old Sam Archer has just been selected to join a new counter-terrorist squad, the Armed Response Unit. And they have their first case. A team of suicide bombers are planning to attack London on New Year's Eve. The problem? No one knows where any of them are.

THE GETAWAY
Archer is in New York City for a funeral. After the service, an old familiar face approaches him with a proposition. A team of bank robbers are tearing the city apart, robbing it for millions. The FBI agent needs Archer to go undercover and try to stop them.

BLACKOUT
Three men have been killed in the UK and USA in one morning. The deaths take place thousands of miles apart, yet are connected by an event fifteen years ago. Before long, Archer and the ARU are drawn into the violent fray. And there's a problem.
One of their own men is on the extermination list.

SILENT NIGHT
A dead body is found in Central Park, a man who was killed by a deadly virus. Someone out there has more of the substance and is planning to use it. Archer must find where this virus came from and secure it before any more is released.

But he is already too late.

ONE WAY
On his way home, Archer saves a team of US Marshals and a child they are protecting from a violent ambush in the middle of the Upper West Side. The group are forced to take cover in a tenement block in Harlem, their ambushers locking them in and sealing off the only way in or out of the building.
And there are more killers on the way to finish the job.

RETURN FIRE
Four months after they first encountered one another, Sam Archer and Alice Vargas are both working in the NYPD Counter-Terrorism Bureau and also living together. But a week after Vargas leaves for a trip to Europe, Archer gets a knock on his front door.
Apparently Vargas has completely disappeared.
And it appears she's been abducted.

GREEN LIGHT
A nineteen year old woman is gunned down in a Queens car park, the latest victim in a brutal gang turf war that goes back almost a century.
Suspended from duty, his badge and gun confiscated, Archer is nevertheless drawn into the fray as he seeks justice for the girl. People are going missing, all over New York.
And soon, so does he.

Also:
CONDITION BLACK (A novella)

In the year 2113, a US 101st Airborne soldier wakes up after crash landing on a moon somewhere in space. All but two of his squad are dead. He has no idea where he is, or who shot him down.
But he quickly learns that some nightmares don't stop when you wake up.

For Anna.

ONE

No one was in Central Park to see the man die.

It was Friday 17th December, a week before Christmas. New York City was a majestic place during the summer but it was equally captivating in the winter. Festive cheer was everywhere. Shop windows were adorned with imaginative seasonal displays, each store trying to outdo the other. Bars served strong punch containing warming liquor, fruit and spices. Speakers were rigged up on lampposts in several neighbourhoods in the outer boroughs through which familiar carols were played during the day. And saplings planted in small soil patches on the sidewalks all over Manhattan were decorated with lights, contributing to the red and golden hue the city adopted every twelfth month of the year.

With soft snow powdering the grass and golden lights sprinkled in trees all over its 843 acres, Central Park epitomised the feel-good seasonal ambience of the city. During the day and early evening, the ice-skating rinks in the Park were in constant use. People could either rent skates or wear their own, some gliding around the ice gracefully, others wobbling their way round far less confidently, treating each completed lap as a small victory. There was the constant *click-clock* of horse's hooves as they pulled carriages along the roads, tourists or couples sitting in the back, taking photographs or enjoying a romantic tour. Small two or three-piece brass bands took up positions beside the paths and worked their way through a repertoire of Christmas songs. And amongst all this, there was a constant stream of people just exploring the sights and admiring the scenery around them. Thirty five million people made their way into Central Park each year and a significant portion of that number came during the winter months.

Nevertheless, once the sun went down the Park started to quieten. A few remaining horse-drawn carriages trundled past, but the activity from earlier in the day quickly decreased as the air grew colder and the night got darker. The Park was open until 1am, but it had been a chilly December and that particular Friday evening was the coldest of the month so far. People were not inclined to hang around.

Coming up to 10pm, the lamp post-lit paths and sidewalks were now eerily quiet.

Snow had just started drifting down from the sky again, adding an extra layer to the white powder that had already blanketed the grass and naked branches on the trees.

During the summer one of the most popular areas in the Park was Sheep Meadow, located to the West between 66th and 69th Street. Fifteen acres in total, the large field hosted hundreds of people every day from early May to the end of September, but apart from the paths running around the perimeter it was shut off during the autumn and winter months to protect the ground and preserve the grass.

That night the Meadow was dark, empty and quiet.

Save for the falling snow and one solitary figure.

At the north perimeter, a groundsman was slowly trudging his way along the fence, heading west. He was working alone. Before starting his shift he'd wrapped up well. He was wearing four layers of clothes accompanied by a scarf, a thick set of gloves and a knitted woollen hat. He'd read somewhere that a human being could lose something like fifty per cent of their body heat through the top of their head, so during the frostier months he always made sure that the beanie was firmly in place before he started work.

Being of Mexican descent, he didn't enjoy the New York winter for a number of reasons. Aside from the obvious, one of them was the emptiness of the Meadow at this time of year. Even though the summer period tripled his workload he still far preferred the warmer, and therefore busier and more sociable time of year. Some places were designed for activity; without it, they seemed neglected and forlorn.

Pausing by the fence, he looked out at the dark field. It had the same deserted feel of a large school on a break for the holidays or an airport Terminal at night.

It was unnatural.

He didn't like it.

Six hours after beginning his shift, the groundsman was almost finished for the evening. He had a number of jobs to attend to in his area of the Park, but emptying the trash cans would be the last tonight. When he was done, he'd punch his timecard, take the A train back up to Spanish Harlem and enjoy a bowl of his wife's homemade soup. He walked along the fence pulling a wheeled cart behind him, a handful of black trash bags tossed inside. Just two more bins to empty. The drop-off point for removal of the bags was at the south-west corner of the Meadow, so once he'd gathered the last two he would dump them all there, return the cart to storage and get his ass home.

He approached the penultimate can, his thick boots crunching in the snow as he walked. He could see the black bag inside was about three quarters full. Coming to a halt, he pulled the bag out of the can, tied off the ends and then tossed it into the cart behind him to join the others. He drew a fresh bag, pulling it off a roll he'd stashed in the cart and replaced the old one.

But just as he was about to move on something on the ground caught his eye.

It was pretty well camouflaged by the snow. He'd almost missed it.

Stepping forward and bending down, he wiped off a layer of snow with his glove.

It was a black shoebox. It looked like someone had tossed it at the trash but missed and walked away, leaving it there on the ground. He was about to scoop it up to throw it inside the newly-replaced bag, but hesitated. He could hear something.

The box was clicking.

The groundsman looked around. All he could see was falling snow and a dark, quiet Park. Whoever had left the box here had long since gone.

Maybe there's an animal inside, he thought.

It was common practice in the city for unwanted pets to be dumped like this. He couldn't just leave the poor creature out here to freeze to death.

He reached forward, pulled a string securing the box and lifted the lid.

The moment he did, the clicking stopped.

There was a *whump.* A small cloud of yellow gas spewed from the box and hit him directly in the face. He instinctively recoiled but inhaled at the same time, the mustard-coloured gas sucked into his mouth and nostrils.

And immediately, he started choking.

He couldn't breathe. Coughing and gagging, he was suddenly overwhelmed by a horrific pain in his chest. It felt as if it was on fire. Every desperate breath he tried to take made the searing, burning sensation worse. He coughed harder, his whole body starting to jerk, blood spraying out of his mouth onto the white snow. He staggered back then collapsed to the ground, doubling over. He curled up in a tight ball in a vain effort to stop the agony, but it was getting worse.

He started to retch, his body spasming violently, blood and pieces of lung tissue spewing from his mouth onto the snow around him. The agonising and uncontrollable spasms increased in intensity, contorting his body and growing more and more violent. Suddenly, there was a loud *crack.*

His spine had snapped.

Immediately going into shock, the groundsman gargled as fluid filled his ruptured lungs.

And thirty seconds after he'd inhaled the gas, the man drowned in his own blood.

His jerking and convulsing ceased.

He was still, blood and bits of lung spattered both on his clothes and on the ground around him.

Crimson against the white.

He was the only person in the Meadow. No one else was around.

And the snow continued to fall silently from the sky.

Across the city, they'd been working on the guy for almost three hours before he cracked. There were two people torturing him, a man and a woman called Wicks and Drexler. Inside the dark house Wicks walked over to the bed and put his hands on his knees, looking down at the bloodied man who was strapped to the frame. The guy had lasted longer than they'd expected. They'd worked their way through every sharp implement they could find in the kitchen, and by the second hour had gotten creative. Wicks reached forward and ripped a strip of duct tape off the dying man's mouth. He did it fast, like pulling off a band aid. Then he peered in close. The guy's eyes were hazy from blood loss and shock trauma.

'Something you wanna tell us?' Wicks asked.

The man coughed weakly, blood around his mouth, his arms and legs taped securely to the wooden bed posts. He mumbled something that was just a whisper.

'Louder.'

'Macy's.'

'Go on.'

He coughed.

'B..Bryant Park,' he said, blood bubbling out of his lips. He must have ruptured a lung.

'And?'

'Pier...17.'

'What time?'

'Around...11. 30.'

Wicks looked into the man's eyes for a moment, then rose.

Drexler stepped forward, a suppressed Glock 21 in her hand and gave the man on the bed six slugs, three to the chest, three to the head. She pulled the trigger fast, the man's body jerking as he took each round, splinters coughing up from the bed frame and floor under the bed as the bullets buried themselves in the wood. The spent cartridges jumped out of the ejection port, tinkling to the floor, each one bouncing and eventually rolling to a stop.

Looking at the dead man, Wicks pulled his cell phone and dialled a number. Someone answered on the fourth ring.

'It's me. He talked. We're in business.'

He listened, nodding, then ended the call and slid the phone back into his pocket. Then he turned to Drexler.

'What time is it?'

Still holding the pistol, the dark-haired woman shot her cuff. '6:25. The sun'll be up soon.'

Wicks nodded.

'Let's go,' he said. 'We've got work to do.'

TWO

'That's the last one?' the removal man asked, three and a half hours later. He was a big, surly guy with a large gut straining against his shirt and a cardboard box tucked under his arm, *Stuff* scribbled in black pen on the side. He was standing in the doorway of a third floor apartment in the East Village neighbourhood of Manhattan.

In front of him, a slim, dark-haired woman in jeans and a red flannel shirt looked around. The apartment had been cleared out, cleaned and emptied. She turned back to the man and nodded.

'That's it. Thank you, Jeff.'

The guy nodded. 'We'll take off now. We should make Chicago by the end of the day. If the weather turns, we'll hole up and be there tomorrow.'

The woman nodded. 'OK. Thank you.'

Jeff turned and left.

On his way down the corridor, he passed a man in his late twenties coming the other way. The newcomer was blond and handsome, dressed in blue jeans, a thick grey hoodie and a green jacket laced on the inside with cream-coloured wool. He watched as the removal guy walked down the stairs whistling a Christmas song, the final box tucked under his arm and glad to be finally on his way. Shifting his attention, the blond man moved into the open doorway of the apartment.

Inside, the dark-haired woman had her back to him and didn't see him arrive. He knocked gently on the doorframe and she turned.

'Oh,' she said. 'Hey.'

'Hey.'

He stayed where he was, the empty apartment in front of him. It seemed naked and bare, like one of the trees lining the street outside that had lost its leaves for the winter. It also looked far bigger now that it had been cleared of all the woman's possessions. To the right, the wooden panels of the main bedroom door caught his eye. The entire middle portion of the frame had been replaced, the fresh wood a slightly different shade from the rest.

He remembered the night last year when that door had been blown apart by a shotgun shell and handgun fire.

He glanced back at the woman.

That was the night the two of them met.

'All done?' he asked, forcing a smile.

'All done.'

'So this is it?'

She sighed and nodded. 'I guess so.' She paused. 'I'm sorry.'

'Yeah. Me too.'

'It just wasn't going to work. And I have to think about my and Jessie's futures.'

He nodded. He went to speak again, but there was the sudden blare of a car horn from outside. The woman checked her watch.

'That's me. I need to get over to LaGuardia. My flight leaves just before midday.'

'I'll walk you down.'

She nodded and followed him towards the door, grabbing a coat from the kitchen counter and pulling it on. Before she left, she took one last look at the empty apartment.

For a second, the place was busy, full of her memories.

Leaving the spare key on the side, she turned and shut the door for the last time, following the blond man along the corridor and down the stairs to the building exit.

Outside, the sun was shining but the air was cold, icy winds blowing down East 13th Street. City maintenance had already done their rounds this morning; snow had been cleared off the roads and sidewalks, piled up to the side to allow access for cars and pedestrians. The streets had then been salted to allow traction for wheels and grip for shoes. To the left, an endless stream of vehicles flowed up 1st Avenue, a faint Christmas song audible from the radio in a deli on the corner of the street. The beating heart of Manhattan on a typical New York December day.

A yellow taxicab was waiting by the kerb outside the apartment building, as close as the banked snow would allow.

The woman pulled up the collar of her coat and turned to the blond man.

'Good luck,' she said. 'With everything.'

He nodded. 'You too.'

They embraced, then parted. Turning, the woman stepped through a gap in the snow and pulled open the door of the cab, climbing inside and slamming the door. She turned to him and smiled, waving as the taxi pulled away and headed off down the road. The man raised his hand in farewell. The driver paused at a red light at the end of the street, waiting to join the stream of traffic heading up 1st Avenue. The light flicked green and the taxi turned right.

Then it was gone.

The blond man stood still, the sharp wind ruffling his hair, looking down the street.

Just like that, he thought.

He felt a purr in his pocket as his cell phone started ringing. He pulled it out and answered.

'Archer.'

'Arch, its Josh.'

'Hey. What's up?' he said, starting to walk down the sidewalk towards the traffic stream on 1st Avenue.

'Shepherd wants us in immediately.'

Archer frowned. 'What's going on?'

'I don't know. But it sounds serious. Want me to pick you up?'

'No, I'm in the city. I'll hitch a cab.'

'OK. See you there.'

Archer ended the call and walked along the icy sidewalk until he arrived on the corner of 1st and 13th. He raised his arm and an approaching taxi in the right-hand lane slowed and drew to a halt beside him.

As he stepped forward, pulling open the door, he checked the time on the black Casio on his wrist.

9:56 am. Saturday. His day off.

His eight years of experience as a cop told him that whatever this was, it wasn't going to be good.

'Shit,' he muttered, stepping inside the taxi and slamming the door.

And the vehicle moved off up the street.

Thirteen miles away in New Jersey, a slender grey-haired man in a dark coat stepped out of his brand new Mercedes and shut the door. The car was a black CL-Class that had set him back over 100 grand but as far as he was concerned it had been worth every cent. He was planning on taking a trip to DC with his wife over the Christmas break when he'd have a chance to really put his foot down and see what the Mercedes could do on the open road.

Clicking the locks shut, he tucked the keys in his pocket and headed towards the entrance of *The Kearny Medical Institute*, a three-floored laboratory complex located just off the town of Kearny in Hudson County.

His name was Dr Jonathan Bale. Although he was too modest to acknowledge it, Dr Bale was widely considered to possess one of the top scientific minds in the United States. He and his six-man team were responsible for some pioneering work at the institute. They worked closely with medical organisations around the country, as well as interacting with the US Army and their Medical Research Institute. Dr Bale was fifty eight, enjoyed good health and had no immediate intention to retire. He had four things that he loved in his life: his wife, his job, his new Mercedes and golf. He'd just come from an early nine holes at Liberty National and had shot a very satisfactory 37. The low score had given him an extra spring to his step and he was feeling good.

Approaching the entrance, a briefcase in his hand and a folder under his arm, he pushed open the glass door. As he walked in, he was surprised to see a new security guard behind the front desk. The man looked tall and rangy and sported a strange haircut. Blond, it was on the verge of being a mullet, short at the sides and longer on top.

Bale hid a smile.

Must be some kind of new fashion, he thought.

'Good morning, sir,' the guard said, a Southern twang to his voice.

'Good morning.' Bale looked around. 'Where's Joel?'

'He took sick. I'm covering his shift.'

Bale nodded.

The guard had a pad and pen in his hands. 'Your name please sir?'

'Dr Bale. My team should already be here.'

'Yes, they're all upstairs. You're the last one. I'll just buzz you in.'

The guard pushed a button under his desk and the glass panel beside the desk slid back. He smiled warmly.

'You have a good morning, sir.'

Bale nodded as he walked forward and approached the lift, pushing the button. The door in front of him opened immediately. He stepped inside and pressed *3*, mentally running through all the tasks he and his team had to work on today. A few seconds later, the lift dinged again and the doors slid open on the third floor.

He walked forward, looking at the folder in his hand and his mind on the day ahead, but suddenly sensed someone standing in front of him.

He looked up.

A large man with thick black curly hair was blocking his path.

No one else was around.

The man's arm was outstretched; he was gripping a pistol aimed straight at Dr Bale's forehead.

Bale dropped his folder and briefcase, shocked, and raised his hands instinctively.

Behind the handgun, the man's face was cold and hard. He nudged the pistol to Bale's right.

'Move.'

Dr Bale did what he was told, staring at the weapon, too scared to object.

'Keep going.'

Dr Bale kept walking.

He arrived at a colleague's office. The door was closed.

'Open it.'

Dr Bale did.

As the door pushed back he saw with horror that a pile of bodies had been dumped inside, all of them shot in the head. They were all the members of his team, dumped one on top of the other. Amidst the heap he caught a glimpse of a security guard's uniform. *Joel.*

The white-tiled floor was pooled and caked with dried blood.

'Whh-what-,' he stammered, fear making his vocal cords seize up.

'Inside.'

Trying not to faint, Dr Bale did as he was told. At his feet, he could see the dead faces of his colleagues and friends. Some of the most brilliant scientists in the country.

Their eyes open and lifeless.

'Against the wall.'

Bale moved back to the wall, but self-preservation kicked in. He started trying to reason with the man.

'Please. I'm beg-'

He never finished the sentence. The weapon in the other man's hand was a modified Glock, an illegal trigger catch turning the weapon from a semi-automatic into an automatic. With an extended magazine slapped into the base of the weapon, he had thirty two bullets to work with.

Lowering the weapon in anticipation of the muzzle climb, the man pulled the trigger. The weapon drained the mag in just over a second, and Dr Bale took every single bullet to the face.

When the gun clicked dry and the echo of gunfire ceased, the body collapsed to the floor, cordite in the air, blood and brains and small black holes sprayed all over the wall behind where he'd been standing. The curly-haired man pulled the empty clip from the weapon and tossed it to the ground. Then he walked out, shutting the door behind him. He pulled a fresh magazine from his pocket and slapped it into the weapon, snapping the working mechanism forward and loading a shell in the chamber.

He walked across the empty lab towards a chair and took a seat directly in front of the lift.

Waiting for whoever came next.

THREE

Fifteen minutes after Archer had stepped inside the taxi, it turned off Vernon Boulevard in Queens and began to move down a side street, passing a long junkyard and several auto-body shops. In the back, Archer looked out of the window to his right. The snowfall here had been pretty heavy last night, the same as in Manhattan. The white stuff had been shovelled and ploughed to the kerb to clear the way for vehicles, piled a couple of feet high in some places.

They paused at a red light for a few moments, then crossed the street and continued to head south. Before long, a long red-brick building slid into view on the left. It was unmarked and looked innocuous, blending in with all the other structures on the block.

'Here's good,' Archer said.

The driver looked at him through the rear-view mirror. 'Right here?'

'Yeah.'

The driver shrugged and pulled to a halt by the kerb. Archer paid the fare and tipped the guy then climbed out and slammed the door shut behind him. As the taxi moved off, turning the corner and disappearing out of sight, Archer looked around. He could see why the driver had been confused. The whole neighbourhood was pretty much deserted, just the faint sound of a radio hanging in the air from one of the auto-body shops nearby.

He walked straight towards a set of glass doors that led into the red-brick building and pulled one of them open, moving inside.

A second glass door was directly in front of him, this one electronically controlled. He drew an ID card from his pocket and swiped it down a card reader. It *buzzed*, a green light on the boxed-panel flicking on; he pushed the second door open and walked into the Counter Terrorism Bureau for the New York Police Department.

The bustle and hum of activity inside the building couldn't have been in greater contrast to the quietness of the street. To the left as you walked in was a large technical area containing a team of some twenty analysts. On the wall in front of them was a myriad of LED news tickers, electronic maps, digital world clocks and television screens tuned to various news channels both from within the United States and from all over the world. Some of the analysts were wearing headphones, monitoring foreign broadcasts and communications, constantly on their guard for anything that so much as hinted at a threat. Others were working closer to home, running key words through domestic calls and internet searches, scouring communications for anything that seemed at all unusual. The rest were working on a variety of jobs such as threading through intelligence, tracking potential suspects or working with field teams based out of the building. Open twenty four hours a day, seven days a week, the Bureau epitomised both the way the world and technology had changed in the last few years and also how the NYPD now conducted its affairs.

Since that terrible day in September 2001 when the city had come under attack, New York's security systems had undergone a multi-million dollar transformation. The Mayor,

Commissioners, Police Chiefs, Lieutenants and street police had collectively done one hell of a job. Crime-wise, New York was now regarded as the safest big city in the United States, just ahead of El Paso in Texas, a real triumph considering where the place had been back in the 80s and early 90s. The number of criminal incidents across the city had plummeted in the past decade and scores of gangs had been driven out of the State due to intensive policing by city law enforcement.

However, New York was still the number one US target for terrorist activity. With over eight million residents, it's standing as the financial and business capital of the nation and with a subway system used by three and a half million people every day, the city knew it had a large red target painted on its chest. Protecting it was a constant and sometimes almost overwhelming challenge. But it was one that was an absolute necessity.

The work was relentless. Like most counter-terrorist work, ninety-nine per cent of the time the public never knew about the successes. They only knew about the failures. From his position near the entrance Archer watched the tech team work. They were like their own tribe, working on assignments, talking to each other in a foreign language of technical jargon, coding and in-house slang, surrounded by some of the most advanced technology available to any police force in the world. The information they gathered was invaluable. It both protected the millions of people who lived in the city and also enabled the 125 detectives who worked out of the building to do their job effectively.

Given that the NYPD had precincts spread across the five boroughs and around 35,000 officers to call upon, the detectives in the Counter Terrorism Bureau had different responsibilities. Much of their work involved threat assessment on major city landmarks, public and private properties and areas in the city deemed vulnerable to terrorist attack. They conducted security audits, ensuring that every appropriate defensive measure was in place and that there weren't any chinks in the armour that could be exploited. They had informants and undercover detectives infiltrating the criminal element in the city, their objective to gather any information on terrorist sleeper cells.

It was like a deadly game of chess. Although the city was now protected like a fortress, it was a certainty that there were groups out there desperate to find a weakness in its defences. The 125 detectives were separated into divisions with various assignments. Archer was part of a five-man detail which was at the top of the food chain when it came to emergencies and casework. Given that he'd been a counter-terrorist task force cop in the UK just seven months ago, how Archer happened to land here now was partly luck, but was mostly down to a stroke of good timing and his old boss in the UK.

Archer had left his police team in London, the Armed Response Unit, in May. Being half-American and therefore bypassing any visa issues, he'd decided to move to New York City for the foreseeable future. Once in New York, he'd intended to apply for the NYPD and if accepted, begin re-training and then work his way up through the ranks from the ground. He needed at least five years on the street before he could attempt his goal of qualifying for the Emergency Service Unit, the NYPD's SWAT team, but it was something that he was fully prepared to do. His father had been an NYPD cop and he'd recently discovered an ambition to follow in his footsteps, to experience what it was like to police *the capital city of the world,* as his dad had called it.

But a few days after he'd arrived and was prepping his application, Archer had received a call from Director Tim Cobb, his boss at the ARU in London. When Archer had explained his reasoning for handing in his notice back in May, Cobb had promised to try and help speed up his process of induction. He'd worked quite extensively with members of the NYPD in the past and had the sort of professional connections that could help Archer out.

However, the proposition he'd made in that phone call was beyond anything the younger man could have imagined or hoped for.

In its new era of law enforcement, the NYPD now had detectives placed in major cities all over the world, in locations such as Lyon, Hamburg, Tel Aviv and Toronto. It wasn't a secret to the police forces in those countries; the detectives weren't on clandestine operations. They were there to work closely with the major intelligence departments in each city and act as tripwires, giving immediate heads-up warnings whenever they were alerted to something relevant to New York City's safety and security. It was a crucial part of the new age of the NYPD.

If something was coming, they wanted to know about it as soon as possible.

Cobb told Archer that he'd contacted one of his colleagues in the Department concerning Archer's situation. The guy had then passed Cobb on to Lieutenant General Jim Franklin, the man who ran the newly-formed Counter Terrorism Bureau. Although the two men had never had dealings in the past, they'd quickly realised that an agreement between them would benefit both parties considerably. Franklin already had two men in the UK working with New Scotland Yard, but given that the ARU was at the forefront of London's fight against terrorism he'd realised that stationing a man at the Unit's headquarters in North London could prove very beneficial.

A deal was proposed.

If Cobb took a man from the NYPD, then Franklin would be happy to take Archer.

When Cobb had rung that night, he told Archer about the planned exchange. He didn't even need to ask if the younger man would say yes. The next day, the swap was given the green light. An NYPD detective was heading to the ARU in London and Archer was joining the Counter Terrorism Bureau in New York City. However, admission wasn't guaranteed. He'd endured extensive background checks and been enrolled in a federal police programme down in Georgia. Given that he'd been a frontline cop in the UK for almost a decade, he'd cruised the training and enjoyed every minute, learning some new techniques and honing some old ones. Once he'd passed the course, the deal was done and at the end of July he'd been formally presented with his badge. It was a huge moment for him.

It meant 3rd Grade Detective Sam Archer was now a member of the NYPD's Counter Terrorism Bureau.

Moving further into the building, Archer turned right and headed into the workplace for the detective squads. This portion of the building was spread over two floors. The lower level was where the working areas were located. Upstairs there were a series of Briefing Rooms and Lieutenant General Franklin's office, all of which lay behind a fenced railing that looked down into the detective pit.

That morning, the place was humming. The weekend shift was hard at work, scores of people at desks, phone conversations taking place and fingers tapping computer keyboards. With the New Year approaching in a couple of weeks, many of the detectives had been assigned security roles for the crowds that would gather in Times Square. Given that there was always an upcoming celebration, parade, sporting event or political visit in the city, there was no such thing as a quiet shift when you worked in this building. Amongst the organised melee, Archer saw that someone had made a half-hearted attempt at putting up Christmas decorations. Token strips of gold and silver tinsel had been draped over a number of partitions separating each cubicle, and a Christmas tree with golden lights had been placed by a wall up ahead. Beside the tree, Archer saw his partner Josh Blake pouring himself a drink from a machine. Archer smiled and walking around the detective area, headed towards him.

Josh was twenty nine, black, and just about the nicest person who worked out of the Bureau. Everyone in the building called him by his first name, not his surname, a testament to the high regard in which he was held. He had a cool head and a maturity befitting a much older man. In the five months Archer had known him, he'd never seen him lose his temper. Originally from New Orleans, Josh had relocated to New York after Katrina had hit in 2005. A Pace University graduate with four years of street experience, he was married with three kids and had a balance in his life that Archer often felt was lacking in his own. Everyone liked Josh. He was strong and calm, with a measured approach to everything he did. He was also a serious weightlifter and had forearms like Popeye. It was always a gamble when a cop was assigned a partner and Archer had hoped that he and 3rd Grade Detective Josh Blake would get along. He needn't have worried. The two of them had hit it off from the moment they met and had since become very good friends.

As Archer walked towards him, Josh sensed someone approaching and turned. He had two foam cups in his hands. Like most in the Department, Josh had been a routine coffee drinker when he and Archer had first met, but his new partner had got him hooked on tea. Now he drank it every morning and had become quite an aficionado, much to his wife's and Archer's amusement.

He passed one of the cups to Archer and winked.

'Earl Grey, no milk, no sugar. And good morning.'

'Thanks,' Archer said, taking it. 'You too. Am I the last one here?'

Josh shook his head.

'You're number four. No sign of Shepherd yet.'

The drinks machine was near where their five-man team was stationed in the detective area. Archer glanced over his shoulder and saw that none of their team was at their desk.

'Where are we meeting?'

'Briefing Room 5,' Josh said, motioning up with his head. 'C'mon.'

The two men turned to their left and headed up a metal stairwell to the second floor. When they reached the top of the stairs they turned right and moved down the walkway, entering Briefing Room 5. In the centre of the room was a long rectangular table, chairs either side. A large screen was mounted on the wall straight ahead, hooked up to a computer terminal which was positioned down the far left of the table, ready and waiting for any member of the analyst team who needed it.

Following Josh into the room, Archer saw two other members of the detail had already arrived, Jorgensen and Marquez. Both of them were wearing off-duty clothes, Jorgensen in a thick navy-blue fleece and jeans, Marquez in a black coat, black sweater and grey trousers. They were sitting on the left of the table. Josh and Archer took seats opposite them on the right.

Across the table, Jorgensen glared at Archer.

'Finally,' he said, confrontationally. 'Where the hell have you been? At the salon getting your hair done?'

Archer smiled at him. 'No, I was with your sister. She says hi.'

Marquez and Josh both chuckled. Jorgensen's eyes narrowed in hostility.

His full name was Dave Jorgensen. Queens born and bred, he was an imposing guy, six foot three and about two hundred and twenty pounds. Before he became a cop he'd been a real up-and-coming American Football player, a starting linebacker at Rutgers for three years. By all accounts he'd been a red-hot prospect and had all the potential to go into the NFL after he graduated, but like many guys before him and many to follow, one injury had destroyed that dream. He'd blown his knee out in his final year and any promise of a professional career had instantly vanished. When he'd managed to get off crutches and walk again, he'd done two things. He'd applied to join the NYPD and had developed a large chip on his shoulder that he'd never managed to remove. He was short-tempered and confrontational, and a lot of people in the Bureau avoided him as a consequence.

But he had a special dislike for Archer. It had been evident from the minute Archer had walked in five months ago. Given his background, he'd been expecting some heat and initial opposition to his inclusion in the Bureau, despite the fact that his father had been NYPD. He hadn't been disappointed. But Jorgensen in particular really hated him, so much so that it had taken Archer by surprise, although he could guess the reason. Archer knew that close to a thousand cops had applied for positions in the Counter Terrorism Bureau after its inception. Josh had told him over a beer that Jorgensen's best friend, an old team mate at Rutgers, had applied for one of the spots but had just missed the final cut. Judging from his attitude, Archer guessed that Jorgensen felt his friend would have been a more valuable addition to the team than him.

He met the big detective's glare across the table and stared straight back, not intimidated in the slightest. Archer just thanked God that the two of them hadn't been assigned as partners. That would have been awkward.

Sitting beside Jorgensen was 3rd Grade Detective Lisa Marquez. She was an entirely different case from him altogether. The only woman in the team, she was also one of the most natural detectives Archer had met, on both sides of the Atlantic. Born in the Bronx and just turned thirty two years old, Marquez was a great mix of Latina passion and incisive thinking. Although she was only five six and about a hundred and thirty pounds, she was just as tough as Jorgensen and didn't take an ounce of his shit, which was just as well considering that the two of them were partners. She was perceptive and sharp; Archer had liked her from the moment they'd met. The feeling was mutual.

She looked across the table at him and nodded, giving a quick smile.

'Morning, Archer,' she said.

'Morning.'

Just as Jorgensen was about to speak again, there was movement behind them at the door and the head of the team entered the room, Sergeant Matt Shepherd, dressed in a cream-coloured fleece and dark blue jeans. In his mid-thirties and with almost fifteen years of experience under his belt, Shepherd was one of those guys who would be just as comfortable in a gunfight in a crack den as he would be delivering a presentation to the senior heads of the Police Department in shirt and tie. Previously Josh's sergeant at Midtown South, Shepherd had made the transfer to the Bureau with him. He was similar in build to Jorgensen, over six feet tall with a powerful frame, but that was where the similarities between the two men ended. Shepherd had a far more likeable demeanour and was also one hell of a leader.

The team had recently been forced to make do without him for a month. He'd returned two weeks ago from an unexpected leave of absence. No one knew why he'd been forced to take time off or where he'd gone, but once he'd returned they'd picked up straight away that things weren't right. Usually an engaging and charismatic guy, Shepherd hadn't smiled once since he'd returned to duty. He seemed distracted and slightly aloof. Everyone on the team was concerned, but no one had dared broach the subject with him. He'd talk when he was ready. And right now, he obviously wasn't.

Stern-faced, he walked past the detectives to the head of the table, followed by a computer analyst named Rach. In her early thirties, with blonde hair and a kind but somewhat plain face, Rach worked with the team as their main analyst. She was diminutive and unassuming but was just as valuable as every other member of the team. Hollywood frequently portrayed their heroes working alone against seemingly insurmountable odds but the reality was very different. None of the detectives in the room could do their job without Rach's assistance. Jorgensen might have outweighed her by a hundred pounds, but she was just as important as he was, perhaps even more so.

As she moved past Jorgensen and Marquez, taking a seat behind the computer terminal, Shepherd nodded at Archer to shut the door. The room was quiet, the only sounds coming from Rach as she started tapping away at the computer. Sitting back down, Archer took a mouthful of tea and watched the screen on the wall spark into life, the NYPD login page appearing and Rach quickly typing herself in.

Shepherd stood to the right of the computer screen. He had that now familiar grave look on his face.

But this morning, he looked even more serious.

FOUR

'Morning everyone,' he said. 'Listen up.'

He looked over at Rach and nodded. She hit a key and a photograph came up on the screen.

'At just after 8 o'clock this morning, a corpse was found alongside the fence at Sheep Meadow in Central Park. Take a look.'

The team examined the photograph. Archer knew Sheep Meadow well and saw from the background that the shot had been taken facing east. Yellow tape had been drawn up around a shape on the ground, the area cordoned off with small orange cones. The victim was mostly covered with snow, but patches of brown trouser and black boot were partially visible through the white. Archer saw that the body was lying near a trash can, a trolley loaded with black bags abandoned beside it.

'An early-morning jogger stopped for a breath of air and spotted something unusual on the snow by the fence,' Shepherd continued. 'She walked forward to take a closer look and saw that it was a body.'

Rach tapped a key and the shot changed. This photograph had been taken immediately above the corpse. What looked like blood was faintly spattered around him, but the guy had been there for some time. His body and the blood were mostly covered by snow which had fallen overnight.

'Was he shot?' Josh asked.

'No,' Shepherd said. 'He wasn't.'

He nodded at Rach who hit a key.

The shot changed to a third photograph, the snow cleared off the man's face. His eyes were open but dim, lifeless. Blood had dried around his mouth and lower part of his face, like a little kid who'd been eating ice cream from a cone.

'CSU checked his body. They couldn't find any knife or gunshots wounds, so HAZMAT and National Health Services were called. They set up a perimeter in the Park and screened the body right there on the snow. I'm afraid what they found is concerning.'

He pointed to the photograph.

'This man was infected with a Type-3 Pneumonic virus. It's a strain that no one at Health Services has seen before. They think it's some sort of a bastardised form of tuberculosis.'

The team took this in, as Rach changed the photograph back to the first one.

'CSU found a small empty pressurised vial hidden in a shoebox placed here,' Shepherd said, tapping the screen, pointing at a small shape by the trash can. 'Apparently it was rigged up to a disturbance switch. The victim was a groundsman who emptied the trash in the Meadow area each weeknight. It looks as if he opened the box and it sprayed some kind of gas right in his face.'

The shot changed to a close-up photo from above the box. A lid was lying above it. Archer saw the empty vial, lying horizontally along the upper portion of the shoebox and what must have been the disturbance switch lining the open lid.

'But we got lucky. HAZMAT said that despite the strength of whatever was in that vial the shot of gas was insignificant and not prolonged. It was snowing at the time, so the moisture in the air disseminated what gas there was before it could spread. Fortunately, no one else was in the immediate area when it went off last night. But if it hadn't have been snowing and there'd been a wind blowing, we'd be in a very different situation right now. We'd probably be down at the city morgue tallying the dead.'

'What about the runner who found him, sir?' Marquez asked. 'Is she OK?'

'She's fine. Once the host is dead, it's not contagious. It's only transmittable via the air.'

'Has anyone claimed responsibility?' Archer asked.

'I've been trying to catch a lead,' Rach said. 'But so far, nothing. No threats or ransom demands.'

'Could it be international?'

Shepherd shook his head. 'We think it's domestic. Nothing has come up on the radar. You know how good Rach and everyone next door is. We contacted Interpol and MI6 earlier this morning but they haven't picked anything up either. Nothing from our people in Asia, the Middle East, or South America.'

He tapped the screen, pointing at the boxed shell of the detonated bomb.

'Whatever this is, it's coming from inside the country. Appropriate departments around the city have been warned. Health Services are working on the victim's body trying to isolate the strain that killed him and see if there's an existing antidote but they're not hopeful. They've never seen anything like this before.'

He looked down at his team.

'But we need to find out where the hell this shit came from and who has it. And we need to do it before any more is released. The next time we may not be so lucky. Lieutenant General Franklin has ordered that we are the investigating team. This is our responsibility.'

He paused.

'Pull up the victim's profile, Rach.'

She tapped several keys and a driving licence appeared on the screen. Archer saw a middle-aged Mexican man in the photograph. With jet black hair and skin the colour of coffee, he looked like a nice guy, completely harmless. And totally unrecognisable from the bloody frozen husk of a human being who'd died out there in the Meadow.

'His name was Luis Cesar,' Shepherd said. 'Fifty two years old, immigrant from Mexico, worked as a groundsman in Central Park for eleven years. Leaves behind a widow and five kids. He and his wife live in an apartment up in Spanish Harlem.'

The room was silent as they looked at the dead man's photo.

Shepherd turned to Jorgensen and Marquez.

'I want you two to head up there. His wife called 911 early this morning saying that her husband didn't come home last night. She hasn't been told what happened. I want you to deliver the news.'

'Shit,' Jorgensen said.

'Are we telling her the truth?' Marquez asked.

'Save the specifics. He died from unknown causes. Tell her he didn't suffer. Leave it at that.'

'OK,' Marquez said, scribbling down the address from the driving licence.

'If you can, find out if anything out of the ordinary has been going on lately,' Shepherd added. 'Anything strange in her husband's behaviour or unusual phone calls, that sort of thing. I'm almost positive this was just wrong place, wrong time, but we need to make one hundred per cent sure he wasn't a deliberate target.'

Shepherd shifted his attention to Archer and Josh.

'There's a research laboratory located on West 66th and Amsterdam. It's called *Flood Microbiology*. I want you two to head over there. A Dr Peter Flood is expecting you. Find out if he or his team recognise these symptoms or have any idea where this could have come from.'

The two men nodded.

'This room will be the base of operations. Rach and I will work out of here, staying close to the line with Health Services. All precincts across the city have been notified of the threat. ESU and Chemical Response Teams are on standby but we're the ranking team on the case.'

He pointed at Cesar's licence. His already tense face hardened.

'Make no mistake. We're going to find out who killed this man. No one does something like that in this city and gets away with it.'

'What about Central Park security cameras?' Marquez asked. 'They might tell us who planted the device?'

'Two techs next door are already checking them,' Rach said. 'But there isn't any CCTV in the immediate Meadow area, and over ten thousand people went in and out of the Park yesterday. It's like finding a needle in a haystack.'

Shepherd nodded, checking his watch.

'We need to get going. Questions?'

There were none.

'Remember, its seven days until Christmas. There're eight million people living in the city right now with a shitload more tourists on top.'

He tapped the screen.

'Someone out there did this for a reason. We're going to find out who they are and take them down.'

He looked at his team and nodded.

'Let's go to work.'

Across Queens, three men were sitting in a booth in the middle of a diner just off the 30th Avenue subway stop in Astoria. All three were dressed in an assortment of jeans, coats and thick sweatshirts, a half-filled cup of coffee in front of each of them. Their bodies were full of nervous energy. Between them, they'd only managed a few hours sleep last night.

There were two reasons for that.

One of them was anticipation of the task ahead of them this morning.

And the other was that there were meant to be four of them there in the diner. One of their team was missing.

He'd gone out late last night to get some pizza and had never come back.

His disappearance had seriously unsettled each member of the trio. One of them, the leader of the group, was doing his best to eat something from a plate in front of him. It was a slice of apple pie doused with cream, more dessert than breakfast. He'd ordered it out of habit but it wasn't going down. Watching him struggle with the pie, the man sitting across from him frowned. Dark-haired and wiry with a forgettable face, he was dressed in a thick jacket and sweater, the faint wispy lines of some tattoos visible just above the collar.

'How the hell can you eat right now, Bleeker?' he asked.

The man called Bleeker glanced up at him. He hesitated, then admitted defeat and tossed the fork on the plate, grabbing his coffee and forcing down a mouthful of caffeine. Around the cup, his knuckles were red and bruised.

His first name was Paul but everyone called him Bleeker. Even his mother. At twenty eight years old, he was a complete and utter failure in every aspect of his life. He'd dropped out of high school with no qualifications. He had no girlfriend. He lived alone and was overweight. He'd never held down a job for longer than a couple of months and that was only if they took him on in the first place. Being a convicted felon didn't help his cause. The only thing he had in his life that meant something was membership of a certain organisation; after a stint upstate two years ago, he'd joined the group his first week inside and had been a member ever since. He'd signed up partly out of curiosity and a need to belong, but mostly out of wanting to survive his prison term and avoid getting gang-raped in his cell or shanked out in the yard.

However, he'd been pleasantly surprised at the perks that had followed after he was released. Given that he'd done legit time, he found he wasn't at the bottom of the food chain for once. Suddenly he had some authority and people willing to do what he said. For the first time in his life, Paul Bleeker had a say in something. That unfamiliar feeling of importance had increased over time, to the point where he now didn't take shit from anybody.

And if he saw an opportunity, he took it.

All those factors had put him in the diner this morning and set in course what would take place in the city later that day. His bruised knuckles tightening around the mug, he drank from his coffee, thinking of all those years when he'd been treated like shit and how he'd had to put up with it.

After this morning, that would never happen again.

The diner was reasonably busy, people drifting in and out, the bell above the door frequently dinging and a blast of cold air accompanying each entrance and exit. Christmas music from the sound system filled the air, mingling with the murmurs of low conversation and the noise from the kitchen around the back. A tired-looking middle-aged waitress wandered over to their table, giving them a perfunctory smile, a pot of coffee in her hand.

'Refill?'

Bleeker nodded, pushing his cup towards her. The woman filled it, then looked at the other two men. Neither responded and she moved away.

'You think he got cold feet?' asked the man sitting beside Bleeker, looking at the empty space in the four-man booth. He was the youngest of the group, just turned twenty years old with a slight frame and a weak face. His eyes were darting nervously around the room, his leg jiggling under the table.

The man across the table shook his head.

'You know Ray. He isn't a pussy.'

'So where the hell is he?'

'Forget him,' Bleeker said. 'Whether he ran or not, we've got a job to do. You need to focus. We do this and we do it right.'

Silence followed. Bleeker drank some of his fresh coffee, then looked at his watch.

'Time check.'

The other two looked at their watches.

'10:25.'

'Check.'

'Check.'

Bleeker took a deep breath. 'So let's do this thing. Donnie, pay the tab.'

Bleeker and the other man slid out from the booth. The kid called Donnie pulled a twenty from his wallet and trapped it under a glass, then moved out and joined the others. Together, the three men walked to the door of the diner.

Each of them carrying a white plastic bag containing a rectangular shoebox.

FIVE

'Don't let Jorgensen get to you,' Josh said, turning the steering wheel. 'He's an asshole.'

He and Archer were in one of the Bureau's blacked-out Ford Explorers. They were just moving onto the Queensborough Bridge which led across the East River and into the east side of Manhattan. It was a sunny morning, but it was still damn chilly. They had the heating going in the car, but it was taking a while to warm up.

'Believe or not, he's actually good police,' Josh continued. 'He's just deficient in his personality.'

Archer shrugged. 'One less Christmas card I have to write this year.' Reaching forward, he cranked the heating up a notch.

'So Katic left this morning?' Josh asked.

'Yeah. She's gone.'

'You say goodbye?'

Archer nodded. 'I was over there when you rang.'

Josh glanced at him. 'How'd it go?'

'It was fine.'

'That's it? It was fine?'

Archer shrugged again. 'She and I met on one of the most dangerous nights of our lives. Then I left. Once I came back and with all that adrenaline gone, we both realised we'd moved on.'

'She's a Fed, right?'

'Yeah. She's taking up an Agent-in-Charge position at their field office in Chicago. Her family are there too. Her kid's starting school there in the New Year.'

Josh nodded, sensing Archer didn't want to talk any more about it, and a silence fell in the car.

Archer looked out of the window and watched the thick pillars of the Bridge pass by, the icy-cold East River running fast below. Moving to New York from the UK wasn't a decision he'd taken lightly. He'd been more than happy in his prestigious position on the First Team of the ARU. They were one of the leading counter-terrorist task forces in London after all, and he'd worked alongside some of the best men and women out there. His great friend Chalky. Porter, Fox and Deakins, top guys who were more family than work colleagues. Nikki, a tech analyst who was both a close friend and an old flame. And Cobb, the best boss a man could ask for.

But a big factor in coming here had been FBI Supervisory Special Agent Mina Katic. Ever since they'd met last summer she'd been constantly in his thoughts. He'd arrived in New York seven months ago and initially everything seemed to be fine; but then Archer had realised it just wasn't working. Something was missing. Aside from just feeling 'off', they both worked insanely unpredictable hours. They'd been separated by an ocean before, but now they were in the same city they still barely saw each other. Like embers on a dying fire, their romance had slowly dimmed and faded.

Soon enough, the spark was gone.

Her job offer in Chicago had been a blessing in disguise. He'd sensed for a while she'd had enough of New York and wanted to move back to where she'd grown up with her daughter, Jess, who would be starting high school in the next couple of years. When she'd first mentioned that she was thinking of leaving, Archer hadn't felt any desire to ask her to stay.

That was when he knew it was over.

The period leading up to her departure, much like their goodbye this morning, had been very civil with no acrimony or hostility. Neither felt any anger towards the other. But for whatever reason, be it personal or professional, what they had obviously wasn't destined to be a long-term thing. It almost seemed to Archer that a man in this career had to pick between his work and his personal life. You couldn't have both. But then he glanced at Josh and realised that wasn't true. You couldn't find a happier married man or a more doting father. Josh was getting it right. Archer wanted to find out what his secret was.

The horn of a passing car blared, bringing Archer back to the situation at hand. They'd just moved off the Bridge and were now in Manhattan. Josh drove down 59th, headed west, past 1st, 2nd and 3rd Avenues. Then Park, Madison and 5th. Central Park rolled into view on their right. Everywhere he looked there were red and gold Christmas decorations, shoppers wrapped up in thick coats, many of them laden with bags as they made their way to a coffee shop or back to their hotels. A group of carol singers had taken up a position on the sidewalk by the south-east entrance of Central Park and he caught a glimpse of an ice-skating rink through a gap in the trees as they drove down the street. New York did Christmas damn well. There were throngs of people everywhere, all enjoying a festive weekend.

All of them blissfully unaware that a man had died a horrific toxic death across the Park last night.

'You got plans Christmas Day?' Josh asked.

'Haven't thought about it.'

'What about your sister? She's in DC, right?'

'She's having a hot one. Going off with the family to the Caribbean.'

'Never understood that. It wouldn't feel right having a barbeque on Christmas Day.'

'Right now I wouldn't mind.'

Josh grinned. 'You should come over. We'd love to have you.'

'I can't do that. Christmas is family time.'

'Yeah, but now I won't be able to fully relax. When I'm sitting by a warm fire with a cold beer and a plate of food, I'll think of you alone in your apartment looking pathetic, pulling the ring off a can of soup.'

'OK, I'll think about it.'

Josh shook his head. 'It's not your decision anymore. I'll tell Michelle. The moment I do that, it's a given. Otherwise she'll head over to your place on Christmas morning and march you over to our house herself.'

Archer laughed. They stopped at a red light at Columbus Circle, then once it turned green drove around the monument and headed uptown on Broadway.

'Where is this place?' Josh asked. '66th, right?'

'66th and Amsterdam.'

From Columbus to around West 86th, Broadway was positioned at a right-diagonal that eventually straightened out. Given its slant, the road met 9th Avenue on 64th Street. Josh held at a red light, then took a left across the intersection and headed down 65th. The next Avenue over was Amsterdam. When the light was green, Josh moved out and over to the left hand lane. He pulled up to the kerb just past 66th, applying the handbrake and killing the engine.

The two men stepped out of the car, Archer hunching into his coat and pulling his collar up against the blast of the cold wind. Being on the west side of Manhattan, they were close to the Hudson River and the wind had an extra bite to it. Slamming his door and jamming his hands into his pockets, he walked around the front of the car and joined Josh on the edge of the sidewalk. Several stores and a frozen yoghurt place were lined side by side up the block, but the building in front of them had to be the address they were after. Judging by the entrance, a number of different businesses and companies had office space here. A series of company names and logos on metal placards lined the walls either side of the entrance, all in different swirling calligraphy and fonts.

Archer looked up at the building as Josh walked forward to check out the plates. About a third of the way down, in plain, printed, no-bullshit style was *Flood Microbiology*.

'Bull's-eye,' Josh said.

Archer didn't respond.

Josh looked over his shoulder. 'Let's head-'

He stopped mid-sentence.

Archer's head was tilted back and he was staring up at the building in front of them.

There was something wrong.

'Arch?'

'*Look*,' he said.

Josh frowned and stepping back to join his partner, tilted his head to see what had caught Archer's attention. The building was about twenty storeys high, but he immediately saw what Archer had spotted.

'*What the hell?*' he said.

The two men backed up quickly, moving out onto the street beside the car to get a better look.

They could see a man standing on the edge of the roof.

Eleven blocks uptown, a man in his early thirties was just finishing cooking a late breakfast, some eggs and bacon sizzling in a pan. He lived alone in an apartment on the Upper West Side. He wasn't a social guy and had never been particularly comfortable around women, so he much preferred his own company in his own private place to having people around. It had been a long week and he was looking forward to relaxing all day by himself, just the way he liked it.

But suddenly, the doorbell rang.

It made him jump. He wasn't expecting a guest. Maybe it was a delivery, or someone from downstairs.

'One second,' he called, tipping the frying pan and sliding his breakfast onto a plate. Turning off the cooker and wiping his hands on a cloth, he walked over to the door and pulled it open.

There was a man and woman standing there.

The man had bleach-blond hair, with a sharp jagged scar across one eyebrow. In contrast to his hair, he had dark, emotionless eyes that wouldn't have looked out of place on a shark.

The woman was dark-haired with a harsh face, her hard eyes emphasised by thick black eyeliner.

They stared at him, expressionless.

The man had a roll of duct tape in his hand.

And the woman was holding a silenced pistol.

SIX

The lift inside the building on 66th and Amsterdam dinged, opening on the 20th floor. Before the doors had fully parted, Archer and Josh sprinted out. The door to the stairwell was straight ahead; Archer wrenched it open and the two men raced up the stairs that led to the roof, bursting through the last door and running out onto the rooftop.

Fifteen yards away, they saw up close what they'd caught a glimpse of from the street.

A man was standing on the very edge of the rooftop. Ten feet behind him was a young woman, her hands covering her mouth.

Both of them were in lab coats.

The woman turned when she heard the two newcomers arrive. She looked distraught and terrified. She was standing beside a smoking oil can, bits of burnt paper swirling around her, catching the wind and whipping off into the air. Archer pulled his badge and showed it to her silently, walking forward. She nodded, her eyes wide with fear. As he moved closer, Archer saw that they were also filled with tears. Josh motioned for her to walk over and join him. She passed Archer as he walked past her slowly, approaching the man on the edge of the roof.

He was completely motionless, his back turned, staring down at the Manhattan street far below. Apart from the whistling of the wind, it was quiet. All the street noise down below was a distant murmur. But the situation was highly dangerous. There was no building or windbreak cover and the gales blowing in from the Hudson were strong, rifling through Archer's hair.

Looking down, he saw the roof under his feet was icy and treacherous. At any moment, the man on the edge could be blown off or slip.

As could he.

Moving towards him ten feet to the right, Archer didn't say a word. The man didn't react or respond when Archer came into his peripheral vision. The wind was snapping through the folds of his white lab coat as if it was a sail.

Archer came to a stop, his hands up in a non-threatening gesture.

Standing there in silence, a few feet from the edge, he looked at the man.

He had grey hair and glasses.

He looked terrified.

'Sir, I'm a detective with the NYPD. My name is Archer.'

The man didn't respond.

'My first name's Sam. What's yours?'

There was a long pause.

'Peter.'

Silence.

The only sound was the wind and the noise Peter's coat made as it was whipped around his body. Archer glanced to his right and looked out over Central Park. From up here he could see all the way up to Harlem. He felt his stomach lurch and fought down vertigo. Turning his attention back to the rooftop, he saw Josh standing with the woman near the door, arms wrapped around her in comfort but also to keep her from moving towards Peter and startling him.

Both of them were watching the tense exchange in silence.

Archer turned back to Peter. Looking down, he noticed that the tips of the man's shoes were over the edge of the building, just his heels keeping him in place.

'Peter, if you step back, we can sit down and talk,' Archer said, slowly and reassuringly. 'I'm sure that whatever's wrong, we can fix it. Together.'

'No. We can't.'

Silence.

'Do you have a family?' Archer asked.

Silence.

'I'm sure they'd want you to move away from the edge,' he said, taking his time, choosing each word carefully. 'Whatever has happened, I'm sure they'd understand.'

He paused.

'Nothing could be worth this.'

For the first time, the man turned his head and looked at Archer.

His eyes looked haunted behind the glasses.

'You need to get out.'

'Out?'

'Of New York. You need to leave right now.'

'Why?'

'Thousands of people are going to die.'

'Why, Peter? What's going to happen?'

Silence.

'Talk to me, Peter.'

Silence.

Archer glanced back at Josh.

And Peter took a step forward.

Across the East River in Astoria, the doors to a Manhattan-bound N train opened and the three men from the diner stepped inside the carriage. Given that it was the weekend the service had been delayed and they'd been waiting on the 30th

Avenue platform for a while. The trio stood together by the doors across the carriage. There wasn't a word of conversation between them. The train was moderately full but no-one gave the men a second glance. There was nothing unusual about them; they blended right in.

By the far doors, Bleeker grabbed a support pole with a meaty hand and looked down at the white bag he held in the other. He saw the shoebox tucked inside.

His ticket to a whole new life.

A female voice came over the intercom. *Stand clear of the closing doors.*

A second later, the doors slid shut.

And the train moved on towards the city.

SEVEN

A police cordon had been set up on Amsterdam just outside the building off 66th. Several officers in uniform were standing with their backs to some blue wooden barriers, preventing any pedestrians who were unwise enough to want to see what had happened from getting any closer. It was easier said than done.

The body was covering about an eight foot radius, concealed under a series of hastily placed sheets. The impact of the fall had left a grisly aftermath. Luckily, no one had been hit by the falling man, although a handful of people had been walking nearby on the sidewalk at the point of impact. They were all in an ambulance nearby being cleaned up and treated for shock.

Inside the lobby and relieved to be back down on street level, Archer looked at the spread of white sheets covering the ground. A four-man team from the CSU, the forensics specialists, had arrived. Archer had just finished speaking to two of them, providing them with the details of what had happened up on the roof, including every word that had been spoken between him and Peter. Standing with the pair of investigators, he watched as a third member of their team knelt down and lifted the sheet with a latex-gloved hand. The fourth dropped to a knee beside him and took photographs of whatever was underneath. Some detectives from the 20th precinct had arrived and were standing together watching the investigators work. Although the death was on their turf it wasn't a homicide, so they were letting Archer and Josh take the reins on this one.

The two CSU investigators thanked Archer. He nodded, then turned and walked back into the main building. A large group of workers from upstairs had gathered in the lobby, some asking what had happened, others trying to catch a glimpse as building security and two other NYPD officers kept them from going outside. Given that the possibility of terrorism was on everybody's mind these days, New Yorkers liked reassurance and word had clearly spread fast about the number of police officers, squad cars and ambulances suddenly gathered outside their building.

To the left of the cluster, Archer saw Josh approaching, clicking off a cell phone and tucking it back into his pocket.

'I just spoke to Rach,' he said. 'His full name was Dr Peter Flood.'

'Flood Microbiology.'

'Exactly. He owned the company. He was the senior scientist and the man we were supposed to be meeting.' Josh looked over Archer's shoulder at the scene outside. 'Poor guy.'

'You hear what he said?'

'You need to get out of New York right now. Thousands of people are going to die.'

'I don't like this. It's too coincidental.'

'You think it's related to the dead guy in the Park?'

Archer nodded. 'I looked into his eyes. Something was scaring the shit out of him.'

'Well Rach is checking out everything she can find on him. We'll know more about him soon.'

Archer looked past Josh and saw the young woman who'd been up on the roof when they'd arrived. She was sitting across the lobby on a bench against the wall, a navy-blue NYPD jacket draped over her slender shoulders. She was alone, staring straight ahead with a cup of coffee in her hands. She'd been hysterical after the man had stepped off the roof to his death, but now seemed to have cried herself out. Josh noticed his partner watching her.

'Her name's Maddy,' he said. 'Twenty eight years old. She's a doctor too.'

He paused.

'And Peter Flood's daughter.'

Archer looked at him. 'Oh shit.'

'Yeah. That's her daddy out there on the sidewalk.' He paused. 'Hey. You did a good job up there, by the way.'

'Yeah, right,' Archer said. 'Perfect outcome.'

'He'd made up his mind. He was stepping off regardless. Nothing you could have done or said would have changed his mind. Was he your first jumper?'

Archer nodded. He went to say more but felt his phone ringing in his pocket. He pulled it out and took the call as Josh turned and headed across the lobby towards the female doctor.

'Archer.'

'Arch, it's Shepherd. I heard Rach speaking to Josh, but I wanted to get your take too. How's everything going?'

Archer looked over his shoulder at the white-sheeted area cordoned off on the street.

'Getting cleaned up. CSU and some local detectives are here. It's going to take a while.'

'How's the girl?'

Archer watched Josh take a seat beside the woman. He was talking to her quietly.

'Better. She's calmed down.'

'We're drawing a blank over here. Rach can't find anything on Flood or his company that could be relevant to this virus. But I think there's a connection.'

'Yeah, I'm getting that feeling.'

'We need her to fill in the blanks and find out why he took a dive.'

'Yes, sir. Anything from Marquez?'

'Yes. CSU found a set of fingerprints on the box from Central Park. They belong to a man called Rashad Cantrell. He's a low-level street dealer based up in Harlem. They're headed over to get him now.'

'That's good.'

'Keep me posted. And get that girl talking.'

'Yes, sir.'

The call ended. Archer tucked the phone back into his pocket. Then he headed over to join Josh and Maddy Flood in the corner of the lobby.

At the Counter Terrorism Bureau, Shepherd put his cell phone back on the table, then examined the computer screen mounted on the wall of the briefing room. Beside him, Rach was tapping the keys, searching through every database she could access.

'Still nothing?

'Not on our system. I think plain old Google could be our friend on this one,' she said, pulling up the website homepage and typing in Flood's name.

The search immediately brought up a number of hits. She clicked on several, lining them up on the screen. Shepherd saw they were newspaper articles and not just from periodicals. *The New York Times, The Washington Post, The Sunday*

Times. Every headline was interesting but one of them was particularly pertinent. It came from a UK paper called *The Guardian.*

American doctor thinks cure for lung cancer is just around the corner.

'Hold up,' Rach said, centring the article on the screen. 'This could be something.'

As the two of them studied the screen, there was a knock on the door behind them. Shepherd turned and saw the head of the Bureau, Lieutenant General James Franklin, standing in the doorway. Franklin was a commanding presence, a thirty year veteran, as tough as redwood with a thick grey moustache and a leathered face, the result of many years of active service for the Department. He was well-known as having been a real bruiser back in the day. He was a guy who didn't answer to anyone in the building, but he never stood on ceremony with anyone and was a good boss to have, especially considering the daunting responsibilities he carried. He also shared a striking resemblance to the actor Sam Elliott. A lot of detectives referred to him as *Wade*, the name of Elliot's character in the cult movie *Road House*. They never did it to his face, though.

'Morning, sir,' Shepherd said.

'Morning, Shep,' Franklin said. 'Can I have a word?'

Shepherd nodded. 'Of course.' He turned to Rach. 'Keep searching.'

He followed his boss outside, joining him by the railing on the walkway. Down below, the desk area for the field teams was busy, detectives milling everywhere.

Facing him, Franklin patted Shepherd on the shoulder.

'How you doing?'

Shepherd nodded, trying to force a smile. 'OK, sir. Bit of a tough morning.'

'How's Beth?'

Shepherd looked away. All attempts at a smile faded.

'I don't know. We haven't spoken in a while.'

'When was the funeral?'

'Last week.'

Franklin nodded. 'How's this virus situation?'

'We're working on it.'

'Good. I know it's your day off, but you're the man I want in charge. That's why I called you in.' Shepherd looked back at Franklin who held his gaze. 'And all bullshit aside, if you want to talk to me, you know where I am.'

'Thank you, sir. I need to get back to work.'

Franklin nodded. Shepherd turned and headed back into the briefing room to re-join Rach.

Franklin remained where he was, watching him walk away.

In New Jersey, another car swung into the parking lot at *The Kearny Medical Institute* where Dr Bale and his team had worked. There were four people inside the vehicle, two men and two women. They weren't a group, however.

Two of them were Wicks and Drexler.

Wicks was behind the wheel. He stopped outside the doors of the three-storey building and pulled on the handbrake. In the back seat, Drexler was sitting on the right, her silenced Glock in her hand, the barrel of the silencer buried in the armpit of the other woman who was sitting beside her. She was shaking with fear.

Drexler pushed open her door, stepped out, then reached back inside and grabbed the woman by her hair. She dragged her out, shoving the silenced pistol into her back while keeping a firm grip on her hair. Wicks hauled the last member of the group, a man, out from the other side and with his pistol jabbed into the guy's spine, they marched the man and woman into the building.

As they were pushed through the entrance and into the lobby, the two captives saw a tall man behind the front desk in a guard's uniform.

'Morning, sir,' Drexler said.

The man didn't respond. He looked at the woman whom Drexler was holding.

'Who the hell is she?'

'Think she's his girlfriend.'

He looked at them, then nodded. 'So take them up. He's waiting.'

Twenty seconds later, they arrived on the third floor. The large man with black curly hair was standing by the doors of the elevator, a pistol in a holster on his hip. Wicks and Drexler pushed the two captives out onto the level and they stumbled forward. Regaining his balance, the man immediately put his arm around the woman protectively, both of them uncertain and scared, glancing around nervously.

The curly-haired guy looked at the newcomers and grinned. He focused on the man.

'Good morning, doctor.'

The male captive didn't respond. He was distracted, puzzled by the lack of activity around him. The large man jerked his head, indicating the two captives should move forward. They walked slowly across the polished tiled floor towards the main laboratory. As they passed him, the large man grabbed the woman and motioned the doctor to keep walking. He came to a stop just outside the main lab.

It was empty.

'Inside,' the man ordered.

The doctor turned. 'What is this about?'

The large man's face darkened.

He grabbed the pistol from his holster and put it to the woman's head. He pulled the trigger and the weapon buzzed angrily, a cloud of blood and brains spraying in the air.

'NO!' the man shouted in horror.

Her body dropped like a stone, blood spattering all over the white floor. Then the curly-haired man swung his pistol to the doctor, aiming at his legs.

'Get in there and wait, asshole. You move or make a sound, you lose a kneecap.'

Numb with shock, the doctor stumbled backwards into the lab behind him. He stepped just inside the doors, which slid shut again in front of him. Behind the glass, he stared at his girlfriend's corpse on the tiled floor.

Outside, the man with the gun turned to Wicks and Drexler. 'Tibbs?'

'Handled,' said Drexler.

'Were you seen?'

She shook her head. 'Used the fire escape.'

'But we had a problem,' Wicks said. 'Kruger wasn't home.'

The man thought for a moment, then shrugged. 'This guy can do what he does.' He checked his watch. 'But you two need to get back to the city. The doctor can't work without a sample.'

His hit-team nodded.

'Before you go, get rid of the bitch,' the man said, jabbing his pistol at the dead woman on the floor. 'Dump her in the room with the others.'

EIGHT

'Is there anything you can tell us about why this happened?' Josh asked the young female doctor gently, sitting beside her. Archer had joined them, squatting on his haunches. It was still busy across the lobby, office workers, cops and CSU forensic investigators everywhere, but the trio were far enough away that they could have a quiet private conversation in the corner.

The woman looked at Josh and nodded.

'Call me Maddy.'

'Can you tell us why this happened, Maddy?'

'Do you know who my father was?' she asked.

Josh looked at Archer.

'No. I'm afraid we don't.'

'He was very well-known in our circles. Both here in the States and around the world. He was a pioneer in his field. He gave a lecture at a conference in Washington two months ago and over three thousand people attended. He had dinner that night at the White House.'

She paused, looking down at the lukewarm cup of coffee in her hands.

'My mother died of lung cancer when I was five,' she said, speaking slowly. 'The physician attending her didn't test for it early enough. If he had, she possibly could have survived, or at least lived a whole lot longer. My father could never move past what happened to her. It ate away at him every day. And once he became truly established in his field, much of his career objectives completed, he began trying to find a cure.'

'For cancer?' Josh asked.

The doctor shook her head. 'No. There are many different types. There isn't just one cure for all. It doesn't work like that.'

She paused.

'Cancer is a shocking sickness. It's something we all fear. It seems to appear out of nowhere and can strike in any part of your body. And you have to remember that in the grand scheme of things, modern medicine is still in extreme infancy. We've made more advances in the past hundred years than we did in the previous thousand, but it's still not enough. Thousands of scientists and doctors have tried to come up with ways of combating the disease. Only a few treatments have been proven to work.'

'Like chemotherapy,' Josh said.

'Yes. That's one. Using radiation to kill the cancerous cells. It's one of the most commonly used and the one most people are aware of. But ask anyone who has ever endured chemotherapy treatment about their experience. I guarantee it won't have been pleasant.'

She paused and sniffed.

'Chemo annihilates the cancerous cells, but it also kills other cells too. That's why some patients lose their hair for example. It works but it destroys healthy cells in the process. My father was desperate to find a middle ground for treating lung cancer, given what happened to my mother. Something that could combat the cancer without affecting the patient in other ways. He was convinced that it was possible.'

She paused.

'He tried many different things. None of them worked. He ended up down so many blind alleys, forced to go back and start all over again at square one. Time and again the same insurmountable problem cropped up that he just couldn't navigate around.'

'Which was?'

'The strains he developed were too weak. They either didn't work, or the cancer just overran them and ate them for lunch. So he decided to use an even stronger pathogen as a base. Something that if he could engineer and cultivate correctly, he knew for sure would annihilate the cancerous cells.'

'Which was?' Josh asked.

'Tubercle bacillus.'

'What's that?'

She looked at him.

Then, for only the second time, she glanced at Archer.

'Tuberculosis.'

Twenty four blocks downtown, the N Train carrying the three men from the Astoria diner swept into Times Square 42nd Street, the main transport hub in Midtown Manhattan. It eventually ground to a halt with a screech and the doors slid open. People started exiting the train and the three men carrying the bags joined them.

Moving down the platform, they walked up the stairs to the next level, the access floor for the various lines headed to different parts of the city. There were several cops up there, as well as some MTA employees and it was busy as hell, people walking in all directions, focused on getting to their destination.

No one paid any attention to the three men.

Anonymous in the crowd, the trio walked into the middle of the concourse and came to a halt, facing each other, all of them fighting the churning nervousness in their guts.

This was it.

Bleeker looked at his two companions.

'Do what you need to do, then leave. Don't hang around. We meet at the safe house, pack our shit and then we're out of here.'

The men nodded.

Then they parted and headed off in three different directions.

The bags containing the shoeboxes held tightly in their hands.

'This is bullshit!' the skinny drug dealer shouted. *'Bullshit, man!'*

He was being led out of a Harlem tenement building on West 134th towards an NYPD Ford Explorer parked against the kerb. Several people were watching from the street, as well as an audience from the windows of apartments in the building, some of them wolf-whistling, others shouting abuse at the two detectives. Jorgensen had about ninety pounds on the dealer and almost carried him to the car, a large bear-paw of a hand enveloping the man's upper arms on each side.

Arriving at the vehicle, he pulled open the rear door and pushed the drug dealer inside, sliding in after him and pulling the door shut. Behind them, Marquez had just stepped out of the building carrying a plastic bag stuffed full of various items. She walked around the front of the car to the driver's door, then climbed inside and shut it, turning to face Jorgensen and the smaller man, the three of them alone and the interior of the car quiet.

'You can't do this, man,' the skinny guy said, his hands cuffed behind him, sitting in the middle seat of the car. 'I've done nothing wrong.'

'Oh really?' Marquez said. She pulled something out of the plastic bag.

It was a large, thickly-packed transparent bag of marijuana leaves. The bag was about the size of a pillow case.

'Then what do you call this?'

Pause.

'That isn't mine.'

'What about these?' Marquez said.

Reaching into the bag again, she pulled up a second thick bag of marijuana and a .45 handgun.

Cantrell swallowed.

'Well, Pinocchio?' Jorgensen asked him.

'They aren't mine either. You planted that shit.'

'Do you even understand how finger-printing works, numb-nuts?' Jorgensen said. 'That's how we found you. You're telling me that if we run one layer of dust over those bags and the gun that your prints won't show up?'

'Don't matter. You're gonna take me to jail anyway!' Cantrell said dramatically.

'Listen!' Marquez said, firmly, looking him in the eyes. 'You're right. You're going to get charged for the weed and the gun. And I'm guessing this isn't the first time you've worn a set of handcuffs.'

Cantrell didn't answer.

'However, luckily for you, we've got much bigger shit to deal with today,' Marquez continued. 'If you start co-operating, I'll make sure that this is just a mark on your record. Nothing more. I promise. I'll say we found just an ounce of weed and no gun. But unless you want to spend Christmas in orange overalls, you better start talking.'

'About what?'

'Tell us about the shoebox,' she said.

Cantrell looked at her, then at Jorgensen beside him. He closed his eyes.

'Oh shit.'

'Exactly,' Jorgensen said.

'You know about that.'

'Yes. We do.'

'Goddamnit. I knew that shit was a mistake.'

'It would be pretty hard for it not to be,' Marquez said. 'A man died last night because of you.'

Cantrell frowned. '*What?*'

'Don't play cute,' Jorgensen said. 'Your prints are all over that box. You just admitted you knew about it. A family man is now lying on a slab at the morgue because of what you did.'

'What the hell are you talking about? I didn't kill anybody.'

'You placed it in the Park!' Jorgensen said.

'Yeah, only because some white boy paid me to.'

Marquez flicked a look at Jorgensen. 'Someone asked you to put it there?'

Cantrell nodded. 'Yeah. I had no idea it could kill anyone. It was only a box. Otherwise I'd have told the guy to find someone else. I'm not a murderer. Never killed anyone in my life.'

'Right. Start from the beginning,' Marquez said. 'What happened?'

'Yesterday, some guy calls me up. He'd heard that I was a good man for fixing things. See, funnily enough you were right about this not being the first time I've worn these bracelets. I did six months upstate last year for a misunderstanding between me and a gentleman from the local precinct. But take a look at me.'

He glanced down at his body, then looked up at Jorgensen.

'Unlike you Detective, I ain't built for confrontation. A guy like me in a place like that better have something to offer. Otherwise things are gonna get real unpleasant real fast, you know? So I became a fixer. That was my job in the yard. Take something one guy wants, trade it with something another guy wants and keep a tiny profit. Made me useful and saved my ass, if you know what I mean.'

He paused.

'Anyway, this guy calls me yesterday. He said I'd been recommended by a man I shared a cell with in the joint.'

'What was his name?'

'The dude from prison? Hurley.'

'Is that his real name?'

'That's what the boys in the yard called him. The guy on the phone said he had a proposition for me. Four hundred bucks for one job. He had a box he wanted me to deliver beside a trash can in the Park.'

Jorgensen frowned. 'And you didn't think something might be suspect about this?'

'I don't know what the city is paying you, man, but four bills for one gig is good money,' Cantrell said, looking up at him. 'I wasn't asking questions. And besides, I've done this before. You guys are always tailing someone who needs to keep his business going and a man has to feed his family. I figured there was a gun or some drugs inside for someone else to pick up.'

'Why didn't you ask what was in the box?' Marquez said.

'Wasn't any of my business,' Cantrell said. 'Gentleman told me best not to look, so I didn't.'

Marquez looked at Jorgensen, both of them assessing what Cantrell was saying.

'OK, so where did you get the box from? Did you pick it up from somewhere?'

'No, he gave it to me.'

'You saw him?'

'Yeah.'

'What did he look like?'

'He was a white boy. Kinda fat. He was covered up though, from the cold. Had one of those stupid hats on, with things coming down over his ears.'

'What about his clothing?'

Cantrell thought for a moment.

'Nothing special. His jacket was red. Like the ones those guys with axes wear.'

'Lumberjacks.'

'Yeah, that's right.'

Marquez nodded, pulling her phone. 'Keep going.'

'Anyway, the man gave me the box. It was all wrapped up with string. Told me not to open it and to place it at the drop-off point. A trash can in Central Park, halfway along the fence down at Sheep Meadow. He paid me on the spot too, which was kind of dumb. Most guys in my position would have just taken off with the cash and whatever was in the box.'

'So why didn't you?'

'I got a reputation to uphold. All a man has in his word. In my business, most guys lose it real fast. And once it's gone, it ain't ever coming back.'

'It saved your life,' Marquez said, pushing *Redial* and lifting her phone to her ear. 'Would you recognise this guy if you saw him again?'

Cantrell nodded, flashing a smile. 'You make the weed and gun just a bump in the road, I'll point him out in a crowd for you, Detective.'

Marquez nodded as the call connected to Briefing Room 5 at the Bureau.

'Rach, I need your help,' she said. 'We need to track someone from last night using the city camera system.'

As she spoke, Cantrell turned to Jorgensen.

'She calls the shots, huh?'

Jorgensen looked down at the smaller man.

'You have no idea.'

NINE

Downtown at the *Flood Microbiology* building, Archer and Josh were absorbing what the doctor had just told them.

'Tuberculosis?' Josh repeated.

She nodded. 'TB. One of the world's most infectious diseases. It killed 1.4 million people in 2011. You mentioned chemotherapy. People generally know that radiation can be used to treat cancer in very high doses. But as I said, it can be severely debilitating. Healthy cells die too. Medical physics is constantly trying to find a way of targeting radiotherapy more accurately. And that's where my father came in.'

Josh and Archer listened closely, concentrating, tuning everything else out. Although the lobby behind them was noisy, it might as well have been empty.

'Given what happened to my mother, his interest lay in curing lung cancer. His idea was to create a radioactive virus that could be inhaled. Once in the lungs, the virus would irradiate cancerous tumours from the inside. The TB would act as the cell in which the virus could replicate. Like a breeding ground and a vehicle to get into the lung tissue.'

'Is that possible?'

'Technically, yes. And if it worked, it would be revolutionary.'

'When did he start working on this?'

'He first broached the subject to us eighteen months ago. At first we thought he was crazy, but then we realised it could actually be feasible. And if it worked, it would change lung cancer therapy forever.'

She paused.

'Our team here are biochemists. What we do isn't glamorous. We spend all our time working out how and why little proteins work and their roles in long drawn-out cascades of reactions. So what my father outlined was very different and very exciting. He wanted us to find how a small amount of radioactive material could be incorporated into the capsid of a virus.'

'Capsid?'

'Protein shell.' She paused. 'Still with me?'

Josh nodded. 'I think so. He wanted to get a radioactive substance inside a shell which would then be incorporated into the virus. That would then be grown along with the tuberculosis and inhaled, allowing it to get inside tumours in the lung.'

She nodded. 'Spot on.'

'You said radioactive material. Like uranium?'

'No, no. That would be a terrible idea. When uranium is mixed with hydrogen it forms plutonium, which isn't exactly an ideal atom to use in medicine. It also degrades into lead which is highly poisonous.'

'So what did you use?'

'Cobalt. It's a metal which has a radioactive isotope which emits gamma radiation. It's radioactive and worked medicinally for our cancer treatment. We spent last summer and fall figuring out how to combine the cobalt with the protein shell. It took us six months. But we did it.'

'So what came next?'

'We needed a virologist to take what we had, combine it with a strain of tuberculosis and culture the resulting virus into something strong enough to destroy a cancer cell but which wouldn't infect the patient with TB. We had our own man here who is very good, but my father needed a top-level expert to work with him. He wanted a specialist. He went to South Africa and recruited one. His name is Dr Kruger.'

'He came over here?'

'Yes. He joined our team a year ago, working with our own virologist Dr Glover. Together, the two of them cultured the radioactive virus with the tuberculosis strain. I couldn't even begin to tell you the specifics about how they did it. Kruger is a brilliant man. He modified the TB to grow at a much faster rate and neutralised its potency, making it the perfect vehicle for the cobalt. He taught Dr Glover a lot just by working alongside him.'

'How many of you work here?'

'Five.'

'Names?'

'Myself. My father. Dr Kruger, Dr Tibbs and Dr Glover.'

Josh glanced at Archer, who nodded, making a mental note of the names.

'This all happened earlier this year. And my father was obsessed at this point. He would stay late, long after we had all gone home, working with Dr Kruger. He began sleeping at the lab. And I started to worry about him. He was neglecting himself and his own health started to suffer.'

She shook her head, looking up with red-rimmed green eyes.

'My mother's death, haunting him every day.'

She paused and sniffed.

'Anyway, four weeks ago they both called us all in on a Wednesday night. They were excited. Dr Kruger figured he'd made a huge breakthrough and struck gold. The radio-virus had cultured and was ready for testing. That evening he was preparing to test it on infected cells in mice. He wanted us all there to watch.'

'What happened?'

'It was devastating. We knew it the moment those poor mice began to react to the gas. I'll never forget it. It turned out that he couldn't have been more wrong.'

She swallowed.

'Unstable atoms degrade and release energy. That's what causes radiation. And the radiation from the virus had knocked out some of the genes that made Dr Kruger's genetically-modified TB safe. It was intended to attack tumour cells, but instead it went after normal blood vessels in the lung. Once inhaled, infection spread at an obscene pace, bursting the pulmonary capillary bed.'

'What does that mean?' Josh asked.

'Basically, you cough so hard that you hack up pieces of lung tissue. The spasms are so strong that you break your own back. The healthy vessels in your lungs rupture and you drown in your own blood.'

'Jesus.'

'It was horrifying. It condensed the infection period from weeks or months into thirty seconds. Dr Kruger and my father had made a terrible, terrible error.'

Her eyes were distant as she thought back.

'Dr Kruger realised how badly they'd gone wrong. He was willing to throw in the towel there and then. But my father said no. He said if anyone on our team touched the virus they would be fired on the spot. And that's when he became darker. He lost a lot of weight. He barely ate. He didn't interact with the rest of us. He was so distracted. He started to obsess about the Atomic bomb. He thought that what he created would have the same devastating effect if it was ever unleashed.'

'So why didn't he just destroy it?'

'I begged him to. Dr Kruger offered to dispose of it. But my father said no. This had been a year and a half of work. He refused to give up. He thought that his ideal medicinal version of the virus was only a few steps away. Maybe only one.'

She paused.

'He told me he was so close to one of the greatest medical breakthroughs the world has ever seen and he wasn't giving up now. But the rest of us were thinking clearly. We knew that if this virus got into the wrong hands it would be one of the most lethal biological weapons ever created. My father would be remembered not as a pioneer, but as a monster.'

'That explains what he was saying,' Josh asked. 'Just before he jumped.'

'Your friend should know. He was standing right there,' she said, looking down at Archer.

He held her gaze.

'Thousands of people are going to die,' Josh said. 'But why would he say that? The virus is devastating but it's contained here, right?'

Archer saw the anger in her eyes fade. It was replaced by something else.

Fear.

She looked at Josh. 'Upstairs, in our main lab, we have six separate vials of the virus. On my father's orders.'

She paused.

'And when we arrived this morning, five of them were missing.'

Thirty two blocks downtown, Paul Bleeker stepped into a changing room on the third floor of Macy's Department Store and pulled the door shut behind him. He was holding a shirt, a random one he'd grabbed from a rail, as well as the plastic bag containing the box. He put the hanger holding the shirt onto a hook then placed the bag gently on the ground.

The changing room's design meant that there was a wooden ledge at the opposite side from the door that customers could use as a seat. Kneeling, Bleeker pulled out a small screwdriver from the pocket of his thick red jacket and started working the screws off the corners of the panel. He worked quietly and methodically. Soft Christmas music played from speakers mounted on the walls in the changing rooms, intermingling with the rustle of clothes being changed in other stalls and the occasional cough or sniff from someone with a seasonal cold.

He worked the last screw out of its home, then placed it alongside the other three in a neat line. Tucking the screwdriver back into his pocket, he quietly lifted off the panel and leant it against the wall.

Under the lid, there was an assortment of electrical wiring, but also a square ledge beside a small air vent.

There was already a box in there, identical to the one he had in the bag. He'd placed it here yesterday in preparation.

He lifted it out, putting it on the floor by his feet, then took its twin out of the bag. He carefully placed the new box inside the compartment, laying it on the ledge. Then he lifted the lid and tucked it underneath the box.

This bomb was different from the one left in Central Park. It had no disruptor or disturbance reactor; it also contained much more of the virus in the vial rigged up to the detonator.

The device he'd given to the drug dealer was just a tester. He'd had a small sample of the virus extracted from one of the main vials and transferred into a pressurised cylinder. He'd made a small bomb, something he could do in his sleep. He wasn't the most intelligent guy out there, but certain things he knew how to do just fine. But he'd needed to see the virus at work, to ensure everything he'd heard wasn't just bullshit. He knew from a job he'd held briefly in Central Park last year that the groundsman in the Meadow area, Luis Cesar, emptied the trash like clockwork between 9:45 and 10:10 every weeknight.

He'd been watching the Meadow from an upper floor corridor of a hotel on West 67th at 10pm last night. He'd seen Cantrell deliver the box earlier. He hadn't opened it, which Hurley had assured Bleeker he wouldn't, and it meant Bleeker wouldn't be on any security cameras mounted inside the Park. Through binoculars, he'd seen the groundsman approach, spot and open the box. He'd watched in fascination at the devastating effects of the virus as it killed the man, blood spraying from his mouth as he fell back and died out there on the snow. It wasn't a hoax and it hadn't been exaggerated.

This poisonous yellow shit was the real deal.

He looked down at the bomb in front of him. At the top of the box was a long vial. Inside the glass cylinder was a portion of noxious-looking yellow liquid. Below it was a digital timer, pre-set at *15:00* in lime-green numbers on a black display.

Fifteen minutes would suffice. It would give him enough time to get out of Midtown and be on his way back to Queens by the time it detonated, was sucked into the air ducts and killed everyone in the building.

Reaching forward, his finger rested on a small button on the side of the timer.

He coughed as he pressed it, covering the beep.

The countdown started silently.

14:59.

14:58.

14:57.

Reaching beside him, Bleeker lifted the panel and put it back in place, then quickly replaced the screws. When he'd finished, he slid the other shoebox into the plastic bag and rose. He grabbed the shirt on the hangar and pulled open the door, walking out of the stall.

Outside, Bleeker moved down the aisle to where the changing rooms met the main shopping floor. A female employee was standing behind a counter, a half-filled rail of clothing behind her.

She gave him a courteous smile which he didn't return.

'Any luck?' she asked.

'Not today,' he said, passing over the shirt.

She took the garment from him, turning to place it on the rail behind her. Bleeker didn't hesitate;

he moved back out into the store and walked rapidly towards the escalator across the level.

He stepped onto the metal stairwell headed to the ground floor and within a few moments he disappeared out of sight.

TEN

At the Counter Terrorist Bureau, Shepherd was leaning on the table beside Rach, watching her work. She was logging into the NYPD's advanced security camera network; they were connected on speakerphone to Marquez and Jorgensen, who were still in their Ford Explorer in Harlem with the arrested street dealer, Rashad Cantrell.

Rach typed in her password and a grid of security cameras came up on the screen. Each one was from a different vantage point in the city and all were moving in real time.

'Right. We're in,' Rach said. 'Where did he meet the man, Lisa? And what time?'

'You heard the lady,' Marquez said, talking to Cantrell. There was a quiet murmur. Then Marquez came back. *'Corner of 72nd and Broadway. Around 9:30 last night.'*

'Which side?'

Pause.

'South-east.'

Rach nodded, and her fingers went to work.

One of the newest improvements in the NYPD's fight against crime was to have high-tech security cameras placed all over the city. It was now impossible to walk around the Lower Manhattan area without your movements being recorded and documented by CCTV. The software was some of the most advanced available and one of its key functions was clothing recognition; it allowed effortless tailing of a suspect. If you wanted to follow someone, all you had to do was freeze a frame and draw a box over a piece of clothing that the suspect was wearing. With one command, the computer would scan through its recent footage and pull up any other recording of the article of clothing in seconds. Worlds away from the old school methods, it saved hundreds of man hours trawling through grainy CCTV recordings and meant the cops could track a suspect's movements with relative ease, either in the present or in this case, the past.

Rach found the relevant camera, and the shot came up on the screen. It was a vantage point from a post, probably three quarters up a street-light, *72nd/Broadway* in white letters on the upper right of the screen.

It was a current feed, showing crowds of people and vehicles moving across the intersection, the usual daytime hustle and bustle. Rach scrolled back to last night, everything moving in reverse at hyper speed, the day turning into night. Although the screen was now darker, the plethora of street lights and festive lighting meant the whole area was clearly illuminated.

'Check the time,' Shepherd said, pointing at the bottom right corner.

Rach looked down and saw it showed *20:54:02*.

She pushed a key and the clock started whirring forward, past *21:00:00*.

Everything in the shot moved in a blur, cars stopping at lights then moving off at high speed, people scurrying in and out of shot.

Rach paused at *21:29:32*, then hit *Play*.

'Right. Here we go,' Shepherd said.

They watched in silence.

The intersection was dark but still busy. There was a constant stream of people and cars, but nowhere near the same quantity as during the day.

People were wrapped up against the cold, but there was no sign of anyone wearing a red coat.

'Any luck?'

'Hang on, Marquez,' Shepherd said.

They waited.

Then Cantrell appeared. He walked into the shot from up the street, his hands stuffed deep in his pockets, his collar pulled up and a cigarette in the corner of his mouth. Taking his right hand out of his pocket, he took a final drag then dropped the cig to the sidewalk, crushing it with the toe of his shoe. He was facing south-east, towards the camera, his face lit up by a streetlight. Shepherd had the man's file open on the desk. He glanced at the mug-shot, then at the slender man on the screen.

'It's him,' he said, loud enough so Marquez and Jorgensen could hear. 'Cantrell just entered the shot. So far, so good.'

Then the man in the red lumberjack-style jacket arrived.

He had his back to the camera and was carrying a box under his arm. He joined Cantrell on the corner. They didn't shake hands.

Nothing happened for a few moments as the two men seemed to talk, their heads moving slightly as they spoke.

Then the man passed over an envelope which Cantrell quickly tucked into the inside breast pocket of his jacket. He took the box and immediately walked off, headed east, out of the shot and towards Central Park.

'Cantrell wasn't wearing gloves,' Rach said. 'That's when his prints got on the box.'

'He's telling the truth,' Shepherd told Marquez. 'The trade happened like he said.'

'Can we ID the guy in the jacket?'

'He has his back to the camera,' Rach said. 'Hang on.'

They watched the shot. Now Cantrell was gone, the man in the jacket raised his gloved hand, hailing a taxi. He climbed inside and shut the door, but his hat was obstructing the view of his face. The car sped off, out of frame, and just as soon as they'd arrived, the two men were gone.

'Shit,' Rach said.

'What about other cameras?'

'That's the only one at the intersection,' Rach said. ''I'll run clothing recognition.'

As she worked, Shepherd's cell phone started ringing. He pulled it and looked down at the display. It was Archer. As he pushed the *Answer* button, he tapped the computer screen with his other hand.

'We need to find out where he went.'

'I can do better than that, sir,' Rach said. 'If he's still in the city, I'll find out where he is right now.'

As Shepherd turned, taking the call, Rach ran the tape back then froze the frame of the man talking with Cantrell. He had his back turned but the fabric and pattern of his coat was lit up perfectly by the street lamp.

She drew a box around the image, then tapped a few keys and hit *Enter.*

Bleeker had ditched the jacket in a trash can less than a minute earlier. Wearing a zip-up dark hoodie and jeans, a Yankees cap over his head, he was just about as anonymous and now cold as a man could be in New York City. He'd left Macy's through the south entrance and was standing on the sidewalk on West 34th between 7th and Broadway, the building directly behind him. The temptation to stay and watch the effect of his work in the store was almost overwhelming, but he knew he needed to get the hell out of here. The winds were blowing strong today. No use watching the bomb go off if he got infected with the virus as well.

Particularly after seeing what it could do.

As Christmas shoppers and tourists moved past him either side, he shot his cuff and checked his watch.

He had thirteen minutes.

He stepped to the kerb, raised his hand and a passing taxi slowed to a stop. The driver lowered his window as Bleeker stepped forward.

'Where to?'

'Queens,' Bleeker said, entering the cab and slamming the door shut. 'Earn your tip.'

'TB, sir,' Archer said to Shepherd on his cell, standing in the lobby of the building on West 66th. 'That's what she told us. Apparently her father was trying to create some kind of revolutionary cure for lung cancer but it went badly wrong.'

'*Tuberculosis?*'

'Yes.'

'*But that's curable, right?*'

'Not this type. It's been grown with a virus.'

'*Did she explain?*'

'Yeah. I just about kept up. Radiation in the virus knocked out some elements that made the TB medicinally safe. Basically if you breathe in this shit you cough so hard you rupture the blood vessels in your lungs. You spew out pieces of lung, break your own back from the spasms and drown in your blood within thirty seconds of inhalation.'

'Jesus Christ. How on earth did this stuff get out of the lab?'

'She doesn't know. But when she and her father arrived at the lab this morning, five of the six samples of the virus were gone. Then they got a phone call from us.'

'So that's why he stepped off the roof. He knew.'

'And that's what killed the groundsman in the Park last night.'

'Who else works at the lab?'

'Only five people apparently. Peter Flood, his daughter, and three other doctors.'

'Names?'

'Kruger, Glover and Tibbs.'

'I'll tell Marquez and Jorgensen. We'll locate and bring them in. In the-'

He suddenly paused, mid-sentence.

'Hang on.'

Pause.

'Wait a minute, Arch. Stay on the line. Rach just got something.'

Pause. Archer looked back at Josh, who was still with Maddy Flood, comforting her.

Shepherd came back. *'Listen. Rach found the man who arranged for the package to be left in the Park last night on surveillance. She's located him again this morning via his clothing.'*

'Where?'

'He was in the subway station at 34ᵗʰ Street about twenty minutes ago. He got off a Downtown-bound R train. She's speeding up the tape. Wait.'

ause. In the meantime, Archer caught Josh's attention; he beckoned his partner to come over quickly.

'*We've got him on the street, walking through Herald Square. He's carrying a white plastic bag with something inside. It looks rectangular.*'

'Like a shoebox,' Archer said.

Then realisation dawned.

'*Oh shit.*'

'*He went into Macy's twelve minutes ago.*'

Josh joined Archer, seeing the look on his face.

'What's going on?' he asked.

'*I'm calling it in,*' Shepherd said. '*Get down there now!*'

ELEVEN

Located on 34th Street and taking up an entire city block between Broadway and 7th Avenue, Macy's billed itself as *The World's Largest Store*, a huge red banner draped down the side of the building claiming so in white letters. It wasn't lying. The monolithic department store offered close to two million square feet of retail space. Hundreds of top-flight designers and clothing companies had concessions inside, from Tommy Hilfiger and Ralph Lauren to Armani, Versace and everyone else in between. The building had ten floors, a selection of coffee shops and restaurants, and thousands of customers passing through its three entrances every day of the week, each week of the year. It was also the setting for several nostalgic movies, including *Miracle on 34th Street,* where a little girl discovered that the store Santa Claus was real.

However, as Archer and Josh jumped out of their hastily pulled-up Ford Explorer on 34th and 7th, their thoughts weren't so pleasant.

With lights flashing they'd cut through traffic and got down there in four minutes flat to find evacuation of the building was already underway. There were scores of pedestrians flooding the sidewalks outside the 7th Avenue entrance, ushered out by efficient store security and cops from Midtown South. Archer saw that an ESU truck had already arrived, the NYPD's SWAT team, the officers already inside the building. Several Hercules Teams, armed Special Forces-type units, had also shown up and were spread out on the sidewalks, talking into radios and scanning the crowds. Showing their badges to the

s, Josh and Archer pushed their way through
e glass doors and made their way into the
building.

Inside, it was a similar scene to the sidewalk
outside. There was a sea of people, men, women
and kids, all of whom were being quickly herded
towards the exits. The two detectives saw a large
pool of ESU officers and store security guards
gathered to the left, listening closely as they
received orders from their Lieutenant who was
standing in front of them, like a sports team
receiving a half-time talk.

Archer and Josh fought their way towards the
group, but the gathering disbanded just as they
got there. The ESU officers and Macy's guards
headed off with purpose, some moving swiftly
towards the upwards escalators, others headed
downstairs to the basement. Standing beside a
guy who looked like the head of store security,
the ESU Lieutenant had spotted Archer and Josh
pushing their way towards him. He was in his
forties, dark haired, dressed in police fatigues, a
Colt AR-15 assault rifle slung over his shoulder
on a strap.

'Blake and Archer,' Josh said, showing his
badge. 'Counter Terrorism Bureau.'

'Hobbs,' the ESU Lieutenant said, shaking their
hands quickly. 'You the two guys who've come
from the lab?'

'That's right.'

'I spoke to your man Shepherd. He said a box
containing a bomb might have been left
somewhere in the building. Mind telling me
what's inside?'

'It's a Type-Three Pneumonic virus,' Archer said. 'Once it enters the human body, the host is dead within half a minute.'

'Jesus Christ. Hang on.' He grabbed his radio. 'All teams, gas masks. This is a biological threat. I repeat, a biological threat. Put on your gas masks.'

'One viral bomb already went off in Central Park last night,' Josh said. 'It killed a groundsman.'

'I've got my men and the store team searching the building,' Hobbs said. 'We know the shape, or anything distinguishable about this box?'

Josh shook his head. 'Rectangular. Like a shoebox. That's it.'

'Shit. I've sent them out in teams, working their way through each floor. But I need reinforcements. You have any ideas as to how we find this thing?'

During this exchange, Archer had gone quiet.

Something Maddy Flood had said earlier surfaced in his mind.

'Wait,' he said.

Hobbs and Blake turned and looked at him.

'Every ESU officer carries a radiation detector, right?'

Hobbs nodded. 'One of the Department's newest regulations. All my men have one. Why?'

'We can use them.'

'How?' Josh asked. 'It's a virus. Nothing will show up.'

Archer shook his head. 'The doc said that the virus was cultivated using cobalt. That stuff is radioactive.'

Josh looked at him. The penny dropped.

'You think it'll show?'

Archer nodded. 'Those things are sensitive. It'll show.'

Hobbs listened to the exchange, then lifted his radio again. 'Attention, all teams. Use your radiation detection equipment, I repeat, use your radiation detection equipment. The package we're looking for will give you a gamma reading.'

He put down the radio. Behind them, more police and a Chemical Response Team had just arrived through the doors, carrying their gear and making their way through the remaining crowd towards the command post. As they approached, Hobbs reached to his belt and unclipped a small radiation detection device, about the size of a stopwatch.

He passed it to Archer. 'Here. I'll fill these guys in. You two better get searching.'

Archer took it with a nod.

Then he and Josh ran for the escalator.

Three floors above, the viral bomb continued to count down silently, hidden from view under the wooden panel.

4:02.

4:01.

3:59.

3:58.

Inside the briefing room at the Counter Terrorism Bureau, Shepherd and Rach were still working on trying to find out where the man in the red jacket went after he left the store. Rach had him walking out of the south entrance on 34th Street, a streetlight camera in front of him, but he'd turned to his left and moved out of the shot.

'Damn,' Rach said, scouring the cameras.

'What?'

'Outside Macy's is the last I can find of him. Look.'

She ran back the tape and hit *Play*. Shepherd watched the man walk out of the store, checking his watch, then turning and heading down 34th. He switched his gaze to the next camera shot.

But the man never reappeared.

'Damn it,' Rach said. 'Blind spot.'

Shepherd tapped the shot on the left. 'Go to this camera in real time.'

'Now?'

'Now.'

She did, and the shot came up. People were flooding the street, all of them milling outside Macy's, waiting to be allowed back in.

'Find the trash,' he said.

She tapped the keyboard and watched as shots appeared on screen. She held the down arrow and the camera slid down. She held the right arrow and it moved to the right. Shepherd tapped the screen.

'He ditched the coat. Look.'

Rach peered closer and could make out a piece of the familiar red fabric. The jacket had been dropped into a trash can, just out of sight of the initial view of the camera.

'Shit,' she said, pulling the camera up to its original shot.

'Track back,' Shepherd said.

She nodded and went to wind back the tape, but something in the corner of the computer screen caught her eye and made her stop.

'Wait a minute, sir,' she said.

She brought up a shot from the top right corner. It was from about thirty minutes ago, the white lettering in the corner of the shot stating it was at *Times Square 42nd Street Sub*.

'Look,' she said, tapping the screen. 'This is from earlier. Ten minutes before he entered the store.'

Shepherd looked closer, examining the shot. Amidst the hustle and bustle of the station in the footage, he saw the man in the red jacket, the white bag containing the dark box in his hand.

He was with two other men.

They were each carrying an identical bag.

'Oh no,' Shepherd said. 'No, no, no. Not good.'

Shepherd and Rach watched the trio split up and move off in separate directions. There was a moment's silence as the implication of what they'd just seen hit them.

Then Rach looked up at Shepherd slowly.

'Sir, we're not just dealing with one bomb.'

'We're dealing with three.'

TWELVE

Archer and Josh had just arrived on the third floor. The building had been cleared; the only people in sight now were ESU officers or store security scouring each level. They'd had to make a flash decision as to which part of the store they concentrated their search and figured the guy would have wanted to blend in when he planted the device. The men's department seemed to be as good a place as any to start.

The task-force guys were working in small teams, holding their radiation detectors and sweeping their designated area. Archer started doing the same. Holding the device, he watched the reading on the monitor closely as he walked around the floor. Meanwhile, Josh had moved ahead and was searching the old fashioned way, quickly checking under piles of clothing, behind rails and around cashier desks, searching for any sign of the box or the bag. However, like the rest of the store the third floor was huge, rails and displays filled with clothes everywhere you looked.

Josh ducked down, searching behind a counter, then cursed and reappeared.

'Anything?' he called.

Archer shook his head, watching the radiation reading. 'Nothing.'

What he'd said earlier was true, but only to a point. The bomb would give off a gamma reading, but he didn't know how strong. Thankfully, the detector's sensors were extremely sensitive. They reacted to fire alarms as well as to other equipment emitting even tiny levels of radiation. Since the device had come into use, there'd been many occasions when a suspected threat somewhere in the city had been called in, ESU and CRT teams deployed, only to find the reading was coming from an innocent member of the public who'd been undergoing radiotherapy treatment. And here, they could be dealing with an even smaller amount. Tiny even. Archer guessed that Flood and Kruger had not used much cobalt in cultivating the virus. He didn't know if they were all wasting their time.

Time they didn't have.

He rounded the corner, the escalators immediately to his right, and looked down at the handheld monitor. The numbers on the display were hovering on *45*, the normal readout.

Having just searched under some clothing displays, Josh loped over and joined him.

'Shit,' he said, looking around at the amount of floor that still needed to be searched. 'We need more people up here.'

Archer nodded, looking down at the monitor. 'We'd better try the next level.'

The two men quickly walked forward towards the rising escalator, stepping on.

'Hey!' a voice suddenly shouted from behind them.

They looked at each other, then immediately ran back down.

They saw a pair of ESU officers ten yards away, each holding a radiation detector. One of them had momentarily pulled off his gas mask in order to shout and get the detectives' attention.

'We've got a reading!'

Running forward, Archer and Josh looked down at their own reader in Archer's hand.

The man was right.

The reading had jumped to *52*.

'Here we go,' Josh whispered, side-by-side with Archer.

The ESU officers took the lead, the two detectives following close behind. The four men moved silently, not taking their eyes off the monitors. They moved agonisingly slowly, their heads down, ignoring their immediate surroundings, just focused on the sensor reading on the machines.

56.

58.

61.

The two ESU guys had walked into an area filled with men's shirts on rails. The place was deserted. Music was still playing quietly from the speakers. Archer and Josh followed close behind, watching their own reading on Archer's borrowed detector.

'It's getting stronger.'

64.

68.

The guy who'd alerted Archer and Josh pushed his pressel switch, talking into his radio with his gasmask still raised.

'Lieutenant, this is Hicks. I'm in menswear on 3. We need CRT and back-up up here right now. We've got a reading.'

The four men moved forward through the menswear section, Hicks pulling his mask back into place. The reading kept rising.

Following it, the ESU officers turned a corner and headed into the changing room area.

72.

75.

They went into the first cubicle on the right, then stepped back out, studying the detector. They tried the second and third.

Then they tried the fourth.

'Whoa,' Hicks said, his voice muffled under the gas mask. 'We got something.'

Archer and Josh looked at their own reader.

It was at *95*.

They tore their gaze from the detector and looked at the cubicle in front of them.

It was empty, but the radiation equipment was telling a different story. Behind them they could hear the sound of running feet. *'In here!'* Hicks called. Then he pointed at the seat in the cubicle. 'Get that panel off.'

Hicks' partner dropped to one knee, pulling a screwdriver from his tac vest. He started working the screws out of the four corners one by one. He removed the fourth just as two CRT specialists appeared in the changing room.

The ESU man grabbed the panel and lifted it.

All six men saw the viral bomb inside.

It was nestled beside some wiring and a small air vent. Archer and Josh recognised it immediately as a replica of the one used in Central Park, except that this one had a timer and no lid. Under a cylindrical vial of yellow liquid was a timer with a series of lime-green buttons.

00:31.

00:30.

00:29.

'Back up!' one of the CRT specialists ordered, the sound distorted by the helmet of his suit. The ESU pair and Archer and Josh were already moving out of the way, making room. Neither

Archer or Josh had a gas mask, but neither of them was leaving.

The CRT team worked like quicksilver. As the specialist on the left ran his hands along the sides of the package, the man to the right laid down a thick black containment case that he had brought with him. It was empty. He clicked open a lock on each corner and pulled off the transparent glass lid.

In front of them, the timer on the bomb ticked down.

00:21.

00:20.

00:19.

'No disruptor or motion sensors,' the specialist on the left said. He kept feeling the package. 'I'm moving it. Box ready?'

'Ready.'

He took hold of the bomb either side and gently lifted it off the panel.

They all held their breath.

It didn't go off.

00:12.

00:11.

00:10.

The man lifted it out steadily and placed it carefully into the black container beside him.

00:07.

00:06.

'Seal it!' he said, withdrawing his hands.

The other guy grabbed the lid, sliding it into place, and together the two of them clicked the four locks, sealing the container and locking it airtight.

'Box secure!' the second man said.

Standing behind them, Archer and Josh saw the countdown on the timer through the glass lid.

00:03.

00:02.

00:01.

THIRTEEN

The bomb detonated.

There was a sudden puff of yellow as the cylindrical vial cracked open and released the modified tuberculosis virus, but the containment box prevented it from entering breathable air, sealed airtight in the protective case. Through the glass, the six gathered men watched the yellow gas swirl up to the lid of the box, slowly and malevolently searching for any cracks or gaps.

Kneeling beside it, the two CRT specialists took a simultaneous deep breath. Both guys were sweating. The tech on the left turned and looked at the ESU pair, then at Josh and Archer.

'It's secure,' he said. 'Just in time. Great job, fellas.'

He grabbed a radio from the ground and put in the call.

'Device is located and is secure. I repeat, device is located and secure.'

He lowered the radio, taking in some deep breaths.

And silence fell as all six men looked at the lethal virus drifting around the box.

Across the city, another bomb was just about to be planted.

A second member of Bleeker's trio, the guy with the tattoos, was walking down a stone path on the east side of Bryant Park, just off 42nd Street and 6th Avenue. He'd ducked into a coffee shop restroom moments earlier, armed his bomb and initiated the ten minute countdown. There was no disturbance switch on this bomb, just the vial and a timer. With the lid back in place and tied securely with string, the man was now approaching an ideal drop-off point for the device, a trash can on the south east of the Park, a stone's throw from the Public Library. Leaving it anywhere else might attract attention. The place was busy and the cops weren't dumb.

He was ten yards from the can, blending right in with the shoppers and the people watching the ice-skaters on the rink to his right. It was relatively central and would be a perfect place to plant the device, achieving maximum impact and fatalities.

He walked towards the can as casually as he could.

Five yards away, he raised the bag and prepared to drop it inside.

But suddenly, someone grabbed his arm from behind, pulling him to an immediate halt. Something was jabbed into the folds of his coat, shoved hard into the middle of his back.

'Don't move, asshole.'

He froze.

As the hand gripped his arm and what had to be a pistol rammed against his back, another person stepped in front of him.

It was a woman. Dressed in jeans and a leather jacket, she had a harsh face, dark features emphasised by cold reptilian eyes. Her nose looked as if it had been broken a number of times. The only trace of femininity was long hair that was half-tied back, several strands hanging over her face, but somehow it made her look even more intimidating.

She examined his face, then looked over his shoulder and nodded.

'It's him.'

'Check it.'

The woman turned to the man holding the bag. 'Pull out your wallet.'

He did so hesitantly, very aware of the gun pressed into his back. The man behind him was up close so no one nearby could see the weapon. She took the wallet and flipped it open.

'Nathan Hansen.'

She nodded, tucking it back in the man's pocket. Without a word, the guy with the gun came up around him, tucking the pistol under his coat and burying it into Hansen's armpit, the weapon hidden in the layers of clothing. Hansen looked at the man and saw he had bleach blond hair, almost white. Glancing down, he also saw that the pistol stuffed under his arm was silenced, the man's finger tight on the trigger.

'Move.'

Walking side by side, the three walked out of the Park and headed across the street onto 42nd. They stopped in front of a French patisserie. The woman pulled open the door and they moved inside.

The restaurant was straight ahead, but the toilets were behind a wooden screen to the right. The trio moved towards them. The man and woman took Hansen into the men's restroom, then locked the door.

Once they were inside, the bleach-haired guy pulled out the pistol from his coat and stuck it in Hansen's face, pushing him against the wall. The handgun was a Glock, a fat silencer on the end of the weapon an inch from Hansen's nose.

'Don't move.'

The woman grabbed the bag from Hansen's hand, then placed it on the ground. She gently slid out the box, untied the string securing it and carefully opened the lid.

She saw the bomb inside. It had been armed, the numbers on the timer counting down.

8:23.

8:22.

8:21.

'Son of a bitch,' she said.

She clicked a switch on the inside of the box and the timer shut down. Then she picked it up and placed the switched off bomb carefully against the wall by the toilet bowl. Hansen watched her do it, then turned his attention to the blond man with the gun. He went to speak but the woman rose and suddenly slapped a rear choke on him, hooking her legs around his hips and pulling him back. They hit the ground with a thump and she tightened the squeeze, the leather on her jacket creaking. Hansen gagged and clutched at her forearm desperately as it blocked his airway.

He passed out after six seconds or so. Drexler held the choke for another thirty seconds until he suffocated. Once he was gone, she released him and rose, dusting herself off. Wicks tucked his pistol into a holster under his coat then knelt down and broke Hansen's neck, just to be sure. One grip and one sharp wrench.

Drexler crouched down and retrieved the box. She separated the vial from the bomb and rose, examining it in her hand. The toxic yellow liquid was gathered at the bottom, a small amount, seemingly innocuous yet horrifyingly dangerous.

'Now we're talking,' she said.

With the dead man slumped on the ground, his head at a strange angle, Drexler unlocked the door and stepped out. Wicks flicked the lock back on as he followed then pulled the door hard behind him, sealing it shut.

Together, the two of them headed out of the patisserie and back out onto the street.

The vial containing the virus held securely in Drexler's hand and tucked safely into her right jacket pocket.

FOURTEEN

Archer and Josh watched as the two CRT specialists carried the glass container across Macy's third floor, stopping outside the lifts. One of them pushed the button and the doors to a cart slid open immediately. The two men moved inside, the boxed virus between them. One of them jabbed the button for the ground floor and the doors shut, the two men disappearing out of sight.

Across the level, members of the ESU team, HAZMAT and store security had gathered, talking quietly with each other. The area had been cordoned off and HAZMAT were preparing to screen it to ensure there was no toxicity or any traces of the virus in the air. It was a set procedure which had to followed, but they were fully aware that if even a tiny amount of the virus had escaped they'd have known all about it by now.

Josh pulled his cell phone out and called Shepherd as Archer stood watching the group.

'Sir, we found the device,' he said. 'The son of a bitch hid it in a panel in a changing room.'

'Defused?'

'No, but it's secured. The CRT team put it in a protective casing just before it detonated.'

'But it went off?'

'Yes. It did.'

'Jesus.' He paused. *'Good job, but listen. We're not done with this yet.'*

'What do you mean?'

'This guy isn't working alone. Before we found him, he was with two other men inside the subway at Times Square. Each of them was carrying a

bag which we're certain contains a box. We think each one is a bomb. We're working on finding the other two now.'

Josh swore, then turned to Archer.

'There could be two more of these things.'

'Aside from the guy in red, none of them are wearing distinctive clothing. Rach is having a hard time tracking them. They also used the subway so could have stepped off at any station. I'll call you back.'

Josh lowered the phone as Shepherd ended the call.

'Two more. Shit, we only just got to this one.'

Archer nodded grimly, looking around the store. 'Something about this is weird.'

'How do you mean?'

'You saw that bomb. It wasn't high tech. It was homemade, same as the one in the Park. Crude as hell. It was in a shoebox for Christ's sake.'

'So?'

'How the hell does someone so amateurish get hold of something so dangerous?'

'He wasn't exactly amateur, Arch. He was thirty seconds from succeeding.'

Archer went to answer, but Josh's phone rang. He answered immediately.

'Sir?'

'Got one! He stepped off a 6 train and headed towards the South Street Seaport ten minutes ago. Rach is alerting the area response teams.'

Josh started running for the escalator, Archer close on his heels.

Forty three blocks uptown, completely unaware of events in Midtown, Marquez and Jorgensen walked down the fourth-floor corridor of a five-storey apartment building on the Upper West Side, on 77th Street between Amsterdam and Broadway. They weren't far from *Flood Microbiology*, which made sense as this was where Dr Kruger's apartment was located. He didn't have a police file but Rach had found his address via the DMV.

They came to a stop outside 4D. The corridor either side of them was long and empty.

Jorgensen looked at Marquez, who nodded, and he knocked on the door a couple of times.

'Dr Kruger? This is the NYPD. Open up, please sir.'

Nothing.

'Dr Kruger?'

He looked at Marquez.

'Dr Kruger?' she called.

Nothing.

Jorgensen thought for a moment, then stepped back. He dipped his shoulder and suddenly rammed into the door. Given his size and muscle memory from days on the Rutgers defensive line, the lock was no match for the force that all two hundred and twenty pounds of him generated. The door splintered open, smashed back like so many quarterbacks who'd played against him back in the day.

He recovered his balance and together, the two detectives moved inside.

The apartment was lavish, the living area straight ahead, the kitchen to the left.

But it was also empty.

They separated, checking the place, then met up a few moments later.

'No sign,' Marquez said.

'You think he left town?' Jorgensen said.

She shook her head. Looking around, she saw a wallet on the mantelpiece and a set of car keys on the marble counter-top. She pointed at them.

'His stuff is still here.'

'Maybe he stepped out. Maybe he'll be back in a minute.'

'Perhaps,' she said, pulling her cell phone and calling Shepherd. As she did so, she opened the wallet on the counter and pulled out Kruger's driver's licence. The photo showed a handsome man, tanned and blond with a square jaw.

'Sir?'

'Yes?'

'We're up at Dr Kruger's,' she said, passing the licence to Jorgensen. She looked around the empty apartment. 'He's not here.'

'OK.'

'Want us to stay and wait? See if he comes back?'

'No. Get over to Dr Tibbs',' Shepherd said abruptly.

'Everything OK, sir? How are Archer and Josh getting on?'

'I'll update you later. I don't have time right now. But find me these other doctors.'

'Yes, sir.'

The call ended. Marquez slid the phone back into her pocket, then turned to Jorgensen, who was examining the driver's licence.

'We're out of here. Dr Tibbs is next. Got his address?'

Jorgensen nodded, still looking around. 'Be nice to have a place like this.'

'With your salary? Maybe in twenty years.'

Jorgensen returned the licence to the wallet, then the two detectives turned and made their way out of the empty apartment. Marquez looked at the lock as she stepped outside. Jorgensen had annihilated it.

'Make it twenty one years. They're gonna make you pay for that.'

Jorgensen pulled the door back into place behind them, and jiggled it, trying to keep it closed.

Eventually it held and he slowly withdrew his hand. Then he looked at her and shrugged.

'I tripped.'

Sitting in the back of a taxi, his heart pounding, Donnie looked back over his shoulder as the cab headed over the Brooklyn Bridge out of Manhattan. He couldn't have felt more relieved to have planted the bomb and got away. Carrying it around, he'd just been waiting for a cop to stop him.

He watched as Lower Manhattan moved further and further away.

It would go off any second now.

FIFTEEN

As luck would have it, Tibbs lived just around the corner from Kruger. The journey only took Marquez and Jorgensen a couple of minutes.

Unlike Kruger's building, this one had a reception and they walked over to the counter, Marquez showing the guy behind the desk her badge and telling him the reason they were here. The man said he hadn't seen Tibbs this morning, which meant he was probably upstairs. As a precaution Marquez asked him for a key-card, which he agreed to provide on the condition that he join them. Marquez understood. Scams like this would be a dime a dozen across the city, thieves coming up with elaborate ways to get access to someone's apartment. If he came with them and watched their every move, his ass would be covered.

He walked around the desk to join the two cops, passing Marquez the key-card. She took it, then turned to Jorgensen.

'Save you another doorframe.'

Together, the trio headed for the lifts. Two of them were already open and they rode one up to 13. Once the lift arrived they stepped out and the guy from the reception led them down the corridor. Soon they came to a halt outside a varnished wooden door, 13 E.

'*Dr Tibbs?*' Marquez said, knocking. '*NYPD. Open up please, sir.*'

Nothing.

'*Dr Tibbs?*'

Nothing.

She took the key-card and slid it into the lock, opening the door.

The moment she pushed it back, all three saw that Dr Tibbs was indeed inside the apartment.

And he wasn't going anywhere.

He was laid out in the living area, a strip of duct tape across his mouth. He'd been shot a number of times, twice to the sternum, twice to the head, blood pooled around him and four empty shell casings lying in the red. As the hotel worker covered his mouth and stared in horror, Marquez and Jorgensen simultaneously drew their side-arms and moved into the apartment, their weapons up.

But just like Kruger's, the place was empty.

Although the Counter-Terrorism Bureau standard-issue Ford Explorer had no light on the roof, it had blue and red lights behind the front and rear fenders. When activated, they sent a clear message to other drivers: get the hell out of the way. Taking the FDR, Josh roared downtown, weaving in and out of traffic as they moved at a controlled but furious speed. He swung off the highway to the right onto South Street and screeched to a halt at the South Street Seaport, alongside Pier 17.

Being the focal point of the entire area, the Pier had been transformed in the 1980s from an old fish market into a three-storey glass pavilion shopping centre, surrounded by a wooden boardwalk and promenade that looked out over the East River. It was one of the busiest shopping areas in Manhattan and also one of Archer's favourite spots to spend his days off. He used to come down here with Katic and her daughter. It had something for everybody. The shopping centre on the Pier was an assortment of different stores, bars and restaurants, some of which served arguably the best seafood in the city. A large pirate ship was docked beside the Pier, acting as a great tourist attraction and entertainment for kids, a number of tour guides dressed up as pirates adding to the spectacle.

Beside the ship, a brass band and group of carol singers were standing on the promenade with their backs to the water. The choir was singing as a crowd watched, people stepping forward to slip money into donation boxes collecting for charity. As he slammed the car door and moved onto the boardwalk, Archer recognised the carol. It was an old classic. *Silent Night.*

Josh joined him, both of them looking at the Pier. A second ESU and CRT team were already here; the music was serving as a distraction, so not many people had noticed the quiet but efficient evacuation beginning around them.

Cursing, Josh pulled his cell, calling Shepherd.

'Sir, we're here. Where the hell are we looking?'

Given that the Seaport was merely a stone's throw from Wall Street, the waterfront primarily catered for the wealthy. A number of stores had set up shop here in order to cash in on all that money. One of them was a trendy clothing brand which had worked increasingly hard for a number of years to establish itself as a provider of top-tier casual wear. Much of their clothing was slim or muscle-fit, a deliberate ploy to discourage anyone who was overweight wearing their stuff, and each article cost anywhere from forty to over a hundred bucks. You almost had to earn the right to wear their clothes. However, such design and marketing strategies has succeeded in giving the brand a certain image and prestige and their garments were popular, particularly with teenagers and young adults.

The store was about twenty five yards from the Seaport and the water. Inside, the manager liked to keep the lights low and the music thumping. Given that it was a week before Christmas the place was doing a brisk trade. They had eight very busy employees assisting customers and processing sales, all of them wearing store-brand polo shirts and jeans. The tills were working flat out and the clothes were flying off the shelves. One of the employees, a twenty two year old NYU student working at the store over the Christmas period to earn some extra money, was carrying some fresh merchandise from the storeroom out back. He laid out an assortment of shirts and jeans, draping them across a wooden stand and adjusting them neatly as he had been taught, displaying the items to their best advantage.

As he was finishing, he caught a familiar whistle coming from the second level. He looked up and saw a colleague motioning for him to come and help her. He quickly headed up the stairs. By the time he got there she'd already moved back to her position behind one of the tills, but he could see why she'd called him. There was a long queue of customers waiting to be served in front of her and the line was growing.

But as he walked over to log in to the till beside her, something caught his eye.

A white shopping bag was sitting on the floor by a table stacked with merchandise to his right. It was unattended. Someone must have put it down to check out some clothing, then walked off and forgotten it. It happened all the time.

He went over to retrieve the bag and put it aside for collection when the forgetful customer had realised what they'd done. But as he bent down to pick it up, he looked closer and frowned. He thought his eyes were playing tricks on him in the low lighting of the store.

Some kind of yellow gas was seeping out of the bag.

SIXTEEN

'OK,' Marquez said, ending the call, still in Dr Tibbs' apartment. She turned to Jorgensen. 'CSU are already on their way. They should be here any minute. Apparently Archer and Josh are onto something downtown.'

'Onto what?'

She shrugged. 'Check the TV.'

Jorgensen turned, then using his sleeve to shield his fingerprints, grabbed the remote for the television off the couch and pushed the power button. Flicking channels, he found Fox News.

'Holy shit.'

The report was showing footage from 34th and 7th, outside Macy's. There were civilians, ESU, Hercules Teams and CRT specialists everywhere, as well as news crews. They looked at the headline.

Breaking: Macy's evacuated after bomb threat.

'Looks like we're missing the party,' Jorgensen said.

Outside in the corridor, the guy from the front desk was still recovering from the shock of seeing Tibbs' corpse. He turned as the sound of approaching footsteps came from the corridor; Jorgensen flicked off the TV and tossed the remote back on the couch as a four-man CSU team quickly entered the room, each carrying a suitcase containing their gear. Both Marquez and Jorgensen knew the team. The lead investigator walked over and shook both detectives' hands; then she looked down at Tibbs' body.

'This is how you found him?'

'Walked in and this is what we saw,' Marquez said.

'Four gunshot wounds. Tight groups. Must have been silenced, otherwise everyone in the building would have heard.'

Behind her, her team started pulling on their gear.

'We'll get to work,' she said, hinting that she wanted them to leave.

'We need to head out anyway,' Marquez said to Jorgensen, who nodded. She looked out of the apartment and saw the guy from the front desk out in the hall. She turned back to the CSU investigator. 'The receptionist saw the body when we did. He might need a few minutes.'

The woman nodded.

'We'll get him out of here. I'll have someone stay with him.'

'Thanks.'

'I'll contact Shepherd when we get something.'

The two detectives nodded, stepping past the CSU team and walking out of the apartment, quickly headed down the corridor to the lifts. As they walked, Jorgensen pulled a pad from his pocket and checked the next address.

'Frankie Glover. Lives across town on 70th and 3rd. Dr Number Three.'

Marquez nodded and they stepped into the open lift, pressing the button for the ground floor. In the silence, both of them thought about the dead doctor laid out in the apartment they'd just left.

A strip of duct tape across the mouth. Two to the sternum, two to the head.

'Poor bastard,' Jorgensen said. 'Not a good way to go.'

'Is there ever a good way?' Marquez replied, as the doors slid shut.

Josh and Archer were just heading out onto the Pier when they heard the screams.

They swung round and saw a handful of people staggering out of a store twenty five yards behind them. They were all choking. Several of them collapsed to their hands and knees, heaving and hacking blood onto the sidewalk.

'No!' Archer shouted, turning and running towards them.

People standing closer to the store stopped and stared as they suddenly saw people falling out of the doorway in front of them, retching and gasping for air. Blood was starting to leak and spray from their mouths, their bodies fitting and spasming violently as the people watching began to scream and back away.

Some members of the ESU and CRT teams had been close by. They reacted fast, sprinting across the street. Archer and Josh had almost reached the store when a CRT guy turned and ordered them back, blocking their path.

'Remain where you are!'

Obeying orders, Archer and Josh watched in despair as people who'd made it out of the store writhed and flailed on the sidewalk, their mouths and chins covered in blood. The ESU, gas masks firmly in place, were frantically pushing people away from the area. Other members of their team had already raced towards the front of the store and had pulled the doors closed, holding them shut. It took three of them. The remaining people trapped inside were desperately trying to force their way out and the trio had to fight to keep the doors secure in order to contain the virus.

Several members of CRT were trying to help the five people on the ground, but it was useless.

Two of them were already dead and the others were about to join them, their bodies stiffening, blood erupting from their mouths. The guy who'd ordered Archer and Josh to stay back was dragging what looked like fabric tenting from the back of the CRT van with the help of two other men.

An ESU officer ran over to the entrance of the store with a bully ram he'd pulled from their truck, the other three officers still holding the doors shut. They lodged it across the entrance bars, providing a makeshift block. People were still thumping the other side, more weakly now, but they weren't getting out.

Having moved back, standing with a crowd of civilians watching in dawning horror, Archer and Josh could hear screaming from inside the store.

But it was fading.

And soon, it stopped.

SEVENTEEN

Jorgensen drove fast at the best of times, but the discovery of Dr Tibbs' corpse had put an extra few ounces of pressure on his pedal foot. They sped across town, lights on the fenders flashing as they cut several reds. Before long they pulled to an abrupt halt outside Dr Glover's address, an apartment building on the Upper East Side on 70th and 3rd. Unlike Dr Tibbs' apartment building there was no reception, which also meant they had to wait for someone to let them in. Standing on the cold street they scanned the occupiers list beside the buzzer. They found *F. Glover* beside Apartment 2D. Luckily, a resident exited the building less than a minute later and Jorgensen jammed his arm in the door before it could shut.

Moving quickly up the stairs, the two detectives headed down the second floor corridor towards Dr Glover's apartment.

However, as they approached they saw that the door was ajar.

Marquez was first inside, checking the apartment through the top sight of her pistol. Jorgensen followed her in. They cleared the place, the same as before.

And just as before, the apartment was empty. No sign of Dr Glover.

After a few moments they met up in the living area, holstering their weapons and looking around. The television was on, showing the news. There was the beginnings of breakfast on the kitchen counter, a couple of cereal bowls and two pastries. One of them had a bite taken out of it.

'Someone was just here,' Jorgensen said.

Marquez nodded in agreement. As Jorgensen moved to the kitchen to take a closer look around, Marquez saw several photo-frames placed on a table in the sitting room. She approached them, and noticed that the same man was in all three. Picking up the middle frame, she examined the photo. He was blond, in his thirties, standing on the deck of a yacht. Dressed in a white polo shirt, cream shorts and deck shoes and holding a green bottle of Heineken, he was smiling at the camera. It had been a beautiful day when the photo was taken and she saw nothing but blue sea and horizon behind him.

'Here's our guy,' she said.

'The kettle's still warm,' said Jorgensen, his hand on the jug. 'He was here recently.'

Feeling uneasy, Marquez looked down at the photograph, at that broad grin on the man's face. She thought of Dr Tibbs, flat on his back, four gunshot wounds to his head and chest.

Where are you, Dr Glover?

Wherever it was, she had a gut feeling that he wouldn't be smiling.

Marquez was right. At that moment Glover's face was a mask of wide-eyed shock, fear and confusion.

He was still sitting inside the lab at *Kearny Medical* across the Hudson River in New Jersey. His initial shock at his predicament was fading and was now being replaced by an ice cold fear and disbelief. Melissa's body had been dragged away and dumped in a room across the level. He was trying not to stare at the blood stain it had left on the floor, smeared on the white tiles. Outside the lab Glover saw the man with the black curly hair watching him from an office next door, his face expressionless, his feet up on a desk and that strange machine pistol clasped in his hand.

Suddenly the lift dinged. It opened and Glover saw the man and woman who'd kidnapped him walk out and head towards the large man. They were a terrifying pair.

He and Melissa had just woken up and had been preparing breakfast and planning their day when someone had knocked on the door. Glover had opened up and been punched hard in the face. He'd fallen back and the man and woman had entered, a silenced pistol trained on him and Melissa, who'd been sitting at the kitchen counter eating a Danish. They'd forced them out of the apartment, taking them downstairs and hustling them into a car outside, then brought them straight here. He watched as the dark-haired woman pulled a small vial from her pocket. Glover recognised what it was straight away and his blood ran cold.

It was Dr Flood's virus.

The curly-headed guy took it from her, raising it and examining the vial in the light.

He turned the cylinder, peering at it from all angles.

Then he looked over at Dr Glover and a broad grin spread across his face.

*

Back at the Pier, the screaming inside the store had long since ended. The ESU and several Hercules teams had formed a cordon with a fifty yard radius. CRT had opened up a secure containment tent, rigging it up to the outside of the building and sealing it airtight to ensure that any remaining gas was contained. The bodies of the five victims who'd made it out of the store had been quickly covered before the news cameras got there. Respective news teams had arrived, but they were being kept well back along with everybody else.

Having shown their badges to an ESU officer guarding the barrier, Archer and Josh were standing inside the cordon, looking at the entrance to the store. Neither said a word. A CRT specialist stepped out from the tent and walked towards the two detectives. The man pulled off the helmet of his bio suit, running his gloved hand through his hair. His face was grim. The two men moved forward to meet him.

'What's the damage?' Archer asked.

'Fifty nine dead. No survivors.'

Silence.

'You have any idea who's responsible for this?'

'We're working on it.'

'Well work faster. I think the youngest in there is about twelve.'

Pause.

'What about containment?' Josh asked.

'We sealed the place before it got out. Believe it or not, we got lucky. The bomb went off on the second floor, so it bought us some extra time. We shut down the building ventilation system and the tent is keeping the place airtight. Luckily, there are no windows in there so the gas had nowhere else to go. We're still working on filtering the air.'

'What's the cover?'

'A chemical pipe ruptured. If the truth gets out we'll have a major panic on our hands.'

Without a word, Josh pulled his cell phone, turning and walking away, leaving Archer and the CRT specialist alone.

'Do you have a spare suit?' Archer asked.

The guy nodded.

'Follow me. I'll give you a mask.'

The interior of the store was dark. Incongruously, the music was still thumping and the lights were flashing. It looked like an abandoned nightclub. Archer moved inside slowly, letting his eyes adjust to the dim lighting. He had a gas mask sealed to his face, his air filtered and protected through the respirator. Although he'd trained with a gas mask at the ARU, he hadn't worn one in a while and felt claustrophobic and uncomfortable with it pulled tight to his face. No way was it coming off, however.

The floor was littered with bodies. Corpses, shopping bags and personal belongings were scattered everywhere. Amongst the twisted and contorted dead, Archer could see a few who were obviously trying on clothes when they got hit but who must have abandoned the fitting rooms in panic, desperately running for the doors and the air outside. They lay there half-dressed, many of them with arms outstretched, blood around their mouths and all over the ground beside them. Archer moved further into the store, stepping carefully past the bodies, making sure he didn't touch any of them out of respect.

The CRT specialist led him up to the second floor. The scene was much the same as downstairs, the place strewn with infected victims, people of both sexes and all ages. Then the specialist pointed to a white bag beside a stand.

'There it is,' he said, his voice muffled.

Archer walked forward and dropping to one knee, peered inside. He saw one of those now familiar boxes, the lid askew and the remains of what had been the vial just visible, the glass cylinder cracked in two. Its terrible job had been accomplished.

Rising, Archer turned and saw Josh walking towards him through the dim store. He was moving slowly, staring at the horrific scene around him, a gas mask over his face. He came to a halt beside Archer and the CRT specialist but didn't say a word.

With the darkness and thumping music, the grisly scene lit by flashing lights, it looked like something out of a nightmare.

The three men stood there in silence.

Surrounded by death.

Josh had just called Shepherd to inform him of the situation but he needn't have bothered. He and Rach had Fox News up on the screen and were watching the initial reports on the disaster.

Breaking: Chemical Pipe ruptures in clothing store by Seaport, kills 59.

The TV pictures were showing people being held back behind the cordoned-off area, some watching with ghoulish fascination, others who had family members unaccounted for being interviewed by reporters, desperate to be allowed inside to find their loved ones. But the ESU teams were continuing to keep them back. The front of the store had been tented off. Nothing was visible and no one was getting closer.

'We were too late,' Rach said quietly.

Shepherd watched the screen for a few moments longer, his face expressionless.

Then he turned to her. 'The shot of the Macy's bomber when he dumped his coat. Pull it up again.'

She nodded, then started tapping away. The television shots disappeared, replaced by the city camera feed. It took her less than thirty seconds to find the right camera and pause it at the moment the man appeared.

'Play.'

They watched as he moved out of the store, shrugging off the identifiable jacket then dumping it in a can. He raised his hand for a taxi but the vehicle was just out of shot.

'Any cameras facing east or west?'

Rach tapped and another box appeared. It was a camera from 34th and 7th, facing east.

'Match the time,' Shepherd said. Rach did and hit *Pause*. She then zoomed in, closer and closer. The shot was pixelated.

'Render.'

She hit *Enter*. There was a second's delay, then the screen cleared. A series of numbers and letters were now as clear as crystal on the screen.

The taxi's licence plates.

'Got you, you son of a bitch,' Shepherd said, pulling his cell and moving to the door. He turned back to Rach as he walked. 'Find that third bomber fast!'

Across Queens, Donnie entered a run-down house off Ditmars Boulevard and shut the front door behind him. It had been their hideout last night but they were only occupying the ground floor. He walked down the corridor, passing a sitting room on his right and moved into the kitchen.

He found Bleeker waiting in there anxiously, watching the midday news on the television. He was sitting on a stool and had a Remington 870 12 gauge shotgun resting on the kitchen table within easy reach. Donnie looked at the screen and saw a *Breaking News* item from the Seaport.

'Did it work?'

'They found mine,' Bleeker said. 'They didn't find yours.'

Looking at the screen, Donnie blinked. He smiled.

'So that's good, right? At least one of them succeeded. This is what you wanted.'

'So where the hell is Nate?'

'He didn't come back?'

'No. And his bomb should've gone off by now. It should be all over the news like yours.'

Donnie didn't speak. Bleeker swore and checked his watch.

'Anyway, mission accomplished. Pack your shit. We're out of here, with or without him.'

'What about your deal with the Brit?'

Bleeker shook his head. 'Screw him. I don't need his money anymore. After what just happened, you and I are going to be richer than we could have ever dreamed.'

Stepping out of the containment tent at the Seaport, Archer pulled off the gas mask and sucked in a deep, cleansing breath of fresh air. He walked over to the CRT truck and passed the mask back to a man inside, thanking him. Josh followed him out. Archer saw him take off his own mask and fumble in his pocket. He pulled out his cell, taking a call and holding it to his ear.

'Sir?'

He listened for a moment. Archer watched his expression.

They had something.

Still listening, Josh moved forward, tossing the gas mask to the CRT guy in the truck and nodding his thanks, then ended the call.

'Shepherd called the cab company. Apparently the Macy's bomber was dropped off outside a house just off Ditmars in Astoria about twenty minutes ago.'

Without another word, both men ran for their car, the CRT specialist watching them go.

EIGHTEEN

At the house, Bleeker and Donnie had almost finished packing. Neither of them lived there. It belonged to Bleeker's brother Hurley who was doing time upstate for armed robbery, and had been an ideal hide-out last night, totally off the grid and no obvious connection to the four men. Bleeker was on the ground floor in one of two side bedrooms beyond the kitchen. He'd already ditched his ID and bankcards, planning to get some forgeries once they left the state. As he quickly stuffed his belongings into a holdall, he glanced over at the last remaining bomb resting on a bed beside the bag. Ray's bomb. It should have gone off on the platform at Times Square 42nd Street this morning, but Ray stepped out late last night and had never returned.

His disappearance was confusing and unnerving. Ray was tough, and not the kind of guy to get cold feet. Bleeker had a gut instinct about what had happened to him and who had done it, and that meant he and Donnie had to get the hell out of there right now.

He reached over to the make-shift viral bomb and carefully unclipped the cylinder. Keeping it in his hand and scooping up the bag with the other, he walked quickly into the kitchen. Placing his bag on a chair he stepped over to the fridge and pulled open the door.

Inside, beside some milk and a half-drunk six pack of Miller, was the last vial of the virus.

Bleeker hadn't anticipated Ray's no-show but despite that, their current situation was still pretty good. He and Donnie now had two vials to sell and this morning's work was a clear demonstration to any potential buyers of the virus's power. The price had just gone up exponentially; there would be plenty of people out there willing to pay it. He took the other vial off the shelf in the fridge and studied it. This small, harmless looking glass cylinder was worth far more than the house he was standing in.

Maybe more than the entire street.

He carefully wrapped both vials in cotton padding, then placed them in a box which he sealed and tucked into his bag. Then he moved over to the sink and opened a cupboard by the window, reaching inside and pushing some cereal boxes out of the way. He pulled out a Beretta handgun and a magazine with fifteen 9mm Parabellum shells pushed inside. He slammed the mag into the pistol, pulled the top slide and checked the safety then slid it into the bag too. He checked his watch and glanced at the television showing footage from the Seaport. There were ESU cops and what had to be NYPD detectives in every shot, crowds of onlookers filling South and Water Street.

They'd already be hunting for whoever left the device inside the store.

As would others.

'Let's go!' he called to Donnie, urgency in his voice.

Speeding down 33rd Street in Astoria, the subway line overhead, Josh and Archer saw Shepherd waiting for them around the corner on Ditmars Boulevard, pulled up to the kerb on the left. He'd already strapped a black bulletproof vest over his torso, *NYPD* clearly visible in white letters on the front and back. He was loading a Mossberg

590A1 shotgun while standing by the trunk of his car. Parking behind him, Archer and Josh jumped out of their own Ford and moved rapidly to the back of their vehicle, just as a third Ford pulled up behind them. Turning as he fastened a bulletproof vest in place, Archer saw it was Marquez and Jorgensen.

His vest on, Josh pulled out two Mossbergs from their stowed positions in the trunk and started loading them. Designed by OF Mossberg and Sons, a Swedish immigrant's company based up in Connecticut, the 590A1 was a modification of the 500 model. With an eight shell magazine chamber and metal trigger guard and safety catch, the black aluminium and steel pump-action shotgun was an old favourite of the US Army and a new one of the NYPD. The old Department-issue Ithaca 37 was being slowly phased out and in the next few years every squad car in the five boroughs would have a Mossberg up front by the radio. Mossberg and Sons claimed it was the only weapon of its kind to pass the Army's military specifications tests for shotguns and it wasn't an outlandish claim. The 590A1 was sleek, smooth to load, didn't have too much kick and had the stopping power of a Claymore mine; eight mines technically, considering the ammunition in the magazine.

Josh finished loading the shotguns; he tossed one to Archer, who caught it and racked the pump and within twenty seconds the entire detail was gathered with Shepherd by his car, *NYPD* vests on their torsos and Mossbergs in their hands. This extra gear was Department procedure for a house breach of this kind. They had no idea what kind of weaponry they were facing inside and that meant they needed sufficient firepower to counter it.

'What's the plan, sir?' Josh asked.

'The taxi company put out a call to their drivers,' Shepherd said. 'Apparently two men matching our guys got dropped off around the corner at Number 18. The house is registered to a Hurley Bleeker. Rach is running a check and trying to locate the third man.'

'Do we know the layout?' Marquez asked.

'Doesn't matter. We go in through the front door. We don't have time to waste. One of their team is still out there.'

'It could be a bottleneck,' Josh said. 'They'll be expecting. They could drop us one-by-one.'

'Hold up,' Archer said.

The team turned and saw where he was looking. A mail van had just pulled up across the street, a woman stepping out of the truck and heading over to one of the properties to deliver a parcel.

'I've got an idea.'

Inside the house, Donnie and Bleeker had finished packing and were standing in the kitchen making sure they had everything they needed. They'd have to leave Hurley's Remington here. No way they could carry a 12 gauge shotgun covertly on a train, but they still had the Beretta in case things got physical.

'I've got the last two vials,' Bleeker said. 'We get out to Long Island, then take the train south. When we're out of the state I'll put the word out about what we're selling. We can hook up with Chapters in Pittsburgh or Baltimore.'

Donnie nodded.

'What about our guest?' he asked, pointing to the main bedroom.

Bleeker turned, having momentarily forgotten about the man inside.

'Shit. Good catch. I'll take care of him.'

He pulled the Beretta from his holdall, flicking off the safety and walked into the room.

A man was sitting in a chair, tied up, his mouth gagged. His eyes widened as he saw Bleeker walk in and grab a pillow. Bleeker held it to the man's face then pushed the barrel of the pistol into the other side.

'Time's up.'

But before he could pull the trigger, there was a sharp knock at the door down the hall.

'Delivery.'

Bleeker froze, the gun and pillow held to the gagged captive's face. The man was squirming and making muffled sounds under the gag.

There was another knock.

'Delivery. C'mon man, it's cold,' the voice called. Female. *'I haven't got all day.'*

Bleeker looked at Donnie. He took the pillow off the captive's head then passed Donnie the Beretta, grip first. The younger man took the weapon, then moved down the corridor. He walked towards the door slowly and risked a glance through the spy hole.

A dark-haired woman was outside on the step, dressed in UPS gear, wrapped up against the cold.

'Who's it for?' he asked.

He watched her look at a package in her hands. 'Hurley Bleeker.'

Donnie thought for a moment, then opened up.

'I'll take-'

Suddenly, the woman dropped the package and rammed the door back hard, throwing Donnie off balance and sending him reeling down the corridor. She pulled a Sig Sauer pistol from underneath her coat, an *NYPD* bulletproof vest on her torso.

'NYPD! Don't move!'

Bleeker was watching from the kitchen as Donnie fell to the ground. He ducked out of sight as Donnie, flat on his back, quickly raised his pistol and aimed at the woman's legs.

NINETEEN

Marquez saw the guy lifting the gun but she was faster. She shot him twice in the chest and watched him thump back to the floor, dead. She moved inside the house swiftly and kicked the gun away from his hand, his palm open and his fingers loose. She focused her attention down the corridor to where the other guy had been standing as Jorgensen and Shepherd moved in behind her, Mossbergs in their shoulders.

'NYPD!' she shouted, looking through the sights of her Sig Sauer. *'Come out with your hands up!'*

There was movement up ahead.

Something appeared around the corner.

The barrel of a twelve gauge shotgun.

Jorgensen and Shepherd were already diving for cover. Marquez launched herself into a room to her right as the guy pulled the trigger. The blast was deafening, a thousand splinters and dust spraying into the air as the shell hit the main doorframe, forcing Jorgensen and Shepherd to retreat and Marquez to stay in what was a small sitting room.

Forced back outside the house, with their backs to the wall each side of the door, Jorgensen and Shepherd tried to move in again to back up Marquez, but the guy in the house fired again, pinning them down, pieces of the door frame spraying in the air. He had command of the corridor.

'Back off!' a voice screamed from the kitchen. *'I said back off!'*

Standing next to Josh to the right side of the door, Archer thought fast.

He swung away from the others and headed to the house next door.

'Back off!' Bleeker screamed again, aiming the Remington down the corridor. He looked at Donnie's lifeless body on the ground up ahead and roared with rage. He racked the pump and fired the shotgun again, splinters and plaster filling the corridor as the shell annihilated the wall by the door. But even though he appeared to have the upper hand, Bleeker knew he was pinned down. It was just a matter of time. Keeping the barrel of the weapon on the only entrance, he looked around frantically, desperately trying to think of a way out. The bitch cop appeared from the sitting room, trying to get off a shot. Bleeker aimed and fired, just missing her and destroying the door frame.

'Back up!'

Then he remembered he had the last two vials of the virus in his bag, sitting on the stool behind him. That was a serious bargaining tool. He could threaten them with that.

Firing again and working the pump, he ran to the bag. But just as he unzipped it and went to grab the box inside, he caught a movement through the kitchen window from the corner of his eye. He swung to his left, raising the shotgun, and caught sight of a figure in the house next door.

That wasn't unusual except this one had white letters on his black vest.

NYPD.

It was the last thing he ever saw.

The Mossberg in Archer's shoulder had a trigger pull of around seven pounds. He squeezed as the man turned towards him and the weapon boomed in his shoulder. The buckshot smashed through both sets of windows and hit the guy full in the chest. He wasn't wearing a vest and the shot hurled him back into the counter behind him. Watching the man slump to the ground, Archer racked the pump on the Mossberg, his ears ringing from the shot.

'Clear!'

He turned, and looked at a couple huddled down on the floor behind him, the owners of the house. They had their hands over their ears.

'Sorry about the window,' he said.

Inside the house, Marquez and Jorgensen were in the lead, sweeping and clearing each room. As they moved into the kitchen, Marquez dropped down to the man Archer had shot, pulling his shotgun from his grasp and checking his pulse.

He was dead.

Jorgensen headed straight to a door ahead, kicking it open and moving forward, all the while looking through the sights of his Mossberg. It was a bedroom, dank, the bed unmade.

But there was a man inside, tied to a chair. He was sitting on the left of the room, his eyes wide with shock. He'd taken a severe beating, his face cut up and bloodied, a piece of black duct tape pulled across his mouth. Jorgensen stared at the man for a moment, recognising him immediately as Marquez joined him inside the room. Lowering their weapons, the two detectives moved forward and Jorgensen pulled the strip of tape off the man's mouth.

'What's your name?' he asked.

'Reuben,' the man said, between deep gulps of air. 'Reuben Kruger. I'm a doctor'.

*

Across the water in Manhattan, a long line had formed outside the men's restroom in the French patisserie at Bryant Park. As she fulfilled a drinks order, a busy waitress noticed the queue and frowned. Irritated, she placed her tray down and quickly stepped past everyone, arriving outside the men's room door. She knocked on it briskly.

'Sir? Is everything alright?'

Nothing.

'Sir?'

Nothing.

No sound from inside.

She tried the handle but it was locked. Turning, she caught the attention of a waiter and motioned him over.

'He's not answering,' the waitress said, as the man joined her. He put his ear against the wood, listening for a moment, then grabbed the handle and tried to force it open. It wouldn't budge. He made a decision and stepped back. He dipped his shoulder and hit the frame. The force overpowered the lock and the door flew open.

As he stumbled into the restroom, they both saw a man slumped on the ground. His body was limp, his head twisted at almost a right angle. Beside him was an empty box. His dead eyes stared across the room.

The waitress covered her mouth, but didn't quite manage to stop a scream.

TWENTY

Thirty minutes later, the house off Ditmars Boulevard was filled with CSU investigators photographing the crime scene before the bodies and weapons were bagged and tagged. A preliminary search inside an unzipped holdall sitting in the kitchen had revealed the third and fourth vials of the virus. That left one to go, in the possession of the third bomber who Rach was currently working hard to find. Given Dr Flood's unexpected suicide, the murder of Dr Tibbs and the disappearance of Dr Glover, Health Services were taking the reins on trying to work up an antidote.

They had another fifty nine infected dead to work with.

A two-man team from their lab had arrived at the house five minutes ago, taken the virus and left as quickly as they had arrived. Everyone inside was relieved to have found the vials, but were even more so when the virus left the house.

Shepherd, Archer, Marquez and Jorgensen were gathered in the bedroom in front of Dr Kruger, who was still sitting in the chair they'd found him in. His binds and gag had been removed and a medic was patching him up. The woman was attending to his face, clearing off the blood, using antiseptic to clean the wounds and then applying several butterfly stitches to the cuts on his cheekbones.

Standing near the door, Archer examined the doctor. He was in his late thirties or early forties and looked in good shape, blond hair and green eyes with overnight stubble on his neck and cheeks. He was wearing a blue shirt and some corduroy trousers with black shoes but the shirt was specked with blood from the injuries to his face. He looked solid; he wasn't in shock. He wasn't staring at the dead body visible through the doorway in the kitchen. And he was alive. That was the most important thing considering that two of his colleagues had already died this morning.

'How are you feeling?' Shepherd asked.

'I'll live,' Kruger said. Only two words, but Archer picked up a strong South African accent.

'So what the hell happened?' Shepherd asked.

'You tell me. Last night someone knocks on my apartment door. I open up and a gun is stuck in my face. They take me downstairs, stuff me in a car and bring me here.'

'What did they want?'

'At first, I had no idea. I thought maybe it was kidnap, but I don't come from a wealthy family and certainly don't mix in high circles. No one would pay much for me.'

He nodded out of the room.

'The fat boy took my key-card for the lab from my pocket, then left. He came back an hour later with five vials of Peter's virus.'

He flinched as the doctor dabbed at a cut on his cheekbone.

'When he got back he took off my binds and shoved a gun in my face. He'd brought some equipment from the lab and ordered me to use it to extract a small sample of the virus and place it in another vial, which was then pressurised. He made me do it right here. They weren't taking any chances and were all wearing masks. I had to do it without. Then I saw them start soldering together those things.'

He nodded to the bed. The team saw a shoebox containing a timer and rack for the vial. A carbon copy of the other bombs.

'It didn't take a genius to work out they were planning some sort of atrocity. Once I was done, the leader took the package with the smallest amount of the virus I transferred for him and was out for a while. He didn't come back with it.'

'It detonated in Central Park,' Marquez said. 'Killed a man.'

Kruger stared at her but didn't respond. The doctor went to unbutton his shirt and check his torso for injuries but he caught her hands. 'I'm fine, doc. It's just my face.' He seemed resolute and tough. Archer liked him already.

At the door behind them, Josh ducked his head into the room. 'Sir?' Shepherd turned. 'I've got some news. The third bomber has been found. He's out of the game.'

'What do you mean he's out of the game?'

'He's dead. He was found in a restroom of a café near Bryant Park. His neck was broken.'

'His bomb?'

'That's the problem sir. The device was there. But the vial containing the virus was gone.'

Thirty five miles to the south west, a New Jersey farmer pulled open the door to a large barn where he always took his lunch break. Despite being in his early seventies, he'd been up since first light, something he had to do if he wanted to make the most of the season and prepare for the spring.

He'd just finished his work for the morning. He owned a large spread of land and the shed he was standing in was almost like his office. It was also excellent storage for his retirement gift, an

Antonov An-2, a single engine biplane. Given that it was a Russian model, built back in 1946, the duster was a favourite of collectors and aircraft aficionados. The farmer was the latter, although he'd never flown the plane. A pilot couldn't fly an Antonov in the United States without an experimental certification which the farmer was currently working on attaining. He'd spent most of his retirement fund on the duster, much to his wife's fury, but was planning to sell it as soon as he'd taken it up in the air just the once. After he experienced that, he'd be happy. An expert had come by last month to give him an evaluation and told him that the plane could be worth over $60,000 to the right collector. The farmer was elated. He'd bought it for two thirds that price.

Leaving the door to the barn open behind him, he walked towards his old armchair. It was beaten and worn, much like the farmer himself, but over time the seat had adjusted to his body shape and now was the most comfortable thing he'd ever sat in. He relaxed back into the chair, his knees creaking, enjoying that moment when the pressure was taken off them. Beside him on a table was a radio, a newspaper and his lunch. His wife had made him a sandwich wrapped in foil. He clicked on the radio then snapped out the newspaper on his lap; reaching over, he picked up his sandwich and unwrapped the foil. It was a Reuben, his favourite, corned beef, cheese, sauerkraut and Russian dressing on thick-cut bread.

Warm and comfortable, he picked it up and went to take a bite.

'That's quite a plane,' a voice suddenly said, startling him.

He looked up and saw two people standing in the doorway of the barn. It was a man and a woman. They'd appeared silently and out of nowhere. He didn't recognise either of them and they definitely weren't rural folk. The man had white blond hair, almost like an albino, most of it sticking straight up. The woman looked the tougher of the two, her face hard, lank dark hair that looked like it needed a good scrub and a brush. Both were in jeans and leather jackets.

Both were staring at him.

'Can I help you?'

'What kind of model is that?' the man asked, pointing at the crop duster.

'Antonov. An-2.'

'How much is it?'

'It's not for sale.'

'You don't know how much I'm willing to offer.'

The farmer didn't reply.

'Who are you?' he asked instead.

'You got any pesticide?' the blond man asked, ignoring the question.

The farmer's eyes narrowed. 'Now what would you want with that?'

'How much you got?'

'Enough.'

'Well show us what you have and I'll tell you how much I'm willing to pay.'

The farmer hid his excitement. He had much more than he needed and could make a tidy profit here which would please his wife. He pretended to think for a moment, pondering the offer. Then he pushed himself out of the chair and walked over towards them.

Up close, he got a closer look at the pair. The white-blond haired guy had a thick scar over his eyebrow which told a story that the farmer didn't want to know. The woman had a face that looked weathered and hard. *Not city folk.* They lacked that softness.

And there was something about them that was unnerving.

'You don't look like farmers.'

'We're from out of town,' the woman said, her eyes fixed on him.

'The plane's not for sale. But I can sell you some pesticide. For the right price.'

'Let's see it first.'

The farmer looked at them for a moment, then beckoned the pair to follow, leading them out of the barn and to another shed next door. He undid the lock, taking the wooden bar off the front and placing it to one side, then pulled open the doors.

He had six thick canisters of the pesticide stored inside. Each barrel was about the size of a beer keg, a yellow toxic sign on the side of each one.

'There you are,' he said, turning. 'Now let's talk about the price.'

The blond man grinned.

'Ok. How about we take it all off your hands for free?'

The farmer looked at him, to see if he was joking.

He wasn't.

'Are you crazy?'

He suddenly realised the woman had her hand behind her back.

She whipped it round and the farmer found himself looking down the end of a silenced pistol.

She pulled the trigger. The back of the farmer's head blew apart, spraying blood and brains into the air in a mist and he collapsed to the ground with a thud, sinking slightly into the mud. Drexler gave him two more rounds for good measure as Wicks stepped past the body and grabbed a wheeled dolly placed beside the canisters.

Stepping past the dead man, Drexler walked up to the first tank of pesticide. She tipped it onto its side and Wicks slid the dolly underneath, loading it up.

TWENTY ONE

In the bedroom at the house off Ditmars, silence had followed Josh's revelation that despite finding the third bomber the last vial was still missing. A race that had been looking set to close was now wide open again. Shepherd had sent him out to call Rach with fresh orders, to find out who went into that café with the dead bomber and broke his neck. Inside the bedroom the medic applied a final butterfly stitch to the cut on Dr Kruger's right cheekbone, then clicked her case shut.

She rose and turned to Shepherd. 'All done. He should be fine. Maybe a mild concussion, but no lasting damage.'

She passed Kruger a small capsule full of paracetamol.

'Take two of these every four hours for the headache and keep your heart-rate down.'

'Easier said than done today,' Jorgensen said, as Kruger took the capsule.

The woman turned and left the room, leaving them alone.

'Why did they do this?' Marquez asked Kruger, pointing to the damage to his face. 'Did you talk back to them?'

Kruger shrugged. 'Guess they didn't like me. The leader struck me as a bully. Literally.'

'So what went on this morning?' Shepherd asked.

'The door was shut,' Kruger said. 'But they all left pretty early. I heard them arguing in the kitchen last night after they'd given me a beating. Something had happened.'

'What was that?'

'I think one of their guys jumped ship. They kept saying *where the hell is he?* Then two of them got into a big argument.'

'You catch a name?'

Kruger shook his head. 'Afraid not. But like I said, I heard them step out early this morning. Two of them got back about an hour ago, the fat boy and the kid. They were about to kill me just before you showed up.'

He suddenly paused.

'Wait. Did you locate the other vials?'

'We got one,' Shepherd said. 'But we missed another. It was released in a clothing store by the Seaport. We're still trying to locate the fifth.'

'How many dead?'

Pause.

'Fifty nine.'

Kruger stared at him for a moment. Then he rose to his feet, wincing as blood started circulating through his lower body for the first time in eighteen hours.

'We need to talk to Peter right away. Where is he?'

Shepherd licked his lips.

'I'm afraid I have some more bad news. Dr Flood is dead.'

Pause. Kruger looked stunned.

'When he found the virus was gone this morning he committed suicide,' Shepherd continued. 'He stepped off the roof of your lab building.'

'You were there?'

Across the room, Archer nodded. Kruger saw this.

'Did he say anything?' he asked.

'You need to get out of New York,' Archer recited. *'Thousands of people are going to die.'*

Kruger bowed his head. The team gave him a moment. All things considered, this guy was having a pretty bad day.

They'd wait until later to tell him about Dr Tibbs.

'We're sorry,' Shepherd said.

'Peter was a great friend of mine. He was the one who brought me here from Cape Town.'

Behind them, Josh suddenly ducked his head in through the door again. He looked straight at Shepherd.

'Sir, you need to come take a look at this.'

Shepherd turned and moved to the doorway. Archer followed him out as Marquez and Jorgensen stayed with the South African doctor to ask him some more questions.

The two men walked into the kitchen, joining Josh who was standing over one of the dead bodies, the man Archer had shot with the Mossberg. A CSU investigator was snapping photographs of the wounding on the dead man's chest. As the camera flashed, Josh pointed down at the body.

'Check it out.'

The guy's shirt had been pulled open, revealing the catastrophic damage caused by the shotgun shell. But that wasn't what Josh was pointing at. The man had several black tattoos on his torso, including a prominent one on his flabby right pectoral. The inking was instantly familiar.

A Swastika.

'What the hell?' Archer said. 'He was a neo-Nazi?'

The CSU photographer overheard the question and nodded. 'Correct. I've run into members of this crew before.'

He pointed at a smaller tattoo on the dead guy's stomach.

It was an *SS*, printed in slanted font.

'They're a white-power group spread across the country. They call themselves *The Stuttgart Soldiers*. That's what the *SS* stands for.' He then jabbed a finger down the corridor at the man Marquez had taken down. 'His buddy has the same tattoo on his arm.'

Staring at the Swastika tattoo on the man's chest, Shepherd pulled his cell phone and dialled Briefing Room 5 at the Bureau. He pushed the button for loudspeaker and held the phone in his palm so everyone could hear.

'*Sir?*'

'Rach, I need you to check something out for me.'

'*What do you need?*'

'I'm at the house off Ditmars. The men in possession of the virus were members of a neo-Nazi group called *The Stuttgart Soldiers*. Run a search and tell me what you find. You're on speaker.'

There was a pause. Archer, Josh and the CSU investigator could hear computer keys being tapped at speed. In the silence, they all examined the dead man's tattoos.

The Stuttgart Soldiers. Founded in 2002; an estimated eight thousand members across the United States. They have chapters in New York, Pittsburgh, Baltimore, Texas, Portland, Arizona and California. Leader of the New York group is

a man called Kyle Gunnar. 36 years old, single.
He lives in Astoria too.'

'Send me his address.'

'*Yes sir.*'

He ended the call and turned to the CSU
investigator, pointing at the dead neo-Nazi at
their feet.

'Does he have any ID?'

The man shook his head. 'None we can find. He
doesn't have a wallet or any passport or driving
licence. The kid down the hall doesn't either.'

Jorgensen and Marquez had just walked out of
the bedroom with Dr Kruger. He stared down at
the dead neo-Nazi lying on the kitchen floor, his
face expressionless. In the meantime, Shepherd
spoke to Jorgensen and Marquez. 'Take the doc
back to the Bureau. Maddy Flood is already over
there. Get him some food and make him
comfortable.'

They both nodded. 'Yes sir.'

Then Shepherd turned to Josh and Archer.

'You two, with me. We're going to pay Kyle
Gunnar a visit.'

*

Gunnar lived about five minutes away, up past
Astoria Boulevard on 43rd Street. The trio went in
Shepherd's car. Turning right, Shepherd pulled to
a stop thirty feet from the address and killed the
engine. Looking down both sidewalks, Archer
saw a few passers-by but other than that it was
quiet, a polar opposite from the mayhem in
Manhattan earlier in the day.

'He lives on the top floor. Apartment 3,'
Shepherd said, all three men looking at the front
door of the house.

'Mossbergs?' Josh asked.

'Leave them here. He's one man. Pistols only. And zip up your coats.'

They did so, covering up the *NYPD* lettering on their bulletproof vests. Then the three men stepped out of the car and shut the doors behind them.

They headed briskly down the street. Archer was the first to the steps leading to the building. He walked quickly and quietly up to the door then tried the handle. In his previous life as a member of the ARU task-force he'd lost count of how many times he'd done this; scores of times he'd seen guys prep a breaching round in a shotgun or a hoist up a ram only to find the door in question was already unlocked.

This one was open too.

He twisted the knob, pushing it back silently and the three men entered the building. There was only one flight of stairs, straight ahead, and they moved up them silently taking care to walk slowly and not announce their presence, keeping their footfalls soft to avoid any loud creaking on the wooden stairwell.

On the first floor, the entrance to Apartment 3 was immediately to the left.

The door was ajar.

Does he lock anything? Archer thought, pulling his Sig.

Pushing back the door, he moved into the apartment followed closely by the other two. Looking through the sights of the pistol, he stepped into a kitchen. It was immaculately tidy, the pots and pans put away, no dishes in the sink, the white-tiled floor clean and shiny. There was one door to the left and one to the right. Once again, the door to the left was open. The room was dark and looked as if nobody was inside. Nevertheless, Josh turned and moved to check it out. Never assume anything. They didn't want to turn their backs and discover it was occupied after all.

There was noise coming from the room to the right. It sounded like a television and the quiet murmur of conversation. Archer and Shepherd moved towards it, both pulling open their jackets to reveal their *NYPD* vests. No need for stealth anymore. They were already inside the apartment.

Standing side by side, Shepherd watched as Archer grasped the handle and twisted it.

As soon as the door fell back, the two men saw Gunnar. And they instantly realised why he was so relaxed about his security.

The man was absolutely enormous. He was over six foot five and built like a brick shithouse, comfortably over two-fifty and closer to three hundred pounds. Shirtless, he was facing the far wall when the two men entered. Archer saw a thick black Swastika tattoo covering the majority of his back. He also had two words printed in bold lettering above the symbol across his barn-door wide shoulders.

DON'T TREAD.

Gunnar turned, calmly and slowly, having heard the two men enter. He was built like a strong man or super-heavyweight bodybuilder, more tattoos spread over the front of his muscular torso. His head was shaved and his jaw looked as if it had been chiselled out of rock.

He looked down at the two intruders, expressionless.

'NYPD. Show me some hands,' Shepherd ordered, his pistol on the man.

Gunnar wasn't the only person in the room. A dark-haired woman was sitting on a couch to his right. Dressed in a white vest and panties, her hair dirty and unwashed, she turned and saw the two men, her make-up smudged around her eyes.

'Pigs!' she screamed, flying up from the couch and rushing towards them.

Josh suddenly stepped into the bedroom, having cleared the room next door. He torso-wrapped the woman, using her momentum to take her forwards and pin her against the wall. She was thrashing and swearing, trying to heel kick him as he kept her trapped to the wall with one arm, holstering his side-arm and pulling some cuffs from his hip with the other.

Watching this, Gunnar smiled, his hands up in the air.

'Baby, relax. It's OK.'

'Get your hands off me, pig!' she screamed again.

Archer and Shepherd kept their pistols on Gunnar, who dwarfed both of them. There was a pause, a momentary standoff even though only one side was armed.

This was going to go one of two ways and that depended on what Gunnar did next.

'What can I do for you gentlemen?' he asked.

Archer couldn't conceal his surprise. Gunnar's voice was incongruously cultured for a man of his size and appearance. He sounded like a Harvard grad.

'We need you to come with us,' Shepherd said.

'Concerning?'

'You'll find out.'

Gunnar nodded. 'Very well.' Frowning, he looked past them at the woman, who was still thrashing and hollering as Josh tried to drag her hands into the cuffs. 'Baby, please. Relax.' Then he turned to Shepherd, offering his hands.

'Front or back?'

'Back,' Shepherd said.

Gunnar nodded, turning and presenting his wrists for the cuffs. Archer stepped forward carefully, holstering his weapon and making sure that Shepherd had his Sig on the man the entire time. He pulled a set of steel cuffs from a pouch above the holster for the Sig. He clicked one side onto Gunnar's left wrist, which was as thick as the business end of a baseball bat. Up close, Gunnar was even more intimidating, towering over Archer. His back was like a damn mountain.

Archer cuffed his other hand and clicked it secure.

'Keys?' Shepherd asked.

'On the table by the door'.

Josh was already hauling the girl outside as she shouted and kicked up a fuss. Gunnar was the polar opposite, calm and co-operative. As Shepherd grabbed a white vest from the bed and a pair of sweats for the girl, tucking them under his arm so they could finish dressing at the station, the huge neo-Nazi turned and looked down at Archer, smiling.

'What's your name?' he asked.

Archer ignored him. As the two men led Gunnar out of the door, Archer glanced around the room. A large American flag was draped across the far wall, taking up most of the space. To the right, he saw a series of notepads stacked together in a neat line on the shelf. Beside them were rows of books. Looking at the spines,

Archer recognised some of the titles, but others were in a foreign language.

However two of them were familiar, resting side by side.

The Bible and *Mein Kampf.*

'Mind your step,' Gunnar said to Shepherd, who was leading him out of the apartment. He'd almost missed a small drop, which would have taken him off balance. Behind the giant, Archer grabbed the house keys off the table. He made momentary eye contact with Shepherd when they paused whilst he secured the apartment. Their expressions said the exact same thing.

Who the hell is this guy?

TWENTY TWO

Twenty minutes later, just as the clock ticked to 1:30pm, the team had reconvened back at the Counter Terrorism Bureau. Over in Manhattan, clean up from the store by the Seaport was in full swing and the entire NYPD, ESU and Chemical Response Teams were on red alert. The CRT had locked down the area where the bomb had detonated, and the bodies had been wheeled out and transported to the lab, their families in the process of being notified.

Macy's had also been shut down for the rest of the day which had severely pissed off its senior executives, some of them calling in and demanding to speak with Lieutenant General Franklin. However, using all his PR skills and trying to calm them down, Franklin pointed out that their building staff had dealt with a potential major incident expertly and with great efficiency. That was good publicity and some compensation for their temporary drop in profit. The Mayor had gone on the air a few moments ago saying that the tragic accident at the Seaport and the situation in Macy's were unrelated and that both events happening so close together was just a terrible coincidence. He assured the city that everything was under control, and offered his sincerest condolences to the families of those killed at the Pier.

Upstairs in Briefing Room 5, Rach was searching for the person or people who'd taken the man into the restroom at Bryant Park and killed him. She'd asked a co-worker to run through the CCTV footage from the lobby at the *Flood Microbiology* building. The analyst had found the man Archer had killed earlier at the house. He'd entered the building and swiped himself in at just after 7pm, exactly as Dr Kruger had said. He'd left ten minutes later with a box under his arm which must have contained the missing vials. The body found at the French café at Bryant Park was on its way to the lab where prints would be taken and hopefully an ID pulled, but that was only part of the puzzle. The number one priority was finding who broke his neck in that restroom and stole the vial from his undetonated bomb.

Downstairs, to the left of the detectives' desks and working areas, was the corridor lined with interrogation cells. Gunnar had been taken into a cell ten minutes ago, his cuffs removed and his white tank-top given to him to put on. He'd been told to sit and wait. The intimidating size of the man and the inking covering his body contrasted oddly with his unrelenting cordiality. Nothing seemed to upset or faze him. Unlike most suspects dragged into the building, he was showing no signs of aggression or resistance, maintaining his air of patience and tolerance.

Watching from a one-way glass window to the side of the interrogation room, his arms folded and with Jorgensen and Marquez beside him, Archer studied the man with curiosity. He'd never come across someone whose appearance was such a contradiction to their manner. Gunnar spoke like a post-grad yet looked like the head of a prison gang.

In fact the only time he hadn't been one hundred per cent compliant since they picked him up was a few seconds ago. Shepherd had gone in to grill him about the dead neo-Nazis but he had flatly refused to talk.

He said he would only talk to the blond guy who'd put the cuffs on him.

That meant Archer was taking the lead whether he liked it or not.

Shepherd stepped outside to the surveillance room, closing the door and joining his three detectives. He passed Archer the folder.

'Guess you're in the hot seat,'

'He's giving me the creeps.'

'Me too. But thank God he's humouring us. I think he could have broken through the handcuffs if he'd sneezed.'

As Shepherd spoke, Josh entered from the door that led out into the main corridor, joining the detail.

'The girl from his apartment is called Kim Baines,' he told them. 'She's a nobody. Only a couple of minors on her file for indecent exposure and possession of cocaine. She's getting cleaned up and drug-tested.'

Shepherd nodded. He turned back to Archer and jabbed a finger at Gunnar, who was sitting patiently the other side of the glass.

'Get him talking, any way you can. The guys we took out at the house are part of his crew. I want names and details.'

Archer nodded. Taking a deep breath, he stepped forward, twisted the handle and walked into the interrogation room.

This is going to be interesting, he thought.

Inside the cell, Gunnar was sitting in the chair facing the door. He smiled warmly when the blond detective entered the room.

'Just the man I wanted to see.'

Archer ignored him, closing the door and taking a seat across the table. He placed the folder on the desktop between them and opened it. There were three photographs inside. He took them out and slid them towards Gunnar, lining them up in a neat row.

The photographs were all fresh from the two crime-scenes, taken directly from above. They showed each of the three bombers' faces.

The giant neo-Nazi looked down at them as Archer watched him closely.

He saw a quick flicker of recognition.

'You know who they are.'

'Yes, I do. Seen them look a lot better though.'

'I need their names.'

Gunnar leaned back and smiled.

'Hold on, handsome. There's no rush.'

'Yes, there is. We need this information now. The longer you don't comply, the longer you'll be here.'

'You have something to charge me with?'

'Your girlfriend's getting drug-tested right now. Something tells me the results aren't going to be good. We could pop a needle in you too. See what shows up.'

Gunnar smiled.

'She's not my girlfriend. Just a girl from my crew. But drug test me if you like. Anything you find will be legally bought and paid for.'

Archer looked at the swollen, muscular frame of the man. His arms and shoulders looked like they were about to burst.

Somehow I doubt it, he thought.

In the silence, Gunnar gazed at him, examining his face. It made him feel uncomfortable as hell but he used all his experience to hide it.

'Damn, you look good,' Gunnar said. 'You should consider joining our society. We'd love to have you.'

Archer glanced at the ink on the man's neck, shoulders and arms. A litany of tattooed hate.

'Sorry. Not my thing.'

'You can't fight nature, my friend. You look better than any poster-boy I've ever seen.' He leaned forward. 'And it would be worth your time. The women in our organisation would go crazy for you.'

'Tell me who these men are.'

'I understand. You're a detective, after all. But think about it. Whenever this investigation is over, look me up.'

'Names.'

Gunnar smiled. He paused for a moment then pointed at the photo on his far left. The face under his meaty forefinger was the youngest of the group, the one Marquez had taken down in the corridor at the house.

'The kid's called Donnie Stahl. The one beside him is Nathan Hansen,' he said, pointing at the guy found in the restroom with the broken neck. 'And the fat guy is Paul Bleeker. '

Archer glanced at the one way mirror to his left and nodded. Outside, Shepherd and the team would already be going to work with the names.

'Did you know them well?'

'No. They were kids. Not my circle. But I've seen them around, at rallies and at concerts.'

He frowned.

'But there's one missing.'

'What?'

'I never saw this group as a three. They were always a four.'

'Who's the fourth guy?'

'He's called Ray. Ray Creek. Think he lives over in Sunnyside.'

He tapped Bleeker's photo, the man Archer had killed.

'Anyway, this guy was the leader.'

Archer pulled back the photo and examined it. 'Tell me about him.'

'Late-twenties. Dropped out of high school, no skills. He was always going to be at the bottom of the heap. Lazy and talentless. But I've seen him around. He tried to intimidate people and throw his weight around. Typical high school bully.'

'But that didn't work with you,' Archer said, looking at Gunnar's bulk.

The neo-Nazi leader grinned and shook his head.

'Very perceptive. Not just a pretty face after all.'

There was a pause. Gunnar looked at him curiously and leaned back, the chair creaking from the weight.

'What's all this about? What did they do?'

Archer didn't reply.

'I caught the news,' Gunnar said. 'The reports from Macy's and the Seaport. Did they have something to do with that?'

'You're going to play innocent?'

Gunnar grinned. 'When you get a warrant you can tear my place upside down, Detective. You can check my phone and see who I've been interacting with. I've got absolutely no idea what they've been up to and there's no way you can pin anything on me that says otherwise.'

He paused.

'But I'm guessing it had something to do with those bombs around Midtown. Right?'

Archer maintained eye contact with the man. He decided to reveal part of his hand.

'Correct. They planted them.'

'But they didn't contain explosives?'

'No. A lethal virus instead.'

'A virus?'

'Bleeker stole five vials of it from a lab on the Upper West Side last night. Do you have any idea how he'd know about something like that?'

'You're the police. You figure it out.'

'Motive?'

'If I had to guess, I'd say racial.'

No shit, Archer thought.

'But these bombs were left in Midtown and Lower Manhattan,' he said.

'So?'

'If this was racially motivated, surely they'd go after Washington Heights or the Bronx? Spanish Harlem? Areas dominated by black or Hispanic communities?'

'There're plenty of non-Aryans in Midtown. And people like myself can't just stroll up into those neighbourhoods you mentioned, Detective.'

'But they would kill hundreds of others. White men, like you. Surely that goes completely against your ideology?'

'Hey, I agree. It's not something I would ever do. I spend my life adhering to those beliefs.' He looked at Archer. 'Look, they must have had their reasons. Don't assume that those reasons were intelligent. Bleeker was as thick as pig shit. God only knows how this virus you're talking about fell into his lap. And given his stupidity, it's almost a guarantee that he would use it in the wrong way.'

Archer clocked Gunnar's facial expression and body language. His geniality was fading. The conversation was just about done.

Archer rose, taking back the photographs and sliding them into the folder. 'We're going to check out these names you've given us.'

'OK.'

'Get comfortable. This could take a while.'

'See you soon,' Gunnar said with a grin. 'And please think about my offer. You'd be surprised who some of our members are.'

At that moment, eight miles to the west, three men were sitting in a line on stools in a bar in Hoboken. The place was called *Texas/Arizona,* a stone's throw from the PATH train that led under the Hudson River and into the east side of Manhattan. The trio had been wandering around the neighbourhood looking for a place with warm heating and cold beer and had stumbled upon the bar, pleasantly surprised by the name.

The joint was starting to get busy, lots of fans in football gear coming in for the NFL games that were already kicking off around the country, but the three men weren't interested. They were dressed all in black with shaved heads and were sitting with a beer in front of each of them. They completely ignored the people gathering around them. They were hardly blending in and were taking up three of the best seats in the house but no one was prepared to confront them about it.

In front of the men, one of the bartenders ended a phone call then grabbed a remote and flicked the television above the bar from an ESPN pre-game show to the news channel. Drinking from their beers, the trio watched in silence. There were several headlines rolling on the screen. It seemed like some crazy stuff had gone down in Manhattan that morning just the other side of the Hudson. There'd been some kind of bomb threat at Macy's and a chemical accident by the South Street Seaport that had killed almost sixty people.

As the three skinheads watched the television, the one in the middle whistled.

'Holy shit.'

The man to his right nodded in agreement. The guy on the left drained his beer and rose from his stool. The man beside him turned.

'Where are you going?'

'Smoke.'

The man walked to the door, heading out of the front of the bar. He pulled a pack of Marlboro from the pocket of his jacket and slid one into his mouth, sparking the end. Tucking the lighter and pack back in his pocket, he took a draw and examined the area around him, blowing out the smoke.

Traffic was coming around the corner from the right, but across the street he saw two cops had pulled someone over. One of them was by the woman's window, talking to her quietly, his partner returning from their squad car with her licence and registration.

The skinhead drew on the cigarette and watched them.

'Hey. Pigs.'

They didn't hear him.

'Hey, piggy, piggies.'

They heard him this time. The officers turned simultaneously and saw him across the road by the bar.

He grinned, standing face on, willing them to take the bait.

The two cops looked at him for a moment. Then they passed the woman's details back to her and started walking towards him. A red light had hit, so the street was clear. They moved across the road with the absolute confidence and authority that their badge and gun provided. Stepping onto the sidewalk, the two cops walked up to him, standing close.

'You say something?' one of them said.

The skinhead grinned, but didn't reply. His two friends had sensed something was happening and were watching the exchange from their seats inside the bar.

'I'm sure you just said something.'

The skinhead didn't reply. He took a long draw on the cigarette instead.

'It sounded like you just called us pigs.'

Turning to the man on his right, the skinhead suddenly blew the smoke in the cop's face.

The police officer blinked, momentarily blinded.

Then the skinhead dropped the cigarette, swivelled and sucker-punched the other cop in the face.

TWENTY THREE

'So what do you think?' Shepherd asked, addressing Marquez, Archer and Josh. 'You think Gunnar's telling the truth?'

They were outside Briefing Room 5, standing beside the railing that looked out over the lower level and detective pit. Given that Rach was already occupied, two analysts across the building were pulling up full profiles on the four names Gunnar had given them. They'd already drawn one, the man Gunnar had said was missing, Ray Creek. He had an address in his name on 33rd Street in Sunnyside, Queens. Shepherd had sent Jorgensen over there with two other detectives to check it out.

'I think he is,' Marquez said. 'He doesn't know what they were up to.'

'Agreed,' Josh said.

'He could be lying,' Shepherd said.

'He seems too smart,' Marquez said. 'He wouldn't be involved in this shit.'

'We could get a polygraph in?' Josh suggested

'What do you think?' Shepherd asked Archer. 'You were in there with him.'

'We got the four names from him but that's all we're going to get. We don't have time to chase down blind alleys. He's a dead end.'

There was a pause. The team looked at the detective pit down below and saw Dr Kruger sitting with Maddy Flood by Shepherd's desk. Their chairs were pulled to the side and they were close enough for their knees to touch, talking in low voices. Kruger was holding her hand comfortingly. Maddy nodded at whatever he was saying, wiping away some fresh tears.

'Let's take a rain check,' Shepherd said, thinking. 'We need to start building a web here. We have two objectives. Number one is locate this last vial. And number two is find out how the hell Bleeker knew about this virus in the first place.'

He turned to Marquez.

'Work with Rach up here. She's trying to find out who took Hansen into that restroom and broke his neck. The moment you have something, I want to know.'

She nodded, stepping back into the briefing room and joining Rach by her computer terminal. Shepherd turned to Archer and Josh.

'I want you two downstairs with the doctors. Find out everything they know. Take one aside each.'

'What about Gunnar, sir?' Josh asked.

Shepherd thought for a moment. 'Let him go. You're right. He's not involved in this.'

Dr Glover was sitting in the lab at *Kearny Medical* when the lift doors opened again. He saw the terrifying man and woman who had kidnapped him unloading a series of canisters from the lift, dragging them across the polished tiles towards the lab. The man with the machine pistol rose from his chair and started speaking with them on the other side of the glass. The trio talked for a moment, the woman scraping the sides of her boots on the white floor, taking off some mud.

Earlier, Glover had been given exact orders as to what was required and why he was here. He'd been informed in graphic detail of the consequences if he failed and had spent the last hour both waiting for these canisters to arrive so he could get started and also praying that police officers would suddenly appear and save him.

But they hadn't.

He watched the trio talk. Then they simultaneously turned and looked over at him. The large man walked over to the lab, his machine pistol in his right hand. He reached into his pocket with his left and pulled out the vial containing the virus. The doors slid open and he walked towards Glover.

'We're ready to begin.'

Not far away, the neo-Nazi who had sucker-punched the cop was hauled into the Hoboken Police Department, his hands cuffed behind him and an officer gripping him on either side. One of them was the cop he'd sucker-punched. The guy's nose had just about stopped bleeding, but it was going to swell up nicely by the morning.

They dragged him over to the booking desk, both of them using more force than was necessary, and slammed him against the counter. The cop behind the desk looked up as if he'd seen this a thousand times before. He probably had.

'Name,' he asked with a bored, monotone voice.

'Listen,' the skinhead said. 'I need my phone call right now.'

'Name?'

'Will Peterson.'

The cop started writing.

'Listen to me guys, I need to make this phone call. It's urgent.'

'Shut the hell up,' the guy he had punched said, dabbing at his face. 'You broke my nose, you asshole.'

'Date of birth and home address?'

'Phone call.'

'Date of birth and home address?'

'Phone call.'

'Screw you,' the cop with the busted nose said.

Peterson cursed. 'Listen to me. I know my rights. Just give me my call. Then you can lock me up for the rest of the month.'

'Jesus Christ, just give him his damn phone call,' the cop behind the counter said, rubbing his temples.

The two cops looked at each other then dragged the skinhead across the reception area to a payphone by the wall. When they got there one of them pulled Peterson around and undid the cuffs, freeing his hands momentarily.

'One call. You've got thirty seconds.'

'Enjoy it,' the guy with the busted nose said. 'You're gonna be in jail 'til next Christmas.'

Peterson pulled two quarters from his pocket quickly, tucking them into the slot. He pushed a number, fast. It was one he always dialled from memory, and one he dialled often.

C'mon. Pick up.

He was in luck. It rang twice then was answered.

'John, it's me,' Peterson said. 'Listen. I need your help and I need it right now.'

TWENTY FOUR

As the clock ticked on into the afternoon, Archer carried two cups from the drinks machine over to Shepherd's desk. To the right, Gunnar was just being released. He'd been taken out of the interrogation cell and was being led towards the exit. Archer felt the man's gaze upon him and was relieved to watch the giant go.

Kruger was sitting beside Shepherd's desk, alone, his head in his hands. Josh was across the detective area, sitting with Maddy Flood at his own desk and talking with her quietly. Archer placed a coffee in front of Kruger then took a seat, drinking from his tea. Kruger looked up, glancing around the building, and Archer took the opportunity to examine him. The medic had patched him up, cleaning off the dried blood and applying some butterfly stitches, but he'd taken a serious beating. It looked like he'd gone twelve rounds for the world title.

'How's the face?'

'Sore as hell.' Kruger reached forward and picked up his cup of coffee. 'Thanks.'

'Has anyone told you about Dr Tibbs?'

Kruger glanced down and nodded. 'I heard.'

There was a pause.

'So what's your story?' Archer asked, changing the subject. 'You said Dr Flood recruited you from South Africa?'

Kruger nodded. 'We met at a conference in Cape Town twelve months ago, almost to the day. I'm a virologist.'

He saw the blank look on Archer's face.

'I study viruses and how they work.'

'OK.'

'Anyway, Peter informed me over dinner about his recent research. He was very excited. He told me that he'd designed a whole new way of encapsulating radioactive isotopes in the protein shells of a virus. He called it *radio viral therapy*. His vision was that it could morph into a ground-breaking treatment for lung cancer, if it had the right cultivation of course. And that was where I came in. He wanted me to come and work with him on the next phase of his project.'

'Which was?'

'Peter had the blueprints as it were. Given my background in viral genetics, he needed me to put everything together and basically grow the virus at his lab on 66th Street. He offered me a position, working alongside him. I packed my bags and arrived in New York three days later.'

'That's a big move.'

'I jumped at the opportunity. Peter was very well known in his field. And it looks as though Maddy is going to be just as successful. She's brilliant.'

Archer glanced over Kruger's shoulder at her. She was sitting facing them.

She sensed Archer looking over at her and glared back.

'Our work continued throughout this year,' Kruger continued. 'The early period was spent finding a suitable base for the virus. Viruses can only grow inside living cells. These can be animal or plant cells, but most are typically bacteria. Given that this was a treatment designed to be administered by inhalation, I found that the only organism capable of culturing Peter's radio virus was TB. Tuberculosis. Understand?'

Archer nodded. 'I think so. But I thought TB was potentially lethal.'

'It is. However, I modified the strain to be fast growing but not capable of harming the lungs. Remember this was supposed to be medicinal, not a weapon. And the longer I worked on the project, the more I realised Peter's vision could actually be feasible. It was very exciting. A virus that would irradiate a cancerous tumour from the inside. Genius. And ground-breaking too.'

He paused, drinking from his coffee.

'However, once we tested it on mice a few weeks ago I realised we must have badly miscalculated somewhere, probably with the radiation and its effect on the virus. I implored Peter to throw in the towel and quit. *It's over,* I told him.'

'But he refused.'

'Not only that. He demanded that I culture six separate samples of it and store them. He felt that the cure was only one mistake or one stroke of luck away. A happy accident, if you will. I agreed, reluctantly. But I could see Peter was starting to unravel.'

He paused, thinking. Archer drank from his tea and continued to listen closely.

'Have you ever heard of a man called Dr Ronald Mallett, Detective?' Kruger asked.

Archer shook his head.

'Can't say I have.'

'He is the world's leading expert on time travel. He's convinced that it will happen before the end of this century. Although he's over sixty years old now, Dr Mallett has made it his life's work, devoting all his energy towards research and theory concerning its possibility. But do you know why?'

Archer shook his head.

'Because his father died prematurely when Ronald was just an eleven year old boy. And to this day, he wants to go back in time and save him.'

He paused.

'People think that men of science like myself, Ronald and Peter are somehow colder. More analytical than emotional. You know the saying: *there are men of science and men of faith.* But Peter's motivations were born of the same pain that Dr Mallett feels. Peter lost his wife decades before she should have died. Maddy grew up without a mother. You lose someone close to you and it unlocks parts of yourself that you didn't even know were there. That alone was all the motivation he needed to pursue this project. He was convinced he was only steps away from altering the malevolence of the virus.'

He sighed.

'Then the next thing I know, I'm kidnapped at gunpoint. Will is dead, Frankie is missing and my friend steps off a twenty storey building to his death. All in the name of science.'

'We'll find Dr Glover and whoever has the last vial,' Archer said. 'That's a promise.'

'Like you did at the Seaport?'

Archer didn't respond.

'Who knew about the virus?' he eventually asked, changing the subject.

'To my knowledge, just the five of us. Unless Peter told someone else.'

'Have you ever spoken about it to anyone? A wife, or girlfriend, or friend? Just one remark?'

'No. I'm not married and don't have a social life outside of the lab. But I guess it's possible that one of the others might have let something slip.'

'Any guesses?'

Kruger shrugged. 'Will- Dr Tibbs- kept to himself. He was a private guy. He was hard to reach outside of work. Dr Glover is the opposite. Frankie likes to go to the bars on the Upper West Side. News of the virus might have come out. Unlikely pillow talk, though.'

He cracked a smile. Archer found himself smiling too, although briefly. Given the events and circumstances of the day, it was unexpected and felt good. Kruger drained his coffee, then shrugged.

'Sorry, Detective, that's all I can offer. If I can help in any other way, let me know.'

Archer nodded. Suddenly a whistle came from above. They both looked up and saw Shepherd leaning over the railing. He was motioning for Archer and Josh to join him.

Archer turned to Kruger. 'Excuse me.'

'Of course.'

He rose, tossing his foam cup of tea in the trash beside the desk. As he walked towards the stairs, Josh joining him, he turned and saw Kruger move over to the empty seat by Maddy and put his arm around her. In the hug, her head on Kruger's shoulder, she and Archer made eye contact.

Her face was cold.

Once they got upstairs, Archer and Josh headed straight into the briefing room. Shepherd was in there with Marquez and Rach, and there was a freeze-frame on the screen on the wall. Judging by the ice rink and familiar surroundings, Archer guessed it was a camera in Bryant Park. He looked at the top right corner and saw *Bry Park 42nd SE*. The clock next to it said *11:35:34*.

'What do we have?' Josh asked.

'Not much, I'm afraid,' Rach said. 'This looks out over the area in front of the café.'

They looked closely. The view should have been unobstructed, but the wooden Christmas stalls and tall decorations had blocked off the view by the rink.

'This is the best shot I can get. And the patisserie doesn't have any CCTV. Trying to find whoever killed Hansen on camera is a dead end.'

Josh swore.

'But we've got something else,' Shepherd said. 'Run the recording, Rach.'

She withdrew the camera shot from the screen and pulled a fifteen second sound clip up instead. She hit *Play*.

'*Bleeker, where the hell are you?*' a voice said, filling the room. '*I've been trying you all morning. You haven't told me where we're meeting tonight and we need to discuss payment. This thing had better be what you say it is.*'

'A tech next door pulled that from Paul Bleeker's cell phone,' Rach said. 'Call came in this morning at 11:05.'

'British accent,' Shepherd said, turning and looking at Archer. 'You recognise a region?'

'Posh.'

'Not the kind of guy who mixes with a low-life neo-Nazi.'

'But sounds like he knows about the virus,' Marquez said. '*This thing had better be what you say it is.*'

'He could be another member of the neo-Nazi group?' Rach suggested.

'They didn't seem familiar,' Shepherd said.

'OK, so someone he met in prison?'

'He didn't exactly sound like a guy who's done time in Gen-pop either.'

'How about employment?' Josh said. 'He sounded superior. As if he's used to calling the shots.'

Shepherd looked at him. Then he turned to Rach. 'Bleeker's file?'

Rach nodded and pulled it up onto the screen.

'Scroll down.'

The team examined the screen. Just like his conviction sheet, the employment history list was long. He'd either quit or been fired from every job he'd had save one, the current.

'Janitor at Lloyd, Garrett and Jacobs,' Rach read. 'Law firm based in the Financial District. Been working there for three months. That could be something.'

She typed the name of the firm into Google and came up with a homepage. She clicked on it, and the page opened up. It was a typical legal firm internet site, a photo of a client and lawyer shaking hands at a desk overlooking Manhattan on a sunny day. There were a series of different headers at the top of the website.

She clicked on *About*. A blurb came up describing how the law firm had come into existence, underneath which was a bio of the three senior partners. Each person in the room scanned them. First John Lloyd, then Simon Garrett. Neither of theirs was relevant. Both men were from West Virginia and both had gone to Harvard, which is where they must have met. The two profile photographs were of middle-aged men sitting at a desk and smiling at the camera, self-assured and successful.

'Hang on,' Marquez said. 'Check out Jacobs' profile.'

They all looked at the bottom of the screen.

Born in Oxford, England in 1975, senior partner Alistair Jacobs was educated at Harrow School and went on to read Law at Cambridge University.

'No way,' Josh said. 'It can't be him.'

Rach scrolled back to the homepage. She hovered the arrow over the welcome video and pressed *Play*. During this, a detective from downstairs had appeared in the doorway. Everyone was so engrossed with the screen that no one had noticed him. He was looking at Shepherd.

'Sir?'

Shepherd was distracted and didn't hear him. The video on the screen was a welcome package, showing footage from inside the law firm and introducing the senior partners. Lloyd and Garrett both introduced themselves, then Jacobs came onto the screen and started talking.

'Here at Lloyd, Garrett and Jacobs, we strive to offer...'

'Holy shit,' Josh said.

Rach looked at Shepherd. 'That's a match, sir.'

'What's his home address?'

Rach got rid of the webpage and started searching. Jacobs didn't have a police department file, but she ran his name through the Manhattan directory phonebook instead. 'Got it. He lives in Tribeca, in a tenth floor apartment on 111 Worth Street.'

'He's a lawyer,' Archer said. 'He might be at work.'

'He's a senior partner,' Shepherd said. 'And it's a weekend. That's unlikely.'

'Sir?' the detective at the door said again.

'But possible,' Marquez said. Rach pulled up the window of the law firm again and scrolled down to their address. She pulled the two windows side by side. The law firm wasn't far away, just off Water Street in the Financial District.

'Contact the 1st precinct,' Shepherd told Rach. 'Have them send a blue and white to both addresses. I want this man here as soon as possible.'

'Sir?' the detective at the door said for a third time, louder and with more emphasis.

The whole room turned.

'Sorry to bother you. But there are two men here to see you. They said it's urgent.'

'Concerning?' Shepherd asked.

'The situation in Manhattan this morning.'

Everyone in the room stared at the detective. Then Shepherd, Archer, Marquez and Josh headed out quickly, following the man down the stairs to the lower level.

When they got there, Shepherd looked around. There was no one standing waiting for him. To the left, Kruger and Maddy Flood were still sitting where Archer and Josh had left them. They watched the commotion with interest as Shepherd turned to the detective.

'So where are they?'

'Interrogation Room 3.'

Shepherd walked quickly down the corridor to the interrogation room. He pushed open the door, walked inside and found a neo-Nazi skinhead dressed in black sitting at the table. A brown-haired man in a suit was beside him, the two of them talking quietly.

Shepherd looked at the suited man.

'You his lawyer?'

The man shook his head, stepping past the desk and offering his hand. At the same time he pulled an ID from his pocket and flipped it open.

'No. My name is Agent-in-Charge John Faison. I'm with the ATF.'

'ATF?' Shepherd said, shaking his hand. 'What the hell are you doing here?'

Faison pointed at the skinhead in the seat, who nodded to Shepherd.

'I'd like you to meet Special Agent Peterson.'

Across Queens, Jorgensen had just arrived outside Ray Creek's address with two other detectives. The three men had already vested up and jumped out of the car, moving straight down the path to the house, a Mossberg in each pair of hands. One detective went down the side alley, careful not to make any noise, whilst Jorgensen and the other made their way to the front.

The second detective took point. Jorgensen nodded, racking a round into his shotgun. The guy twisted the handle; the door was open. He pushed it back and the two men ran into the house.

'NYPD!'

The detective went left and Jorgensen went right. He smashed into what was a downstairs bedroom, looking through the sights of the Mossberg.

He paused, seeing something across the room.

He stared at it for a moment, then lowered the shotgun slowly.

Moments later, the other two detectives appeared in the doorway and froze when they saw what Jorgensen had seen.

'Jesus,' one of them said.

They'd found Ray Creek.

Or what was left of him.

TWENTY FIVE

'How long have you been under, Agent Peterson?' Shepherd asked. He was now sitting in the chair across the table from the ATF agent whose handcuffs had been removed.

'Seven months,' Peterson said, rubbing his wrists. 'Seven long-ass months.'

Leaning against the wall, Archer inspected the guy and was impressed. He never would have guessed that Peterson was an undercover ATF agent. Short for *Alcohol, Tobacco and Firearms,* the ATF was the Federal Control Agency for all three, as well as for explosives. Based out of the United States Department of Justice, the Agency protected communities from illegal trafficking, sale or possession of all three. Standing beside Peterson, Agent-in-Charge Faison looked like one of their typical employees. He was conservatively dressed in a suit, brown haired, sturdy, somewhere in his thirties and looked to be in good physical shape. Peterson had to be late twenties or early thirties and looked the complete opposite to Faison with his shaved head, his pierced eyebrow and pale skin. As Archer watched, Peterson slid off his black jacket to reveal a series of neo-Nazi tattoos etched on his forearms. He had an *SS* inking on the left and an *88* on the right.

88. HH in the alphabet.

Heil Hitler.

'Are those real?' Archer asked.

Peterson looked at his arms and nodded.

'They had to be. You don't just stroll in and out of these groups. But I'm counting the days till I'm reassigned and can get them covered. '

Beside him, Faison nodded, patting the man's shoulder.

'So what can you tell us about the situation in the city?' Shepherd asked.

'We think we know two men who are heavily involved,' Faison said.

'In 2009, there was a Homeland Security report that got a lot of people's attention,' Faison explained, starting from the beginning, as the NYPD team listened intently. 'It made a very substantial and bold claim. It's been the basis of much of our Agency's investigations and operations ever since.'

'What was the statement?' Marquez asked.

'That right wing extremists are now the most dangerous domestic terrorism threat in the United States. And the report was right. Most people like to live in a fantasy land. They don't want to acknowledge the possibility that neo-Nazism is still prevalent in society. We're human beings; we like happy endings. According to the history books, the Nazi regime died in Berlin in 1945 when Hitler killed himself in his bunker and the Allied Forces won the war. But almost seventy years on there are white-power and nationalistic groups not just across America, but all over the world. They are everywhere, they're growing in number and they're extremely dangerous.'

'The hierarchy of these organisations is pretty simple,' Peterson continued, rubbing the knuckles on his right hand then indicating two tiers. 'You've got two levels, the leader and the followers. Just the way it began in Germany all those years ago. You get someone charismatic on the mic who knows what they're doing and who looks good in a suit. He spouts a direct message and sooner or later the right person listens. And passion breeds followers.'

He paused.

'So many teenagers and young adults in this country lack stability or structure in their homes. They grow up being told they'll never amount to anything. So a disciplined and hierarchical organisation can seem attractive as hell. It allows them to vent their anger and feel like they finally belong to something. This following spreads, attracting more and more kids, and before you know it you've got a major, potentially violent situation on your hands.'

'You're talking about skinheads?' Shepherd said.

'At the bottom, yes. They're all about thrash metal, aggression, intimidation and violence. In Eastern Europe a lot of these groups masquerade as fans of soccer clubs. But not everyone gets pulled into the hate groups from the street. Others do it for survival.'

'Survival?'

'These organisations are rife in prison. If you're looking at a long jail term you need to make friends. And if you're part of a white-power group, you've got protection.'

'The men and women who run these groups may be twisted and extreme in their views, but they're far from stupid,' Faison said. 'They know they need to find a bridge into society and politics. They've jumped all over the anti-immigration issue to try and drum up followers. They organise marches, rallies, public book burnings. The day I saw a group marching through the centre of Washington waving

Swastikas was the day I knew this was something serious.'

'They can get away with that?' Archer asked.

'Yes. They're protected by the First Amendment. Freedom of speech and peaceful assembly. As long as they don't riot they're not breaking any laws.'

'Jesus.'

Faison nodded. 'It's scary. Membership of these groups is growing fast across the nation. This isn't a foreign enemy trying to breach our borders. These are home-grown people, men and women who truly think they're doing what's best for the country. As you can guess, these groups operate well under the radar. And whenever that happens, illegal activity is sure to follow. Gun-running, drug trafficking, vandalism. A number of the Texas and Arizona factions take it upon themselves to tool up with rifles and patrol the borders looking for any immigrants. They see themselves as soldiers protecting the flag from *domestic enemies* as they call them.'

'Like a militia,' Shepherd said.

'Exactly,' said Faison. 'Some horrible shit goes on out there. Murders, hate crimes. Sometimes rape. The boys in the trucks dub it *rahowa*, short for a *racial holy war*. Some of them are really convinced that they're carrying out God's work. The people leading them cherry-pick lines from the Bible and twist them to suit to their ideology. They're making hate holy.'

He shook his head.

'Considering the amount of illegal weapons handling these groups engage in, my team and I were tasked to bring down one of the largest neo-

Nazi border gangs in Texas. They call themselves *The Stuttgart Soldiers*.'

Faison pointed to the *SS* tattoo on Peterson's forearm.

Shepherd nodded. 'Gunnar's organisation.'

'You know Kyle Gunnar?'

'We had him in here twenty minutes ago. Nothing stuck. He's clean.'

'Of course. He epitomises the leadership of these groups. They're smart as hell. As you all know, the most intelligent criminals put distance between themselves and the crime. Even if they get caught, it'll never get traced back to them. It's like any successful criminal enterprise. Mafia bosses did it for years.'

'Tell us about the Texas chapter,' Shepherd said.

'They operate out of a town called Roller, located near the border. They run guns and pump dope back and forth, in and out of Mexico. We think they have entire caches of illegal weapons stashed in the area, which is where we come in. A cache of Glock pistols was recently stolen from a weapon's storage facility outside San Antonio. Less than a week later the entire Chapter were walking around carrying the pistols, but modified.'

'Modified how?'

'An auto-selector switch mounted on the weapon. Highly illegal. Turns a semi-automatic into an automatic pistol. One squeeze drains an extended clip in about a second.'

'Who runs this Chapter?' Josh asked.

'Two men. Finn Sway and Bobby Rourke.'

Shepherd glanced at Marquez, who nodded, making a mental note of the names. Without a word she turned and stepped out of the room, shutting the door behind her.

'Are they similar to Gunnar?' Archer asked.

'Physically?' said Faison. 'No. Not at all. Sway's tall and kind of skinny. He's got a mullet haircut, short on the sides, bit of length on the top.'

'What about Rourke?' Shepherd asked.

'He's a seriously nasty piece of work. He's a creep. He uses the club for sexual favours. He tells female prospects that it's a necessary part of joining the organisation and that they have to do everything he orders. It's his vice. He did two years at Dallas State for rape. He and two other members ganged a sixteen year old schoolgirl.'

'What about Sway?'

'He's not a rapist, but he's a murderer. He leads those militia trucks out in the desert, shooting anyone who isn't white Caucasian. Both of them are killers.'

'How do they finance all this?' Josh asked.

'They run meth-houses and move weight back and forth across the Mexican border,' Faison said. 'They rob any drug dealers they haven't already driven out of the area or sell their own product. Classy stuff, right? A real holy war.'

'How many in their Chapter?'

'I'd say thirty or so. Sway and Rourke at the top.'

'Do you interact with them personally?' Shepherd asked Peterson.

He nodded. 'My cover pushed me up the food chain. To them, I'm ex-US Army just back from the Middle East. These gangs are always looking for ways into Army bases and camps to try and leech some weapons from the quartermasters. I told them that I still have contacts inside and can get them rifles and ammunition. Right now they're kissing my ass.'

'You're supplying them?'

'No. We haven't passed over a single weapon. But they almost don't need us to. The Brady Law passed in '93 demands a five-day waiting period and background checks when purchasing a handgun. But these boys are already running around with modified Glock machine-pistols and assault rifles.'

Peterson paused.

'A big trade has been brewing for the past month or so. I told them my guy inside Fort Hood could smuggle out thirty M16s and a load of ammo. We've been in the process of setting up a deal. That's when an Agency Task Force would take over and bring them all down at the scene. The trade was being planned for this weekend.'

'So what happened?' Shepherd asked.

'This is where it gets relevant to you. Rourke called me into his office last weekend. He said the deal would have to be delayed.'

'You think he was on to you?'

'No way, otherwise I'd be dead. He was excited. Rourke's got three weaknesses. Money, teenage girls and the fact that he can't keep his mouth shut. He just loves the sound of his own voice. I showed interest and asked him what had come up. I didn't think he'd tell me. But he did.'

He paused.

'He said something had fallen into his lap. It was bigger than anything the Chapter had encountered before. He was being cryptic, but I could tell he was desperate to talk about it. He and Sway called a meeting in the club room that night, a week ago today. Everyone was there. They said that we were heading to New York for this weekend. A new business opportunity had arisen, one that could make us all wealthier than we'd ever dreamed. He said it was for a huge meth deal but I could tell that was bullshit. I knew it was something else. And afterwards, I overheard him talking with Sway outside the clubhouse. They were speaking quiet, but there was one word they repeated several times.'

'Which was?'

'Virus.'

'You're sure?'

'Positive. Plus these boys never go farther north than Carolina. To come all this way something major really must have been on the cards.'

He paused.

'Then I caught the news earlier and saw there was some kind of bomb threat at Macy's. And a *chemical pipe accident* by the Seaport. And two neo-Nazis were shot dead at a house off Ditmars Boulevard. All this is one day? There has to be a connection.'

'Hold up,' Archer said. 'This doesn't make sense. You're saying Rourke and Sway want to make money from this virus?'

'That's right.'

'But it's already been released. They're pissing away all their potential profit.'

Peterson shook his head. 'That's the thing. Rourke told me that the club was going to make a fortune. I don't think he knew about or signed off on what those boys were doing this morning.'

He paused.

'I think someone screwed them over.'

TWENTY SIX

There was a pause. The room absorbed everything Peterson and Faison had just said.

'What can you tell us about this virus?' Faison asked.

'It's Type-3 Pneumonic,' Shepherd said. 'If you inhale it all the blood cells in your lungs rupture. You break your own back and drown in your own blood.'

'Jesus Christ.'

'Five vials of it have gone missing from a lab complex in Manhattan. They were stolen by a man called Paul Bleeker. He's a *Stuttgart Soldier* too, from the New York Chapter. Have you heard of him?'

Peterson shook his head. 'Afraid not.'

'He was working with three other members from the New York group. Each of them had a bomb with a vial of the virus. We found one in Macy's. The other went off at the Seaport, killing all those people. We recovered the third and fourth vials at a house raid, killing Bleeker and one of his men.'

'What about the fifth vial?'

'Still unaccounted for. But the bomber who had the vial was found in the bathroom of a Bryant Park café. His neck had been broken. And the vial was missing.'

'Shit.'

'Exactly.'

Peterson looked up at Faison. 'That sounds like Wicks and Drexler's work.'

'Who are Wicks and Drexler?'

'Sway and Rourke's hit-team. Members of the club. I'd bet everything I own that they did it.'

'We can't find anything on CCTV that could confirm it.'

'It fits though,' Peterson said. 'Think about it. If Rourke and Sway found out Bleeker stole the virus, they'd want it back fast. They didn't come all this way for a meth deal.'

Shepherd thought for a moment.

'How would they know one of his men would be at Bryant Park at that time?'

'Gunnar said the fourth member of Bleeker's group was missing, sir,' Archer said. 'Maybe they got to him and made him talk?'

Shepherd, Faison and Peterson all nodded.

'This is starting to make sense,' Shepherd said.

'Where's the Chapter holed up?' Archer asked Peterson.

'We've set up camp on an empty industrial estate in New Jersey. The whole crew's there. They're treating it as a weekend-long party.'

'Including Rourke and Sway?' Shepherd asked.

'Haven't seen either of them since we arrived. Or Wicks and Drexler for that matter. But they'll be back at some point. The vehicles they rode up in are still there.'

Shepherd turned to Faison.

'Do you have any men on the camp-site?' he asked.

He shook his head. 'Just Peterson right now. He's my eyes and ears. Our whole operation was set for this coming weekend so my team is still down in Texas. I'm the only agent who came up here to follow. But that was when we thought this was a straight arms deal, before we knew about this virus threat. I can call in back-up from the New York or Newark office at a moment's notice.'

Shepherd nodded, and turned to Josh, who was standing behind him.

'I want eyes on the camp-site. Find Sergeant Hendricks and tell him I need to speak with him.'

'Yes, sir,' Josh said, pulling open the door and leaving the room. Shepherd turned back to the two ATF agents.

'I don't want to encroach on your operation gentlemen, but I'm sure you understand that the NYPD now has a major interest in Bobby Rourke and Finn Sway.'

'We all want the same thing here,' Faison said. 'And forget M16s and boxed ammunition. If we catch them in possession of a lethal virus, that takes it to a whole new level. Not only do we secure the virus, we'll bury the entire Chapter for good. I'll call the New York office and get a Task Force on stand-by. We'll stake out the camp with your team. If we can confirm the virus is at the location, we'll move in and take 'em all.'

'And I'll go back undercover,' Peterson said. 'Try to find out what's going on.'

'The rest of them won't wonder where you've been?' Archer asked.

Peterson shook his head. 'I had to get arrested to get to you. It's given me a window.'

'What did you do?'

'Slugged a cop in Hoboken.' He looked up at Faison. 'How is he?'

'Broken nose and pissed off that I got you out. I'd send him a Christmas card.'

'I'll tell the group that my girlfriend posted bail,' Peterson said. 'My story will check out.'

Shepherd nodded. 'OK.'

'Before we continue, there's something else,' Faison said.

'Which is?'

'This needs to be ATF's collar.'

Shepherd looked at him. Both men knew that ATF already had jurisdiction, but Shepherd appreciated the courtesy. He nodded.

'Agreed. At the campsite, the ATF will take the lead. The NYPD will offer back-up.'

'Appreciate that.'

Shepherd glanced at the hate tattooed on Special Agent Peterson's arms.

'You've definitely earned it,' he said.

Peterson rose. Shepherd did the same and shook hands with him and Faison.

'Do you have any other leads on where this last vial could be?' Faison asked.

'We're following up on one right now,' said Shepherd. 'When I know more, I'll fill you in. When Sergeant Hendricks arrives, we'll brief his team and draw up a game-plan. Can you both sit tight until he gets here?'

Both ATF agents nodded.

Faison pulled his cell phone. 'I need to make some calls.'

Fourteen miles to the west at *Kearny Medical*, Bobby Rourke stood side-by-side with Wicks and Drexler, watching the kidnapped doctor working inside the lab. They had their arms folded and were all standing in line. To the right, Drexler glanced at her watch.

'How long's this gonna take?'

'He'll be done by sunset.'

'You know we could have done this ourselves,' Wicks said.

Rourke shook his head.

'Pointless risk. This is dangerous shit. And I need him later anyway.'

There was a whistle from an office to their right. The trio walked forward and found Finn watching a television. It was *NY ONE News* running the bulletins from the day.

'Check this out,' he said.

Breaking: Chemical Pipe ruptures in clothing store by Seaport, kills 59.

They watched the pictures in silence, showing a clean-up operation down by the waterfront. The shot was filled with NYPD cops, detectives, ESU officers and lab teams.

'Chemical pipe my ass,' Rourke said.

'At least we know it works,' Wicks said.

The headline rolled to another. *Two suspected neo-Nazi extremists killed in police raid in Astoria.* The shot changed and they watched footage from outside a house off Ditmars Boulevard. The news cameras were being kept well back, but two body-bags had been wheeled out. CSU teams had taped off the area and were moving in and out of the property.

'So that's where they were hiding,' Wicks said.

'Good job pigs,' Finn said. 'Save us the trouble.'

As the others watched the television, Drexler glanced out of the window to her right, which was overlooking the front of the building.

'Hold up,' she said. 'We've got company.'

The group all looked out of the window.

A car was pulling into the parking lot.

Mary Bale wasn't one to cause a fuss, but her husband hadn't been answering his phone all morning and she'd wanted to arrange a good time to bring in his lunch. They only lived a fifteen minute drive from the lab complex so the journey wasn't an ordeal. She saw all the familiar cars of his team outside the building, including her husband's new pride and joy, a Mercedes CL-Class.

She pulled into an empty slot, then applied the handbrake and turned off the engine. She picked up a brown bag beside her containing a couple of cold-cut sandwiches and some potato chips. Jonathan's favourite. It was after 2pm but they could still enjoy a late-lunch together before heading out to see their daughter at her home in Elizabeth this afternoon.

She stepped out of the car, shutting the door, then walked towards the entrance. She entered the building and saw a lean, slender guard with a short mullet haircut behind the front desk.

'Good afternoon, ma'am,' he said, with a Southern accent and a smile.

TWENTY SEVEN

In the Battery Park area of Lower Manhattan, a nine year old goalkeeper took a run-up and hoofed a soccer ball up a field. It was the middle of the second half of a kids' little-league game, the score at 7-8. As the boys ran around on the pitch, swarming after the ball like a flock of headless chickens, their parents watched on the side-lines, wrapped up against the cold and cheering them all on.

One of them was a senior legal partner in his late forties called Alistair Jacobs. He'd been out all morning with his son and hadn't seen the news reporting the bomb threat at Macy's or the incident at the Seaport. Seeing that he only had the boy for one day a week, he always turned his phone off until the late afternoon so he could give the lad his full, undivided attention. It was common knowledge that you couldn't reach Jacobs on a Saturday. Most people never even bothered trying.

Including his ex-wife, which was something he savoured.

Just recently divorced, the court had decided that the boy live with his mother, largely due to Jacobs' work commitments and unpredictable hours. His allotted timeslot for spending time with him was from Friday night until Saturday night. Seeing the boy tackle someone and steal the ball, Jacobs shouted encouragement, the expensive leather gloves on his hands muffling his enthusiastic clapping.

Watching the game, Jacobs seemed just as engaged as all the other parents standing beside him on the side-lines. However, his mind was somewhere else entirely.

Today was a big day.

He'd set up the law firm with Lloyd and Garrett five years ago, making the move across the Atlantic from London. At the time his marriage had been in pretty good shape and he'd relocated to New York with his son and American wife, not anticipating a messy and expensive divorce. The firm had built an extremely strong reputation and client list since their inception, dealing with everyone from movie stars and professional athletes to Wall Street bankers and Financial District bigwigs. Forty seven years old, good-looking, well-dressed, successful and now single, Jacobs knew that many people at the firm envied him. All the trainees and junior partners looked at him with a mixture of jealousy and respect, believing his life to be perfect.

It wasn't.

In reality, Jacobs was in deep, deep shit. A series of bad investments, a serious gambling habit and a high-maintenance wife who'd dragged him through the divorce courts had combined to drain his once considerable savings. With an expensive Manhattan lifestyle to maintain and a spiralling debt, he couldn't just walk into the bank and ask for a loan. And given his gambling addiction which he was currently fighting, he owed serious money to people who were just as serious about collection. Although he still had seven figures in his bank account he was down thirteen million this year.

Not exactly an amount you could ask HSBC to spot you for.

Moving his attention from the soccer match, he glanced around the Park.

He'd been sent an envelope in the mail four days ago containing a series of photos of his son. Someone had snapped them at the game here last week, but a crosshairs had been neatly drawn over each photograph in black pen, centred on the boy's head.

The people who had sent it were men to whom he owed seven million dollars.

A note inside the envelope told him he had seven days to pay it.

He couldn't go to the cops. If he did, the people he owed would kill both him and the boy without a moment's hesitation. And if he got arrested for illegal gambling, he knew they had connections inside. He wouldn't last a night in jail. Desperate and scared, he'd been searching for a solution. Something. Anything. It had been the longest four days of his life, but in other ways it had been the shortest. Every night since the envelope had arrived at his office he'd sat behind his desk at the firm long into the early hours, frantically trying to think of a way out. He'd fought the urge to gamble further, but it was just as hard as a junkie avoiding the needle and spoon.

You'll win it back at the table, the voice inside his head kept saying.

You just need a few lucky hands.

Fighting the compulsion, he'd searched for an alternative. His projected solution, as embarrassing as it was, had been to ask the other senior partners for a loan. The firm had enough money to cover what he owed and he would figure out a way to pay it back. Hell, he'd win it back. But right now, he needed to be alive by this time next week to do so. Survival was his priority. He'd met with Lloyd and Garrett on Thursday night and asked them outright. He didn't mention who he owed the money to though. Both partners had been aghast. *Seven million dollars?* Lloyd had repeated, incredulous and horrified. Garrett had just looked at Jacobs and shaken his head, speechless. Both men had not only refused point blank. They'd also said that they were going to *take steps* to secure the firm's reputation.

That had been Thursday.

Payment was due this Tuesday.

Both Lloyd and Garrett had walked out that night and left Jacobs alone in his office. He'd sat at his desk completely out of ideas and with nowhere to turn. His last option was to gamble what he had left and hopefully win a load back. But even as the thought crossed his mind he knew he would have to go on the streak of a lifetime. Alone, scared, in debt and with his life in danger he'd sat there in his office with the photograph of his son on his lap. His only other resort was to flee the country with the boy, but then he'd be hunted for abduction seeing as his wife had custody.

But as he sat there, a miracle had happened. It was like a gift from God and from the most unlikely of sources.

His janitor had walked into his office to empty his trash.

Jacobs had seen the man around although he'd never taken much notice of him. He was pudgy, scruffy and looked bad-tempered. He worked the nightshift, cleaning the offices and emptying the rubbish every weeknight. It was out of character for Jacobs to be sitting there doing nothing at that time of the evening and the janitor had noticed the Englishman's unusual agitation. He'd asked if everything was OK. More as a throwaway comment than anything else and with two glasses of whisky in him, Jacobs had asked the guy if he had any idea how to make seven million dollars in the next five days.

But it was as if fate, or luck, or something higher had sent that man into his office that night. Jacobs still couldn't believe it. The janitor didn't just look at him as if he was mad.

He'd said *Yes. I do.*

Jacobs had assumed the man was joking, but his face was serious. Unbelieving and more out of curiosity than anything, Jacobs had asked the man how.

The janitor had placed his bag on the ground, then stepped forward and offered his hand, introducing himself. *Paul Bleeker.* Taking a seat across the desk from Jacobs, Bleeker told him that he knew two men who were about to get a hold of something that was worth a hell of a lot of money. They'd put an asking price out on the street of two million dollars. Bleeker snorted, saying it was worth ten times that and proposed that if Jacobs put the money up for the item, Bleeker could purchase it then let it be known in the right quarters that it was available and sell it on. They'd make enough to not only cover Jacobs' debt but a whole lot extra.

It'll happen fast, Bleeker assured him. *Opportunities like this come along once in a lifetime.*

Jacobs' gambling instincts had been instantly aroused.

He'd asked Bleeker what was in it for him. The scruffy janitor had simply asked for a 50 per cent cut of the profits Jacobs would make when they sold it on. In return, he would act as a go-between and set the deal up. Bleeker wanted money. Jacobs wanted to save his son. He'd asked Bleeker what this mysterious item was. Apparently it was some kind of deadly virus.

Desperate and with nowhere else to turn, he'd suppressed any moral objections, agreed to fund the purchase and had gone to bed that night both relieved and slightly bewildered at his sudden good fortune. And yesterday, everything had gone according to plan. Bleeker had messaged him saying that the sellers were in town.

But then Jacobs and Bleeker had been scheduled to meet at his office last night to discuss the details of the trade.

And Bleeker had never showed.

Now, the day of the planned exchange, Jacobs was nervous and confused. His gambling addiction had led him into dangerous waters in the past, but the illegality and danger of what he was embarking on here was whole different territory. He didn't even want to know the type of people Bleeker would sell this virus on to or consider the consequences. And as with all illegal dealings, he knew the usual rules wouldn't apply. These were dangerous men he was planning on meeting with later. Bleeker hadn't revealed much about them, save that they were coming up from Texas.

Watching the kids chase the ball around the field, Jacobs took a deep breath.

Relax. This time in three days all your debts will be cleared.

No more threats.

Pulling out his cell phone, he turned it on. He'd left an anxious message on Bleeker's answering machine a few hours ago. He still didn't know where the trade would take place tonight. Checking the display, he saw that Bleeker still hadn't called back.

Shit.

On the pitch, the referee checked his watch and blew his whistle. Jacobs tucked the phone back into his pocket and started clapping with all the other parents. All the kids shook hands with players from the other team, then his son ran over to him.

'I scored, Dad,' the boy said. 'Did you see?'

'I saw,' Jacobs lied, ruffling his hair. 'You're a natural. David Beckham better watch out.'

The boy beamed as Jacobs checked his watch.

'Some of the other kids are going to get pizza. Can we go too?'

Jacobs looked at him. 'I actually need to head off for an hour or so, buddy.'

He saw the dismay on his son's face.

'Don't worry, I'll be back by three o'clock.'

He looked over at another of the parents, a woman called Marie. She was friendly, and from the way she looked at him Jacobs guessed that she knew he was back on the singles market. Her son was friends with Jacobs' boy and she seemed to have overheard what Jacobs had said.

'I can watch him for you, Ali,' she said, giving him her best smile.

'Are you sure?'

'Of course.'

'Thank you so much, Marie. I appreciate it.'

She smiled, and he looked down at his son.

'I'll be back in an hour or so,' he said, forcing a smile. 'Then we can get some ice cream, or go to the cinema if you'd like.'

The boy smiled eagerly. 'OK, Dad.'

Jacobs turned and walked away from the soccer field, pulling his cell phone from his pocket. Heading towards the Park exit he tried Bleeker again but it went straight to voicemail.

He cursed and hung up, striding across the grass.

Bleeker, where the hell are you?

At the Counter Terrorism Bureau, Shepherd finished clarifying some extra details with Agents Faison and Peterson, then stepped out of the interrogation cell and made his way to the stairs. He saw Kruger and Maddy Flood sitting at his desk in the detective pit and took a quick detour, moving over to them.

'How are you both feeling?'

'We're OK,' Kruger said.

'Good news. We've got some leads.'

'What is it?'

'One of the bombers, Paul Bleeker, worked as a janitor at a Manhattan law firm. He's got a message on his cell phone that indicates one of his bosses knows about the virus. We've got two police cars on their way to pick this guy up and bring him in.'

'What about the fifth vial?' Maddy asked.

'Two gentlemen from the ATF just arrived. They know the two people who we think are in possession of it. We're trying to locate them.'

The two doctors took this in, then nodded. Shepherd turned and headed back up the stairs to the briefing room. Inside, he found Rach at her desk working with Archer and Josh. On the screen, he saw that she'd pulled up files relating to the English senior partner, Alistair Jacobs. Shepherd saw a driving licence and some press articles.

'This is all I could find, sir,' Rach said. 'He's a big-league lawyer. Judging by one of these newspaper articles, he's also recently divorced.'

'No charges?'

'Nothing. Not even a parking ticket.'

Shepherd nodded. 'Lawyers are good at making sure their records are clean.'

'A little too clean,' Archer said.

'Not everyone has a police file, Arch,' Rach said.

'No, but he's interacting with Paul Bleeker. That means he's got something to hide.'

'When did he move here?' Shepherd said, looking at the screen.

'According to the paper, five years ago. Before that, he was a partner at another firm in London.'

Shepherd scanned the screen. 'We need to know more about this man.'

Archer thought for a moment, then rose and pulled his cell phone.

'I'll handle this, sir,' he said. 'Gimme five.'

He walked out and passed Marquez on the way, who looked serious as she entered the room.

'Sir, I just spoke with Jorgensen,' she said. 'He found Ray Creek at his home.'

'Alive?'

'Far from it. Six gunshot wounds to his head and chest. He'd also been tortured. CSU used ballistics fingerprinting to compare slugs and cartridges from the scene with those at Dr Tibbs' apartment. They also compared wound pattern. They were a match.'

'So whoever killed Creek killed Tibbs.'

'Yes, sir. CSU checked CCTV at Tibbs' apartment building but they couldn't find anyone entering the building who didn't live inside. They think whoever killed Tibbs used the fire escape. Unless another resident capped him.'

'OK. Tell Jorgensen to get back here.'

'Yes, sir.'

She turned and walked out, passing Archer who was standing on the walkway. He'd just finished dialling a long number and put the phone to his ear.

Walking up through Tribeca, Jacobs swore and ended another attempted call. Bleeker still wasn't picking up. His entire future and the safety of his son depended on this deal going down tonight. If Bleeker pulled out or got cold feet, Jacobs would go find whatever rock he was hiding under and drag him out. If he had to, he'd tear apart the city looking for him.

Turning right, he walked down Worth Street, headed towards 111 and his apartment. From upstairs he could log into the law firm's admin database and find Bleeker's address. He'd go over there himself and get the information he needed. As he walked, he decided to quickly check his emails. He opened the Internet browser, but a *Breaking News* banner on the homepage caught his eye.

He read it as he pushed back the glass door and walked into the building.

Breaking: Macy's evacuated after morning bomb threat. Chemical accident by Seaport kills 59.

He froze.

Then he looked up and saw two cops in uniform standing there in the lobby.

The two men were looking straight at him, their expressions hard.

Jacobs sensed movement behind him and turned.

Two other cops had walked through the doors, blocking him off.

The four police officers stood there, boxing him in, the clips on all four holsters undone, their hands resting on the grip of each pistol.

Oh shit.

TWENTY EIGHT

Up on the walkway at the Counter Terrorism
Bureau, Archer swore and called the number
again. He'd been trying to get through for over
five minutes, but the guy on the other end was an
unreliable correspondent at the best of times and
wasn't picking up. Archer checked his Casio. It
was mid-afternoon, just coming up to 3pm which
meant it would be around 8 pm in the UK.

C'mon, he thought, Jacobs on his mind. *Pick
up, idiot. We need information on this guy.*

Finally, someone answered. Abruptly.

'What?'

'Is that any way to answer the phone?'

'Archer!' Chalky said. *'Jesus Christ, you
withheld your number. I thought you were an ex-
girlfriend.'*

'How are you?'

'Not bad. Yourself?'

'I've had better mornings.'

*'Yeah, I saw the news. There was a bomb threat
at Macy's? And a load of people died at a
clothing store?'*

'Rings a bell.'

'You all OK?'

'Yeah, we're fine. But the thing at the store
wasn't an accident. And I need your help with
something.'

'What's that?'

'Five vials of a pneumonic virus were stolen
from a lab in Manhattan last night. It's some
seriously nasty shit. We've secured all but one of
them.'

'OK.'

'But one of the bombers has a message on his cell phone. It sounds like someone else is involved. And he's English.'

'Oh dear. What's his name?'

'Alistair Jacobs. You heard of him?'

'No. But someone else on the team might have.'

'Are you at the station?'

'Yeah. Nightshift.'

'We've got this guy's file up on the screen here, but it's looking pretty clean. A little too clean, if you know what I mean.'

'Tell you what, I'll get one of Nikki's team to run a search. Gimme a couple of minutes.'

'OK. Thanks.'

Archer ended the call. He turned and walked back into the briefing room, re-joining Shepherd, Josh and Rach.

'I've got someone pulling information on Jacobs. I'll call him back in a moment.'

Shepherd nodded. 'Good.'

Marquez appeared, re-entering the room. 'Sir, they just picked up Jacobs at his apartment building. They're bringing him in now.'

'Great. Background information on Rourke and Sway?'

'Agent Faison arranged for their ATF files to be transferred to us. They should be here already.'

Rach looked down at her terminal, then pulled up a large file she'd been sent from next door. The team watched as she opened it and pulled up both men's jackets, side by side on the screen. They saw vital statistics, addresses, known family, felony records and a mug-shot of each man. Both were in orange jumpsuits, standing up against a height chart, holding a placard with their full name and prison ID in white on the front. The team paused and took a good look at the men they were hunting.

On the left of the screen, Rourke was staring grimly ahead. He looked unhealthy, his black hair messy, his face flushed. The black chart behind his head said he was five-eight. To the right, Sway was taller, over six foot with that short mullet haircut that Peterson had described. He looked lean and angry, his eyes hard as he stared into the camera like the lens would shatter if he did it hard enough. Under the vital stats came the charges against the two men. The lists were long.

'Send out the photos and profiles to every precinct in the NYPD,' Shepherd told Rach. 'Let's get a manhunt going.'

'Yes, sir. There are two more files here too.'

She pulled them up. Rourke and Sway's files disappeared, replaced by two others, a man and a woman. They were both in orange overalls too. It seemed prison service was a prerequisite for joining *The Stuttgart Soldiers*. The man had bleached white hair and dark eyes with a nasty scar across his eyebrow. The woman was dark-haired and looked tough as hell.

'The man is called Ryan Wicks,' Rach read. 'In and out of prison the last few years. Suspected perp in several homicides in the San Antonio area.'

'What's the scar from?' Archer asked.

'Someone tried to stab him in prison.'

'The woman?'

'Natasha Drexler. Former prostitute and heroin addict. Did time for assault and battery. Lead suspect in four unsolved murders in Southern Texas.'

'Jesus Christ,' Josh said. 'Not exactly Romeo and Juliet, are they?'

Shepherd turned to Archer.

'Try your friend again. I want information on Jacobs before he gets here.'

Archer nodded, pulling his cell and pushing *Redial*. The call connected, and he put it on speakerphone.

'Chalk?'

'Yeah, I'm here mate.'

'Good. You're on speakerphone.'

'OK. I'm with one of the analysts now. CID have a file on Jacobs. It's not as clean as you thought.'

'Shoot.'

'CID did an investigation a couple of years ago into a loan shark operating out of Canary Wharf. They pulled his list of clients and one of them was your man Jacobs. They've got him tagged as a gambling addict and therefore possible blackmail material. They think he's owed well into seven figures on occasion. He's always managed to pay the debts and keep his record clean but it's been close a couple of times and he attracted CID attention as a consequence. He's never been charged with anything though.'

'That's why he's still able to practise as a lawyer,' Archer said, as Shepherd nodded.

'Apparently his divorce hasn't helped his bank account either.'

'Anything on his ex-wife?'

'Hang on. Bringing her up now.'

Pause.

'Nothing relevant. He dodged a bullet there though, Arch.'

'How so?'

'I'm looking at a picture of her. He must have married her after losing a bet. She's a dog. Got a face put together like a ransom note.'

The comment was so inappropriate and unexpected that Marquez, Josh and Rach burst out laughing, immediately quelled by a look from Shepherd.

Archer fought hard to hide a smile and shook his head.

'Anything else?'

'Yeah. He's got a kid that he was battling to get custody of but it was awarded to his wife. The gambling is his kryptonite though. If you want somewhere to push, there you go.'

'Alright, thanks.'

'I'll call you next week. Stay out of trouble.'

'Later.'

Archer hung up, then turned to Shepherd. 'So he's a gambling addict. And he's got a kid. That's stuff to work with.'

'Maybe that's why he's involved in this,' Marquez suggested. 'He needs the money.'

Jorgensen suddenly appeared at the door. Shepherd saw him arrive. 'Welcome back.'

Jorgensen nodded.

'I passed a blue and white outside, sir. The lawyer you were after just arrived.'

At *Kearny Medical*, Dr Glover tried to blink fear out of his eyes as he worked, forcing himself to focus. It wasn't easy. He'd just seen the woman who'd kidnapped him shoot a lady in the head as she stepped out of the elevator. The woman's body had been dragged off and dumped in a room with Melissa's. Glover had caught a glimpse of a whole pile of bodies inside when the door was opened. He felt as if he was in a nightmare.

Sitting at the desktop and wearing a bio suit, Glover was working on the distinct orders the curly-haired man with the gun had given him earlier. He'd demanded that Dr Flood's virus be mixed with a nutrient broth already here at the lab. The resulting mixture would then be tipped into the six canisters the man and woman had brought, all of which had been emptied and cleansed of the pesticide they'd held previously. Unfortunately, the man with the gun had done his homework. The strength of Dr Flood's virus would devour the bacteria in the broth like giving it a free lunch.

Within a couple of hours, it would turn one vial of the virus into an entire canister.

God only knew what they were planning to do with it.

Glover was doing what the man ordered but was deliberately drawing the process out, trying to give himself time to think. He was working on the sixth canister, the last one, but was desperately trying to work out a means of escape. Once he was done they'd kill him. He was sure of it. But he was trapped and unarmed. There was nothing in the lab he could use as a weapon and they all had guns. Besides, he wasn't a fighter; he was a doctor. The only thing he had at his disposal was the virus. He was trying to think of a way to lure them all into the lab without wearing protective clothing. If they inhaled the gas, it'd be game over and he could get the hell out of here and contact the police immediately.

To his left, Glover heard the door to the lab slide open. He felt a glimmer of hope which died when he saw that the big guy was wearing a bio suit as he walked in. He also had that machine pistol in his hand.

'And?'

'Almost done.'

'You're lying. You're finished. You're stalling.'

Silence.

'Will it work?'

'I think so.'

Behind the protective helmet, the man grinned.

'Well we need to find out.'

'Find out what?'

'If it works.'

Glover looked at him, confused. The man stepped forward. Glover didn't see the punch coming and it smashed into his stomach, knocking air out of his lungs and winding him. He fell to the ground, gasping. The man grabbed Glover's helmet and ripped it off, tucking it under his arm. Then he turned and walked towards the exit, scooping up the vial containing the last few drops of the virus.

He tossed it over his shoulder.

Hunched over, Glover watched the vial flying through the air, heading towards the ground and certain death. He made a desperate dive to catch it but just missed it. The vial smashed open as it hit the floor. Instantly the yellow virus started seeping out into the air.

Staggering to his feet, Glover ran forward to the doors, but they'd already clicked shut, locking him in. He pounded on the glass.

'Please! Let me out!' he screamed.

The other man ignored him, and removed his helmet, taking in a deep breath of clean air outside the lab. Glover turned and saw the yellow virus drifting across the room, coming towards him. Although only a small amount had been released, that was more than enough. He took a deep breath, holding it and looking around the lab desperately for anything he could use as a respirator. It was hopeless. There was nothing.

He turned again, looked outside and saw the man with the pistol watching curiously. Glover felt his oxygen running out, desperate to take a breath, the yellow gas coming even closer.

He fought and fought, but his body couldn't resist.

And he breathed in.

TWENTY NINE

Although Archer had only been with the Counter-Terrorism Bureau for just under half a year, he'd seen all manner of suspects and criminals processed through the building. Murderers, members of sleeper terrorist cells, suspected suicide bombers, physical monstrosities like Kyle Gunnar. But the sight of a good-looking English millionaire in a smart grey suit being led into the station in handcuffs was definitely a first. His shoes probably cost more than Archer's entire wardrobe. He had short-cut grey hair the same shade as his suit and a white shirt with a long black tie under a black coat. Moments ago he'd been led into the cell which Gunnar had just vacated, his pockets emptied and placed in a tray next door. Shepherd was in the seat across from him as Archer leaned against the wall to his right, his arms folded.

Jacobs was still in his chair, his hands on the desk, his face calm. Archer examined him.

A man accustomed to getting his own way.

'Before you begin, let me save you some time,' Jacobs said. 'I'm not saying a word until my lawyer arrives.'

'It'll be an old colleague or friend, right?' Archer said.

Jacobs looked up at him, surprised. Not at his statement, but by his accent.

'MI6?'

Archer shook his head. 'NYPD.'

'How the hell did you end up here?'

'I could ask you the same thing.'

'Here are the concrete facts,' Shepherd said. 'We have a recorded message on Paul Bleeker's phone which you left several hours ago. I think you know about a certain virus and you were planning to do something with it.'

Jacobs didn't speak.

He also didn't ask *what virus.*

'What if we let your partners know this is happening?' Archer asked. 'A good lawyer might get you off the hook. That's a very distant *might.* But do you think all your clients will still want to do business with a suspected terrorist?'

'Go ahead. Once I get out of here, I'll sue each one of you for everything you have.'

'From the sounds of it, you need the money.'

'What's that supposed to mean?'

'We know all about your little gambling problem. How much do you owe this time?'

Jacobs shook his head. But his demeanour had changed slightly. He studied the table in front of him. Archer had struck a nerve.

'Have they threatened you?'

Silence.

'Have they threatened your son?'

Jacobs kept his eyes on the wooden desk but the look on his face answered Archer's questions. He may have been a good lawyer but Archer could see why he wouldn't be good at the card table. He wasn't exactly hard to read.

'If you work with us, we can help you,' Shepherd said. 'We can bring the boy in and put him in protective custody. Something tells me the men you owe aren't the type who follow the rules. You help us out, we can make that all go away.'

Pause.

'No. You can't.'

'A man was killed in Central Park last night. He was gassed with a small dose of the virus we think you're involved with. Two other viral bombs were left across the city this morning. Paul Bleeker arranged it. If you work with us, we can secure the remaining sample of this virus before anyone else is killed.'

Jacobs looked up at Shepherd. He seemed genuinely surprised.

'Wait a minute. Bleeker already had the virus?'

'Yes, he did.'

'Where is he?'

'The morgue.'

Jacobs dropped his head. 'That son of a bitch.'

'What was your deal?' Archer asked.

Shepherd suddenly rose from his chair, and walked out, closing the door. Jacobs and Archer were left alone.

'What was your deal?' Archer asked again. 'How did you end up in this?'

Jacobs didn't reply. A few moments later, the door opened, and Shepherd reappeared, something in his hand. He closed the door and moved back to his chair. He slid a photograph across the table towards Jacobs. It was a shot from the morgue of the groundsman from the Park, Luis Cesar, taken from above the steel tray he was laid on.

'This is the man who died in Central Park,' Shepherd said, as Jacobs looked down. 'He had a wife and five children. He drowned in his own blood.'

Pause.

'Right now, you can help us. I'm sure your lawyer will be the best of the best. He'll wrestle these charges down to something manageable.

Two years in a private facility, maybe less. Maybe you'll never see a prison cell. But if you don't start working with us, hundreds, maybe thousands more people could die like this man.'

Silence.

'Talk to us!' Archer said. 'Cut the shit. We don't have time for this!'

Just then, the door burst open and a lawyer walked in, a briefcase in his hand.

'Not another word, Mr Jacobs,' he said, moving forward and placing the briefcase on the desktop in a smooth motion.

Archer and Shepherd looked over at the English lawyer, who'd seemed on the verge of speaking. Then he looked up at his lawyer and nodded.

He wasn't going to be talking any time soon.

At *Kearny Medical* in New Jersey, Bobby Rourke was looking through the glass at the body of the dead doctor inside the sealed lab. He'd finally stopped twitching, blood and pieces of lung tissue surrounding him, some of it sprayed on the glass. He'd watched the man's death with fascination.

The virus sure as hell worked.

Behind him, the lift dinged and opened. He looked over his shoulder and saw Finn walk out, heading towards him. As he approached, Sway noticed his friend wearing the protective suit minus the helmet and saw the dead body inside the lab.

'Why didn't you just shoot him?'

'I wanted to do a test. '

Finn looked at the six canisters sitting on the desktop in the lab. He pointed.

'OK, genius, so how do we get them out now?'

'Relax. One of the doctors showed me how to filter the air before I shot him. I push a button, it'll be clean in less than a minute.'

Finn nodded. 'OK. We're halfway there.'

'No, we're all the way there. The doctor cooked up six canisters for us and Bleeker's dead.'

'Yeah, but his contact isn't.'

'Wait. You still want to go through with that?'

'Yeah. I do.'

'Do you have his number?'

Sway nodded. Rourke turned to him.

'Think for a moment. We need to be careful. You and Bleeker set this up to con the money out of the Brit. That was before Bleeker screwed us. What he did this morning will have alerted every cop and Federal agent in New York.'

'Relax. It doesn't affect our plan. It just means we'll do it with an early two million in our back pockets.'

'You sure he'll pay?'

'Bleeker said the Brit's in seven figures with a Triad gang. He's been given one week to front the money or his kid dies. He won't back out.'

'Could be a set up.'

'Look at it this way. Bleeker served his purpose by making introductions at the rally. Now he's dead, which saves us the trouble. And we get another $2 mil added to the pot.'

'I still don't like it.'

'But I do. There's two million on the table. I'm not walking away from that.' He pulled his cell phone. 'I'll set this thing up.'

He pointed at the sealed-off lab.

'Do me a favour and clean that shit out of there.'

Back at the Counter Terrorism Bureau, Archer and Shepherd had re-joined Josh and Jorgensen in the observation room of the interrogation cell. Marquez was upstairs working with Rach. The four men were standing in silence, watching through the glass as Jacobs talked with his lawyer inside the other room.

'Shit,' Jorgensen said. 'He's not going to be talking any time soon.'

'We had him, sir,' Archer said to Shepherd. 'He had no idea what Bleeker was up to this morning.'

'Your comment about needing the money rattled him,' Shepherd said. 'And the photo of the dead man shook him further. He's not in this for terrorism.'

'He's in it for money,' Josh finished.

'He said something strange in there,' Archer said.

'What was that?'

'*Bleeker already had the virus?*'

'So?' Jorgensen said. 'Why's that strange, genius?'

'Because he was surprised. I think he and Bleeker were planning to buy it from someone else.'

'But Bleeker already had the virus.'

'Only because he stole it.'

'You think he was double-crossing Jacobs?' Shepherd asked.

'I think he was planning to.'

As the men thought about this, Marquez stepped into the room, closing the door behind her. Shepherd turned to her.

'Any updates?'

She nodded. 'CSU found a pay-as-you-go cell phone in a drawer at Dr Tibbs' apartment. It has a very interesting call history.'

'Interesting how?'

'There's only one number on there. Paul Bleeker'.

'Oh shit,' Jorgensen said. 'So Tibbs is the missing link?'

'He has to be,' Marquez said. 'Apparently the calls stretch back for the last couple of weeks.'

'Get the two doctors,' Shepherd asked.

Marquez ducked out. Moments later, she reappeared with Kruger and Maddy, the pair joining the team in the observation room for the interrogation cell.

'What's going on?' Kruger asked.

'A cell phone was found at Dr Tibbs' apartment. He's been in touch with Paul Bleeker for the past fortnight.'

'What?'

'He was the leak in your team,' Shepherd said. 'That's how Bleeker knew about the virus. Tibbs must have told him.'

Kruger and Maddy both looked shocked. Shepherd gave them a moment. In the silence, a cell phone started ringing but the room ignored it. Kruger looked surprised and took a seat while he thought the revelation through. Archer glanced at Maddy and saw her frowning, shaking her head. Marquez had noticed it too.

'Will was such a quiet, gentle guy,' Maddy said. 'I can't believe he'd do something like this.'

'Never underestimate the appeal of money,' Jorgensen replied insensitively.

The phone kept ringing.

'Jesus Christ, will someone answer that?'
Shepherd said.

They looked at each other; it didn't belong to
any of them. Then they all turned in the direction
of the ringing cell.

It was rattling and vibrating across the desk
behind them, the screen flashing.

It was Jacobs' phone.

Jacobs and his lawyer were mid-conversation
when the door to the interrogation room burst
open. Shepherd's whole team moved swiftly
inside, followed by Rach carrying her laptop. A
wire was hooked up to Jacobs' Blackberry, which
was still ringing. Rach placed the laptop on the
table quickly whilst Shepherd slid the phone in
front of Jacobs. It sat there, purring and shifting
on the table as the call continued.

Private Number was on the display.

The lawyer turned to the group. 'This is-'

'Answer it,' Shepherd told Jacobs, pointing at
the phone. The English lawyer was taken aback.
He froze, as the phone continued to ring. '*Answer
it!*' Shepherd shouted at him. 'On speaker.'

His change in tone jolted Jacobs into action. He
lifted a finger and pushed *Answer*.

'Hello?'

Pause.

'Jacobs?'

The voice was Southern.

'Yes. How did you get this number?'

'Bleeker's dead.'

'Yes. I know.'

'We'll still meet tonight.'

'Bleeker never told me where the meet would
be.'

'What?'

'He never told me where the trade would happen.'

Pause.

'Tonic East. 10pm. Third floor. You got the money?'

'Yes.'

'Two million. I want it transferred into an offshore bank account. I'll give you the details when we meet. Then you get the item. If you're a minute late, I'm gone.'

'Yes. How do I know what you look like?'

Pause.

'I'll find you.'

And he hung up.

A moment of silence followed. Then as one, the room exhaled. Shepherd grabbed the phone, making sure the call was disconnected.

'Now we're talking,' he said. 'Did you get a trace, Rach?'

She shook her head. 'Too quick.'

Shepherd turned to his team.

'Tonic. You guys know that place?'

'Yes, sir,' Jorgensen said. 'I do. It's a football bar, corner of East 29th and 3rd. Turns into a club at night.'

Shepherd checked his watch. 'It's 1530. The meet is at 2200. That gives us plenty of time to prepare.'

He looked down at Jacobs.

'You're going to make that meeting.'

The lawyer, startled by all this, tried to interject. 'My client and I-'

'Everyone, follow me,' Shepherd said, ignoring the man and moving to the door.

At *Kearny Medical*, Sway had just ended the call.

He remained where he was, looking down at his phone.

'What?' Rourke asked.

Sway didn't answer.

'What's up?'

Sway stared at the phone for a few moments longer, thinking.

Then he turned to Rourke. 'Nothing. We're on for tonight.' He pointed at the canisters inside the secured lab. Rourke had activated the purification system and the air was now cleaned. 'We need to get them stowed.'

'No rush,' Rourke said. 'I'm not going anywhere until you get back from the meet.'

'What about this place?'

'Before we leave I'll rig it up.'

'If we blow it tonight, that'll get attention. Set the timer for tomorrow.'

Rourke grinned. 'Trust me. I know what I'm doing.'

Sway nodded.

'I'm going to go prepare,' he said, walking off towards the lift.

'Wait. Don't you need a sample of the virus?'

Sway turned and grinned.

'Trust me. I know what I'm doing.'

THIRTY

Less than an hour later a whole host of people had gathered inside Briefing Room 5 at the Counter Terrorism Bureau. Rach was at her terminal, same as before. Beside her were the two doctors, Maddy Flood and Kruger. On the left side of the room were Archer, Josh, Jorgensen and Marquez. Sergeant Hendricks and his four-man team were on the other. Archer looked over at Hendricks and felt reassured by his presence.

Dark-featured and with a face that rarely broke into a smile, Hendricks was as tough as nails, one of the hardest cops Archer had ever seen. He was a burgeoning legend within the NYPD. Before he came to the Counter Terrorism Bureau, Hendricks had run his own team out of the 75th in Brooklyn which was regarded as the most dangerous precinct in all of New York. The surrounding area was plagued by violence, bombed-out buildings, barbed wire and almost a daily murder count. But the scary thing was that Hendricks had requested a transfer to the precinct.

He'd wanted to go there.

There were all sorts of rumours about stuff he'd done and most of them were true. His team was gathered beside him, standing in silence. Hendricks had handpicked them himself and they were like a damn wolf-pack, all as gritty and stern-faced as he was. They were the perfect team to work with tonight. Faison and Peterson were also on the other side of the table, sitting and talking quietly between themselves. With his shaved head and hate tattoos Peterson looked incongruous amongst everyone else in the room, but he was arguably the most important person there. He was going to be their eyes and ears at the New Jersey camp tonight.

They all suddenly quietened as Shepherd walked in. He closed the door behind him and walked to the front of the room, standing beside the screen.

By the time he got there, the room was silent.

'Everyone here?'

He looked around, met with a series of nods.

'Right. Listen up. I'll summarise so we're all on the same page. Late last night, five vials of a lethal pneumonic virus were stolen from a lab complex on the Upper West Side called *Flood Microbiology*. We've accounted for four of these vials and taken down those responsible. Our goal tonight is to secure the fifth and arrest the people in possession of it.'

He pointed at the screen. Rach had pulled up Jacobs' DMV licence.

'This man, Alistair Jacobs, was intending to purchase the remaining vial at 2200 tonight. He's downstairs in one of the interrogation cells. The deal will proceed as planned and we're going to apprehend the sellers at the trade.'

'Where, Shep?' Hendricks asked.

'A bar stroke nightclub called Tonic East. It's on the corner of 29th and 3rd. My team and I will be there. When the sellers show up, we'll take them in and secure the virus.'

Rach pulled up Sway and Rourke's prison mug shots.

'These are the two men we're looking for. Bobby Rourke and Finn Sway, both twenty nine years old, both born in Roller, Texas. They are known leaders of the Texan Chapter of a neo-Nazi group called *The Stuttgart Soldiers*, a group in which Special Agent Peterson is currently embedded.'

Rach then changed the shot to Wicks and Drexler.

'These two may also be involved or at the scene.'

The room was silent as everyone examined the mug-shots. After a moment, Rach flicked the shots back to Rourke and Sway.

'How's the trade proceeding?' Faison asked.

'Sway told him the meet happens on the third floor. Jacobs will call his secondary who'll begin the transaction into Sway's offshore bank account. When the transfer's been confirmed, Sway will hand over the vial containing the virus.' He turned to his detail. 'But that call is coming through to Rach here. My team will be dispersed in the crowd undercover. Jacobs will be wearing a wire so we'll hear everything he's saying.'

'How do we know he won't give Sway a signal?' one of Hendricks' team asked.

'Leverage. Jacobs knows he's in deep shit. He told us he owes over seven million dollars to a gang who work off the books in the Financial District. Without us, he and his son will be dead by Tuesday night.'

'But what about when the money doesn't show up in the account?'

'By that point, it won't matter. Jacobs is going to ask to see the vial first. All we need is visual confirmation that Sway has it. Then we take him before he has a chance to move or react.'

He pointed at the screen.

'We'd move in and take these sons of bitches right now, but nobody knows where the hell they are or where this last vial is. We'll have to wait for the trade to flush them out. But we do know where their back-up is. And that's where the rest of you come in.'

Rach clicked a button, and it changed to a map of an industrial estate in New Jersey.

'The ATF have a man undercover in the group, Special Agent Peterson here. He informed us that Sway and Rourke's entire Chapter has set up camp on this estate.'

Shepherd looked over at Hendricks.

'Jake, I need you and your team to stake out the camp, working with Agent-in-Charge Faison and under the ATF's orders. The virus may show up here if the trade is cancelled or Sway and Rourke have a change of heart. If we can confirm it is at this location, we're moving in and taking down the whole campsite.'

Hendricks and his team nodded. 'You got it.'

'Agent Peterson is going back undercover. He'll be wearing a mic so you'll hear everything that's going on down there. This will be two operations working at the same time. I'll lead the group at the club. Agent-in-Charge Faison will take charge at the campsite.'

'What if they plan to release the virus at the club, sir?' Josh asked. 'It could be a trap.'

'That's highly unlikely. There are two million dollars on the table here, and neither Rourke nor Sway is wealthy. We all know the way criminals think. They won't pass it up. Questions?'

There were none.

'My team, stay here. We'll go into detail about the arrangement at the club. Sergeant Hendricks, you and your squad liaise with Agent Faison and sort out your own arrangements. We're under their jurisdiction tonight. And remember people, our objective is to secure this last vial of the virus. That precedes everything else.'

Pause.

'That's it.'

The room stirred. As Faison, Peterson and Hendricks' team walked out, taking the opportunity to introduce themselves, Shepherd moved towards Kruger and Maddy Flood. They'd sat through the briefing in silence.

'I know you've both been to hell and back today,' he said. 'But if possible, I'd like to keep you around on advisory roles.'

They looked at each other. Neither was convinced.

Maddy turned to Shepherd. 'To be honest, I just want to go home.'

'It might be dangerous.'

'I don't care.'

Shepherd nodded. 'OK. I understand.'

He looked at Kruger, who nodded. 'Me too. I just want a shower and to put an icepack on my face.'

'Very well. But some detectives go with each of you for the time being. Until this is over, you both have protection.'

Outside *Kearny Medical* Wicks, Drexler and another man listened in silence as Finn finished outlining his plan. They were standing just outside the entrance, their arms folded against the cold. The newcomer had arrived fifteen minutes ago. Wicks and Drexler had met him before. They were happy to see him and also knew without a doubt that they could trust him.

Finn finished his explanation, then turned to the newcomer.

'What do you think?' he asked.

'Shit, Finn,' the man said. 'Where's this side of you been hiding? You're cleverer than I thought.'

Sway grinned.

'This ties all up all the loose ends,' he said. 'When this is done, and Bobby's loaded up the canisters, we're out of here. There's plenty of room for you if you want to hitch a ride. Bob's got some buyers interested in Juarez. We'll sell the virus then be out of Roller before the end of the week.'

'That sounds good. I'm sick of this place.'

'So you'll do it?'

'Of course.'

Sway looked at Drexler.

'You?'

She hawked and spat, nodding. 'I'm in.'

He turned to Wicks, who nodded, taking a drag on a cigarette. 'Let's do it.'

'Great. Now listen close. I'll outline it one more time.'

THIRTY ONE

Saturday night in any Manhattan bar was easily the busiest time of the week. Make it seven days before Christmas and pretty much every place with alcohol and a dance floor was packed. That night, Tonic East was no exception. The place had three floors. There were bars on 1, 2 and 3, televisions mounted all over the walls on 1 and 3 whilst 2 was dominated by a large dance-floor and DJ booth. Although it was winter the place was buzzing, the heating and the proximity of other human bodies helping to keep everyone in the place warm.

Shepherd and Marquez were parked around the corner with Jacobs, getting him ready. But they had a man on each level inside the bar. Jorgensen was on 3, Josh on 2. Archer was on the ground floor, facing the entrance, his back to the bar and ignoring everyone around him.

Seeing as the building was heated he'd left his jacket in the car outside and was dressed in a grey hoodie and blue jeans, blending right in with the mass of NFL fans scattered around him. He had his right hand by his hip, covering the Sig in the holster hidden under the loose-fitting top. He didn't want anyone touching or grabbing it by accident. The team were all hooked up with ear pieces and mics tucked into their sleeves so they could communicate instantly without having to pull out a cell phone.

The two doormen checking for ID had been informed of the situation. The manager of the bar had needed a lot of persuasion to convince him to let the detectives take their weapons inside and to allow the trade to happen. But at the end of the day this was an NYPD operation and the outcome was inevitable. He'd accepted he just had to shut up and put up.

Leaning against the bar, Archer shot his cuff and checked his watch.

9:54 pm.

Jacobs would be sent inside any minute now. Archer scanned everyone he could see from his position, but there was no sign of either Rourke or Sway anywhere.

Shepherd's voice suddenly came up over his ear piece. *'Report.'*

'Nothing up here,' Jorgensen said.

'Me either,' said Josh.

'No sign,' Archer said.

'OK, get ready. We're sending Jacobs in. Sway or Rourke could appear at any minute.'

In the Ford, Shepherd watched Marquez place a sticky mic under the collar of Jacobs' suit. As she worked, Shepherd glanced at the English senior partner's face. He looked strained and had been asking to speak to his son. Earlier, he'd been permitted to call a woman looking after the boy and had asked her to watch him a little longer. She'd agreed pleasantly, completely unaware that he was making the call from an NYPD interrogation cell with a group of detectives staring down at him.

'I want to speak to my son,' he repeated to Shepherd. 'Please.'

'Once this is over,' Shepherd said. Marquez finished adjusting Jacobs' collar. The mic was invisible. She grabbed a set of headphones and put one of the sides to her ear, pushing her forefinger into her other.

'Please. Just one quick call.'

Marquez turned to Shepherd. 'We're good. Sound is 100 per cent.'

'Once this is done, you can use my cell and talk to him all night,' Shepherd said. 'But you give Sway or Rourke one signal, you won't speak to the kid again until I decide so. Clear?'

Jacobs looked at him, then nodded. Shepherd checked his watch.

9:55 pm.

'Showtime. Out you go.'

Jacobs pushed open his door and stepped out, trying to stay cool and breathe.

Less than a minute later, Archer saw the lawyer walk in.

'Eyes on Jacobs.'

The constant jostling of people getting to the bar meant Archer was jammed in, which was good for camouflage but not so good if he had to move in a hurry. In the dim lights, rap music thumping from the sound system, he watched Jacobs closely. He looked nervous as hell. The stairs were straight ahead of him, which he approached and started to climb.

Switching his attention back to the level, Archer scanned everyone who was walking in and around him.

Nothing.

'I see Jacobs, but no sign of Rourke or Sway.'

'We've got the door covered. Get up to 2 and stay on him.'

Archer nodded, stepping away from the bar and making his way to the stairs.

And with all his focus on Jacobs, he didn't notice a dark-haired woman in a leather jacket watching him from the corner of the bar.

The second floor was where the dance floor and nightclub were located. People were milling about everywhere, dancing and sitting around drinking as house music pounded out of the speakers, the lights low and flashing.

When Archer arrived on the second level he saw Jacobs to his left, cutting his way through the dance-floor. He was meant to be on his way to the roof, not staying down here. Josh was here somewhere too but Archer couldn't see him.

'Jacobs is headed the wrong way. He's going through the dance-floor on 2.'

'Where the hell is he going?' Shepherd asked. *'Follow him.'*

'Josh, where are you?'

'To your right.'

Archer looked over and saw Josh leaning against the wall by a booth, watching the stairs.

'Follow Jacobs,' he said. *'I'll watch for Rourke and Sway.'*

Archer moved into the dance-floor, cutting his way through the crowd, keeping his hand over his Sig protectively. He saw Jacobs turn a corner to the left. Archer quickly followed, but when he got there Jacobs was gone.

Shit.

Then he realised that was where the door to the unisex restroom was. Jacobs must have ducked inside.

'Jacobs is in the restroom,' he said, enunciating clearly so the others could hear him over the pounding dance music.

He checked his watch.

9:56 pm.

They didn't have time for this. If Jacobs was late, the trade wouldn't happen. Archer stepped back, casually taking up a position near the wall facing the door. In front of him, the song changed to a pulsing dance track, the lights flashing in time to the music.

Just as Archer was contemplating breaking open the door and hauling him out, it opened and Jacobs reappeared. His hair had been tidied and it looked as if he'd splashed water on his face. He didn't notice Archer and headed back down the side of the dance-floor, moving towards the stairs. Archer went to talk into his mic but realised he was beside a speaker. He stepped to his right so the others could hear what he was saying.

'We're in business. Josh, he's on his way to you.'

Watching Jacobs move through the crowd, Archer went to follow.

But suddenly, his path was blocked.

Amongst the flashing lights and dancing people, three huge guys seemed to appear out of nowhere. They merged together from through the crowd, a human wall of bulk and intimidation, thick beards on their faces.

All three of them were staring down at Archer.

They had their big fists clenched, thick golden rings on their fingers serving as makeshift knuckle-dusters. Each guy was built like a fridge-freezer, way over six feet and two hundred pounds. Comparatively, Archer was around six foot and one eighty five, and there was only one of him.

Looking up, Archer caught the edge of what looked like a black Swastika tattoo on one of their necks.

This wasn't a coincidence.

THIRTY TWO

Cornered just off the dance floor, Archer pulled his badge but one of the thugs slapped it out of his hands before he could even flip it open. The only other option was his gun, but he would never pull it in a place that crowded.

He glanced at the goon on his left and saw he was holding something in his large fist.

A knife.

The middle neo-Nazi pushed him backwards towards the wall, which counted as striking a detective and gave him carte blanche to respond. But he was outnumbered. To his right, a small queue had formed for the restroom, everyone watching as the trio encircled Archer. The song on the speakers beside them changed, David Guetta, Flo Rida and Nicki Minaj thumping out. *Where Them Girls At?* the lyrics of the song asked, pounding around the room. He looked up at the three skinheads. No girls around here.

When tackling someone one-on-one or even two-on-one, Archer liked to use jiu-jitsu and chokeholds to disable them. It was quick, bloodless and nullified any size discrepancy. A guy can't punch you if he can't breathe and he can't sue you for assault if he doesn't have a mark on his body or even clearly remember what had happened. A tough guy could take a punch but no one on the planet could hold out from a choke. But he was outnumbered three to one here and by a hell of a lot of poundage.

He needed to even the odds to at least two.

He glanced past the group, over the shoulder of one of them. He had one shot, otherwise it would be like in the movies when someone shouted *what's that?* and the bad guys turned to look.

He did it right.

Instinctively, the trio glanced behind them, just for a second.

And backed up against the wall, Archer targeted the guy with the knife.

His right fist hit the thug's jaw like a freight train that was running late. He tagged the neo-Nazi just as he turned back, a hundred and eight five pounds of survival behind the punch. The guy hadn't been braced, the muscles of his neck not ready to absorb the blow and the punch laid him out.

He dropped to the floor, the blade spilling out of his hand as he fell.

The others reacted instantly. The middle one didn't take a swing. He just ducked his head down and drove Archer into the wall, trying to slam him to the ground where he could pin him down and attack him. Archer stiffened his back and legs and looped his right arm quickly around the guy's neck, grabbing his right hand with his left and locking his grip. The guy was strong and Archer felt himself going for a ride.

But as the guy slammed him down, he unwittingly worsened his own position. Archer hooked his feet behind the guy's back and started squeezing his arms as hard as he could, the thug's head caught in a guillotine headlock. The music was pounding, strobes flashing, people queuing for the restroom shocked as they watched the fight. Archer was now beside the speaker and Nicki Minaj pounded into his ear. His body was pumping with adrenaline, locked onto the neo-Nazi and not letting go. His head caught in the headlock, the thug used his hands to try and prise Archer off his neck but Archer intensified the pressure, using every muscle fibre and sinew in his body, gritting his teeth with fierce aggression, putting a crushing vice on the guy's neck.

His back to the ground, every muscle in his body in the choke, Archer saw the second guy coming towards him in distorted staccato images in the strobe lighting. Archer was about to release the goon he had in his grip to defend himself, but the thug was yanked back as an arm suddenly appeared around his neck.

Josh's arm.

Archer's guy was trying to pull his head out of the headlock, but he wasn't going anywhere. He lost consciousness around the same time as Josh's guy, who Josh lowered to the ground near the corner and out of the way of the dance-floor. Archer let his victim go, the man's body limp, and scrambled to his feet panting hard. He grabbed his badge from the carpet to his right then pulled his handcuffs and slapped one side over the big skinhead's wrist, locking the other side to a radiator. Josh did the same with the other two, scooping up the knife and tucking it in his pocket. Without a word or moment's hesitation, the two detectives cut their way back through the side of the dance-floor, headed for the stairs. Josh took the lead, Archer following, taking deep breaths. He checked his watch.

9:59 pm.

One minute until the trade.

But as he looked up, he met an arcing elbow an inch from his face. It smashed into his nose, taking him by surprise just as his punch had done to the neo-Nazi behind him a few moments before. Stumbling back and falling to the floor, his eyes watering from the pain, he tried to make out who'd struck him as blood started to pour from his nose.

Seeing double, he could just make out a dark-haired woman walking fast to the stairs, pulling a cell phone from her pocket.

Drexler.

Partygoers knelt down to help him to his feet. Archer wiped blood off his face, trying to recover his senses.

But by the time he looked over at the stairs again, the woman was gone.

Upstairs and unaware of what had been happening immediately below, Jacobs was standing in front of the bar on the roof. Although it was a cold night, the roof top had several burn heaters and walls on three sides acting as windbreaks. There were people standing and sitting everywhere, but none of them paid him any attention.

Jorgensen was on one of the benches to the right, his left hand in his pocket on the pressel switch, his other resting on the bench within easy reach of his pistol under his jacket. Given that he was dressed in plain clothes, he blended right in with everyone else. He pushed the pressel.

'Jacobs is in place,' he said quietly.

Releasing the switch, he glanced to his left, towards the stairs, then scanned the level around him.

Sway, Rourke or their hit team could be here already, making sure Jacobs had come alone.

Where are you, assholes?

Eight yards away, Jacobs suddenly felt his phone purr in his inside breast pocket.

He reached into his jacket and withdrew it, taking the call.

'Yes?'

'I told you to come alone. You just made a big mistake.'

At that moment, Archer arrived on the third floor, joining Josh. Jacobs had his back to them, standing straight ahead facing the west.

They saw he had his phone to his ear.

What happened next occurred in a heartbeat. Jacobs was standing perfectly still, then suddenly jolted backwards, like someone had hit him with a strong uppercut. A pink cloud appeared in the air behind his head. There was a *thump* beside Archer as a young woman chatting with her friends took a bullet in her upper arm.

Her body carried the momentum from the round, knocking her over. Jacobs hit the ground at the same time, but he was already dead, shot through the forehead.

One bullet, two impacts, two casualties.

Then about thirty screams.

Outside in the van, Shepherd and Marquez heard the screaming. At the same time, both their earpieces started going off.

'Jacobs is down!' Jorgensen said. *'Jacobs is down! Someone took him out with a rifle!'*

'Shit!' Shepherd said, as he and Marquez pulled the door back and jumped out of the van, running around the corner.

As they arrived outside the club, they saw people starting to spill out of the doors screaming and shouting in panic. Both detectives had to clamp a finger to their ear to hear what the trio upstairs were saying.

'Is he alive?' Shepherd shouted.

'He's gone, sir,' Jorgensen said. 'Shot between the eyes.'

'What direction was the shot?'

'From the west.'

Less than a hundred yards from the roof of the nightclub was a newly opened apartment building. It was an ideal location for precision shooting. Many of the apartments inside were yet to be filled or rented and CCTV was yet to be installed.

The shooter was already on his way down in the lift. He was alone and carried nothing with him save for a rectangular brown box with a stamped address and a cell phone in his pocket.

It couldn't have gone better.

He'd taken a call, learning that the trade was a set-up, then fired from inside a bathroom through a gap in a window that was half open, set up deep inside the room to avoid detection. The rifle was a Winchester 270, a suppressor in place to dampen noise and muzzle flash. He'd also used sub-sonic ammunition so the British lawyer never even heard the shot that killed him. The bullet had hit the man right through the centre of the forehead. The moment he'd seen Jacobs take the round through the scope, the rifleman had exhaled, then placed the rifle back into its case. The spent cartridge was still inside the weapon which meant he didn't have to fumble around looking for it. Sealing the case and package he'd scooped it up and promptly left the empty apartment, heading for the stairs.

He got down to the ground floor in less than twenty seconds. Pushing open the door, he walked into the building lobby. It was empty, no reception desk and more importantly no CCTV. He placed the rectangular parcel by several others by the mail drop-off point so it was instantly camouflaged.

Pushing open the door to the street he heard sirens and faint screaming in the distance.

Turning in the opposite direction, the shooter pulled up his collar and disappeared into the night.

Upstairs at the club, Archer and Josh were with the injured woman, blood pulsing from the wound to her arm. Josh was calling for an ambulance whilst Archer pulled off his hoodie and wrapped it around the woman's bicep, knotting the sleeves and cinching it tight in a makeshift compression bandage. He clamped his hands either side of the wound. The hoodie was made of thick cotton, but blood slowly started to stain the grey red. She was bleeding badly but the makeshift tourniquet was doing its job.

'Ambulance is on its way,' Josh said, putting his phone back in his pocket. Archer looked over his shoulder at the city rooftops.

'Son of a bitch,' he said. 'It was like target practice. He knew this was a set-up.'

In the mayhem, Josh looked at his partner and noticed his bleeding nose for the first time.

'What the hell happened to you?'

THIRTY THREE

Ten minutes later the wounded girl was on her way to Murray Hill Medical. The CSU were up on the third floor, snapping photographs of the crime-scene and Jacobs' body and trying to establish where exactly the shot had come from. The three neo-Nazis who'd come after Archer had been taken outside and bundled into several police cars. None of them were saying anything. Whilst Jorgensen and Marquez were downstairs talking with backup, Archer and Josh were up on the roof, watching the CSU work. Shepherd moved up the last flight of stairs and walked over to join them.

'How are we doing, sir?' Josh asked.

'Every cop in Manhattan is looking for Sway and Rourke. We'll get them.' Shepherd looked at Archer's nose. 'You OK?'

'That bitch Drexler tagged me. Didn't see it coming.'

'Sure it was her?'

'Positive.'

'She must have got out in the stampede after the shot. We missed her.'

The three men looked over at Jacob's body.

'Shit,' Shepherd said. 'There goes our lead.'

'And we're no closer to getting our hands on that virus,' Josh said.

Archer grabbed a bottle of water from a table and poured it over his hands, washing off some dried blood, his and the girl's.

'Any word from Hendricks or the ATF?' he asked.

Shepherd shook his head. 'Not yet. They're all in place. We've got more people watching that camp than a damn soccer game. This virus sample has to show up somewhere tonight.'

Suddenly, Marquez's voice came up on each man's earpiece. *'Sir?'*

'Yes?'

'Good news.'

'What is it?'

'A man was just picked up and arrested ten blocks from here.'

She paused.

'It's Finn Sway.'

'Take these off me, pigs!' snarled Sway, his hands cuffed in front of him. He'd been dumped in the back of a Bureau Ford Explorer outside the club. Marquez, Archer, Josh and Jorgensen were standing there watching him, a street officer in the car beside Sway to make sure he didn't try to escape.

'Where's the rifle?' Marquez asked.

'What rifle?'

'You're a bad liar.'

'What the hell are you talking about?'

'Don't waste our time. Where is it?'

'Shut your mouth, bitch. I don't deal with your kind.'

'HEY!' Jorgensen said, pointing at Sway. 'Cool it.'

Sway glared back at him. Standing next to Marquez, Archer studied Sway. Although they were yet to confirm that he was the shooter he certainly fit the profile. Peterson had given an accurate description of the guy. He was tall, six-three on the file, and was dressed in blue jeans and a thick cotton coat. He wasn't wearing a hat, but Archer recognised the distinctive short sides and long-top haircut from his ATF file.

'What the hell is going on?' Sway asked.

'A man was just shot dead on the roof of this nightclub with a rifle,' Archer told him. 'And we know you were coming to meet him.'

'No I wasn't.'

'Bullshit,' Marquez said. 'You're in the area ten minutes after the shooting.'

'So?'

'Damn coincidence, isn't it?'

'Guess that's exactly what it is.'

He looked at Archer.

'You got a murder weapon, pretty boy?'

'Not yet.'

'What time was the guy shot?'

Marquez rolled her eyes and answered. '10 o'clock.'

Sway smiled. 'Then I couldn't have killed him. I wasn't even in this part of the city. I only just got down here. Then you guys sprang these cuffs on me like a goddamn bear-trap.'

'Where were you?' Jorgensen asked.

'At a coffee place uptown.'

'You're going to have to be more specific than that.'

'Shit, it was the green one. Starbucks.'

'What time?'

'I don't know exactly. But I was there around 10. Go ask the people who work there. They saw me.'

'Which Starbucks was it?'

'The one by Port Authority. That big-ass bus terminal.'

'Corner of 39th and 8th,' Josh confirmed.

'So if you weren't the shooter what are you doing in this part of town?' Archer asked.

'Taking a look around, man. Is that against the law?'

'Why are you in New York?'

'Visiting. I've never been here before. After all this shit, I'm never coming back. I'm not lying. Go ask the people at that coffee place. Hell, they must have cameras. Check them.'

Marquez looked at Sway, then walked away to one side with Archer, Josh and Jorgensen. Beside them, the gurney carrying the black body-bag with Jacobs inside rattled as it was pushed off the sidewalk and onto the street, rolling towards the back of a waiting ambulance. Beside it, Shepherd finished talking with a CSU investigator then walked over to his team.

'From the trajectory, the team upstairs think the shot came from that building there,' he said, pointing at what looked like an apartment building about eighty yards from the club. 'CSU and detectives are already over there clearing the place.'

'Any sign of a rifle, sir?' Marquez asked.

Shepherd shook his head. 'Nothing.' He looked over at Sway, who was glowering in the back of the Ford. 'Has he talked?'

'Yeah. He's claiming that he was uptown at the time of the shooting.'

'Whereabouts?'

'A Starbucks.'

'You got the specific one?'

'Yes, sir,' Josh said. 'It's opposite Port Authority.'

'Anything in his pockets?'

'No vial if that's what you mean.'

'OK. You and Arch head up there. Ask the serving staff. If they have CCTV, check it. We'll know within twenty minutes if he's lying or not.'

The two men nodded and walked off. Heading towards their car, Josh turned to Archer.

'I'm driving.'

*

Parking around Midtown New York was always a nightmare and never more so than at Christmas. However, being NYPD had certain advantages and that night it meant that Josh and Archer could pull up to the kerb right outside the coffee shop. Archer felt the icy wind the moment he got out of the car and was glad that he'd grabbed his coat before they headed off. This was three or four layer weather and he'd lost his hoodie using it as a tourniquet on the girl's leg. He headed straight for the entrance with Josh.

Given that they were in plainclothes and their side-arms were mostly concealed, the barista behind the counter didn't immediately realise they were NYPD. It was much warmer in here and the two detectives relished the change in temperature as they stepped up to the counter. A young blond girl dressed in the standard green apron and black hat was waiting for them by the till.

'Good evening. What can I get you?' she asked with a smile.

It faded slightly when she saw Archer's busted nose.

Josh showed his badge. 'We're with the NYPD. We have some questions.'

Further along the counter, a woman in a white shirt had seen them arrive. She overheard Josh and walked over to join them.

'What's going on, Kelly?' she asked.

'You the manager?' Archer asked.

She nodded cautiously.

'Relax,' he said. 'You're not in any trouble. We're here about a customer who claimed he was here earlier.'

'A customer? What did he do?'

'Can't tell you that. But he's saying he was in here at 10pm. Were you on duty then?'

The woman nodded. 'I wasn't on counter though. That was Jay. You just caught him. He's out back getting changed.'

She turned to the barista.

'Go grab him, Kelly.'

Kelly nodded and walked down the counter, disappearing out of sight.

'What does this guy look like?' the manager asked.

Josh pulled a piece of paper from his pocket. On the page were four prison mug shots of Sway, Rourke, Wicks and Drexler. Each member of the team had taken a printout of the four suspects before they left the Bureau earlier. Josh folded it so only Sway's shot was visible, then passed it over. The woman took it in her hands and examined it closely.

'Recognise him?'

She frowned, then shook her head.

'Afraid not. He's definitely not a regular. Jay'll be the one who can help you.'

Down the counter the guy called Jay appeared, a tall black guy who looked like a college student. He'd changed out of his uniform, wearing jeans and a brown leather coat. He walked towards them and Archer showed him his badge.

'What's going on?'

'Sir, we need to ask you a few questions concerning a customer who was in here almost an hour ago.'

'OK.'

The manager passed Jay the sheet and pointed at Sway. 'Do you recognise him?'

Jay looked down. He nodded straight away.

'Yeah. I do. That guy was in here.'

Archer glanced at Josh. 'You're sure?'

'Yeah. He had a real strong accent. Sounded like a Southern boy.' He looked up over his shoulder, and pointed at a camera mounted on the wall facing the counter. 'He had the camera in his face too. Check the tapes.'

'I think we need to,' Josh said.

The manager nodded, and stepped away from the counter.

'Follow me.'

Five minutes later, Archer walked out from the security room and pulled his cell phone. The call connected to Marquez downtown.

'It's Archer. You're not going to believe this. Our boy is telling the truth.'

'What?'

'We've a sworn witness who says he was in here the same time as the shooting. He's also on the CCTV. I just watched the tape. It's him. He even looks up at the menu-board and you can clearly see his face.'

'Shit.'

'We matched the time. He was here at the exact same moment that Jacobs went down. His story checks out.'

'But we need to take him back to the Bureau, right?'

'We don't have anything to charge him with. We don't have any proof that he has the virus or knows where it is. He's got nothing incriminating on him.'

He paused.

'We have to let him go.'

'OK, I'll tell Shepherd. He's going to be pissed.'

Archer ended the call, then looked back as Josh joined him.

'Damn it. I thought we had him.'

'Me too.'

'Shit.'

'So now what?'

Archer checked his watch. 'The club situation is being handled. Jacobs is dead. Sway's off the hook. No sign of Rourke anywhere. I guess we wait on orders from Shepherd or pray that the virus shows up at the campsite.'

Josh nodded. He glanced at the barista and manager who were just stepping out from the tape room.

'You guys still serving?'

THIRTY FOUR

A couple of minutes later, the two detectives were sitting across from each other at a table on the second floor in the coffee shop. Despite the lateness of the hour there were still some people scattered around, most of them engaged in either quiet conversation or tapping away on netbooks. Archer knew most of these places shut at 10pm, but given the winter season they must have pushed it back by an hour or so to capitalise on the extra business. He and Josh had both ordered a drink and a quick bite. They'd been on the go all day, no time to grab anything to eat, and the old army adage held water. Whenever there's a break in battle eat something. You never know when you'll get the chance again.

'I still don't believe this,' Josh said, biting into a Danish and wiping some icing from the corner of his mouth. 'That was one nasty son of a bitch. I thought he was a slam dunk.'

Archer shrugged, taking a bite from an oatmeal cookie. 'His alibi checked out. Nothing we can do.'

'And now Jacobs is dead. You catch the way Sway was getting at Marquez? Racist asshole.'

'Our profile of him as the shooter was purely based on Peterson's assumptions. Hendricks called in and said there're about thirty of them on that estate and they're coming and going all the time. Any one of them could have pulled the trigger. Until we find a murder weapon or a witness, this is all just a guessing game.'

'So why don't we bring them all in?'

'Two reasons. ATF has jurisdiction. We move when they say we move. Catching Jacobs' killer isn't the priority here. The virus is. And also, no one has any idea where Rourke is. We can't arrest him if we can't find him. And if we arrest his entire gang, he might disappear for good.'

'But you heard the call Jacobs took at the Bureau. We just heard Sway talk. They had the same accent.'

'He had *an* accent. And he didn't mention the virus during the call. It's all hearsay. It would never hold up.'

Josh considered this, looking down at his cup of coffee. 'Shit, you're right.'

Pause.

'But that son of a bitch knows something.'

'But he also now knows we're onto him. If he's got half a brain cell, he'll leave town immediately with the rest of his crew.'

'That's going to screw up ATF's operation.'

'Or it might help it.'

'How?'

'Sway's not going to hang around. He knows we're breathing down his neck. And any man who's under pressure and in a rush is much more likely to make a mistake.'

Josh's phone rang. He was mid-mouthful of Danish, but grabbed the phone and answered it.

Pause.

'Yeah, I'm with Arch,' he said. 'We're still at the coffee shop.' As he spoke, Archer put the remaining piece of cookie in his mouth, then picked up his tea and leaned back, considering the situation.

Josh was right. Sway was a home run. He ticked all the boxes, fit the profile perfectly. It was clear from his dismissive attitude towards Josh and Marquez that he had no time for anyone not white Caucasian. But he was here at the time of the shooting. It was on camera and an eye witness backed it up. It was a rock-solid alibi. He couldn't have fired the rifle. Which meant somewhere, they'd missed something. They needed to go back and reconsider the evidence. Adjust their train of thought.

There was an answer here.

They just had to find it.

Josh ended the call. 'That was Marquez. They let Sway go. CSU are still trying to pinpoint exactly where the bullet came from. No one saw a muzzle flash and no one heard the shot.'

'The rifle must have had a silencer.'

Josh finished his Danish and wiped his mouth with a napkin. 'So what now?'

'We forget about Jacobs and pray that we get a lead at the campsite.'

Silence followed. The Starbucks had music playing; considering the hectic day they'd had so far the normality of the atmosphere was welcome. A moment of calm in the eye of a storm. Archer looked around at the other customers. They had no idea what was going on right now and the potential danger they were all in. He thought back to this morning. Seeing Katic off for the last time. It didn't even feel like the same day. He ran through everything that had happened since watching her taxi leave. The initial briefing. The ride into Manhattan. Peter Flood's suicide. Macy's. The Seaport. The house. Kyle Gunnar. Tonic. He reached up and felt his nose gently. It was sore as hell.

'She got you good,' Josh said, watching him. 'You and Kruger look like twins.'

Archer shot him a look and he thought back to the fight in the club. 'Thanks for your help by the way. I thought they had me.'

'No problem. Hell of a day, right?'

'Yeah. Thank God we've got Shepherd back.'

There was a pause. Archer thought for a moment.

'What?' Josh asked.

'Can I ask you something?'

'Shoot.'

'Why did Shepherd take time off?'

Josh's expression changed. He looked across the table at Archer, instantly serious.

'You think I know?'

'You and him go back a long way.'

Josh watched Archer closely. A long moment followed. Then he nodded.

'This stays here. Understand?'

'Of course.'

'At the end of October, Shepherd was asleep in bed with his wife, middle of the night. Something woke him up. He heard a noise from downstairs. He was burgled at the beginning of the year so he thought they'd come back for another slice. He pulled his nine and crept out. None of the lights were on in the house. He went downstairs and saw a figure dressed in black, holding a gun. Shepherd shot him twice in the chest. Killed him on the spot.'

Josh looked down.

'Turned out the guy was his son.'

Archer's mouth opened. *'What?'*

'He'd snuck out to go see his girl. The gun in his hand was one of his brother's toys that the kid had left on the rug. He'd picked it up off the floor to put it away and then Shepherd had appeared and put two in his chest. He was only eighteen.'

'Jesus Christ. Shepherd killed his own son?'

'That's why he took the time off. That's why he hasn't been the same since he got back.'

Archer's mouth was open in shock. He couldn't believe it.

'How's his wife?'

'She hasn't spoken to him for weeks. She kicked him out of the house. He's been staying with Hendricks.'

'Shit.'

'Yeah,' Josh said. 'Hell of a thing. Man tries to defend his home, ends up killing his own boy.'

With that the conversation ceased, Archer still shocked at the revelation. Both men sat there in silence.

Then Josh shot his cuff and checked his watch. 'We should get back downtown.'

'OK. I'll be a few minutes behind.'

'Where you going?'

'We need a lead. Something more than the campsite.'

'So where else are you gonna find one?'

'We never checked out Flood Microbiology, did we?'

Josh thought for a moment. 'No. We didn't.'

'I want to take another look around the lab. See if there's anything we missed.'

Josh nodded and drained his coffee. 'Want me to give you a lift?'

Archer shook his head.

'I'll walk. Need to clear my head anyway.'

'Hey! Look who it is!'

Peterson grinned as he walked onto the industrial estate, a taxi behind him pulling away and speeding off into the night. A bonfire was going in the centre of the area, thrash metal coming out of some speakers, bottles of liquor and cans of beer being passed around. Three of the guys walked towards him, shaking his hand one by one. The man in the middle was one of his two companions from the bar in Hoboken.

'You crazy son of a bitch,' he said. 'How the hell did you get them to let you out?'

'My girl posted bail,' Peterson said, with a grin. 'Arraignment is in a month.'

The trio laughed, two of them patting him on the back.

'C'mon, dumbass. Let's get you a beer.'

Peterson walked off with the trio towards the main campsite. Behind the bonfire, the doors to one of the meth caravans opened. A big bearded guy stepped out; he pulled down his mask, then grabbed a can of Bud and took a swig.

'Idiots,' the man beside Peterson said. 'Cooking product next to our campfire. *Hey!*'

The big guy looked over at him.

'You want to take that shit somewhere else?'

The cooker gave him the finger and drank some more beer. During this exchange, Peterson glanced over his shoulder.

But all he saw were old abandoned buildings and dark forestry beyond.

'You hearing this, OK, Sergeant?' came Faison's voice quietly over the radio.

Sixty yards from the main campsite, hidden in the shadows of the hedge-growth with the members of his team, Hendricks scooped up his radio and answered.

'Copy that,' he said quietly. 'Loud and clear.'

Peterson was wearing a small, imperceptible sticky mic tucked away under his collar. From now on they could hear every word he was saying down there. One of Shepherd's people had just contacted them to report that the British lawyer had been shot dead at the nightclub before the trade took place. Someone took him out with a rifle. They'd arrested Finn Sway who'd been found near the scene but his alibi had checked out and they'd released him. Shep had wanted to keep him in custody regardless but given that this was an ATF operation, Faison ultimately called the shots. He'd requested that they let Sway go. And so he had.

Hendricks had agreed with that decision. He knew people like Sway. Even if he didn't kill Jacobs himself, he would've been implicated. And he was involved with this last vial of the virus somehow. Hendricks had heard the briefing and it all made sense.

Looking down at the camp, his eyes narrowed in anticipation. Now, Sway would be twitched knowing the NYPD was up his ass.

All they had to do now was sit back and wait for him and his crew to make a mistake.

THIRTY FIVE

It was too cold for Archer to walk all the way up to the lab on 66th. Besides, he couldn't take too long or Shepherd would be pissed. He managed about four blocks, then threw in the towel and hailed a cab.

The journey took a couple of minutes. As the taxi pulled up outside the lab building on Amsterdam, Archer saw a lone figure sitting outside on a bench, wrapped up in a dark coat.

Maddy Flood.

She was sitting not ten feet from where her father had died. The point of impact on the sidewalk in front of her had been cleaned up and the team who were here earlier were long gone, all traces of the suicide removed. Archer paid the fare, then stepped out of the cab and shut the door, and the vehicle headed off uptown.

He walked slowly towards her, well aware of the hostility she'd been directing his way all day. He stopped six feet away from her, his hands buried deep in the pockets of his coat.

'I thought you were meant to have a detective with you?' he said.

'He went to get us some food and I left. I wanted to be alone.'

'Are you OK?'

She looked at him, then sniffed. 'What happened to your nose?'

'Jacobs is dead.'

'What? How?'

'The meet at the club was a set-up. They killed him with a rifle.'

She thought about what he said, then looked back at him. 'What are you doing here?'

'I wanted to take a look around upstairs.'

He watched her closely. Her anger seemed to have softened a touch. He took a chance.

'Feel like showing me around?'

Across the street, a man watched the pair walk into the building. He pulled a cell phone from his pocket and dialled a number.

'It's me,' he said. 'I checked out the lab. It's clear. The bitch arrived a moment after I got out. She just went inside.'

'Alone?'

'Some asshole is with her. He just showed up. They're going up together. Young guy.'

'Is it rigged up?'

'It's been prepared. I used the bug and keypad like you showed me. When they go in the main lab, they'll die.'

'Good. Using what's left and what we don't need to get rid of her. I like it. Well done.'

'What about Kruger?'

'Wicks couldn't get to him. There were detectives in the corridor outside his apartment.'

'Is that a problem?'

'No. Won't be an issue. Get back across the water. I'll see you at Kearny.'

'Are you OK.'

'I'm fine. The pigs arrested me but my alibi checked out.' Pause. *'Nice work brother.'*

*

Flood Microbiology occupied the 17th and 18th floors in the building. Once the lift arrived on 17, Archer and Maddy stepped out and walked towards the entrance to the lab complex. Downstairs, the building security had changed to the night shift, but the guy behind the main desk had barely looked up from his newspaper as they walked in.

Up on the 17th floor, there was another reception desk but no one was manning it. Straight ahead was the entrance to the lab. The door and the walls were all made of transparent glass, which meant Archer could see inside. It was dark, lit only by faint green and red glows from equipment around the complex, but even in the poor light Archer could see that everything was clean, polished and sterilised. Maddy pulled a key card and swiped them in, pushing the door back.

'Let's go to Dad's office,' Maddy said, as Archer followed.

She led him all the way down the main corridor, then turned right. *Dr P Flood* was printed on a gold-coloured tag pinned to the door of a private room. It was already unlocked and she pushed it open. The office was of average size, containing a desk with a comfortable-looking chair behind it. Filing cabinets were standing against the wall to the right beside a series of clothing hooks for lab-coats. Books were stacked neatly on shelves on the wall to the left, medical journals and such, nothing Archer recognised. He moved to the right and pulled open the top drawer of one of the filing cabinets. Everything inside was labelled alphabetically.

'Did he have a file on the virus?'

'He did. But he destroyed it.'

'Paper shredder?'

'No. Burned. That's why he was up on the roof in the first place.'

He turned.

'When we arrived this morning, we saw that all but one of the vials were missing,' she explained. 'Then we got a call from one of your people saying that a man had been gassed and killed in Central Park. When they described how he died, Dad immediately put the two together and knew it had to be his virus.'

'What did he do?'

'He went into a frenzy and started destroying everything. Then I found him up on the roof, torching all his papers in a trash can. I turned my back for a moment and when I looked back he was standing on the edge of the building. Then you and your partner showed up.'

Archer nodded and slid the drawer of the cabinet shut. He moved around Peter Flood's desk and sat down in the swivel chair. The padded leather gave a slight wheeze as it took his weight, the air decompressing. It was comfy. The desktop was sparse, save for a computer screen and a picture frame to the right. It was a shot of Peter with Maddy on what had to be her graduation day. Dressed in a black gown, a mortar-board on her head, she was holding a scroll. Her father had his arm around her and they were both smiling proudly at the camera.

'Yale,' she said. 'Five years ago.'

Archer's mind flashed back to the expression on Peter's face up on the roof. The fear. The red-rimmed, tired eyes behind those thick glasses.

Thousands of people are going to die.

He looked up at her. 'I'm sorry about what happened. I mean it.'

'I know.'

Turning his attention to the computer, Archer grabbed the mouse and gave it a light swivel. The screen flicked into life. No password required. He clicked on Firefox, then went to *Browsing History*.

It was empty.

'Did he have an email account?'

She nodded and moved around the desk. 'He used the company one. He wasn't particularly good with computers.'

Leaning over him, she hit a few keys and the company logo came up beside a username and password box. She tapped the keys again and after hitting *Enter* the screen changed to Flood's inbox. As she concentrated on the screen, her hair tumbled forward and Archer caught her perfume. He focused on the screen.

Empty.

'Shit,' Archer said. 'He deleted everything.'

'No. There is something. I realised it this morning. Everyone kind of hurried past it.'

'What is it?'

'In his hurry, Dad went to destroy everything. Old files, emails, notes, messages on his phone. He took all the information in his head with him. But in his hurry, he forgot the most important thing of all.'

She looked down at him.

'Do you want to see it?'

'See what?'

'The virus.'

Archer looked at her for a moment, then rose and nodded. They walked around the desk and headed back outside into the corridor.

'He forgot to destroy the last vial?'

'He wasn't thinking clearly. And it was locked away in the freezer. It must have slipped his mind.'

She led them down the corridor, then arrived at a keypad facing what had to be the main lab. The first door led into a small cubicle. There was an ultraviolet glow inside. Maddy saw him looking up at the lighting.

'Helps show any traces of bacteria on our suits,' Maddy said. 'The shower and air-system take care of most of it, but we need to be sure.'

'Do we need to suit up?'

She shook her head. 'Don't worry. I took the vial out this morning, but locked it in a Class III cabinet. No one can get to it other than me. It's secure.'

She tapped in a quick six digit code and the glass door buzzed, sliding open.

Archer followed her inside. They were forced to stop as the first door closed, the two of them standing close together in the shower cubicle. Then the second one opened and they walked into the lab.

The door slid shut behind them.

The laboratory was rectangular. There were white worktops lining the walls, all sorts of equipment placed incrementally along them. Although the main lights were turned off, the lab was illuminated by a faint glow from some LED lights and the UV lighting in the decontamination shower. Straight ahead against the far wall there was a rectangular shaped freezer with a glass door. It was big, about the size of two refrigerators stacked side by side. Archer saw racks of test tubes and beakers inside containing different coloured fluids.

And just to the left of the freezer, he saw what had to be the virus.

He walked forward slowly beside Maddy and looked into a thick containment cabinet. It was octagonal, glass panels separated by thick strips of metal. There were several holes with long black rubber gloves leading into the glass case to allow the doctors to work on the materials inside.

Towards the back of the airtight case was a rack with six slots.

Five of them were empty.

In the centre of the rack rested the last remaining vial.

'Bleeker stole every one he could see,' she said. 'The only reason he missed this one was because I'd stored it in the freezer.'

Archer stared at the vial, like a moth drawn to a flame. It was about the size of a large shot glass. The liquid inside was muddy yellow, resting on the bottom of the glass like river silt giving off its own little caramel glow. It looked so inconsequential.

However, Archer thought back to the store by Pier 17, standing amongst the fifty nine infected dead, blood and pieces of lung tissue around them.

Looks could be deceiving.

'Tomorrow, I'll come in and destroy it for once and for all.'

Archer nodded, but cocked his head. 'What's with the receiver?'

'What receiver?'

He pointed. 'Behind the vial. Look.'

She turned and looked closer.

There was a little electrical bug clipped to the back of the cabinet. It was about the size of a small pencil sharpener.

She frowned. 'That shouldn't be there.'

Archer's eyes widened.

He grabbed Maddy's shoulder.

'Step back,' he said, sharply.

Confused by his change in tone, she moved away from the cabinet. Archer stared at the bug. It looked like a receiver. *But for what?* He examined the cabinet, then lowered his gaze to the cupboard under the worktop. He dropped to his knees, facing the drawers.

He took the handles and pulled them open.

There was a timer inside, red numbers this time. They were counting down.

0:54.

0:53.

'What the hell?' Maddy said.

Archer rose, moving back. 'Is this room secure?'

She nodded quickly, staring at the timer. 'Yes, it's airtight.'

'We need to get out of here right now and lock it down.'

Maddy didn't need to be told. She was already making for the door. Archer turned and followed her. She pushed in her code on her keypad.

But a red light buzzed above it.

It wouldn't open.

'What? This should work!' she said, incredulous, frantically trying again.

Buzz.

Red light.

'Someone's locked us in,' Archer said. He turned, and saw a camera mounted in the corner of the room. 'Try and get the guard's attention on the camera.'

As she ran over and waved her hands frantically, mouthing *Help*, Archer looked back at the timer.

0:42.

0:41.

'Wait!' Maddy said. 'There are bio-suits in here. We'll be safe.' She turned from the camera and ran across the room, pulling open a locker.

But there was nothing there. The rail was empty.

'Someone's taken them!' she shouted. 'They should be right here!'

Together, they looked back at the clock-face.

'Oh my God!'

0:37.

0:36.

0:35.

'Archer, what are we going to do?'

He didn't reply, looking around the lab.

Think, man. Think.

He moved back over towards the device, examining it. It was at *00:29.*

'Quick, defuse it!' she said.

'I'm not a bomb tech!' he said. 'I can't touch it. It might go off.' He turned and grabbed a chair, running over to the glass wall. 'We'll have to smash our way out and run for it.'

He hammered the chair into the glass, but it just bounced off. He kept trying, but the glass was reinforced. There was no way he was breaking it.

Dropping the chair, he pulled his pistol and fired three times, but all it did was leave three white dented splodges on the glass.

It wasn't breaking.

'Shit!'

He turned and looked around as Maddy ran back to the timer.

'Twenty seconds!' she screamed. 'Oh my God, we're going to die!'

Across the room, Archer looked around frantically.

Think!

Think!

'Archer, what do we do?'

Scanning the room, his heart racing, he looked for a solution.

And suddenly, he had an idea.

He ran forward to the cryogenics freezer, ripping the doors open. He started pulling all the beakers and racks of test tubes off the shelves, placing them quickly on the desk top. He didn't know if the gases inside were flammable or toxic, but took them out as quickly and carefully as he could.

'Ten seconds!' she screamed.

He ripped out all three shelves, throwing them out of the way.

They clattered to the floor across the room.

'Five seconds!' she screamed, unable to tear her eyes off the countdown. *'We're going to die!'*

Archer ran to his left and grabbed her. He tore open the door to the freezer and dragged her inside with him, then pulled the door shut.

It closed and the plastic seal formed.

Then the bomb detonated.

Archer and Maddy saw the vial and cabinet shatter from the bug clipped to the back. The destroyed glass showered to the worktop and floor and the yellow virus started to seep out.

It slowly drifted out into the room, giving the air a toxic golden tinge.

Panting, Archer and Maddy stared at it, protected behind the glass and watching the evil miasma spread into the lab.

THIRTY SIX

The sealed door had saved them from the virus but now they were trapped. Inside the freezer, it was unbelievably cold. It was designed to hold and preserve chemical liquids, not living human bodies. The adrenaline was starting to pass, their heartbeats slowing and both Archer and Maddy's bodies were starting to react to the freezing temperature.

They were shivering hard. They'd pulled their collars up, folded their arms and closed their fists, trying to preserve any warmth their bodies created and protect their fingers from frostbite. But the cold was unremitting. It made the temperature out on the street seem almost tropical.

Archer pulled his cell phone, taking utmost care not to nudge the door and break the seal, the only thing protecting them from the virus. Beside him, Maddy looked out of the glass door into the lab.

'Anything?' she asked.

He cursed. 'Nothing. There's no signal.' He moved the phone around the freezer as much as he could, taking care not to hit the door and keeping his eyes on the display. No bars. No service. *'Shit.'*

He tucked the phone back into his pocket and wrapped himself up, trying to retain his body heat.

'So what now?' Maddy asked.

'We wait until someone finds us.'

'How long could that take?'

Archer didn't respond. He was looking through the glass at the toxic yellow air.

'Someone set this up.'

'How did they know we'd be in here?'

'The receiver was a bug. I've seen them before. When you entered the code on the keypad to get in, it set off the countdown. When it ended, the bug shattered the glass.'

'Who would do something like that?'

'I don't know. But they wanted to kill whoever came in here next. That's why they took the suits.'

He looked at her beside him.

'All the documents are gone. The computer's been wiped. Your father and Dr Tibbs are dead. Dr Glover is missing. They were about to kill Dr Kruger before we showed up.'

'They're killing anyone who knew about the virus,' Maddy finished.

Archer nodded. 'It must have been one of Rourke and Sway's people. They knew only you and Kruger have access to the lab. They figured both or either one of you would be the next people to come in here.'

Maddy didn't reply. Shivering, Archer lifted his arm carefully over her.

He felt her tense.

'Relax. I'm not making a move. We need body heat.'

He felt her stay rigid for a moment. Then she slowly relaxed and leaned into him, the two of them shivering together.

Waiting.

Downtown, the rest of the detail was still gathered outside Tonic East. The CSU had been able to work out from the trajectory of the bullet that the shot had come from a newly opened apartment building south and west of the bar on

Lexington Avenue. They were over there now, trying to find the exact window from where the shot had been fired, but the rifleman had thought of everything. He hadn't left any evidence behind, certainly not a cartridge or a rifle, and nobody inside the building had seen anyone suspicious. There was a chance that he was still hiding out somewhere inside so ESU were working their way up each floor, clearing each apartment which was slow, painstaking and disruptive work.

Sway had been released, much to Shepherd's annoyance. He'd wanted to keep him in custody but Faison was calling the shots and told Shepherd that he needed to let him go. He'd said that Sway could lead them to Rourke but Shepherd wasn't convinced. The man now knew for a fact that the NYPD had been tailing him. Catching him with the virus now was going to take some work. Furious, Shepherd had watched Sway walking away, his handcuffs taken off and a smirk on his face. He'd willed him to hail a cab in front of him so he could catch the plates but Sway had walked around the corner and disappeared out of sight.

Standing with Jorgensen and Josh, Shepherd shook his head at the memory. Things were not going well. Marquez approached the three men, tucking her cell phone back into her pocket.

'The three boys who jumped Archer are on their way to the station.'

'Are they saying anything?' Josh asked.

'Not a word. But at least that's three of them off the street tonight.'

'Peterson's back under at the camp,' Shepherd told them. 'Hendricks and Faison are in place. We're heading over there to join them.'

'What about the shooter?' Jorgensen asked, nodding at the apartment building where the shot had come from.

'The virus is our concern. CSU and ESU will handle this.' Shepherd paused, then looked around. 'Wait a minute. Where the hell is Archer?'

'He went back up to Flood Microbiology, sir,' Josh said. 'He wanted to take a quick look around.'

Shepherd checked his watch. 'We're going to the campsite now. That's our next best lead. Marquez and Jorgensen, you'll ride with me. Josh, go pick him up, then follow us.'

The team nodded, separating, and Josh pulled his cell phone. He dialled Archer's number.

But he couldn't get through.

At that moment Sway was crossing the Hudson River in a taxi, headed for *Kearny Medical* in New Jersey where Bobby would be packing up the canisters. They needed to get out of the State. The pigs had been onto him in a flash and although they couldn't pin the shooting on him, they weren't as dumb as they looked.

It was only a matter of time before one of them caught on and realised what had happened.

*

Inside the freezer, Archer and Maddy had slumped down in the cabinet. He had his arm around her, her head in his shoulder, both of them trembling hard from the cold as icy air continued to blast relentlessly into the cabinet. It was well below freezing and it was starting to take its toll.

'I'm so cold,' she whispered slowly, shaking. Archer rubbed her arm slowly with his right hand, trying to generate some warmth as best he could.

'Someone will find us. Just hang on.'

Silence.

They both looked outside. The laboratory air still had that yellow haze, laden with the virus.

'Thank you,' she said quietly, trembling.

'For what.'

'For saving my life. For a while, anyway.'

Pause. Each moment of conversation was followed by longer moments of silence.

'Dad said we were going to die. He was right.'

'We're not going to die. Someone will find us.'

'Who?'

'Someone.'

Pause.

She nestled her head into his chest, mist coming out every time they both exhaled.

Archer didn't tell her, but he was worried.

Downtown, still outside Tonic East, Josh withdrew his phone from his ear and looked down at the screen, confused. Just as she was climbing into a car with Jorgensen and Shepherd, Marquez noticed Josh's hesitation and paused. She stepped out, slamming the door and turned to Shepherd, who was firing the engine.

'I'll ride with Josh.'

Shepherd nodded, pulling off the handbrake and the Ford moved off. Marquez walked over to Josh, who was trying to make the call again.

'Everything OK?'

'I can't get through to Archer.'

Marquez noticed the tone in his voice.

'I'll drive,' she said.

THIRTY SEVEN

All conversation in the freezer had stopped. Maddy was huddled in under Archer's arm, wrapped up in the folds of her coat. All their movements had slowed, the cold making them sleepy. Archer was feeling warmer which he knew was a bad sign. It didn't matter that they'd cheated the virus. If they didn't get help, they would both be dead in fifteen minutes.

Suddenly Maddy spoke.

'I'm sorry.'

'For what?'

'For being...so hostile to you today.'

Pause.

'I just...'

She paused again. The cold was fragmenting her sentences. Talking was becoming harder and harder.

'He died...And I wanted it to be...someone's fault...other than his.'

Silence.

'And I never...got a chance...to say...goodbye.'

Pause.

'He must have been...so scared.'

Every time she exhaled, her breath turned to mist as the temperature condensed the water vapour.

Archer didn't reply.

He just hugged her close, both of them shaking.

A long moment of silence followed.

'Tell me...about you.'

He looked down at her. *'What...do you want...to know?'*

'Anything. Tell me about your family....Do you have...any... brothers or sisters?'

'A sister.'

'What's her name?'

'Sarah.'

'What about...your parents?'

'They're gone.'

Silence.

'How?'

'My mother had cancer. My father was...murdered.'

Pause.

'I didn't get to...say goodbye either.'

Silence.

Frost had gathered on the edges of their clothing and in their hair. There was a rustle as Maddy tilted her head, looking up at him. He met her gaze.

She was pale.

'I just...realised something.'

'What?'

'I don't even know your name.'

He forced a smile. *'Archer.'*

'No...I mean...your first name.'

He looked down at her. Her lips were looking blue.

'Sam... it's Sam.'

He felt her move into him slightly closer. He felt warm, and sleepy.

Talk, idiot.

Stay awake.

If you fall asleep, you won't wake up again.

'Hold on,' Archer whispered. *'Won't...be long now.'*

They sat there in silence.

Shivering.

Waiting.

*

Having pulled up outside the building, Josh and Marquez moved into the lobby seventeen floors below. The night security guy was at his desk, engrossed in a *New York Post*. The guy flicked his eyes up from the rear pages then looked back down.

'What floor is Flood Microbiology?'

'17 and 18,' he said, not looking up from the paper. 'You got an appointment?'

Annoyed by his attitude, Marquez pulled her badge and showed it. 'We don't need one.'

That got his attention. He snapped up in his seat, putting the paper away. 'I'll buzz you in.'

'Thank you.'

Inside the freezer, Archer's eyes were just about to close when he saw movement the other side of the lab in the main corridor.

It looked like Josh and Marquez.

Both figures were staring at him, pressed up against the glass, Marquez with her phone to her ear. Josh was up close to the glass, shouting something, but Archer couldn't make out what he was saying.

Shit, I'm dreaming, he thought.

It can't be them

They're downtown.

Under his arm, Maddy had gone quiet and still. She wasn't shivering any more.

I'm dying, he thought.

No, you're not. Keep your eyes open.

I'm about to die in a damn deep freezer.

I'll just close my eyes.

Just for a second.

THIRTY EIGHT

Sergeant Jake Hendricks was a thirteen-year man within the NYPD who took great pride in two things in his life. He had never taken a shortcut. And his five-man team were renowned as one of the toughest groups inside the entire Police Department.

His fierce hatred for any illegal activity stemmed from when he was a kid. He'd been walking home from the movies with his father on Halloween night when they were set upon by a gang on some sort of initiation. They'd kicked the absolute shit of his dad right in front of Jake, who'd watched on helplessly. His father had been hospitalised for the next six weeks, half of it in a coma. Every boy thinks his father is indestructible but that illusion had been stamped and trampled out of Jake by the gang that night. Sitting beside the hospital bed, watching his father lying there unconscious, the younger Hendricks had felt rage boiling inside him at the injustice of it all. And in the nineteen years since, he had never forgotten what had happened that night. It had been the impetus for him becoming a cop.

Criminals and gang-members often thought they had the upper hand when it came to the police because cops had to follow rules and they didn't. Some of them saw it as a game; Hendricks viewed it as warfare. If you dealt drugs to kids Hendricks would see to it that you'd be sucking your food through a straw for the next six months. You had girls working corners for you, he'd send them away and then send you to the Emergency Room. His ruthless reputation definitely preceded him, both in the Department and on the street. It had landed him in hot water a number of times, his superiors nervous of the legal ramifications or consequences of such ruthless justice. But deep down, Hendricks knew they all secretly supported him. He just had the balls to do what most others wanted to do.

He hadn't applied to join the Counter-Terrorism Bureau. He'd been approached. Lieutenant General Franklin had called him in for a meeting at the beginning of the year and offered him his own hand-picked team. Franklin was old school and had policed New York when it was a far more dangerous place to live. He admired and respected Hendricks, especially in the no-nonsense way he tackled the streets. He'd operated the same way himself back in the day. Hendricks had thought long and hard then accepted the offer, taking four of the best people from his team at the 75th with him, and they'd set up shop across the River in Queens. One of Hendricks' informants told him later that once word spread through Brooklyn that he was moving on, a party had almost started.

Hendricks had been a cop for fifteen years and he'd been friends with Matt Shepherd for just as long. They'd started out as partners in their early twenties fresh out of training, riding a squad car together. Their families had shared many Thanksgivings and holidays and Hendricks considered Shepherd to be one of his closest friends. Knowing what had happened to Shep recently, Hendricks had been keen to help him out any way he could. Hendricks was a father too; he had two kids, a boy and a girl. He couldn't begin to comprehend the pain that Shep and his wife were going through. It was an accident that could just as easily have happened to Hendricks himself. So if staking out and taking out this skinhead cesspit was what Shep needed, than that's exactly what Hendricks and his detail would do.

He looked down through his binoculars at the gathering below. He and his team were hidden behind several boulders to the west on a slight elevation. He'd counted twenty three Chapter members down there, including the ATF man Peterson. They were all in the centre of the compound, long abandoned buildings behind them. It was a frosty night and the neo-Nazis had built a large fire in the middle of the concrete, burning anything they could find. Their cars and motorbikes had been parked around and behind them, forming a second layer to the circle. Someone had heavy metal music going, bottles of whiskey being passed around and a ragged circle of the thugs had formed around the campfire. Hendricks also saw many of them were carrying weapons. Not pea-shooters either. He'd counted six sawn-off shotguns, two M16s and a handful of what looked like modified Glock pistols.

That could be a problem.

Straight ahead behind the group were three caravans, Chapter members in protective gear ducking in and out, removing masks and sucking in breaths of fresh air. None of their activity had anything to do with the virus however.

These idiots were cooking meth.

Hendricks had encountered production of the drug like this before. They were called rolling meth labs. Handlers liked to use wheeled labs for a number of reasons. Firstly, they could be easily moved to a secluded location to unpack the crystals that had coagulated on the equipment inside. Also, the cooking process released strong toxic fumes that were easily noticeable in a residential area, so putting the lab on the road was a way of avoiding detection. And once the process was finished and the crystallised meth scraped up and bagged, all the toxic shit that was left could be dumped by the roadside or on abandoned ground like this. The interior of the caravans would be coated with a highly poisonous residue, endangering anyone who passed by within a certain radius. He knew that these assholes would leave the caravans here once they moved on, someone else's problem to deal with.

Not tonight, he thought.

Hendricks watched as a man stepped out of the middle caravan, closing the door behind him. He pulled off his protective face mask, revealing a severe face and a beard. The process of cooking the drug was also extremely dangerous. The chemicals used to cultivate the methamphetamine were poisonous, unstable and flammable and propane was required for the process. Consequently there was a substantial red tank of the stuff beside each caravan. Given the mixing of certain liquids that went on inside these vans, the possibility of an explosion was high. It could happen at any moment.

Pulling his cell and keeping the display hidden behind the rock, Hendricks scrolled through his phone book and found the number for HAZMAT. There needed to be a clean-up crew on stand-by. Virus or no virus, Hendricks didn't want his people going anywhere near the meth trucks before they were secured.

He pushed the call button and put the phone to his ear, looking down on the estate through his binoculars and feeling his anger rise.

Archer opened his eyes.

He was lying down. He realised he wasn't in the freezer anymore. His joints felt sore, but he didn't feel cold. He felt warm.

Am I dead?

He was lying on his back, looking up at a white ceiling. He was warm. Very warm. He realised he was wrapped in what felt like three thick blankets. He grunted and sat up. He wasn't dead. He was in an ambulance, outside on street level. The back doors were open to the sidewalk, and he could see police and HAZMAT teams outside on Amsterdam, the lights on their vehicles flashing in the night.

Amongst the crowd, he saw Josh. His partner saw him sit up and ran over.

'How are you feeling?' he asked, arriving by the ambulance.

'Like a popsicle,' he said, rubbing his chest. 'Did you secure the room?'

'CRT are up there now. They quarantined the entire building. They had to stabilise the lab and purify the air before they pulled you out. You guys got seriously lucky. It was close. A few minutes more and you'd be dead.'

Archer nodded. He had a pounding headache. 'Where's the doc?'

Josh pointed and Archer saw Maddy wrapped up in thick blankets in a second ambulance ten yards away. It seemed she'd woken up before he had. She was talking with a medic standing in front of her. She sensed him make eye contact and looked over.

For the first time since they'd met she smiled at him.

He smiled back.

'What the hell happened?' Josh asked.

Archer rubbed his head. 'We went into the lab. Someone had placed an electronic bug on the cabinet and taken the bio suits. We triggered the countdown when Maddy entered the keypad code and the doors locked behind us. If it wasn't for the freezer, we'd be dead.'

'Someone was trying to kill you.'

'Not me,' Archer said, nodding at Maddy. 'Her.'

Josh went to speak, but spotted Shepherd walk out of the building. He saw them at the ambulance and walked over swiftly, arriving outside the doors.

'You're awake,' he said to Archer. 'Good. Are you OK?'

'Yes, sir.'

'I heard what happened.' He looked over his shoulder at Maddy. 'Someone wants her in a coffin.'

'Where's Dr Kruger sir?' Josh asked.

'I just called him. He's on his way down here. Until this is over, both he and the woman stay with us at all times.'

'Where's Marquez?'

'She's inside, talking with the guard who was manning the desk.'

Rubbing his chest, Archer was starting to feel better. The headache was beginning to pass. Swinging his legs off the bed, he struggled to his feet, shrugging off the blankets. Josh grabbed his shoulder as he swayed.

'Take your time,' he said.

'We don't have time.'

'Who came in this evening?' Marquez asked the reception security guard.

The man shrugged. 'Anyone who works here has a key-card. They can come and go as they please. Visitors have to sign in and out on the call-sheet. It's on this board.'

He passed her a clipboard and she scanned the page. The list was long.

'Busy for a Saturday.'

'Always is. Upstairs we've got legal firms, office space, multi-million-dollar corporations, real estate agencies, bio-chemistry labs. This is New York. Saturday night here is like Monday morning to the rest of the world.'

Archer, Josh and Shepherd had just arrived beside her. She turned and saw Archer was back on his feet. She gave him a quick smile then looked back at the desk guard.

'Any of them catch your eye?'

'Not really. Girl with a nice ass came in. That's about it.'

'Anyone come in for Flood Microbiology tonight?'

'No one who signed in.'

'And this is the only entrance into and out of the building?' Marquez asked.

'Yes ma'am.'

Archer, Marquez and Shepherd scrutinised the sign-in board. Josh thought for a moment, then pulled a piece of paper from his pocket.

'This is a Hail Mary, but do you recognise any of these people?' he asked, unfolding it and showing the four mug shots to the man.

The guard's eyes suddenly widened.

'Wait. Yeah. Yeah, I do.'

The team stared at him. The guard grabbed the sheet and tapped it. 'I recognise this guy. He was in here tonight.'

He was pointing at Finn Sway's photograph.

'Are you sure?' Shepherd asked.

'Positive. We talked about football.'

The team scanned the check-in board but there was no Sway anywhere.

'He must have signed in?' Shepherd said.

The guard shook his head. 'He swiped his way in. Like I said, only way to do that is with a valid key card.'

'Did you see him leave?' Marquez asked.

The guard nodded. 'Yeah. He was only here for about ten minutes.'

'What time?'

The guard thought for a moment. 'Would have been 10:15 or so. The second half of the Giants game was going on.'

'Hang on,' Marquez said. 'You're imagining this. It's impossible.'

'No I'm not.'

Marquez shook her head, pointing at Sway's mug shot. 'This man couldn't have been here. We had him in handcuffs downtown at that time.'

The guard shook his head, adamantly. 'He was in this building, Detective. I'm positive.'

'Impossible.'

'No. You're both right,' Archer said.

'How?' Marquez asked. Then she thought for a moment and looked at Archer. 'Oh shit.'

'What?' Shepherd asked, confused. 'How could he be in two places at once?'

'Because there are two Sways, sir,' Archer said. 'Finn Sway has a brother.'

THIRTY NINE

At his girlfriend's place thirty one blocks downtown, Reese Sway had almost finished packing up his stuff. Or her stuff, to be exact. He was working fast but methodically, going for the most valuable things. Jewellery, money in her bedside drawer, a gold watch. Finn had promised that they would both be millionaires by the end of next week, but Reese had only made it this far by being good at what he did.

And anyway, a grifter stays a grifter, no matter how much money he has.

He and Finn were born three years apart. Before Reese was born, Finn and their parents lived in the middle of Roller, but half-way through her second pregnancy the boy's mother had found out that their dad was screwing other women in town. She'd packed her stuff, got in her car and driven away, leaving three- year old Finn behind with his cheating asshole of a father.

Reese had grown up moving from place to place, leap-frogging from town to town. Eventually his mother had all but given up, living in a trailer in North Carolina and spending her unemployment on alcohol and drugs. When he was fifteen he'd had enough; he packed his shit and left. Two months later, he'd called his grandma and found out that his mother had overdosed on Oxycontin and died.

The moment he'd left home, Reese had been forced to fend for himself. He bounced from homeless shelters to subways and bus stations. A few weeks after he'd first walked out he'd been sitting in a park in Charlotte in the middle of the afternoon, the same bench where'd he slept the previous night, hungry and tired. A nineteen year old blond girl called Christina had sat down beside him. They'd got talking, and he'd given her his story.

But rather than walk away, which he'd been expecting, the girl had been horrified at what had happened to him. She took Reese home and luckily for him, her parents were equally kind-hearted. They'd let him stay in their spare room, fed him and bought him some new clothes from the local store outlet. After countless nights sleeping rough on park benches and under bridges, he lay there between the soft sheets and suddenly realised he had something that other bums didn't have.

Women were attracted to him.

He'd humoured the family, sensing Christina had taken more than just a passing interest in him. That instinct was justified when she snuck into his room late at night about two weeks into his stay. But after a while the situation started to feel claustrophobic. Reese hadn't grown up in a family environment and he sure as hell didn't need one now. He didn't care about anyone but himself and after they'd taken him to church one Sunday he'd realised enough was enough. So, just under a month into his stay at the family's residence, he'd slid open the bedroom window and headed for the first train out of town.

But not before he'd cleaned the house out of as many valuables as he could carry.

And that's where his grifting began. Conning became a game, one he was very good at. And the better he got, the more money he made. Given his youth, people underestimated him. He'd lost count of how many women he'd ripped off using a variety of routines and set-ups. Often it was as easy as going home with a girl from a bar, then robbing her blind the moment she fell asleep. He'd always skip town before anyone realised what had happened or had a chance to call the cops.

However, something his mother had said just before he left home had always lingered at the back of his mind. He'd tried to ignore it, but it kept coming back. He knew piss-all about his father but one night, in a drunken, drug-induced haze, his mother told him that he had an elder brother.

Apparently the guy lived in a town called Roller, down in Texas towards the border with Mexico.

Eventually, two days after his twenty first birthday and with money in his pocket from a successful rip-off, Reese had made a decision. He'd booked a flight to San Antonio then taken a bus out to Roller, arriving just after 9pm. He'd dumped his bag at the only motel in town, then gone to the only bar for a beer. He was planning to have a few drinks, get his head down then ask around and find his brother the next day but the man he was there to find had walked in less than an hour after Reese, with some of his friends. Looking up from his Bud, Reese had done a double take. The guy was the spitting image of him. He'd stepped off his stool and walked over to him, apprehensive.

The man had seen Reese then done a double take himself. The two men spent a few seconds staring at each other. It was like looking in a mirror.

The night that followed was still the most enjoyable of Reese's young life. He'd been apprehensive on the journey down there, wondering if his brother would acknowledge him, whether he'd turn out to be an asshole or if he was even still here. But he needn't have worried; they'd spent the entire night getting drunk and catching up on twenty one years of history. It turned out their father was dead too. After he put all his money in a bad investment four years ago he'd drunk a bottle of Jack, put a shotgun in his mouth and eaten a shell. Finn had enjoyed hearing the tales about his brother's grifting, how he conned his way from place to place and ripped people off.

In return, Finn told him about his work. Six months ago he'd joined a local right-wing chapter called *The Stuttgart Soldiers*. He'd done six months upstate and had been cell mates with one of their members. *They aren't just Nazi dumbasses* Finn had said, seeing the look on his brother's face. This was a business and a civic responsibility, taking the fight to domestic enemies. Reese had assumed all they did was burn books and run non-whites out of town, but Finn told him how they took guns and dope back and forth across the borders. They patrolled the area in trucks, searching for immigrants and then removing them from the land, *taking back their country one wetback at a time*.

Interested, but too self-centred to be concerned with other people's issues, Reese had made the right noises then spent the rest of the night drinking whiskey and having a great time with Finn and his friends. They'd all welcomed him as family. More so than anyone else ever had.

Two days later, Reese had bid Finn farewell but had a new outlook on life. He had a brother, some family he actually cared about and who gave a shit about him in return. In the five years since that night he and Finn had stayed in constant touch. Victims of the young conman assumed that he only cared about one thing: himself. But that wasn't true. He'd do anything for his big brother.

Which is exactly what he'd done tonight.

Reese had been in New Jersey for the past three months, his meagre savings dwindling fast as he rented a motel room over in Elizabeth. He was working on a girl he'd met at a bar in Midtown who had a husband fighting the Taliban and who was bored and lonely. He'd put in some solid groundwork, eventually winning her over, but it had been a lot of effort.

Then a week ago he'd received a call from Finn.

He was coming to New York. Reese was surprised and delighted. He'd asked him why, but Finn wouldn't reveal anything over the phone. He said he'd tell him in person.

And he had. Earlier today he'd asked Reese to meet him at a lab complex in New Jersey. He'd ridden a taxi over there, then taken a few moments to shake hands with Finn's crew, Wicks and Drexler, two of the people he'd hung out with that night in Roller when he'd first met his big brother. Finn had then explained about the virus and what he and Bobby were planning to do with it.

However, he said there was a problem, which is why Reese was there.

Finn was due to meet with a so-called buyer later that night but had a feeling it was a set up.

However, he wasn't going to pass up the chance of getting his hands on $2 million. The plan was to stake the bar out, watching for any pigs who might be undercover. Finn would set up with a rifle nearby. If the bar was kosher, he had Drexler in the club. She'd approach the man, tell him to transfer the $2 mil via wire transfer then once payment was confirmed, pass over a fake vial. The guy would never know it wasn't the virus; he couldn't exactly open it and test it in the club. And if it was a trap, Finn would kill him. But given that he had eyes and ears on him everywhere, Finn needed a solid alibi. And that was where Reese came in.

Finn had asked him to go to a Starbucks at 10pm on the nose, buy a drink, make himself visible on camera, hang about for a few moments and then leave. Reese couldn't have been more willing to help. Anything that was a con or put one over the cops was his bread and butter. *What about our clothes?* Reese had asked. Finn said they'd stop at a retail store on the way to Manhattan and buy a matching set.

Once he was done at the coffee shop, Reese was told to go to some lab on 66th and Amsterdam. Apparently there was one last vial of the virus that had been missed which they didn't need anymore and a bitch doctor who needed to be got rid of. Drexler had offered to find her and take her out but Finn said she'd have cops guarding her. They couldn't waste time looking for her either. They'd been assured that the woman would be the next person to go inside the main lab, so Reese had entered the building and the lab using a key card Finn gave him. He'd headed upstairs and rigged up the virus with a bug and timer as instructed which would be activated once anyone entered the correct code into the keypad. It would kill the bitch and get rid of the last sample of the virus.

He'd taken the bio suits, dumping them in the trash, and left.

Now in the apartment, he checked his watch, then swept the contents of the girl's jewellery box into his bag. Finally, he checked around, making sure he had everything worth taking.

'What?'

'Jesus Christ,' Archer said, shaking his head, leaning back. 'How the hell did we miss this? We had the guy in handcuffs and we let him go.'

'Miss what?' Shepherd said.

'There are two Sways. They're brothers. That's their cover. That's how Finn Sway said he couldn't have planted that bomb at the club. That's how the guy at the coffee shop saw him at the exact same time and how this man says he was in here just afterwards. Sway was the shooter. His brother was at the Starbucks pretending to be him. Then he came here and rigged up the lab.'

The team looked at him and realised how they'd been duped.

'Jesus Christ,' Shepherd said.

'How was this not on the file?' Marquez asked.

'Roller only has a small-town local PD,' Archer said. 'You saw his jacket. He came from a broken home. He could have ten brothers and sisters for all we know.'

'We need to get them both before they leave the city,' Josh said.

Shepherd pulled his phone, pushing *Redial*.

'Rach?' he said. 'Listen. Pull up footage from outside Tonic around 2215. The East 29th Street camera will show Finn Sway. I want you to run clothing rec on him as fast as you can.'

He waited. A few moments later, Rach came back.

'Go on,' Shepherd said, listening closely. A few moments pause. Then he started for the door, ending the call. 'One of the two Sways entered an apartment building off 35th and 8th four minutes ago.'

The entire team ran out of the building and headed for their cars. Dr Kruger had just arrived, stepping out of a taxi, the detective assigned to protect him joining him on the sidewalk. Kruger had changed his clothes, the blood-stained blue shirt replaced by a sweater, brown jacket and fresh jeans. He paid the fare, then slammed the door. 'What's going on?'

'In the car, doc,' Shepherd said. 'You're coming with us.'

FORTY

Reese Sway had just completed a final sweep of the apartment when he heard a series of cars pull up on the street below. The soft squeal of tyres and sudden killing of engines were giveaways. He ran to the bedroom window and saw people piling out of black 4x4 vehicles and run into the building.

Panicking, he zipped up the bag of stolen valuables then ran into the den. The girl's husband kept a weapon in the apartment, a pistol hidden behind some books. He grabbed the gun and a loaded magazine beside it then slammed the clip into the weapon and racked the slide.

He ran to the door, rushing outside into the corridor. Below, he heard the lower door to the stairwell open and the sound of feet pounding up the stairs.

He was trapped.

Turning, he ran up the stairwell, taking the stairs two at a time.

Archer, Shepherd and Josh were taking the stairs, Marquez and Jorgensen the lift. They'd heard movement above them and the sound of someone running up the stairwell. The three men took off up the stairs, taking them two at a time, when they heard the sound of a door being smashed open several flights above them.

Josh was the first to arrive at the already open door. It was the entrance to the roof.

He pushed it back and immediately there was a gunshot. Josh was thumped back as several more shots thudded into the door where he'd been standing.

Archer and Shepherd ducked back to avoid being hit as the lift opened behind them, Marquez and Jorgensen running out. Drawing their side-arms, Marquez, Jorgensen and Shepherd moved forward to the doorway as Archer dropped to one knee, helping Josh to the ground. He'd taken the round in the upper arm.

Archer clamped his hands either side of the wound as Josh grimaced.

'*Shit,* ' he said through gritted teeth. 'This must feel like déjà vu for you.'

On the roof, the three cops took cover as Reese fired again, the gunshots echoing off the buildings all around them. He'd put one of them down. Keeping up the fire, he turned and ran towards the edge of the building. He stopped short and looked around, desperately looking for a way to escape. But the gap between this roof and the next was twenty feet. He couldn't make it. He was trapped.

'*Put your hands up!*' a voice bellowed.

Shepherd, Marquez and Jorgensen had him triangulated, three sights of three pistols trained on his head.

Sway had his back turned, looking out over the roof of the adjacent building.

'*Drop the weapon!*' Shepherd shouted. '*It's over, kid.*'

Sway suddenly spun around.

He had his pistol sweeping up, aiming for Marquez who was the first one in the arc to his right.

Shepherd had no choice. Threaten his team, and he'd take you out in a heartbeat. He fired once.

Not like the movies, where they aimed for the leg or a flesh wound. Sway had a weapon and had already shot Josh. That meant he needed to go down hard.

The bullet hit Sway in the upper chest, the force punching him backwards. He dropped the pistol, which clattered onto the roof beside him, and fell back onto the edge of the rooftop, his back arched over the wall.

Keeping their weapons trained on him, Shepherd, Marquez and Jorgensen moved forward.

Sway was panting, his chest heaving up and down, a growing patch of blood staining the front of his sweater from the gunshot wound. Up close they could see that he wasn't Finn Sway, although the resemblance was very strong. This guy was younger.

The trio all watched him then lowered their weapons. The kid wasn't a threat anymore. He was on his way out.

The young man managed to lift his head and looked down at the wound, his eyes confused. Then he looked up at Shepherd, the man who shot him. The guy was young. Barely a man. A younger Finn Sway. They were even wearing the same outfit.

The younger Sway grimaced, the heaving in his chest decreasing.

Then his head lolled to the side and his breathing stopped altogether.

FORTY ONE

Fifteen minutes later Josh was being loaded into an ambulance on a frame back down on the street. Luckily they were only a few blocks from Roosevelt Hospital and a medical team had arrived fast. Josh had taken the round in the upper arm; the ambulance team said he was going to be fine but they needed to get him into surgery and extract the bullet immediately. They finished locking him in place in the back and were feeding him oxygen.

Standing by the rear doors, Archer and Marquez watched. Lying on the bed, medics working either side of him, Josh saw the two detectives and lifted the hand of his good arm. They raised theirs back in acknowledgement as the doors were pulled shut from the inside. Then the ambulance sped off on its way to the hospital.

Watching it go, Archer turned and saw Shepherd standing alone near the entrance of the building. The street was pretty busy around him but he'd tuned it all out, lost in his own thoughts. They'd just wheeled out Sway's body-bag and were taking it to the morgue in a separate ambulance. His prints had already been taken and a match had come back from Charlotte-Mecklenburg PD. The kid's name was Reese Sway, no middle name. Finn Sway's younger brother. He'd been charged for vagrancy and theft but had never served time. Watching Shepherd, Archer heard Josh's voice in his mind. *Hell of a thing. Man tries to defend his home, ends up killing his own son.* Reese Sway had been young. Archer could imagine the memories pulling the trigger had stirred up. He stepped his way through the assembled throng of police and onlookers, and approached Shepherd.

'Josh is on his way,' Archer said. 'He's going to be fine.'

'Great.'

Archer saw the look on his face. 'You had no choice, sir.'

'There's always a choice.' Shepherd shook his head angrily. 'Stupid kid.'

'He tried to kill Josh. He tried to kill the doctor and me at the lab. He wasn't a kid.'

Jorgensen walked over. Shepherd saw him approaching.

'Where are we with Finn Sway?' he asked.

'Rach can't find him in the city,' Jorgensen said. 'But taxi and bus services have been informed as well as State borders. Dispatch is putting out his description. We'll find him.'

Behind Jorgensen some news teams had just pitched up, hoping for a scoop after a headline-packed day. Shepherd glanced at them. 'I'm going to put the word out. Let's get every New Yorker searching for this scumbag.'

The two detectives nodded. Shepherd rose and stepped towards to the waiting press, thinking of the dead boy.

Stupid kid.

Eleven miles to the west, Finn Sway had just arrived at *Kearny Medical* in New Jersey having taken a taxi. He'd considered using one of the cars left in the parking lot from the dead scientists upstairs, but decided he didn't need the hassle and wanted to be able to jump into a vehicle at a moment's notice. He stepped out and shut the door, paid the fare, then watched the guy leave.

When the car was gone, Finn walked over to the lab complex and pulled open the door.

Rourke was standing inside behind the reception desk. Wicks and Drexler were sitting across the lobby, talking. All three of them turned and looked at Finn as he walked in.

'Jacobs is dead,' Finn said. 'It was a set-up.'

Rourke nodded. 'I heard.'

'You finished?'

Rourke nodded again, slowly. 'Van's loaded. I'll be done upstairs in a few minutes.'

'We need to get out of here right now,' said Finn. He suddenly paused and looked at Rourke. 'What's up with you?'

Rourke didn't answer. Finn looked around.

'Where the hell is Reese?'

Rourke glanced over his shoulder. From where he was standing, Finn could see an *NY ONE* report playing on the screen. The sound was low, but he could make out what the reporter was saying. *'...were given no option but to shoot. The deceased has been officially named as Reese Sway.'* Finn froze. The shot flipped to a dark-haired cop standing on the street, flashing lights and a lot of activity behind him. *Sergeant Matt Shepherd, NYPD Counter Terrorism Bureau* was on the text block below. He started speaking to the reporter.

'We cornered the man. I ordered him to drop his weapon but he ignored me and was about to shoot another of my detectives. We are still looking for another man, the deceased's brother, Finn Sway. We ask all city residents to keep a lookout for this man and to report any sightings immediately.'

Finn's prison mug-shot appeared on the screen.

'I'm sorry,' Rourke said.

Finn ignored him. He kept staring at the screen instead. At the image of the man who had killed his brother.

'That son of a bitch,' he said quietly. 'I saw that asshole earlier. He had me in handcuffs.'

'Stay cool. We need to get the hell out of here now.'

'Sergeant Matt Shepherd,' Finn Sway repeated to himself quietly, ignoring Rourke. He turned and pointed at a computer on the desk in front of Rourke. 'Search him.'

Rourke looked at him for a moment, then decided not to argue and pulled up Google, typing in the man's name.

Finn moved around the counter and watched the screen as Rourke scrolled down.

'Wait,' he said, pointing at one of the first links. 'Here.'

It was a small acknowledgement from the *New York Post*. Rourke clicked on it.

'*Hoboken High School wishes to acknowledge the generous donation to the new music department from Sergeant Matt Shepherd and his wife Beth in memory of their son Ricky Shepherd, who was recently killed in a tragic accident.*'

It continued onto a second paragraph and Finn struck gold.

It gave the family's home address.

Without another word, Finn grabbed a pad and scribbled it down, tearing the sheet off the page and stuffing it in his pocket. Then he pulled Rourke's modified Glock from the holster on his hip and turned to Wicks. 'Keys.'

Wicks nodded, tossing his set to him. Finn swung round and walked to the doors.

'Where are you going?' Rourke asked. 'It's open season on you right now!'

Sway ignored him, pushing open the doors and walking out into the parking lot. He pulled the mag from the Glock, checked the clip was loaded, then slotted it back inside the weapon. He pushed the button on the keys and the lights on a BMW flashed as the car unlocked. He ripped open the door and climbed inside as Rourke ran out of the building after him.

'Finn!'

Firing the engine, Finn swung the car out of the lot and the tyres screeched as it roared off into the night. Cursing, Rourke turned and walked back into the building.

'We're leaving,' he said to his hit-team, who rose. He pulled another set of keys from his pocket and threw them to Wicks. 'You're driving the hot van. All the canisters are inside. Go to the campsite and tell everyone to pack up.'

Wicks looked out into the lot.

There were two white vans out there, parked side by side.

'Which van?'

'The one on the left.'

'What about you?'

He nodded to Drexler. 'We'll be right behind. I need to finish arming the gear upstairs.'

Wicks nodded. 'See you soon.'

He pushed open the door and walked out into the parking lot.

On West 35th, Shepherd had just wrapped up the report he'd given the news teams when Marquez came running up the street.

'Sir!' He turned. 'Taxi company got in touch. One of their drivers told dispatch he took a man matching Sway's description out of the city. He dropped him off less than ten minutes ago.'

'Where to?'

'Kearny Medical Institute. It's a lab complex out in New Jersey fifteen minutes from here.'

'You're driving,' Shepherd said, running to the Ford Explorer containing Maddy Flood and Kruger and pulling open the door. Marquez jumped in beside him and fired the engine.

Jorgensen and Archer were right on their heels, then both stopped and looked at each other. There was one car left. And the two of them.

Which meant they'd be riding together.

FORTY TWO

To say conversation inside the Ford Explorer was minimal would be an understatement. The two men rode in total silence, Jorgensen behind the wheel, Archer in the passenger seat to his right. This was the closest the two of them had ever been for any length of time and neither was enjoying the experience.

Archer suddenly lifted his head and sniffed. He looked over his shoulder into the back.

'Is that weed?'

Jorgensen didn't respond.

Archer rolled his eyes and turning back, looked out into the night.

Silence.

'Shame Josh was the first to the roof,' Jorgensen suddenly said. 'We're down a good cop and here I am stuck with you. Do me a favour and step in front of the bullet next time.'

With that, Archer snapped.

He turned to him. 'You know what? I'm getting really sick and tired of your shit.'

Jorgensen looked over and glared.

'You want to make something of it?' he replied.

'I get it, college boy. You don't like me because I'm foreign. You don't like me because your friend didn't make the squad and I did. But get over yourself. Every person in the entire Bureau thinks you're an asshole.'

'You think that's why I hate you?'

'You want to tell me otherwise?'

Silence.

'My brother was a cop too,' Jorgensen said, his hands tight on the wheel.

'So?'

'He was five years older than me. He was the reason I joined. He put his time in then joined the ESU. He was one of the best guys they had.'

He paused, shaking his head.

'Then last summer, he takes a response call at Flushing Corona Park on a Sunday night in September. Three bank robbers had held up a money truck on its way from the US Open to Long Island.'

Archer froze.

'They tried to take them on but the thieves pulled flash bangs. The whole team was stunned, disorientated. Then one of the robbers drilled him with an M16, right between the eyes. Killed him instantly.'

He paused.

'I have a good friend in the New York FBI Office. He told me this crew had been running the city ragged the entire year. He said someone was put undercover in their group but hadn't stopped them in time.'

He looked at Archer, his jaw clenched.

'Turned out that person was you.'

Archer stared at him.

'I don't know how you ended up in it. I don't want to know. But you could have taken those people down. You could have saved Tommy's life. But you didn't. And because of you, he died.'

Silence.

Archer was lost for words. He hadn't been expecting that.

Jorgensen put his foot down harder, relieving some frustration.

And they sped on through the night.

As they approached *Kearny Medical*, Shepherd called Jorgensen in the car behind and told him that they'd be moving in straight away. As the two cars swung into the lot, the team saw that there were a number of vehicles parked outside the building. The two Ford Explorers pulled up quietly, the engines were switched off and the entire group stepped out, Shepherd's team minus Josh but plus the two doctors. Archer climbed out, his mood rock bottom. The combination of Jorgensen's revelation, Josh taking a round and spending half an hour in a freezer had left him feeling like complete shit.

The group stood there for a moment. Beside them, the building was dark, the lights switched off. The entire place had a stillness that only a complete lack of human activity could emit.

'Looks like we missed him,' Jorgensen said.

'Not necessarily,' Shepherd said quietly, pointing to all the cars parked in the lot. He pulled his Sig and the other three detectives did the same.

Together, they approached the dark building. Shepherd tried the front handle; the door was open. He pushed it back and they all entered the lobby.

The place was deserted. To the right was a reception desk. Straight ahead was a glass panel to prevent unauthorised access. It was open. Stepping through one by one, the group followed Shepherd as he moved forward to the stairwell quickly and silently.

There was no sign of activity on 1 or 2. But when they got to 3, it was immediately clear that someone had been here recently.

It looked as if it was the main floor of the building. Up ahead was a large laboratory with smaller rooms and offices placed around the level. There were signs of occupation. Food wrappers and an empty pizza box had been dumped on the ground. A long smeared bloodstain was running along the polished tiled floor, leading from the main lab and almost drawing an arrow to an office to the right. The door to the room was closed. Archer turned and headed towards it.

The others walked forward. Suddenly, Maddy gasped and covered her mouth, stifling a scream.

A dead body was slumped inside the main lab. It was immediately clear that the virus had killed him, judging by the blood and pieces of tissue surrounding him and sprayed onto the glass walls.

'It's Frankie,' she whispered from behind her hand to Shepherd, silent tears streaming down her face. 'Dr Glover. What the hell is he doing here?'

Marquez, Shepherd and Jorgensen stared at the dead man as Kruger put his arm around Maddy. From behind them, there was a whistle. They all turned and saw Archer standing by the office, the door pushed back. Shepherd walked over with the two doctors and Marquez to see what he was looking at.

There was a heap of dead bodies in the room, eight or nine of them. They'd been dumped in a pile, limp and lifeless. Blood had pooled and caked on the floor underneath them.

'*Jesus,*' Shepherd whispered. 'What the hell was going on here?'

Behind them, Jorgensen hadn't joined the group, mostly out of wanting to stay away from Archer. He was moving towards the main lab instead, walking slowly but purposefully. Shepherd glanced over his shoulder and saw him heading towards the lab doors.

'Careful, Dave,' he warned. 'The air's probably still contaminated.'

'Wait,' Kruger said, moving over to a terminal to the right. He tapped a few buttons and suddenly the air purification system started blasting, filtering the air inside the lab.

'It'll take ten seconds.'

While they waited, everyone by the office looked again at the bodies dumped inside. Archer saw bullet-holes and blood on the wall to his right where they each must have been executed. In the main lab, the purification system stopped. A light turned green. Kruger looked over at Jorgensen and nodded.

'The air is clear.'

Jorgensen took point as Marquez went to follow him. Shepherd, Archer and the two doctors remained by the office containing the corpses. Jorgensen approached the door of the lab.

It slid open. He moved inside.

Marquez was a few feet behind him but before she could enter, the doors slid shut in front of her.

There was a *beep.*

Jorgensen swung around. 'What the hell was that?'

Marquez tried stepping towards the doors again, but they didn't move. She started working on the keypad, but no one knew the code.

'Shit, they locked,' she said.

'Hang on, Jorgensen,' Shepherd said as he joined Marquez at the keypad, both of them trying to force the doors open. Inside the lab,

Jorgensen nodded then turned and looked around the interior. He glanced down at Dr Glover's body to his right. He walked straight forwards. There was equipment covering the work surfaces to his left but he didn't know what any of it was for.

Then he heard a beeping coming from somewhere inside the room. He tried to place it. The sound seemed to be coming from a thick cabinet against the wall up ahead. He approached it. The cabinet was about the size of a large bookcase. The doors were shut. He reached forward and pulled them open.

The inside was loaded with explosives and gasoline and a timer.

00:57.

00:56.

'Jesus Christ.' He turned to Marquez and Shepherd outside, his eyes wide. 'The door triggered it!'

The whole group looked at the explosives and the timer in horror. Marquez was working frantically at the keypad. But it just beeped.

'It's not working! I can't open it!'

Shepherd grabbed a chair from behind him and swung it at the glass as hard as he could. It just bounced off. He did it twice more, then dropped it and pulled his pistol. Marquez did the same.

'Take cover, Jorgensen!' he ordered.

Jorgensen ducked behind a far work station. Behind him the timer ticked to *00:40.* The two of them fired, the weapons flashing as Maddy and Kruger covered their ears. The glass didn't smash, each round just leaving a white dent. Increasingly panicked, Marquez emptied an entire clip into it but it wouldn't give way, all the shell casings tinkling to the tiles at her feet. Staring at the still intact glass, Shepherd swung round to Archer, pointing at Maddy and Kruger.

'Get them out of here now!'

Archer nodded and hustled the two doctors towards the stairwell, the trio quickly disappearing out of sight.

Jorgensen was up by the glass, looking at Shepherd and Marquez desperately for help. The timer kept counting down over his shoulder.

00:35.

00:34.

At the glass, Jorgensen looked back at the timer.

Pause. He bowed his head, as Shepherd and Marquez looked on desperately from the other side of the glass.

'You need to go,' he said.

'No!' Marquez said, hitting the glass with the butt of her pistol.

'Go!'

'No!'

She couldn't stop tears filling her eyes, standing there looking at her partner. To the left, Shepherd was hammering the glass with the butt of his pistol but it wasn't giving way.

00:24.

00:23.

And for the first time in a very long time, Dave Jorgensen smiled. He put his hand up to the glass. Tears rolling down her cheeks, Marquez matched it with hers. They stayed that way, palm to palm, for a long moment. He smiled again.

'Go. And be good, Marquez.'

Openly sobbing, she stared through the glass at her partner. She nodded.

Then she turned and ran for the stairwell with Shepherd.

Alone, everyone out of the building, Jorgensen felt strangely at peace. It was just him. The rest of the team were outside.

Safe.

He sat down with his back against the glass, watching the countdown on the timer across the room. The room around him was quiet and still. There was no movement anywhere he could see save for the constant silent ticking down of the numbers on the explosives.

The timer reached *00:10*.

He knew he was about to die. But he wasn't scared or sad. He thought about his life. Everything he'd done. The best times, and the worst. He thought of his brother, Tommy, and the memories he had of their time together before he died. His time in the Department. His lack of friends.

And Marquez.

He thought back to what he'd said to Archer in the car. He didn't like the guy but he knew deep down what happened to Tommy wasn't his fault.

I've been an asshole for way too long, he thought.

The timer hit *00:05*. Sitting against the glass, he looked across the lab at the bomb and smiled, knowing all the others had escaped.

Finally, you did something right.

Then he thought of Tommy. He pictured his big brother waiting for him. In a place without bombs, or anger, or pain.

I'll be right there, bro.

Up ahead the countdown approached its end.
He closed his eyes.

00:03.

00:02.

00:01.

I'll be right there.

FORTY THREE

Bobby Rourke wasn't a racist.

Growing up with no prospects in a small southern town, his future had been bleak. Life in Roller was just about as boring and uneventful as you could get without being six feet under. There was a saying in the area that a lot of residents hated, but most of them agreed with. *The only good thing about Roller is the road leading out of it*. His father had left when Bobby was a kid. He met some other woman and just took off. Bobby couldn't remember much about him, save that he had hard fists and had a hatred of anyone not white Caucasian. Watching him as a boy Bobby had adopted those beliefs, wanting to please and impress him. But once he was gone and as Bobby grew up, he realised just how wrong his father had been. Society had changed. Equality and human rights now meant people of all colours, races and religions were able to live together, work together, have families together. And despite being the leader of a neo-Nazi hate group, Bobby had a secret.

He didn't have an issue with any of that.

Before his grandfather had died, he'd asked Bobby to come out to see him on his farm on the outskirts of town. He told him that he was going to leave the farm and the house to him in his will. Rourke wasn't under any illusions. He knew the only reason it was being passed to him was that he was the only Rourke still around. He'd asked the old man if the will had already been signed. It had. So Bobby had grabbed a cushion from the couch and suffocated him on the spot. A minute later, the old man was dead and the farm belonged to him.

However, he'd completely underestimated the amount of work it took to maintain a place like that. He quickly discovered the sheer weight of tasks he needed to perform in order to keep the place going was far greater than anything he'd ever encountered before. Lazy by nature, Rourke had hated it. True to form, he'd quickly started neglecting the place when he realised money wasn't just going to fall into his lap and the crops had begun to fail. The house was in good condition thanks to the old man, but to Bobby it was a stop on the journey and not a destination. Every day he woke up trying to think of a way out of that place.

Then one summer night, three years ago, he'd been out on the porch smoking some weed when he'd heard motorbikes in the distance. The noise had become louder and louder until three bikers appeared from the dirt road, pulling up outside the house. Bobby had stayed where he was but his hand had slid down around the pistol grip of a shotgun by his side.

The bikers had dismounted, taking off their helmets. They had shaved heads and Bobby could see prison ink on the necks of two of the men. Bobby had flicked away the joint, then risen, the shotgun in his hands.

'You lost, gentlemen?' he'd said, walking to the front of the porch.

'No need for the weapon,' the lead biker said, pointing at the shotgun.

'I'll decide that.'

'You got time to talk?'

'I can fit you in. Long as those two stay where they are and keep their hands in sight.'

The two men nodded, standing with their arms folded, the sun setting over the neglected crops behind them. The lead biker had joined Bobby on the veranda, taking a seat. Bobby had stayed standing, the shotgun gripped tight in his hands. Then the biker began to explain who they were and why they were here.

Apparently the three of them had done time upstate, during which they had become part of an Aryan brotherhood. Called *The Stuttgart Soldiers*, the club had chapters spread across America. The biker emphasised that he'd been a young man going nowhere, with no direction in his life, but the club had saved him and put money in his pocket.

And they were always looking for new recruits.

He explained that given members of the club were viewed as outlaws and public enemies, they were forced to carry out certain practices to support the club financially, *for the greater good* as the man had said. They ran dope across the border, selling it at a bargain price on the streets and giving the junkies what they needed. They even cooked their own, providing methamphetamines for those who wanted it and were prepared to pay. And another of their recent business ventures had been gun-running. Caches of sub-machine guns, pistols, grenades, ammunition. However, they could feel the ATF breathing down their necks. They'd received a tip that a raid of their stores was imminent. That meant they needed to find another place to hide their weapons for the time being.

The biker had proposed that they do so at Rourke's farm. No one would know that he was a friend of the brotherhood and the ATF would find nothing when they hit the stash-houses. They would be willing to pay five grand, cash, and in addition offer Rourke a blood-free induction into the club. The biker emphasised how rare that was. Normally, initiation meant spilling blood and not your own. Rourke agreed to the proposition, saying he'd take the money, they could store their weapons and he'd think about the offer.

The two men had shaken hands and his group returned later that night with two truckloads of boxed weapons and ammunition. It had all been buried out in the field, hidden by a sea of overgrown crops. True to his word, the biker had paid Rourke cash in hand, five G's. He'd counted out the money in hundreds in front of Rourke, peeling the notes from a stack. Rourke got the message loud and clear.

There was plenty more where that came from if he wanted it.

Four weeks later he was a member of the club. Suddenly he had a purpose. Responsibility. He was invited to club meetings, asked for his opinion and for the first time in his life was listened to. He was paid handsomely and had young female prospects desperate to sleep with him. But as time went on, things changed. The three guys who had come out to his farm that night were now all dead, two of them killed in prison, the guy who'd talked with him on the veranda shot dead in a drive-by. Rourke had already taken over the gun-running operation and after a two year interlude at Dallas State for rape, found himself one of the prominent members of the Chapter when he was released.

During that time, he'd got to know Finn Sway. Finn had gone to the same high school, a year above Bobby, but the two of them hadn't become friends until they met through the club. Finn was head of the militia arm of the Chapter. He and five others would drive out into the desert on roaming patrols with rifles and ammo, searching for immigrants or any non-whites they could find near the borders. They had a high hit-rate. Bobby had gone with the group a few times and seen the process. They stalked and shot them without mercy. Ten minutes later, the man, woman or child would be buried in the sand in an unmarked grave. These were anonymous people who were desperate to slide their way into the country, so most of them had left all forms of identity behind them. No one would ever report them missing, find their bodies or know what had happened to them. Roller PD consisted of only six men and they were so useless they couldn't find a whore in a brothel.

But almost a decade after he'd become a member, Rourke was done with the club's dealings. Most of the guys he'd become friends and brothers with were either dead, in jail or on their way there. Running guns and dope was a business but it wasn't a sustainable future. The ATF and FBI were always circling. Rourke had had enough. He still put on a front when he was with the other members, agreeing with all the racist shit they spewed but deep down he didn't believe a word of it. Besides he liked other colours, green in particular. Especially when it was a bill and had a President's face printed on it.

He'd been looking for salvation for a while.
And it had appeared a fortnight ago.

The entire Chapter had been at an annual rally in South Carolina. All the Chapters from across the country got together for a weekend-long party and hate festival.

During the celebrations, drinking a beer and walking past one of the bonfires, Rourke ran into a brother from another Chapter, Paul Bleeker. They knew each other from a separate rally last year. After they'd spent a night drinking and partying, Bleeker now appeared to assume that the two of them were friends. He was a joke. Rourke knew he was desperate to impress and get noticed, and for some reason he'd latched onto him.

Standing there beside the huge fire and scores of skinheads, Bleeker had told Rourke he'd been looking for him. He wanted Bobby to meet someone. Bored, and with nothing else to do, Rourke had agreed. Bleeker introduced him to another member who Rourke didn't recognise. Bored and uninterested, Rourke had been about to walk away when the stranger said that if Bobby and Bleeker wanted it, there was a way the three of them could make an absolute fortune.

That got his attention.

Rourke had asked him to explain. Bleeker's companion told him about a modified virus which was a fast-acting biological killer. Apparently there were a few samples of it at a lab in New York and the contact knew there would be a lot of people out there who'd be very keen to acquire it and would pay big money. Mid-conversation, Rourke had whistled Finn over and he'd joined them. The four men had talked for almost an hour, learning about this virus and how they could use it to their advantage. At the end, a deal was struck. It was pretty straightforward. The four of them would steal the virus, adapt it for easy use, sell it on and share the massive payout.

The operation was planned for Friday 17th December in New York City, two weeks after the rally. Bobby had planned to go alone to oversee and organise getting the virus out of New York but Finn had wanted to join him. He had nothing else going and he could see his brother who was in New Jersey. Finn had also suggested that having back-up wouldn't be a bad idea. Rourke was reluctant, wanting to keep knowledge of the virus a secret, but Finn said they could just lie to them instead. That would get the whole Chapter on the road and none of them would know the real reason they were going to New York. Bobby had called a Chapter meeting and informed the members of the upcoming road trip. The cover story was a huge meth deal with a Brooklyn drug cartel. The Texan Chapter were renowned for the quality of their product and apparently the New Yorkers wanted in. The club had been enthusiastic; none of them had suspected they were being manipulated.

They'd ridden up to New York and arrived yesterday, Friday 17th, setting up base on an old retail estate in New Jersey. Three of the guys who ran the meth arm of the business set up three caravans to start cooking, using the isolation of the estate to create some fresh product ready for the so-called deal. Rourke had left the estate with Finn as soon as they'd arrived and headed into the city to go and meet with Paul Bleeker and his contact.

However, things hadn't gone to plan.

Bleeker had gone dark, not answering his phone. His contact they'd met at the rally was unreachable. Finn had broken into *Flood Microbiology* but couldn't locate any sign of the virus.

Bleeker and his contact had screwed them.

Bob and Finn agreed they should have guessed Bleeker would do this. He was an unreliable asshole.

But they sure as hell hadn't come all this way for nothing.

Rourke had called Wicks and Drexler and told them to meet him in the city. He'd shared with them the real reason they were here and that Bleeker had fallen off the radar. That had been just after 10:30pm. He ordered them to find Bleeker or one of his known gang before sunrise. They'd done just that. Wicks had called a friend in the New York Chapter and he'd given addresses for Bleeker and the three guys he always hung out with. Bleeker wasn't at home but they'd captured one of his friends. They'd just broken into the man's house when the guy had pulled up in a car and walked straight in.

He'd told them pretty much everything they wanted to know. Apparently Bleeker had decided to steal the vials himself, cutting his three partners from the rally out of the deal. He was planning to use some of them in Manhattan as a demonstration that coming morning then leave town with three of his friends. The tortured man had given the locations and the times. The original plan cooked up at the rally had been to mix the virus with a liquid broth which could then be transported in canisters. Increasing the quantity without losing the quality would drastically increase their margin of profit. Rourke had located a lab in New Jersey which would be an ideal place to do it. They'd never intended to kill the doctors at *Flood Microbiology* and *Kearny Medical*, but Bleeker's double-cross had enraged the two men. Wicks had called and told them what the tortured man had said. He and Drexler had orders to gain a sample of the virus and take out all the doctors who worked at *Flood Microbiology* as well as Bleeker's crew. Rourke wanted everyone who knew about this virus exterminated.

No more chances of getting screwed.

He and Finn had waited outside *Kearny Medical* until the guard arrived, then killed him and let themselves in. Finn had taken a spare uniform from the man's locker out back whilst Bobby went upstairs. They then murdered each member of the team as they arrived for work, one by one. Wicks and Drexler had done well. Before noon, they brought a doctor from *Flood Microbiology* to mix the virus and had also got hold of a vial.

Bleeker was an idiot. He and his three friends had got themselves killed and also attracted the attention of the entire NYPD. Reese's death and Finn's sudden departure were also setbacks. Bobby didn't have any siblings but he knew if some pig killed his brother that he'd want revenge too. He wouldn't want to be the cop who'd killed Reese for all the guns in Texas right now. But not everything was bad. Rourke had received an interesting phone call earlier from

Bleeker's contact. The information that had been passed was interesting and invaluable. The contact had warned Rourke of a situation at the campsite where the Chapter were holed up.

Bobby had taken the appropriate measures to counter it.

So behind the wheel of a white van, moving fast through rural New Jersey, Rourke glanced at Drexler. She was sitting beside him, watching the road. They were the only two in the vehicle.

'How we doing?'

She checked her rear view mirror. 'We're good. Nothing but night.'

He grinned, and put his foot down.

He liked happy endings.

FORTY FOUR

Fire crews had arrived and were battling to put out the blaze at *Kearny Medical*. The explosion had been monumental, everyone outside shielding themselves from the fireball and wave of heat as the explosives and gasoline in the lab detonated. The flames licking up the side of the building were giving the area an orange glow and the air stank of smoke.

Down in the parking lot, Archer spotted Marquez sitting on the back of a car. He walked over and sat beside her. She was staring up at the blaze, the fire lighting up her face, her eyes red-rimmed from tears. Knowing no words would help, Archer took her hand gently. They sat in silence, watching the fire crew attack the blaze. Shepherd approached his two remaining detectives but didn't say anything.

He leant against the car beside Archer, looking up at the burning building, his mood sombre. Then his cell rang. He took it out and answered.

'Shepherd.'

He listened.

'OK. We'll be there soon.' He ended the call, turning to his two remaining detectives. 'A van just pulled into the neo-Nazi campsite. Hendricks thinks there may be something inside.'

'Who's behind the wheel?' Archer asked.

'Wicks.'

Without saying a word, Marquez suddenly jumped off the back of the car. The two men watched her walk over to her Ford Explorer and climb inside.

She fired the engine and roared out of the parking lot, speeding off into the night.

'Are we going?' Archer asked Shepherd.

He went to reply, but his phone rang again. He pulled it out, looking at the number and Archer saw surprise on his face. He took the call, turning and walking out of earshot. Watching him move away, Archer noticed Kruger and Maddy Flood standing together to his left, looking up at the fire and talking quietly.

He stood up and approached them. 'Are you both OK?'

'Yes,' Maddy said, her attitude far friendlier now. Archer glanced to his right to see if Shepherd was ready to go.

But Archer noticed that he'd gone very still, the phone held to his ear.

Suddenly, he took off, racing towards his Ford.

'Sir!' Archer called. 'What's going on?'

Not responding and jumping into his car, Shepherd fired the ignition and pulled a U-turn, the tyres squealing as the vehicle swung hard to the right. Archer ran after the Ford, but Shepherd sped off, barely slowing to turn out of the lot and roaring off out of sight.

Watching him go, Archer shook his head, totally confused. Shepherd had left him and the two doctors behind.

What the hell is going on?

Just like every night for the last six weeks, Beth Shepherd couldn't sleep. She'd tried sleeping pills, but they hadn't worked. She'd tried drinking but that was a path she didn't want to go down any further. Any way she could, she was desperate to fall asleep.

Because it was a release.

In her dreams, she was with her son again.

And for those blissful couple of seconds just after she woke up in the morning, those two words that haunted her weren't running through her mind like the news feed on CNN. But then they came, as they always did.

Ricky's dead.

She was lying on the couch, a blanket over her tired body, the television remote in her hand. There was a DVD in the player, her son's high school graduation from this past summer. Beth's brother had been on hand to film the whole thing, and there was a moment where she, Matt and the two boys posed together for a photograph. She kept rewinding and watching those few seconds, the four of them in a line with their arms around each other, Matt telling everyone to say *cheese*. She'd watched it so many times that she'd almost worn away the white arrow on the *Rewind* button. Her other son Mark was upstairs, asleep. Since it had happened, she'd barely let him out of her sight. She knew it couldn't continue, the way things were, but to move on was to accept that Ricky was dead and never coming back.

She pushed the *Rewind* button again. She'd done it so many times that now she didn't even have to think; muscle memory held it for just the right amount of time. Then she hit *Play* and watched those few moments of bliss again. She noticed different things each time. Mark's shirt was half pulled out. Matt's tie was loose. Ricky's grin was impish and infectious. They all looked so happy.

None of them aware that Ricky would be dead six months later.

She examined her son's face, smiling under the mortar-board on his head, a scroll in his hand.

She hit *Pause* and stared at him, tears welling in her eyes. In the dark room, the glare of the television was like a beacon. She examined his face, his smile, his hair, his clothes. Eventually, she tore her gaze from his face and glanced at the digital clock beside the television.

1:15 am.

She realised she felt tired.

I'll watch it one more time. Then sleep.

She pushed *Rewind* again for just the right amount of time and the shot wound back. But as she went to press *Play*, she suddenly sensed movement to her right.

'Mark?'

She lifted her head and looked over at the doorway.

She jolted back. It wasn't Mark.

There was a tall man standing there.

Staring at her.

And he had a pistol in his hand aimed at her head.

FORTY FIVE

Shepherd's sudden and unexplained departure meant Archer was left alone with the two doctors. As the echoes of the engine of Shepherd's Ford disappeared into the night, Archer turned and walked back towards the medical pair, shaking his head.

'What was that about?' Kruger asked.

'I've got no idea.'

He glanced at the time on his watch. *1:16 am*. It had been one hell of a day and it sure as hell wasn't over yet.

'So many of us dead,' Maddy said, looking up at the burning building. 'All those people up there. Dad, Will and now Frankie.'

She shook her head.

'What the hell was he doing here?'

'They must have kidnapped him,' Archer said.

'But why?'

'I don't know. Did you get a look at the equipment upstairs?'

They both nodded.

'Much of it was the same as ours,' Kruger said. 'Frankie was also a virologist. He worked with me.'

He paused.

'What?' Archer asked, seeing the look on his face.

'There was something else up there too,' Kruger said. 'I saw it inside the lab just before the big detective was locked inside.'

'What was it?'

'There was a canister at the back of the room near the explosives. I've seen them before in

South Africa. I recognised the design and the sticker on the side.'

'So?'

'They hold pesticides.'

'Pesticides?'

'Yes.'

'Where would you get that from?'

'I guess you'd order it.'

'Or steal it,' Maddy said.

Archer thought back to what Shepherd said. Wicks was behind the wheel of the van at the campsite. Not Rourke. Not Sway. Not Drexler.

So where the hell were they?

Archer pulled his cell, dialling Rach.

'Hello?'

'Rach, it's Archer.'

'I heard about Jorgensen. I'm sorry.'

'Yeah. Me too.' Pause. 'But listen. I'm still here in New Jersey. We found the last doctor from Dr Flood's lab here. The virus had killed him. I think Rourke and Sway kidnapped him and him working on something.'

'What?'

'I don't know. But Dr Kruger saw an empty can of pesticide. I need you to check something out.'

Five miles away, the CTB Ford Explorer roared down the street, Shepherd with his foot all the way down. He was holding the wheel with one hand and gripping his cell phone with the other.

'Talk to me, buddy,' he said, turning a hard right.

'I heard someone outside,' his son Mark whispered. *'He's in the house, Dad.'*

'Did you see him?'

'He was tall, lanky. Weird haircut.'

Shepherd paled.

Finn Sway.

'I heard Mum fighting with him. I think he must have knocked her out. It's all gone quiet. Wait.'

Shepherd listened in helpless agony, pushing his foot down all the way, the car hurtling towards his neighbourhood.

'I think he's coming upstairs,' Mark whispered, even quieter.

Shepherd listened.

Then the call went dead.

'I just checked tonight's reports,' Rach told Archer. *'Not much happening in the area. Most of the action is where you are.'*

'There must be something.'

'Hang on.' Pause. *'Most of its minor charges; alcohol, fighting in the street. Someone got shot in Newark. No surprise there. That's about it. The biggest is the shooting and a missing persons report.'*

'A missing person?'

'Man called Doug Craig. Seventy two years old. Wife said he was out working on their farm, but disappeared some time earlier in the day. She's looked everywhere but can't find him. Jersey State PD are looking into it.'

'Where was this?'

'A farm twelve miles from you.'

'A farm?' Archer repeated.

'Yes.'

Pesticide.

'It might not be anything.'

'But it could be something. Send me the address.'

He ended the call, then realised they had no car. He looked around for a vehicle. He couldn't borrow the fire truck.

Then he saw all the employee cars parked in the lot. One of them was a Mercedes that caught his eye. He moved towards it, trying the handle. It was locked. He pulled his Sig, reversing the weapon and smashed the window. It took three goes, but it went and the alarm started blaring. Some of the fire-crew turned, but Archer raised his badge and they turned back to the fire. The alarm wailing, he released the lock and pulled open the door then used a trick employed by so many people he'd arrested in the past. He hot-wired the vehicle. The alarm died and the engine fired. He finished twisting the two wires under the panel into place as Kruger and Maddy watched.

He waved them over and they ran towards him, both climbing into the Mercedes to join him.

A hundred yards from the neo-Nazi campsite, Marquez had pulled up to a halt beside Hendricks teams' vehicles, parking behind a series of thick trees. She'd grabbed a Mossberg and a box of shells from the trunk, shutting the lid quietly and had moved up through the trees to join Hendricks and his team who were crouched down behind a boulder, peering around at the campsite below.

Hendricks turned and saw her arrive. He didn't know her name but recognised her as one of Shep's people, which meant she was good.

'*Evening,*' he whispered.

She didn't respond, looking down at the campsite. She saw a ragged circle of gang members surrounding a large bonfire. Many of them had weapons ready to hand. To the right, she saw the white van mentioned in the call, the bleach-haired man called Wicks standing beside it and talking with several other members.

'What's the situation?'

'They've been going all night so far. Drinking, partying. Few of them went off screwing. But that van just turned up. We think the virus could be inside.'

Hendricks paused, realising the woman was alone.

'Where's the rest of your team?'

Marquez didn't respond.

She knelt down beside him and loaded her Mossberg, sliding red shells into the magazine chamber quietly. He watched her. Something was wrong, but this wasn't the time to ask questions. The woman slid a last shell into the weapon, then looked down at the camp.

'So what's the plan?'

'We wait on confirmation from ATF that the virus is inside the van. If it is, we move in.'

He paused.

'What's your name?'

'Marquez.'

FORTY SIX

Down below, Wicks had stepped out of the van and was spreading the word to everyone around the campsite to pack up. It was met with a lot of disapproval and resentment. Most of them had been drinking and were having a good time and none felt like starting the drive back to Texas tonight. Wicks hadn't been down here since they arrived on Friday but saw they'd set up meth labs beside the camp, not bothering with any safety precautions.

He shook his head at the stupidity just as one of the doors of the caravans opened. A big bearded man the size of a doorframe stepped out. He saw the commotion and pulled his mask down off his face.

'What's going on?' he shouted.

'Pack your shit,' Wicks called back. 'We're leaving.'

'What about the deal?'

'It's off.'

'We're not done yet.'

'Then stay. I don't give a shit'

The bearded man looked around. 'Where're Bob and Finn?'

'They're following.'

'What happened to Harper, Travis and Stacks? We need their help.'

'They're staying. They got arrested.'

'What for?'

'Jesus Christ, who gives a shit? Just pack up or stay.'

Muttering expletives, the man swung round and stepped back into the caravan.

Wicks turned and saw several of the crew had gathered by the white van. They were all looking over at him.

'What's in the back?' one of them asked. He was a guy called Peterson, an ex-grunt. Bobby had taken to him and had been in the process of setting up a gun trade with one of Peterson's old contacts at Fort Hood.

'None of your business,' he said, walking over.

'You drag us up here for three days and we don't even get to find out what's going on?'

'Exactly.'

Peterson went to argue, but Wicks' hand moved inside his jacket, resting on his pistol, his temper flaring. It had been a long night and his patience was almost gone.

'Touch the handle. Please. I'm begging you.'

Peterson saw his hand and the look in his eyes; he took the hint.

'Shit,' Faison hissed, listening and watching the exchange in the shadows. 'We don't know what's inside.'

'Do we move?' Hendricks asked over the radio.

Faison grabbed his own radio. 'All teams, stand by. I repeat, stand by.'

Wicks glared at Peterson for a moment longer then turned and walked off. He pulled a pack of cigarettes from his pocket, drew one out with his lips and replacing the pack, pulled a lighter.

Watching him sparking the smoke, Peterson took his chance. He suddenly grabbed the handle and pulled open the doors.

Behind him, Wicks heard and swung round.

'Hey!'

'Stand by,' Faison's voice said over the radio.

Peterson looked inside the van as Wicks ran over, pulling his pistol.

The back was empty.

Fifty yards to the west a skinhead suddenly appeared from around the boulder, having wandered out of the camp to take a leak. As he unzipped his fly, he looked up.

And stared at Hendricks, his team and Marquez, ten feet in front of him.

It took just over a second for the thug to register what he was looking at. His hand flashed towards a semi-automatic pistol tucked into the back of his waistband but Hendricks was already raising his shotgun. The pistol appeared in the skinhead's right, headed in a sweeping arc towards the trio of NYPD detectives.

And Hendricks fired.

Seconds earlier, Wicks had joined Peterson. But he hadn't fired his pistol. He was staring inside the empty van, confused. There was nothing inside.

'What the hell?'

Then a shotgun blast echoed across the estate. Down by the van, the neo-Nazis all turned.

'Oh shit!' Faison said. He grabbed his radio. *'All teams, move in! Move in!'*

FORTY SEVEN

As shouts of *'ATF!'* and *'NYPD!'* suddenly filled the estate, Hendricks and his squad moved in from the left as the ATF came in from the right. They were approaching fast. Down below, scores of the skinheads were starting to react, pulling weapons from cars or retrieving them from wherever they'd been left around the camp.

'NYPD!' Hendricks shouted, moving past the skinhead he'd just taken down, closing in on the camp. *'Drop your weapons!'*

Instead, the neo-Nazis started to fire.

The night quiet of the estate was instantly shattered by the echoes of automatic and semi-automatic weapons. The ATF agents and NYPD detectives were forced to take cover as bullets and shotgun shells started smashing into rocks and trees around them.

However, Hendricks didn't withdraw, firing his Mossberg and racking the pump. He edged forward, keeping low, seemingly unconcerned as bullets whizzed past him as he returned fire. Straight ahead was a big neo-Nazi, one of the meth cookers, a modified Glock 17 in his hands. It seemed most of them had this weapon. The guy was aiming it at Hendricks which gave him no choice. He pulled the trigger and the shotgun boomed, hitting the thug in the chest and blowing him back.

As Hendricks racked the pump, he realised the Latina detective Marquez was right by his side. Around them, the gunfight was escalating, agents and detectives taking cover, but she seemed completely unfazed. She fired her shotgun at a man running towards them, the blast hitting the guy in the chest and punching him off his feet. She racked the pump and fired again, hitting another man. Hendricks and Marquez's determined approach was causing the skinheads to take cover. The ATF and other NYPD detectives moved up to join them, firing down at the camp. Although the gunfight was now in full savage swing, momentum was swinging the law enforcement's way.

Hendricks and Marquez had worked their way to the edge of the camp but were forced to take cover around the corner of a building on the edge of the estate as they came under sustained attack. Hendricks risked a glance, but bullets from automatic weapons and shotgun shells drilled into the wall beside him, chalk and dust spraying into the air. They were pinned down. None of the neo-Nazis were surrendering. It was a full-on shootout, automatic weapons and pump-action shotguns on each side, the air filled with the sound of gunfire and the stink of cordite. Hendricks and Marquez's position had been spotted and the two of them were under heavy fire.

To their right and further back, some of Hendricks' team saw their boss pinned down and increased the rate of fire, giving him an opportunity to peer round the wall.

He saw bullets hitting the three meth trucks at the back of the campsite, smashing the windows and drilling the walls as scores of the Chapter members returned fire from behind cars or bikes. The caravans were directly behind the neo-Nazis so hitting the labs was unavoidable but extremely dangerous. They could go up in a second.

And just then, Hendricks caught sight of the white-haired guy who'd arrived in the van. Wicks. He was firing off rounds with a silenced pistol. When it clicked dry, he ducked behind one of the cars, the wheels either side of him bursting and deflating as rounds took them out.

Hendricks watched him yank open the trunk and pull something out from the back. It was a case.

He opened it up, and Hendricks' blood turned cold.

It was an RPG.

Hendricks raised his Mossberg, centred on the man and pulled the trigger.

The gun jammed.

'*Shit!*'

He dropped down, gunfire chipping the wall beside him, spraying chalk all over him. He saw the blond man sliding a rocket-propelled grenade into the launcher, clicking it into place. Hendricks cleared the breech, but it was taking forever.

'*C'mon!*'

He watched the blond man turn, using the car as cover and aiming the weapon at the group of ATF agents moving in. He was behind the car. Hendricks couldn't hit him.

But ten yards behind the man was one of the eight pound propane tanks used for cooking the meth.

And there was a lit cigarette five feet from the tank.

His weapon emptied, the jam cleared, Hendricks racked a shell and aimed at the tank as the blond man centred the RPG on the ATF Task Force.

He pulled the trigger.

Across the state, inside the Shepherd family home, Finn Sway had the bitch gagged and tied up. She was on the hall floor, her eyes wide with fear, muffled whimpering coming from under her gag. He had his gun to the kid's head, both of them facing the front door.

'What time does your dad come home?'

'In about an hour.'

'Call him.'

The kid didn't react. Finn cuffed him with the butt of the pistol, and the woman made a noise under the gag.

'Call him or die.'

Mark pulled his phone and pushed Redial, his hands shaking.

'Put it on speaker. You send him a signal, I shoot your mother.'

The call rang twice.

'*Mark?*'

The kid didn't respond. Finn pushed the pistol harder into his temple.

'Hey Dad.'

'*Everything OK?*'

Pause.

'Yeah. Was just wondering when you were coming home?'

'*I'm on my way. I'll be there soon.*'

Across the hall, the woman was making sounds. Sway turned to her, pointing the gun. 'Shut your mouth, bitch.' He looked over at the television and saw a freeze frame of the family at what looked like a high school event.

He looked at the face of the man who'd killed Reese, smiling on the screen.

Finn would make sure that he never smiled again.

Although he'd only just turned nine, Mark Shepherd already knew how to handle himself. Being that Dad and his friend Mr Hendricks were both cops, they'd put all four of their kids through bully-proof classes. Dad had also devoted some time to teaching his sons self-defence. Mark was a typical boy, interested in sports and hanging out with his friends, but he also relished the fact his father taught him things other kids his age didn't know. With the gun to his head, Mom tied up behind him, his heart was beating so fast he thought it would burst out of his chest. He felt like he was going to throw up. He could smell alcohol and smoke on the man behind him. He felt the cold metal of the pistol against his temple.

But as the man had turned to Mom, Mark had glanced to his right down the hall, and seen something at the window.

Dad.

He was outside. He made eye contact with Mark and then quickly disappeared from view. Mark sensed the man with the gun turn his attention back.

'How long does it take him to get home?'

'About twenty minutes.'

'Well one of you gets to live until then. Who's it going to be?'

Mark shivered. He looked over at his mother, helpless on the floor, her eyes pleading with the man with the gun.

'Guess it's you kid.'

Given Mark's height, the man was slightly stooped over him. One arm was encircling

Mark's neck, the other holding the pistol. Mark reached behind him and suddenly grabbed the man's balls, just like Dad had taught him.

Then he twisted as hard as he could.

The man with the gun screamed in pain. Not letting go, Mark ducked his head down then reared up hard, the top of his head hammering into the underside of the man's chin like an uppercut. The man fell back onto the floor.

Shouting in pain and fury he lifted his pistol, aiming it straight at Mark.

'Get down!' a voice shouted.

In agony, clutching his groin with one hand, Finn was just about to pull the trigger when he heard the shout.

The kid hit the floor.

And behind him, outside the hall window, was Shepherd.

A pistol in his hands was aimed straight at Finn.

Oh shit.

Shepherd fired three times, smashing the glass of the window. The three gunshots thumped into Sway, laying him out and knocking the machine pistol out of his hand. His head lolled to the side, facing Beth who stared at him, their faces an inch apart.

His eyes were lifeless.

He was dead.

FORTY EIGHT

Checking his rear-view mirror to ensure they hadn't been followed, Bobby Rourke swung the van through the front gates of the farm and moved across the grass. He headed towards a crop duster parked there on the field, facing south. As he drove, he had his window down and heard what sounded like a massive explosion in the distance coming from a familiar direction.

The tip-off from Bleeker's contact had been right. The camp did have surveillance on it. Sacrificing Wicks and the rest of the Chapter had been necessary to get out safely with the virus and it was a decision he hadn't hesitated in making. The tip-off and decoy had bought him a small window which he needed to use. It wouldn't take long for the Feds and pigs to realise Wicks didn't have the virus.

Rourke pulled to a halt beside the light aircraft. Wicks and Drexler had got it out of the shed earlier and it was resting on the grass, ready to go, just as he'd ordered. The plan had always been to fly back to Texas, allowing them to pass over state borders with the canisters containing the virus stowed in the back. The original intention had been for him, Finn, Bleeker and Bleeker's contact to be in the plane but Bobby was the only member of the foursome who'd made it. No matter. Plans changed and so did people.

'Our ticket home,' he said to Drexler, who nodded. He'd told her earlier about the tip off that police were watching the camp and his plan to send Wicks in driving the decoy, giving him and Drexler a window to escape. She'd agreed in a heartbeat, seemingly not caring that she'd originally been left out of the plan or about Wicks' fate. That was why Rourke found her so useful. She didn't have a compassionate bone in her body. She'd been brought up on a farm and had flown a duster before which was a bonus. He'd have a second pair of hands in the cockpit which could be useful.

They both jumped out of the van. Bobby didn't know about many things other than guns and drugs, but he did know about crop dusters. This one was an Antonov An-2, somewhat of a relic but more than sufficient to get the job done. The plane was durable, light and was the largest single-engine biplane ever produced and still flying. The field was private, belonging to the old farmer Wicks and Drexler had shot and buried, but there was no security and no alarm at the gate. Having seen the place in day light, Drexler had told him there was enough of a runway stretch to get up in the air.

Drexler ran over to the plane, pulling open the cabin door. Rourke was already carrying one of the canisters to the doorway. Moving back and forth from the van, the two of them started loading the barrels, one by one. That task completed, they both jumped back into the car. Rourke fired the ignition, moved off and headed towards the entrance of the field. There was a scrapyard a hundred yards down the road. They'd abandon the vehicle there.

By the time anyone found it and made a connection, they'd have sold the virus-laden canisters and be out of the country.

In the shadows, Archer watched them go.

He'd killed the Merc's headlights long before he approached the farm and had parked the vehicle fifty yards back behind some cover. Neither of the two doctors wanted to be left behind, so the three of them had scaled the fence, shielded from view by the farm buildings, and ran forward using a large shed as cover.

Dr Kruger's suggestion and Rach's report of the missing farmer had been right on the money. Up ahead, lit up in the lights of their own vehicle were Rourke and Drexler. Archer recognised her immediately as the woman who'd smashed his nose in Tonic. From their hiding place in the shadows, Archer and the two doctors had watched the pair finish loading a crop duster with what looked like canisters. When that'd been done, they'd climbed back into their vehicle and swung out of the airfield, driving off down the track leading away from the farm.

They'd left, but they'd be back soon, no question.

With the vehicle momentarily gone, Archer motioned for the two doctors to follow him. The trio moved out from behind the shed, running across the flat grass towards the biplane, which was parked facing the long dark stretch of field ahead.

When they arrived, Kruger ran to the side cabin door; he pulled it open and peered inside as Archer kept his eyes on the entrance to the field, making sure Rourke and Drexler weren't on their way back.

'Detective,' Kruger whispered, beckoning him over.

Archer ran to the plane and stuck his head inside. He saw a large tank at the back, six canisters stacked in front of it in a neat cluster.

'They must contain the virus,' Kruger said. 'That must be what they had Frankie working on at the lab.'

He stepped back so Maddy could look inside.

'Jesus,' she said quietly. 'There's gallons of it.'

'It's OK,' Archer said. 'When they come back, I'll drop them and we'll secure the plane.'

'Not here,' Kruger said. 'They'll see us the moment they get back. The headlights will light us up like we're on stage.'

Archer realised he was right.

'Get inside. The moment he checks his cargo, he gets a Sig Sauer in the face.'

Rourke and Drexler had just dumped the van at the scrap yard. Jogging back, they turned into the field and were running towards the plane when they heard the faint sound of engines in the distance. Rourke turned and saw ten or so headlights approaching, coming down the track. Drexler went to grab her pistol, but Rourke caught her hand.

'Relax,' he said. 'It's good.'

The lights grew brighter as a gang of bikers pulled into the airfield and drove straight towards them, the engines on the bikes growling in unison.

Rourke and Drexler shielded their eyes from the glare and the ten bikers came to a halt in front of them both. They killed their engines, then what had to be the leader kicked down the stand, stepped off his bike and walked towards them.

'Who the hell are they?' Maddy whispered, watching from a window inside the plane.

Archer and Kruger looked out beside her.

'What do we do?' Kruger asked.

Archer pulled his cell phone but there was no signal. He had one pistol with seventeen rounds. Sneaking another glance through the window, he saw the bikers were armed with sub-machine guns, pistols and sawn-off shotguns. He saw the group talking, but couldn't hear what was being said. He started thinking fast, desperately searching for a solution.

If he confronted Rourke, Drexler and the bikers it would be twelve on one. Their gunfire would shred him, Maddy and Dr Kruger to pieces.

They were trapped.

'So are we good?' Rourke asked.

The leader of the outlaw gang nodded. 'I've arranged protection at your refuelling points. You won't have any problems.'

'ATF and the police will be searching for us. Can you handle that?'

The man nodded, jabbing a thumb at his men. 'We all live off the grid. Won't be hard to kill some pigs then disappear.'

'You'll get your money by the end of next week.'

The two men shook hands.

Then Rourke and Drexler turned, heading for the plane.

The rear cabin was a muddy brown colour, a series of seats towards the front and a large tank for pesticide or water at the back. Archer, Maddy and Kruger were huddled behind it, hidden from view. Peering round the edge of the tank, Archer watched Rourke and Drexler climb into the cabin, pulling the door shut. For a horrible moment, he thought they were going to move down in their direction, but they went the other way and settled into the cockpit.

They both strapped on their seatbelts and started clicking buttons to fire up the engine and rotors, running checks at the same time.

The crop duster sputtered as the engine started to burst into life.

Rourke and Drexler were ready to fly.

With three passengers they didn't know about in the back.

FORTY NINE

Five minutes later the plane was in the air and climbing. Behind the tank, Archer watched Rourke and Drexler in the cockpit. He glanced to his left. Beside him, Maddy looked scared whilst Dr Kruger was looking at him for silent guidance. Archer gave them both a thumbs up. He felt his stomach tilt again as they gained altitude.

He would have to put a gun on the pair. Take their weapons and force them to land the plane. It wasn't the best plan but he couldn't think of a better alternative. He took a deep breath and reassured himself. The radio was working. They had plenty of fuel and Rourke's Roller PD file had said that he owned a farm. He knew what he was doing in one of these things, otherwise he wouldn't have been able to get in the air in the first place. He'd know how to land it, assuming that he didn't want to kill them all.

Peering around the tank, Archer saw that both of them had their head-gear on, completely distracted and unaware of their uninvited guests. He stepped out from being the tank, his Sig held tightly in his hands. Beside him, he looked at the six canisters, a pesticide hazard sign slapped on the side.

Quietly, he crept towards the cabin, his pistol trained on the back of Rourke's head.

He had to give it to them. They were smarter than then they looked. Using Sway's brother as an alibi when Jacobs was killed. Sending a decoy to the estate so the ATF and the NYPD would be tailing the wrong van. Flying over the State borders. This was never about terrorism. This was about money. The whole time they'd been here, they'd separated themselves from their Chapter and done their own thing. The Chapter's presence was just a diversion. Keep attention off what they were doing. And law enforcement had taken the bait. It was only by luck and intuition that Archer was here.

With the sights of his pistol on Rourke, Archer heard Agent-in-Charge Faison's words echo in his mind.

The most intelligent criminals put distance between themselves and the crime.

Even if they get caught, it'll never get traced back to them.

And suddenly, Archer paused.

Something from earlier had been bothering him all night, It had never settled with him all day. It hadn't rung true when he'd first heard it and it still didn't now.

Dr Tibbs.

When everyone had him fingered as the missing link, Archer hadn't been convinced. Neither had Maddy and he trusted her instincts.

He was such a quiet, gentle guy, she'd said. *I can't believe he'd do this.*

Then Jacobs' phone had rung and everyone had forgotten what she'd said. But she was right. Mixing with neo-Nazis seemed totally out of character for a quiet scientist who was a loner.

The most intelligent criminals put distance between themselves and the crime.

Even if they get caught, it'll never get traced back to them.

Archer froze.

Comprehension dawned.

And he realised a second too late that he'd been played.

He went to turn, but felt the cold barrel of a pistol press up hard against his neck.

'Drop the gun,' Kruger said, his finger on the trigger.

Archer glanced to his left. He saw a Beretta 92. Behind it, Kruger's cut-up, bruised face had hardened.

He wasn't looking for guidance anymore.

'Drop the gun,' he repeated.

Behind him, Archer saw that Maddy was unconscious, bleeding from a cut to her head. Kruger had levelled her the moment Archer turned his back.

'Drop the gun,' he said again. 'Or I blow your brains out.'

Archer felt the cold metal pressed in behind his ear. He didn't have a choice. He dropped the Sig and it clattered to the cabin floor of the plane.

Kruger whistled and Rourke and Drexler turned.

Archer saw astonishment on their faces. Rourke said something to Drexler, then undid his belt and moved down into the belly of the plane as she took over the controls. Archer stayed motionless, the barrel of the pistol driven into the side of his neck.

'Holy shit,' Rourke said to Kruger, genuinely surprised. 'How long have you been there?'

'We got in when you dumped the van.'

'I sent Wicks to come and get you, but he said you had two pigs outside your apartment. I thought you were staying in New York?'

'This *doos* was sniffing around,' he said, the gun into Archer's neck. 'Thought I'd hitch a ride.'

Rourke looked at Archer. 'Is he a pig?'

'Yeah.'

'So kill him.'

Kruger shook his head. 'Not here. The bullets will put holes in the cabin.'

Rourke tilted his head and saw Maddy lying unconscious on the floor. 'OK. Wait till we're over countryside. Then throw them both out.'

Kruger suddenly pistol-whipped Archer hard, knocking him to the floor of the plane. Rourke grabbed a set of handcuffs from Archer's hip and cuffed his hands behind him to a metal hand-hold. He also took the time to hit Archer in the face several times afterwards, his fists smashing into his already busted nose. That done, Rourke gave him a final kick, then turned to Kruger.

'We're on course. I set up the first pit stop in North Carolina.'

Kruger nodded, then took a seat across the cabin from Archer. Rourke kicked Archer again, then headed back to the cockpit. Archer spat blood out of his mouth and looked across at the South African doctor.

The expression he'd worn all day on his beaten-up face had changed.

All trace of his friendliness was gone.

It had been replaced with a menacing stare.

'You son of a bitch,' Archer said.

'It's a miracle we even made it here,' Kruger said. 'I've been watching all of you run around like morons all night.'

'You're a part of this?'

'Of course. I set it up. Do you know how much this virus is worth?'

He jabbed a finger at Rourke, up front in the cockpit with Drexler.

'I needed someone to package and transport it. Figured I might as well hitch a ride. Luckily you made the connection with the farm after I fed you the pesticide idea. You were quick, I'll give you that.'

Archer glanced at Rourke. 'How the hell do you know him?'

Kruger grinned.

He undid the buttons on his shirt and pulled it open.

Archer saw a thick black Swastika tattooed on one pectoral.

On the other was an *SS*.

Stuttgart Soldiers.

'Surprised?' Kruger said with a grin.

Kyle Gunnar's voice echoed in Archer's mind, a missed warning from earlier in the day.

You'd be surprised who some of our members are.

Suddenly, all the missing pieces of the puzzle started to fall into place.

'You were the one who told Bleeker about the virus?'

Kruger nodded.

'He introduced me to them,' he said, jabbing a thumb at the cockpit. 'At a rally two weeks ago. We had a plan, but then Bleeker got greedy and double-crossed us. Kidnapped me and stole the vials. He wanted it all for himself. I think he was going to kill me at the house just before you and your friends showed up.'

Archer thought back. It all started making sense. In the dark plane, he saw the South African grin.

'You piece of shit. You planted the cell phone at Tibbs' apartment.'

'Very good. Pay-as-you-go, so no connection to me. All I had to do was clean off my prints, visit Will on Thursday night then drop it on his floor before I left. He must have found it, stowed it in the drawer and framed himself.'

Kruger pointed his pistol at Maddy.

'Anyway, be thankful you got an extra few hours. You both should have died at the lab.'

Archer didn't respond. He was thinking back through the day, cursing himself at what an idiot he'd been.

'When Gunnar walked past at the Bureau this afternoon, you ducked down. Put your head in your hands like you were upset. But you were covering up. You knew he'd recognise you and wouldn't be able to hide it.'

'Very good. But what a shame. You're too late. You're going to die. And what a tragedy about your friend at the lab. His coffin will be the size of a tinder box.'

Archer spat blood from his mouth again, glaring at the neo-Nazi doctor.

'Easy now,' Kruger said. 'At any moment, I can open that door and throw you out. I could do it right now.'

The two men stared at each other. Then Kruger checked his watch. Archer glanced to his left and saw Maddy still slumped on the floor. She was out cold. Blood had slid down her face from the wound from the blow to the back of her head.

Kruger suddenly whistled at the cockpit. Rourke heard him and turned. Kruger beckoned for him to come down, so Rourke left his seat and walked down into the cabin.

'How are we doing?'

'We're on course.' Rourke glanced at Archer. 'You want to get rid of him now?'

Kruger didn't reply.

He raised his pistol instead, aiming at the centre of Rourke's torso, and started firing.

Rourke took six rounds. Each impact jerked him back and he collapsed in a torn, bloody dead heap across the cabin. The bullets ruptured holes in the cabin and air started to whistle in. Archer saw Drexler turn, looking at Rourke's corpse, her eyes wide with shock. But before she could react, Kruger was up on his feet, the pistol trained on her.

'Don't move, bitch,' he said, moving down towards her in the cockpit. 'I'll take that weapon.'

Archer saw Drexler stay motionless behind the control stick. Then she reached inside her jacket and passed over what looked like a silenced Glock. Kruger took it, and tossed it into the cabin behind him, the pistol landing near Rourke's corpse.

He started ordering Drexler to do something, the gun to her head, but Archer couldn't hear what it was from the whistling coming through the bullet holes in the plane.

Archer saw her nodding and he felt the plane start veering to the left.

Rourke was slumped across the cabin, torn apart by the gunfire. Archer looked up at Kruger, who was walking back into the cabin, grinning at him.

'Just like that, huh? Kill him and take his ride to Texas?'

Kruger smiled, a strange look in his eyes.

'We're not going to Texas.'

FIFTY

Archer watched as Kruger stepped across the cabin towards him. He grabbed one of the canisters full of the liquidised virus, rolling it towards the tank. He attached the tubing and pushed the pumping mechanism; the big tank started sucking in all the liquid.

Archer watched him work. 'So where are we going?'

'Take a guess.'

Archer thought of their flight path and the veer they'd taken.

'DC?'

Kruger didn't respond.

'Are you nuts?'

Kruger shook his head. 'No. I'm not. I'm going to do something that the Third Reich only ever dreamt of. They fought an entire war with the Americans but never got anywhere near their homeland. By the time the rest of the country wakes up this morning, thousands upon thousands of people in their capital city will be dead. My virus will cleanse that place like a Biblical plague.'

'Keep dreaming. They'll shoot you down before you get anywhere near the city.'

'Doesn't matter. This stuff will still be in the air. Rourke will go down as the man who killed a city. I'll be just an innocent passenger.'

Archer looked at the thickly-built doctor with the hate tattooed on his chest.

Kruger flicked his gaze to Archer. His eyes were gleaming.

'Why the hell are you doing this?'

'What?'

'You're a doctor, for Christ's sake.'

'So?'

He paused.

'You know the history. Apartheid, Mandela, black and white. But you don't know that four black men broke into my house when I was a boy. You don't know that they raped my mother in front of me, then shot her in the head. That they put a shotgun in my father's mouth and pulled the trigger. I would have been next but a neighbour heard the shots and arrived just in time. He killed them and saved me.'

He spat on the floor.

'I was orphaned at eleven years old by those bastards,' he said. 'These men worked for my father. He took them in when they had nothing. Gave them a home, food, water, a job. A purpose. And that's how they repay him.' He sneered. 'And over there, American culture is everywhere. All those guys worshipped it. The rappers, the baseball caps, the pants around their asses. All that shit started here. It's spread, like a disease. Liberal, democratic bullshit. So now, this is payback.'

He looked down at the canisters, then at Archer.

'I'm no different from Peter. He created this virus because he lost someone he loved. Now I'm going to use it for the exact same reason.'

'You won't even make the city,' Archer said again. 'They'll shoot you down.'

'Like I said, it doesn't matter. Hell of a wind blowing today. Headed south.'

He smiled.

'I've thought of everything, Detective. It makes no difference whether I spray this stuff or we take a hit. Either way the virus will be in the air and will be spread for hundreds of miles, floating down onto the city.'

'And you'll be a martyr for the cause, right?' Archer said.

'Correct.'

Silence.

Beside him, the tank sucked up the liquidised virus, the piping sealed tight so none of it escaped into the air.

'Bleeker was a fool. But he was the only one with any balls to use this virus.' Kruger nodded at Rourke's corpse, slumped across the cabin. 'All he wanted was money.'

He paused.

'But not me. Not tonight.'

With that, Kruger moved off and headed up the cabin. He moved into the cockpit, jabbing the pistol into Drexler's neck who nodded and said something to him. Watching him go, Archer felt helpless.

Kruger was right. The gas would be airborne whatever happened, if it was sprayed, they were shot down or they crashed. Hundreds of thousands of people would die.

Archer felt the tight handcuffs around his wrists.

In desperation, he looked over at Maddy who was motionless on the floor.

Suddenly, her eyes flared open.

Maddy had regained consciousness whilst Kruger was talking. She'd heard everything he said, but had played possum, staying still. She looked straight at Archer, who was sitting across from her in the rear of the plane and saw the cuffs holding him to the bar. With Kruger's back to them, assuming his hostages were restrained or out cold and therefore no threat, she quietly raised herself to her hands and knees and crept forward, never taking her eyes off Kruger who was still focused on Drexler and where they were going. She crawled towards Archer, who tilted his hips, mouthing *this pocket.* She reached inside and found the key to his cuffs.

She quickly undid them.

Now free, he went to rise, but Kruger suddenly stood upright. Maddy froze then frantically scrambled back to the rear of the plane and resumed her previous position trying not to breathe too heavily.

Archer put his hands behind his back as if they were still bound.

Kruger moved back into the cabin. He walked up to Archer and stared down at him, a mad light in his eyes.

'Not long now. But you're pissing me off. I think it's time you and the bitch went for a skydive.'

He laughed.

'Just like her old man.'

He placed his Beretta to one side, then moved towards the door. He grabbed a support rail and reached for the handle. As he did so, Archer shouted something to him, but given the noise the whistling wind made from the bullet holes in the cabin, Kruger couldn't hear.

Instinctively, he turned towards Archer, stepping closer.

'What?'

Launching forward, Archer suddenly took Kruger off his feet.

FIFTY ONE

Kruger had done his research. The duster was coming in from the north-west. The wind reading was perfect, blowing south. If they took a hit, the virus would be airborne, drifting down onto the capital city and the surrounding area.

They were beginning to approach a military installation. It was Fort Myer, a military base aligned with the USMC Henderson Hall and the first joint base in the Department of Defense. Although it was the early hours of the morning, the main ops room was busy. A serviceman studying the screen in front of him frowned, peering closer. He pulled off his head-set, then turned.

'Captain?'

A man looked over.

'I've got a small propeller aircraft headed south towards the city,' one of the men said.

'That's restricted airspace.'

'Could be a private airplane off course?'

'I don't care,' the Captain said, walking around the ops room towards the controls. 'He comes anywhere near the city, he's going down. Pass me the transmitter.'

The man did so. The Captain took it and pushed the buttons down on either side.

'Unidentified aircraft, this is the United States Army. Identify yourself.'

Archer and Kruger were grappling furiously on the floor of the crop duster. Drexler had turned, sensing something was wrong, but she had to stay in the cockpit or the plane would dip. As the two men fought, Maddy had reversed the pump; the

liquid was now being sucked back into the
canister. Grabbing a bar to steady herself, she
staggered across the cabin, avoiding the fighting
men and wrenched open the side door.

The noise in the cockpit increased tenfold as
wind roared in the cabin.

Her coat and hair flapping violently in the wind,
she looked down and saw that they were flying
over what she guessed was the Potomac, the
water glinting far below in the moonlight.

She grabbed the canister nearest to her and
using all her strength, heaved it out of the door.

Kruger was as strong as an ox. Archer was
pinned on the floor of the aircraft, trying to attack
the doctor's neck. Kruger was trying to strike
him, but was hampered by the fact that he needed
all his strength to hold Archer down. As they
fought, Kruger became aware of Maddy throwing
the canisters out of the door.

'Bitch!'

With a roar of anger, he lunged for her.

But he made a fatal mistake.

He turned his back on Archer.

Archer leapt on the big South African, hooked
his legs around his lower torso and sunk in a rear
choke, pinning him to the floor. As Kruger
gagged and fought for air, Maddy continued to
drag the canisters across the cabin floor and
throw them out, each one plummeting down and
dropping into the Potomac below. She reached
over for the last. She pulled out the tubing, the
seal instantly forming. She screwed on the
secondary cap as tight as she could, then went to
throw it out of the plane.

Suddenly, three bullet-holes appeared in the big
tank by her head, and she dropped to the floor

instinctively. Archer saw Drexler moving out of the cockpit, her retrieved silenced Glock 21 in her hands. He released Kruger, just as Drexler raised the weapon again but her mag clicked dry. Screaming a curse, she threw the weapon away and moved into the cabin towards them.

Abandoning Kruger on the floor, Archer rose and waited for her. He had a rule about not harming women, but this one had broken his nose and had just tried to kill Maddy. All rules were out the window.

'C'mon, bitch,' he shouted. *'I'm ready this time.'*

She screamed like a banshee and lunged forward but was met with a huge uppercut that took her off her feet, revenge for the shot she broke Archer's nose with. She bit her tongue and lip, the punch sending her backwards and onto the floor in a daze. Watching her drop, Archer suddenly heard the radio up front in the cockpit. He ran forward to the cockpit and could just make out what it was saying over the howling gale.

'Unidentified aircraft, this is the United States Army. You have just entered restricted airspace. This is a verbal warning. If you disregard this and do not turn around, we will shoot you down, I repeat, we will shoot you down!'

'That's the last one!' Maddy shouted behind him, tossing out the final canister.

Drexler was trying to get to her feet, but she was dizzy from the blow, disorientated and weakly spitting blood from her mouth. Archer grabbed the radio receiver. The plane had started dipping and was gathering speed and he felt his stomach lurch.

'This is NYPD Detective Sam Archer, I repeat, NYPD Detective Sam Archer!'

'This is your final warning. If you do not turn around right now, you will be shot down. I repeat, you will be shot down!'

He swung round, frantically searching the cabin.

He saw a parachute hanging by Maddy's head.

'Put it on!' he shouted, pointing at it.

Far below them, the Captain at Fort Myer looked at the screen in desperation.

'What do I do, sir?' the man in front of him asked.

'They've been warned. We have no alternative. *Fire!'*

Just as Kruger and the woman re-gathered their senses, Archer looked through the window and saw lights up ahead and to the right.

The radio had gone quiet.

He turned and ran through the plane, past Drexler and Kruger, who were staggering to their feet. Maddy had just finished securing a parachute, clicking it in place with shaking hands, holding a hook inside the plane as she stood by the open door. Her eyes widened as Archer headed straight for her.

Without stopping, Archer tackled her, driving his shoulder through.

He took them both through the open doorway, and out of the plane into the night sky.

A split-second later, the rocket launched from Fort Myer below.

On their feet in the cabin, Kruger and Drexler looked out of the cockpit window and saw it streaking towards them.

Drexler screamed.

Kruger closed his eyes.

As the duster exploded above them, Archer and Maddy tumbled through the air, plummeting down through the darkness towards the Potomac. They had just the one parachute between them which was strapped to Maddy's back.

She screamed in terror as they hurtled towards the water through the dark night, the wind shrieking around them.

'Archer!'

He didn't answer. He used all his strength just to hang on. If he lost his grip, he'd fall hundreds of feet to his death. Hanging on to the straps above her shoulders, he manoeuvred his legs tight around her. He hooked his right arm into the straps, gripping the far one as hard as he could as they spun down towards the water.

He pulled the parachute release cord.

Nothing happened.

He tried again, the wind howling in their ears.

'Shit!'

The water was approaching with terrifying speed.

If they hit it at this speed, they would both be killed instantly.

'Archer!'

Archer pulled the cord as hard as he could for the third time.

'C'MON!'

It worked. The white parachute unravelled and billowed out with a flurry. The two of them

whiplashed up as the parachute expanded, killing
their speed.

And they hit the water.

FIFTY TWO

Five hours later, the dawn sun was just starting to rise over the horizon. At the New Jersey industrial estate, the leading doctor of a HAZMAT team finished testing the air. He removed his headgear and gave Hendricks the thumbs up. The toxicity had lowered, the strong wind disseminating the poisonous gas. They were good. The area was safe.

When Hendricks hit the propane it had triggered a huge explosion, all three meth trucks and the other tanks of propane going up. Unlike in the movies, propane tanks don't explode unless they're hit with an incendiary round or if there's a source of fire to ignite them. Hendricks had done the latter; his shotgun blast had bled gas from the tank which came into contact with the lit cigarette on the ground. That was all it took.

The blast had killed sixteen of the Chapter members on the spot, and most importantly Wicks, the blond-haired guy with the RPG. The shockwave had blown the remaining thugs off their feet, completely disorientating them, their eyes and ears bleeding, their senses scrambled. Hendricks and most of the other law enforcement were further back and using cover anyway, so aside from a serious ringing in their ears, they'd been pretty well unaffected by the blast. After the explosion, they'd immediately moved in, the handful of remaining Chapter members not putting up any resistance. They were locked into handcuffs, most of them still trying to work out what had happened. Four ATF guys had been hit in the gunfight and ambulances were already on their way, along with HAZMAT. Once the place was secured HAZMAT had ordered everyone off site, their team hosing down the flaming caravans.

As the team withdrew and the arrested neo-Nazis were dumped in the back of an ATF truck, there were reports coming in about a situation over the Potomac River. Apparently six canisters loaded with a deadly virus had been thrown from a crop duster over the water. A NYPD detective and a female doctor had jumped out of the plane just before it was blown out of the sky. A parachute had slowed their descent, but it hadn't released early enough and both had sustained injuries. They'd been pulled from the water and taken to an army hospital. No one knew any more details other than the canisters had been retrieved from the water, intact and secure.

It was over.

Standing in the middle of the smoking estate, Hendricks looked around him. The dawn sun was giving the place a tangerine glow. The Latina detective Marquez was beside him, the embers of the dying campfire ten yards in front of them. Hendricks recalled her fearlessness in the gunfight. *I wish I'd known about you when I'd selected my team*, he thought, glancing at her.

The ATF agents Faison and Peterson walked over to join them. Hendricks and Marquez nodded to the two men and the quartet stood in silence. Hendricks felt his cell phone purr in his pocket. He pulled it out and looked at the display. It was Shepherd.

He took the call.

'Shep, where the hell have you been, man?' he said. 'You missed-'

He suddenly paused, listening.

'What?'

*

'Take it easy, doc!' Archer said, as his leg was elevated in a sling. 'Jesus!'

The army doctor gave him a look, then satisfied, turned and walked out of the room. The hospital sling was supporting Archer's broken ankle, bound and wrapped in a cast.

He'd stayed conscious when they hit the water. Despite the parachute massively reducing their speed, they'd hit the surface hard. Archer had skydived once before. Chalky had bought him a skydive for his birthday a couple of years ago, but little to Chalk's knowledge Archer had booked him onto the jump as well after he'd been told of the present. The night before the jump they'd been out on the town till four am and the two hungover officers had arrived at the airfield the next morning feeling very much the worse for wear. Leaping out of an aircraft was absolutely the last thing on God's earth that they wanted to do right then. In the end, Archer had enjoyed the experience, particularly seeing the look on Chalky's face before they dived and then hearing his yells and promises of retribution as they fell through the air.

However, Archer had remembered one vital piece of information from that day. It'd come from the jump instructor when Archer had aired a concern about parachute reliability. The guy had told him that he'd only suffered dual parachute failure once in his career. He'd survived by signalling to another man he'd jumped with. Falling through the air, the two men had manoeuvred towards each other. The man without a chute had hooked his arms into the other guy's parachute, legs around his waist and had held on as hard as he could as the other man pulled the cord. He'd dislocated his shoulder but they'd both survived.

Little did Archer know at the time that his question would save his and Maddy's life a couple of years later.

Archer knew the duster's low level of flight had saved them. If they'd been higher, they would have reached terminal velocity. The parachute would have ripped off or he'd have broken both his arms trying to stay hooked to Maddy. Or they'd have hit the water without a windbreak, which would have been similar to what Peter Flood experienced when he stepped off the *Flood Microbiology* rooftop. Nevertheless, they'd hit the water hard. So hard it had knocked the wind out of both of them and broken some bones.

Pitched into the ice-cold water, it had been suddenly dark and silent. Archer had still been holding Maddy who'd gone limp. Aware that the parachute was above them on the water he'd kept hold of her and kicked as hard as he could, aiming up and away.

They'd surfaced to the right of the parachute, Archer taking in a mouthful of air. But his joy at being alive was short-lived. In his arms, Maddy wasn't moving and pieces of the flaming crop duster were starting to rain down around them. Minutes later, a DC Metro patrol boat came roaring up the River having seen the parachute landing. The pair were pulled from the water, sub-machine guns trained on them until it could be verified who they were. Then the adrenaline had worn off and the pain had set in.

Once safely on the boat, Archer had looked down and seen his foot was bent at a bizarre angle. Beside him on the deck, Maddy was still unmoving. They'd injected Archer with something that had to be morphine and the pain had disappeared. Then they'd taken him to a hospital in a painless daze. He was only just starting to re-gather his senses.

There was a knock at the door. It opened and a grey-haired man in military uniform entered the room.

'Good morning, Detective.'

'Where am I?'

'Walter Reed Medical.'

The morphine was wearing off. Archer moved and grimaced.

'Jesus. I feel like I got hit by a bus.'

There was a pause. The man in uniform stepped forward.

'My name is Lieutenant Grant. I spoke to your boss, Sergeant Shepherd, at the NYPD. He explained the situation and told me who you are. I wanted to come here and thank you personally.'

Archer looked at the man. 'Did it work?'

He smiled and nodded. 'Everyone's safe. Finn Sway, Bobby Rourke and Reuben Kruger are all dead. A diving team pulled the canisters containing the virus from the water. They're on their way to a military lab where they'll be destroyed.'

'What's the cover?'

The man smiled. 'Farmer lost control of his crop duster. The Army were forced to shoot it down to protect an urban area. He parachuted out before it took the hit.'

Archer nodded.

Then he thought of something. 'Where's the doc?'

'She's in another room down the hall.'

'Is she OK?'

He nodded. 'Some bumps and bruises and a broken leg. Bit of mild whiplash. But she'll be fine.'

Archer nodded, then struggled to get up and out of the bed.

'Take it easy,' Grant said, moving forward to help him.

She was lying in the bed when he entered, fast asleep. Wearing one of the hospital gowns, the same as him, her dark hair was draped over her shoulders. Sunlight was streaming in through the window.

Hobbling in on crutches, Archer moved inside the room as quietly as he could, then shut the door. He watched her for a moment, then moved forward awkwardly on the crutches and sat beside her in an empty chair.

She stirred awake and opened her eyes.

For the first time, he noticed they were green.

'Hey,' Archer said.

She smiled. 'Hey.'

'How are you feeling?'

'My leg kills.'

'Yeah. Mine too.'

She looked down at his foot. 'Jesus, Archer, you should be resting.'

'I am resting. And I wanted to see you.'

She looked at him for a moment. He watched as tears welled in her eyes. She struggled up, leaned forward and hugged him.

'You did it,' she said in his ear, her arms wrapped around him, tears rolling down her cheeks. 'You saved everyone.'

'So did you.'

She withdrew and then noticed something on his forehead. Reaching up, she pushed his hair back gently and saw a jagged scar. It ran from the middle of his forehead down to his ear. She'd never noticed it before. It had always been obscured by his hair.

'How did you get this?'

'Someone tried to cut my face off.'

'When?'

'Earlier this year.'

She looked at him, and saw that he was serious.

'How did you get him to stop?'

'I beat him to death with a door.'

She scanned his face. He wasn't lying.

She couldn't help but laugh. 'There's never a dull moment with you, that's for sure.'

He smiled.

And she leant forward and kissed him.

At the Counter-Terrorism Bureau, Shepherd was sitting with Rach and Hendricks in the briefing room, all three of them exhausted. Once he'd put Sway down, he'd run into his home and freed his wife and boy. Neighbours had already reported hearing shots fired so back-up had arrived within a couple of minutes and taken control of the scene. He'd made sure that Beth and Mark were OK and that Finn Sway's body was removed. He'd had to leave them to close out the rest of the operation, but armed officers were staying at his house until he got back.

It seemed all hell had broken loose suddenly. He'd just got off the phone with an Army lieutenant at Walter Reed who'd filled him in on what had happened to Archer and Maddy. It turned out Dr Kruger had been the missing link. He'd been an extremist in South Africa and joined *The Stuttgart Soldiers* when he arrived in the States. He was the man who'd told Bleeker about the virus at one of the New York Chapter meetings, and together with Rourke and Sway the four men had planned to steal and sell the virus. But Bleeker had got greedy, kidnapped Kruger to gain access to the lab and stolen the vials. Archer had explained to the lieutenant that Sway and Rourke were planning to fly the canisters containing the virus back to Texas, but Kruger had always intended to hijack the crop duster and cover DC with it. Archer and the doc had stopped him just in time.

Josh was out of surgery; he was going to be fine. Shepherd had spoken to him on the phone and the detective was furious that he'd missed out on all the action. Once Shepherd had told Hendricks what happened with Finn Sway at his home, he got a full update of what had happened at the campsite. Apparently the neo-Nazis had almost an entire cache of stolen weapons, so Faison got what he wanted. Firing at a Federal agent was a serious crime so having fired at an entire Task Force, the remaining bunch were going away for a long time, joining their three friends who'd confronted Archer in the nightclub.

However, not all the news was good. The tallied dead at the lab in New Jersey had been eleven; a Dr Jonathan Bale, his entire team, his wife, a security guard and a woman called

Melissa Slade who'd turned out to be Dr Frankie Glover's girlfriend. Glover himself was dead, as was Jorgensen, joining the fifty nine who'd perished at the store by the Seaport. A New Jersey farmer had also been found, hastily buried beside a shed at his farm with a fatal gunshot wound to the head, much like Alistair Jacobs. And of course there was Luis Cesar. The puzzle of the murder weapon from Tonic East was solved when an attentive CSU investigator noticed a rectangular parcel in the lobby of the apartment building from where the shot had been taken. It was addressed to a company in Texas. They'd opened it up and found a Winchester 270 inside, a suppressor on the end, the weapon that had killed the English lawyer.

The phone on the desk suddenly rang. Rach took the call. She listened for a few moments, then thanked whoever was on the other end and put the receiver back on the cradle.

'Good news. Metro PD confirmed the canisters are on their way to the lab.'

'For research?'

She shook her head. 'To be destroyed.'

Shepherd smiled. He went to speak further, but there was a quiet knock on the door behind him. He turned. And saw his wife.

Beth.

'Hi,' he said, rising from his chair.

'Hi.'

There was a pause. Rach and Hendricks got the signal.

'We'll head out,' Hendricks said patting his friend on the shoulder, Rach following him.

'Thank you. I mean it. Outstanding work from both of you.'

They nodded, moving past Beth Shepherd, leaving the husband and wife alone.

'Please. Come in,' he said. She shut the door behind her. As it had done so many times in the past few weeks, a silence fell between them, both of them standing across the room from each other.

Only a few feet apart but an eighteen year old boy's life separating them.

'Thank you for what you did.'

Shepherd didn't reply.

'I heard what happened,' she said. 'Your team saved everyone.'

'Yes, they did.'

'Are they all OK?'

Shepherd looked at her. 'No. Josh got shot. Archer broke his leg.' Pause. 'And Dave Jorgensen died.'

'I'm sorry.'

Pause.

'How are you?' she asked.

'I'm OK,' he said.

Silence. He looked her in the eye.

'I'm so sorry.'

She blinked and turned her head to hide the tears in her eyes.

'I just miss him, Matt,' she said, her voice trembling.

'So do I,' Shepherd said. She started to cry. He took a step closer. She didn't withdraw. He moved closer still. She didn't withdraw.

Then they embraced for the first time in months.

She cried quietly, her head against his shirt.

'I'm so sorry,' she said. 'I know it was an accident. It's not your fault.'

Then she leaned up and kissed him, all her
anger and blame washing away.

He wasn't a murderer.

He was a hero.

FIFTY THREE

Four days later Archer and Maddy were standing on the street in Union Square in the middle of the afternoon. It was just coming up to sundown on Christmas Eve as shoppers, mostly men, rushed around buying last minute presents. A charity Santa was ringing a bell just behind them, set up just outside Whole Foods. The same group of carol singers from Pier 17 were standing across the Square beside the brass band, singing carols and collecting donations for charity.

Wrapped up warm in a new grey hoodie and his same green coat, Archer had his lower leg in a cast, crutches under his arm, a strip of tape over his nose between two black eyes. He faced Maddy, who was standing with her back to a taxi, the rear door open. She lived just off Union Square but her apartment was now empty, her things already on the way to their new place.

'So this is it,' Archer said with a smile.

Maddy nodded.

'Got all your stuff?'

She nodded. She moved forward and kissed him. Then they hugged.

'Goodbye Archer,' she said in his ear.

'Goodbye, doc.'

She kissed him again, then turned and moved into the cab, closing the door. As Archer leaned back on his crutches, the driver pulled away from the kerb and the car moved off down the street, turning left and heading uptown until it was out of sight. Watching it go, Archer had a brief attack of déjà vu.

Then he hobbled back over towards Josh who was standing nearby, watching him with a smile.

He had his arm in a white sling. The wound on his arm was a clean through and through. The bullet had been removed, the damage cleaned and stitched up.

'Off she goes.'

Josh smiled. 'Safe and well. Where's she going?'

'California. She's already been offered a job there in the New Year. Fresh start.'

Josh nodded. He checked his watch with his good arm.

'C'mon. I owe you a beer.'

Together, the two men moved down the street, headed towards a bar just down 14th Street. Josh walked slowly as Archer negotiated the gritted sidewalk with his crutches. The lights and decorations in the windows they passed were festive and welcoming. The city was showing itself off in all its glory. Archer sensed Josh huffing beside him; his partner had spent the last week trying to calm down after missing the finale of the operation and furious at not being there to play his part. Archer looked at him and grinned.

'There'll be a next time.'

'There better not be,' Josh said. 'But you left it pretty damn close, didn't you?'

'You know I like to be dramatic.'

'You should take up skydiving. You're a natural.'

'Clearly,' Archer said, pointing with his crutches.

'You could save them some money. Only one parachute between two people.'

Archer grinned as the two cops walked towards the bar. Josh was the first to the door and he pulled it open, letting Archer in first. Inside it was warm and inviting. As the two of them made their way inside, Archer saw a familiar face sitting at a table.

It was Marquez.

She smiled when she saw them, stepping off her stool and giving them both a hug. Archer lowered himself onto a seat, stowing his crutches whilst the other two shrugged off their coats. Marquez had already got a round in, a glass of wine in front of her, two bottles of ice-cold Miller waiting for the two men.

She looked at them and tried to stifle a smile. She failed and giggled.

'What's so funny?' Josh asked.

'Look at the state of you two.'

She had a point; both of them looked as if they'd been hit by a train. A shot up arm, a broken ankle, a busted nose and two black eyes.

'Maybe take the photos this year instead of being in them,' she said.

They both smiled, leaning forward and taking their bottles of beer. Archer lifted it to his mouth then thought for a moment and made a toast.

'Hey. To Jorgensen.'

The other two looked at him for a moment. Marquez smiled and they touched drinks in a toast.

'Jorgensen.'

'Jorgensen.'

There was a pause as they drank.

'Right, let's get some food,' Josh said. A waitress from the bar was already approaching them, menus in her hands. She'd seen the two men enter and noticed that they both were pretty roughed up.

'What happened?' she asked, seeing the bruising on Archer's face and the white cast on his leg.

'Had an accident,' he told her. 'Skydiving.'

'What happened?'

'Parachute malfunction.'

'It didn't open?'

'I wasn't wearing one.'

She looked at him, then laughed, assuming he was joking.

'Rather you than me,' she said, placing the menus on the table. 'I'd never have the guts to jump out of a plane.'

Archer smiled.

'You'd be surprised what can motivate you.'

THE END

###

About the author:

Born in Sydney, Australia and raised in England and Brunei, Tom Barber has always had a passion for writing and story-telling. It took him to Nottingham University, England, where he graduated in 2009 with a 2:1 BA Hons in English Studies. Post-graduation, Tom followed this by moving to New York City and completing the 2 Year Meisner Acting training programme at The William Esper Studio, furthering his love of acting and screen-writing.

Upon his return to the UK in late 2011, Tom set to work on his debut novel, *Nine Lives*, which has since become a five-star rated Amazon UK Kindle hit. The following books in the series, *The Getaway, Blackout, Silent Night, One Way, Return Fire* and *Green Light* have been equally successful, garnering five-star reviews in the US, UK, France, Australia and Canada.

Silent Night is the fourth novel in the Sam Archer series.

Follow @TomBarberBooks.

Read an extract from

One Way

By
Tom Barber

The fifth Sam Archer thriller.
Now available on Amazon Kindle.

*****

ONE

Two officers from East Hampton Town PD took the call. Both male, they'd joined the Department fresh from the Suffolk County Police Academy three years ago, and after a twelve-week orientation and on-the-job training programme, had been partners ever since.

East Hampton Town PD is made up of fifty-six officers who perform all of the law-enforcement tasks the area requires. The Hamptons are a group of villages forming a part of Long Island that everyone associates with wealth; the rich and famous frequently choose to vacation there, some renting places for the season and others just buying them outright to save hassle. Whichever option they take, the Hamptons contain some of the most expensive residential properties not just on the East Coast, but in all of the United States. There was a reason the region served as a setting in *The Great Gatsby;* the area evokes the glamour and sophistication of a prosperous present and romanticised past.

Given the demographic and the amount of zeroes a person needs in their bank account just to rent a place there, crime is low. Most of those who vacation and live in the Hamptons are the business and social crème de la crème, so any illegal activity tends to be either petty stuff or at the opposite end of the spectrum, serious accounting, fraud or business transgressions which an FBI or a Financial Crimes task force from the city handles. The most common illegal deed is burglary, thieves capitalising on properties mothballed for long periods out of season or when the residents are out of town, making the most of their absence to help themselves to expensive furniture, art and jewellery.

Murder in East Hampton Town is almost unheard of. Until that Saturday afternoon, there hadn't been a single case in the area in over nine years. The PD has no homicide division, which means in the extremely rare event of an unexplained death, a Department squad car answers the call.

In their three years together, the two young men on their way to the callout that day had never attended a murder scene.

But what they found at the villa significantly changed that.

It had just gone 3pm on a beautiful Saturday in early March. The air was warm, the sun shining, summer missing the memo and arriving three months early. The address the two officers were given by Dispatch was a prestigious beach villa an hour's drive from the city. A delivery man had called it in fifteen minutes ago. He'd been sent out to deliver a few additional cases of wine for a party and after no-one had responded to his repeated knocking on the front door, he'd gone around the back.

Inside an East Hampton Town PD Ford Interceptor, the two cops swung into the drive, pulling up beside an ambulance and seeing the delivery man sitting in the back. His own van was parked on the side of the road outside the gates, the rear doors still open. The man had an oxygen mask over his face and was being attended to by a couple of paramedics inside the ambulance.

He was staring straight ahead, his eyes glazed, and didn't seem to notice the two cops arrive.

Sliding on the handbrake and switching off the engine, the two police officers stepped out of their vehicle and slammed the doors. Both were dressed in the dark blue EHT PD police uniform, and were carrying a pistol, cuffs, radio and nightstick on their belts.

The medics looked over at them but didn't say anything, concentrating on their patient.

Approaching the entrance to the house, the officers saw the front door was shut, several cases of wine on a wheeled dolly beside it, the booze abandoned by the delivery guy.

Looking at the door, one of the officers turned and walked over to the ambulance.

'Got a glove?' he asked quietly.

The medic closest to him pulled a latex one from a box, passing it over. Snapping it onto his hand with a silent nod of thanks, the officer re-joined his partner. With the glove protecting against fingerprints, he tried the handle.

It twisted and the door opened.

He eased it back to reveal the interior of the villa.

The house had a Mediterranean feel, light, open and airy with a polished tile floor which would keep the place cool in the hot weather. There were impressive paintings on the walls either side of the hallway, an ornate mirror hanging above a gold gilt marble-topped table to the right, a large crystal lamp and vase of flowers placed on the top.

The two cops stepped inside slowly, taking care not to touch or disturb anything. They made their way down the corridor and passed through an open door to arrive at what was the main living area.

It was spacious and open-plan, conjoined with a large kitchen and separated by a long granite-topped counter. Matching the exterior of the house, the walls were painted white and cream.

It meant the blood spattered all over them stood out starkly.

There were bodies strewn everywhere. Men. Women. Children. It was clear from the remaining foodstuffs on the counter and on a dining table that they'd been killed at or just prior to lunchtime.

Bowls of salad and plates of sliced cold-cuts were sitting abandoned.

Glasses and plates were shattered all over the floor, shards of glass and pieces of bone china lying amongst spilt food.

Bottles of wine and beer had either been fragmented by gunfire or were lying smashed on the counter, table and floor, the liquid mixing with the food and blood.

Deep black bullet holes riddled the light walls and scores of copper shell casings were scattered everywhere, lying amongst the bodies and debris.

The villa had a terrible stillness.

It looked more like an abattoir than a holiday home.

Both cops stood frozen in the doorway. It took each of them a moment to recover from the initial shock. As one stared in horror at the carnage in front of him, the other looked out onto the veranda directly in front of them.

The windows were all intact. One of the doors was pulled open, and the thin cream curtains fluttered gently in the breeze.

The only movement in an otherwise motionless house.

They heard a set of wind-chimes, tinkling softly from somewhere outside as they made gentle contact in the light wind. The villa was on the edge of the beach so the two men could see and hear the waves as they rolled in, seagulls calling from somewhere nearby, the air salty.

The cop to the right stepped forward, picking his way slowly and cautiously round the edge of the room, taking great care not to tread on any evidence. It was easier said than done. When he made it to the window, he drew his nightstick and used the club to push the gently billowing curtains to one side, examining the sand visible beyond the veranda.

There were a series of children's footprints visible, coming back and forth from the water.

But there were also a set of four, maybe five, definite adult prints, leading from the sea to the villa and back again.

He looked up but saw nothing except clear blue sea and horizon.

No ships, no sailboats.

No people.

Whoever did this was long gone.

He turned away from the window and re-joined his partner, who still hadn't moved as he stared at the massacre. He sensed his partner watching him and they made eye contact.

Their priority now was to clear the rest of the residence.

The two men pulled their side-arms and split up, following protocol, checking the villa quickly. They moved fast but worked thoroughly, both of them on edge, inspecting every room. The rest of the house was equally lavish, each room beautifully decorated and well-appointed with expensive furniture. Whoever owned the property was damn wealthy, that was for sure.

It was clear as daylight they also had enemies.

Soon after, the two officers met up again outside the main room. The man who'd stepped up to the window holstered his side-arm and swallowed, his throat dry.

'Found two more upstairs. Both shot in the head.'

'Was this a robbery?'

His partner stared at the blood-stained and bullet-riddled walls around them.

'No. This was an execution.'

The other man looked down at the corpses. The body closest to his feet was a big man in shorts and a white shirt, lying flat on his back. He had a gold chain around his neck, thick chest hair protruding through the gap in the fabric, his hair combed back.

He'd been shot three times in the chest. Blood had dried around him, his lifeless eyes staring up vacantly at the ceiling.

Shifting his gaze, a body ten feet away caught the officer's eye. The guy had a pistol in a holster on his hip, lying face down in a pool of his own blood.

He wasn't the only corpse in the room who had a weapon.

Staying where they were, the two cops both heard the sound of wailing sirens somewhere in the distance. Back up was almost here.

Then a noise came from inside the house.

The two men froze. They pulled their side arms again and looked at each other.

It had come from one of the rooms along the corridor.

They lifted their pistols and stood there, listening.

They heard it again.

A rustle.

Movement.

Keeping their weapons in the aim, the two men moved down the corridor slowly as the sirens outside grew louder. There was the sound of a series of cars screeching to a halt in the drive, the quiet villa about to become a hell of a lot busier.

Behind the two cops, the thin curtains rippled gently in the sea breeze.

And the tinkling of the wind chimes echoed through the house.

*

Two weeks later and almost fourteen hundred miles south of East Hampton, a man twisted a key in a lock and pushed open the door to his second-floor apartment. He lived alone and had just come back from a long day's work. He'd been having a rough time at the office lately and today had been especially gruelling, full of questions and not many answers. He felt like a boxer with his back to the ropes, taking an onslaught of punches, desperately trying to make it to the bell and back to his corner. He was hanging in there.

Just.

Closing the door behind him and ensuring it was locked, the man laid the keys on the side, along with a pistol he pulled from his belt and a cell phone he drew from his pocket. Walking over to the fridge, he yanked the door open and took out a cold Corona from the shelf, unscrewing the cap and tossing it at the trash. Scooping up a take-out menu, he wandered into the lounge and collapsed onto a chair, tired and pissed off in equal measure.

He grabbed the remote control from the arm beside him and flicked on the television, taking a long pull of cold beer. The last thing he felt like doing was concentrating on anything right now, but considering what he did for a living, it was important to stay abreast of current affairs.

He also wanted to see if he or anyone he knew had made the headlines.

He flicked onto CNN and took another swig of icy beer, looking at the take-out menu and thinking about what to order. He glanced at the screen again.

And he froze.

The footage was of a small girl leaving an urban Police Department Plaza in what had to be Washington or Philadelphia or maybe New York. She was being moved quickly, escorted fast by a male and female security team, reporters and journalists being kept well back.

The man scanned the banner headline and the images.

Slamming his beer on the table beside him, he jumped up from the chair and rushed across the room, grabbing his cell phone. Dialling a number, he moved back in front of the television and continued watching the screen, at the little girl being ushered towards a blacked-out car.

Someone picked up the other end.

'Yeah?'

'It's me!' the man said hurriedly.

'What is it?'

'You're not going to believe who I'm looking at right now.'

'Who?'

'CNN, right now. *Now!*'

'OK. Hang on.' There was a pause. A shuffling the other end of the line. 'Hurry!'

Another pause.

Then the man the other end came back.

'Holy shit.'

'It's her,' the man said, staring at the screen. 'It's her.'

****

55422487R00231

Made in the USA
Middletown, DE
17 July 2019